TH… …N

Sisters of Woodside Mysteries

Book 3

A Regency Romance

by Mary Kingswood

Published by Sutors Publishing

ISBN: 978-1-912167-20-3 (paperback)

Cover design by: Shayne Rutherford of Darkmoon Graphics

Author's note:

This book is written using historic British terminology, so *saloon* instead of *salon*, *chaperon* instead of *chaperone* and so on. I follow Jane Austen's example and refer to a group of sisters as the Miss Wintertons.

The Companion: Sisters of Woodside Mysteries 3

About the book: *A traditional Regency romance, drawing room rather than bedroom.*

Margaret is the quiet one of the Winterton family, happy only in her own home with her sisters protectively gathered around her. But her father's death and mountain of debts tear the sisters apart and uproot them from Woodside. As a poor relation, Margaret must become a lowly paid companion to two elderly aunts she has never met. There is no welcome for Margaret at their gloomy house, Pendarreth, but the surrounding woods bring her solace - and unexpected danger.

Mel Haymer is a simple country curate by profession, but his past holds a dark secret. He is quite content to leave the past undisturbed, but then he meets Margaret Winterton, a young lady unlike any other he's ever known. He can't deny his feelings for her, but if he surrenders to love, he will bring disaster to his family. Margaret's coming cracks the fragile shell hiding family tragedies. Can Mel and Margaret find the strength to uncover the truth and turn Pendarreth into a happy home?

Book 3 of the 5-book Sisters of Woodside Mysteries series, each a complete story with a HEA, but read all of them to find out all the secrets of the Winterton family!

About the series: *When Mr Edmund Winterton of Woodside dies, his daughters find themselves penniless and homeless. What can they do? Unless they wish to live on charity, they will have to find genteel employment for themselves. This book is set in England during the Regency period of the early nineteenth century. Book 0 takes place 5 years before books 1-4, and book 5 ten years later.*

Book 0: The Betrothed (Rosamund) (a short novel, free to mailing list subscribers)

Book 1: The Governess (Annabelle)

Book 2: The Chaperon (Lucy)

Book 3: The Companion (Margaret)

Book 4: The Seamstress (Fanny)

Book 5: Woodside

Want to be the first to hear about new releases? Sign up for my mailing list at http://marykingswood.co.uk/

Table of contents

The Winterton family

Hi-res versions of all the family trees available at http://marykingswood.co.uk/.

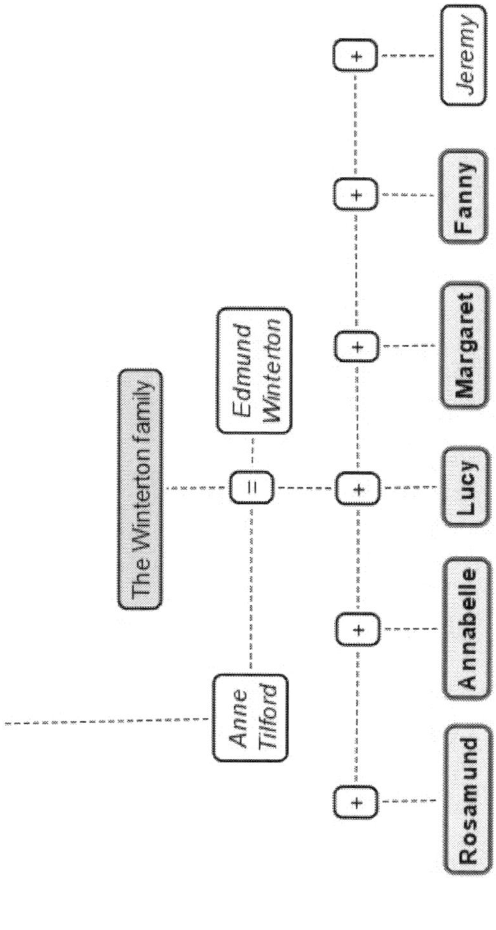

The Dalton family

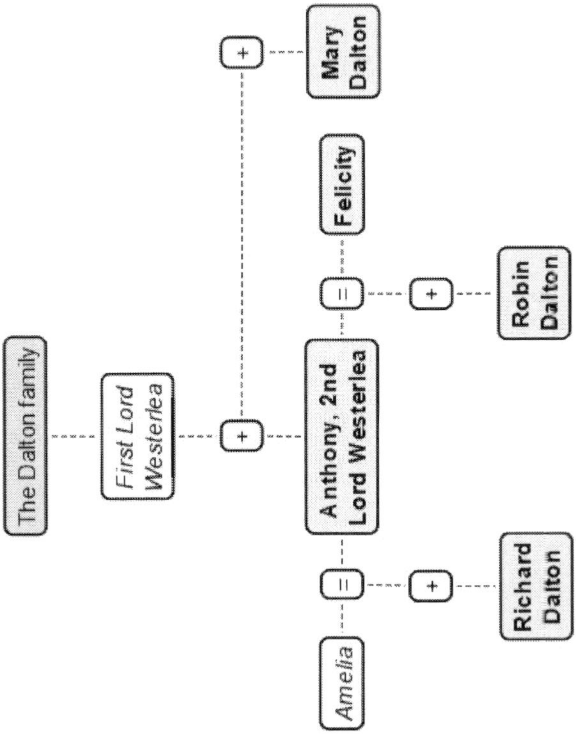

The Tilford and Haymer families

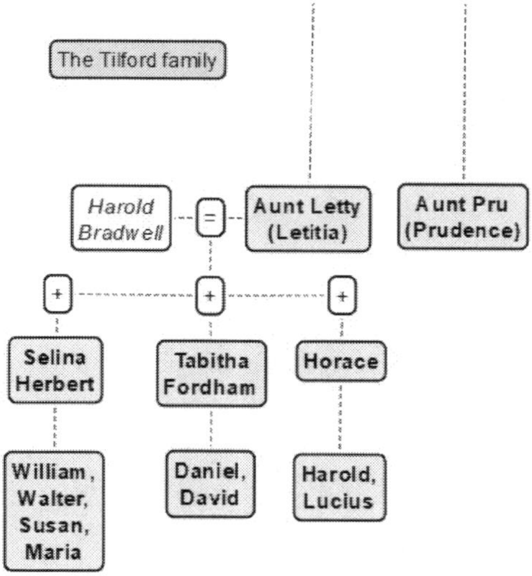

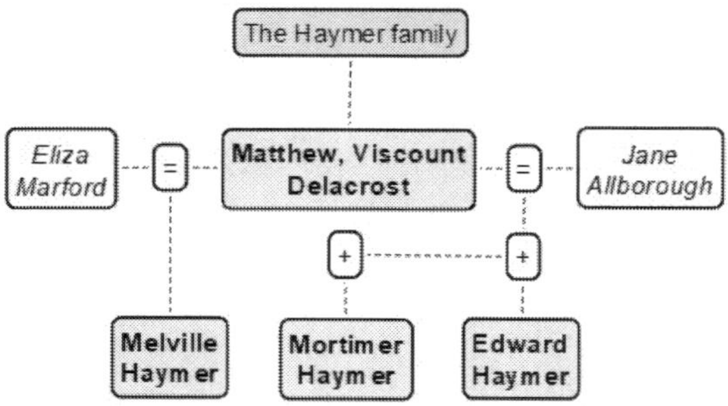

1: The Road To Pendarreth (January)

'My dear niece Margaret, We are all so looking forward to your arrival. You will be such a help to your Aunt Letty, and it will greatly relieve my mind to have you in the house and able to share the burden of caring for her. Not that I regard it as the least burdensome, naturally, for who else should care for her but her sister? But your tender ministrations to your aunt will enable me to devote more time to tending our precious inheritance, which duty I have been obliged to set aside since my dear sister became ill. When I say duty, of course it is the pleasantest of duties and quite lifts my spirits. Your loving aunt, Prudence Tilford.'

~~~~~

JANUARY

Even the birds were silent, the bare branches of the big old oak tree unmoving in the still, crisp air. High up in the branches, Margaret was saying farewell to the tree house. Alone of her sisters, she still came here very often to sit amongst the rustling leaves and be silent, remembering. Today the leaves were gone, and it was too
~~~~~

cold for her to linger, but she could not leave Woodside for ever without sitting in the tree house. Remembering. Or perhaps trying to forget.

Annabelle's voice intruded first. "Margaret, dear! The carriage will be here soon. Come now, dearest, you must be ready when it arrives. You have a long journey ahead of you."

Margaret sat motionless in the wooden house among the now leafless boughs. In summer, no one could see her, even when she sat on the platform outside, her feet dangling over the edge into emptiness. But now she hid inside, wrapped in her old travelling cloak, making no sound, hoping for just a few more minutes of solitude. Peering through the knothole in the wall, she could see Annabelle marching purposefully across the lawn.

Then Lucy's high voice. "Come on down, Margaret. It is time to go."

With a sigh, Margaret got to her feet. There was no point trying to escape Lucy, for she would climb the tree and pull her down, if need be. Slowly she stepped over the edge onto the ladder, skirts caught up in one hand.

"There you are, dear," Annabelle said. "Quickly now, go and get your bonnet on, for you do not want to keep Mr Dalton waiting."

Margaret nodded, and with Annabelle on one side of her and Lucy on the other like gaolers, she made her way back to the house and prepared herself to face the unknown future.

~~~~~

Her brother-in-law Mr Dalton was very kind. Everyone was very kind, but still she could not stop herself from crying. She cried all the first day in the carriage, and then there was a horrid night to be endured in the house where Lucy was to live. Margaret was sure
~~~~~

there were ghosts and could not sleep a wink. She did not in the least like to leave Lucy there. Then onward with Mr Dalton alone, and even though he was unfailingly polite to her, she could not stop herself from crying again, just a little, and she could tell he was not pleased with her.

Yet how could she help crying? Everything was changed. Poor, dear Papa had left his daughters quite destitute, and there was no help for it but to go out and make their own way in the world. The Miss Wintertons of Woodside had never been very high up in good society, but now they were excluded from it altogether. Annabelle was to be a governess, Lucy a chaperon, and Fanny — dear Fanny, so quick and neat with her stitchery — was to be a seamstress and ply her needle for money. And Margaret was to be a companion to two elderly aunts she had never seen.

She wished they could have stayed at Frickham, where all the lanes and fields and woods and streams were familiar, like comforting old friends. There had been talk at one time of Mr Dalton finding them a little cottage in the village, where they could have stayed together and been very snug and kept chickens But the others had not liked to be beholden to him, for he was only a brother-in-law, so it was not right that he should keep them. He had not so much money that they would not be a drain on his purse, she supposed. Four unmarried sisters — it would cost him several hundred pounds a year to keep them in tolerable comfort, and he would be obliged to invite them frequently to dinner, send them game and fish when he had it, and make the carriage available to them. No, it would have been the greatest inconvenience to him. It was generous of him to offer, but it was not to be thought of. Although she did think of it, naturally, in her darker moments.

In the afternoon, the scenery became more rugged, and once they neared their destination and turned off the main road,

Margaret grew interested. This was better! Hills and woods — mile after mile of woods — with hardly a habitation to be seen save one lonely cottage, after which there was nothing but trees. Then they passed between two stone pillars, with the name *'Pendarreth'* engraved on each. They had arrived.

In the gloom of a winter afternoon, the house looked lowering and dark, its latticed windows unfriendly. No light showed anywhere as their vehicle drew to a halt under the carriage porch. Mr Dalton was obliged to descend and sound the knocker, and even then it was some minutes before the door creaked open, and someone peered out with a lantern.

Margaret, waiting in the carriage, heard the murmur of voices, then Mr Dalton came and opened the carriage door for her. "Down you come, Margaret. Here is your Aunt Prudence to greet you. Miss Tilford, this is your niece Margaret Winterton."

Margaret descended and curtsied politely. Her aunt held the lamp up, and by its light her anxious face could be seen, wisps of grey hair peeking out from beneath her cambric cap. Long lace lappets framed her face, and her round gown was unfashionably full-skirted.

"Well, child, how small you are! We expected you days since. Come in, come in at once for you are very late. We have already begun dinner, and Letty so dislikes any delay. Hurry now!"

She hustled Margaret towards the house. No one else was about, and no servants hurried out to help with the luggage. Margaret glanced at Mr Dalton, and with the smallest hint of a shrug, he turned to assist the groom to unload.

Inside, the high-ceilinged entrance hall echoed to their steps. Dark wooden floors and sombre panelling made it as gloomy as a cave, the light from the single lamp flickering so that shadows danced in the corners. Margaret could almost make out the shapes of ghouls shifting restlessly here and there, banished where the light fell on them, only to reappear as soon as the beam passed by.

"Come along, now. Hurry!"

Margaret felt her aunt's rudeness and stopped, looking uncertainly towards the door where Mr Dalton and the groom were labouring to carry one of her boxes across the threshold. As always, she could not speak the words to express what she felt. Any of her sisters could have done it, but her tongue could not shape the words.

Mr Dalton saw her bemusement and gave her a little smile. "Yes, go with your aunt, Margaret. I shall leave your boxes here, and I daresay the servants will attend to them later."

Still she hesitated.

"I shall find an inn, never fear. Nothing else was expected, I assure you."

"Oh no, we cannot accommodate a gentleman," Aunt Pru said. "There is no room for a gentleman here. We keep no manservant, you know. Better go to an inn. Come now, Margaret."

"Goodbye, Margaret," Mr Dalton said. "Be sure to write to your sisters often."

She nodded. The wretched tears were welling up again, rendering her quite incapable of speech, so she hurled herself at him, wrapping her arms as far round him as she could reach. He laughed and hugged her back.

"There, there, now! Off you go."

She allowed him to push her gently away towards Aunt Pru, who turned without another word and set off at great speed down the hall. Terrified of being left behind, Margaret ran after her, and then up some stairs. When she looked back, Mr Dalton had gone, and the hall was quite empty, with only her boxes making deeper pools of darkness in the gloom.

With so little ceremony was the last tie to her home broken.

Up and up the stairs they went, the high windows admitting little light. Then into a vast, empty room, her aunt's slippers making a soft shushing sound on the polished floor, while Margaret's boots thumped loudly. They entered a narrow corridor, doors on one side, windows on the other. A corner, and another, even longer, corridor. A door was thrown open, and suddenly there was light and warmth and voices.

"At last!" a deep voice called out. "The soup will be quite cold."

"So sorry, sister," Aunt Pru said. "Niece Margaret is come, that is all. We can eat now. Rose, set another place for Miss Margaret."

It was an odd sort of room, clearly a bedroom, for the huge bed took up about a quarter of the space. But there were comfortable chairs, desks and small tables scattered about, as well as a small dining table set with two places and groaning with food. There were three maids in the room. One of them opened a drawer in a sideboard and produced the cover and cutlery for a third setting.

"Quickly, child!" Aunt Pru said. "Do not stand there like a statue. Take off your cloak and sit down. Oh, just leave it on that chair there. Come along, come along. Your Aunt Letty is waiting."

Margaret threw aside her cloak and ripped the bonnet from her head without even bothering to untie the ribbons. Hurriedly, she sat down, trying to unbutton her gloves at the same time.

"Good. Now at last we may eat. Serve the soup, Lily."

The two sisters were as different as could be. Aunt Pru was spindly, bent and grey, as old ladies are presumed to be, her face wizened and wrinkled, her black gown old-fashioned. Aunt Letty was large, her face as smooth and round as the moon, her hair still mostly black. Rolls of flesh padded her neck and arms, and her robe of rich red velvet was cut loose to accommodate her rounded stomach.

Aunt Letty said nothing at all to Margaret, applying herself to her food with surprising enthusiasm for one supposedly ill. Aunt Pru, on the other hand, ate like a bird, pecking at this and that, and fussing over whether a dish might be too hot or too cold or too spicy for Aunt Letty. Margaret ate a little of everything she was offered, as she had been taught to do, but enjoyed none of it. There was no wine to drink, only a queer sweet sort of ale, but there were two courses and several kinds of meat, as well as a syllabub, a dish of which Margaret was particularly fond.

She had taken only two mouthfuls of this when Aunt Letty said, "The girl is tired. Lily, show her to her room."

One of the maids bobbed a curtsy and lit two candles from the fire with a taper. Giving one to Margaret, she led her silently to the door. Margaret, quite bemused, remembered her manners and curtsied to her aunts.

"Good night, dear," Aunt Pru said. "Breakfast at ten."

Aunt Letty, busy spooning blancmange onto her plate, said nothing at all.

Margaret scuttled behind the maid, but she had not far to go. Her room was next door to Aunt Letty's. Lily lit several candles, built up the fire to a good blaze and turned down the bed.

"Ye'll get used to 'em, miss," she said. "They's kindly souls, both on 'em. G'night, miss."

With that, she was gone, and Margaret was alone. There was no sign of her boxes, a nightgown, or washing water. She sat for a while, in the hope that one or other of these items might appear. When they did not, she undressed down to her chemise, blew out the candles and slipped into bed, shivering between chilly sheets. It was, she guessed, no later than five o'clock in the afternoon. At Woodside, that was the hour to dress for dinner. Then there would be a leisurely meal with her sisters chattering around her, followed by two or three hours in the drawing room for cards or music or conversation. But here, the evening was over already.

She was tired, though. Aunt Letty had been right about that. Two days of travelling and weeping had exhausted her. She closed her eyes, and sank into sleep.

~~~~~

In the small town of Heston Ford, the day was drawing to a peaceful close. At the coach-builder's cottage, Mel Haymer ducked his head to avoid the low lintel, and passed through the doorway. Even from the porch, he could still hear one of the women weeping upstairs. "Good night, Mrs Williams. I am glad your father-in-law is looking so peaceful."

"Aye, it'll not be long now," Mrs Williams said. "Good night, then, Mr Haymer, sir. Thank you for coming, and for staying so long. It's been a great comfort to him, when he's so near the end." A pause. "Will you look in again tomorrow? Like as not, he'll not last the night, but if he does..."

"I shall certainly call again tomorrow and see how things are," Mel said. "A prayer or two never goes amiss, whether for those leaving the world or for those left behind."

"Aye, that's just like you, sir. You're the best curate we've had here, beyond a doubt. The rector's very lucky to have you, and so
~~~~~

are we. Here's Jed with your horse now, sir. Will you take a lantern with you?"

"No need," he said. "The horse knows his way, and it is only five miles to Dunton Cross, after all."

Just as the horse arrived at the door, a smart carriage bowled past on the main road heading north.

"I saw that carriage earlier this afternoon," Mel said. "It turned down the Pendarreth road."

"Aye, that'll have brought the niece they're expecting," Mrs Williams said. "A Miss Margaret Winterton. You'll have heard the story, I expect. Her father left her without two pennies to rub together, so she's to be companion to Mrs Bradwell and Miss Tilford at Pendarreth. Not a place for a young lady, I'd have thought. Not that it's any of my business, but I can't help feeling sorry for the girl, shut away there with those two queer old ladies."

Mel smiled. "They are not as queer as village gossip makes out, Mrs Williams."

But as he rode slowly home, letting the horse make its own way, he wondered greatly about Miss Margaret Winterton.

He had been on the road through Heston Ford as the carriage had first gone by before it turned towards Pendarreth, and he had had a clear view of the small, pale face inside, peering through the glass. There had been a look on her face of such fear that his heart went out to her, torn away from all she held dear, and brought here to this secluded corner of England.

He had a great wish to know more of Miss Winterton.

2: A Visit From The Curate

Inevitably, Margaret woke early. That was not in the least surprising, having gone to bed at the unconscionably early hour of five o'clock. The fire had gone out, but everything was there to remake it, and she soon had a good blaze going, although the chimney smoked horribly, making her cough. Then she huddled in bed again until the first grey light of dawn crept through the grimy window panes.

Down below, the distant clang of a saucepan told her that the cook was already at work. No one brought hot water, however, nor was there any sign of her boxes being brought up. She tugged on the bell rope, but it came away in her hand, rotted to uselessness.

Now what to do? At home, when she needed anything, one or other of her sisters had somehow divined her need and either taken care of it themselves or summoned a servant. She had always had one or other of her sisters to help her communicate with the world. Never before had she needed to fend for herself. So she waited, hoping that someone would come, but no one did.

Eventually, tired of waiting and very hungry, Margaret threw on yesterday's clothes and set off in search of the servants. Following the direction of the saucepan noises led her past Aunt

Letty's door, where a middle-aged servant was curled up on a pallet, snoring loudly. No doubt she waited there to be summoned because Aunt Letty's bell was broken, too. Margaret had not the heart to wake her, so she crept past and round the corner.

She found herself on a gallery high above a large hall. Above her, thick wooden beams supported an arched ceiling. Down below, three huge stone fireplaces decorated with crests lay lifeless and cold. Margaret hurried on, wishing she had her shawl, for the air was cold as ice. A turn brought her to a long corridor, with closed doors on one side and latticed windows on the other. Through the windows she could see a courtyard with plants arranged in neat squares. A herb garden, perhaps.

Yet another corner led to the big empty room she had passed through the night before. Now she could see that it was a gallery, with the images of stern Tilford ancestors looking down at her unsmilingly, while here and there busts with empty eyes stood in niches, frozen for posterity.

She had her bearings now. To her great delight, the house was symmetrical — a large square with the courtyard in the middle, the entrance hall on one side and the great hall matching it on the other. It was very pleasing. She was comfortable in a square house one with no odd wings shooting off, or unexpected changes in walls and floors, or corners hiding dark secrets. Every part of Pendarreth looked the same. And there was this to be said for Pendarreth, too — that no matter how gloomy or quirky or strange it might be, at least there were no bad memories to haunt her. That part of her life was over for ever.

At least she now knew where she was. Down the stairs she went to the hall, where her boxes still lay exactly where they had been left the night before. Unlocking one, she fished out her shawl.

The layout of the house was now settled in her mind, so she made her way confidently through the ground floor corridors to the baize-covered door which hid the servants' quarters. Unhesitatingly she pushed it open.

Margaret had always liked the other side of a baize door. On the family's side, all was richness and luxury, the wood and silver and brass all polished to a high sheen, with carpets and runners to deaden sound. On the other side were plain druggets, simple furniture and serviceable dark paintwork, and friendly faces who smiled and never said, "Really, Margaret!" in exasperated tones, or, "Do make an effort, Margaret," as Papa had often done, or Rosamund, sometimes. Even Annabelle occasionally said, "I am sure you could manage if you tried a little harder, Margaret." As if one could just stop being terrified because one wished it.

But servants could never scold one. Besides, whether the Pendarreth servants were friendly or whether they were shocked to see her trespass on their territory, as some servants would be, what else could she do, when the bell would not work?

So she passed through the inner hall and on towards another door where she could hear voices, many female voices, all chattering away together and even laughing. That sounded very comfortable.

She pushed open the door. It was the servants' hall, the long table laid ready for a meal, the baskets of bread and pot of porridge already on the table. Eight faces, all women, turned towards Margaret, and all conversation died away. Then, with a great scraping of chairs on the stone floor, they rose and curtsied to her.

Margaret smiled at them, and motioned for them to sit down. The air was full of wonderful scents — freshly baked bread, something fishy, fried meat. She sniffed the air appreciatively, her mouth watering. At Woodside, Mrs Thompson would have understood at once, and invited her to join them, but these women looked at her in surprise.

The one in the cook's apron smiled. "You must be Miss Margaret."

Margaret nodded, pleased to see a smile.

"I'm Primrose, miss, and this is Rose... Lily... Daisy... Jasmine... Poppy... Holly... Heather."

"Flowers!" Margaret said, beaming. How odd, that all the servants should have flower names, even the very solid Poppy, as unlike her namesake as it was possible to be, although perhaps her cheeks and nose were almost poppy red.

The women all laughed. "Aye, flowers," Primrose said. "Whoever heard of a cook called Primrose, eh? But Miss Prudence is like that. She named us all."

"There's Ivy, too," said one of the others. "She takes care of the mistress at night, so she's still upstairs."

They all nodded, and Margaret wondered if, when a housemaid left, the next housemaid inherited her predecessor's name. Some employers liked to do that, so they never had to learn new names.

"What can we do for you, miss?" Primrose said.

Margaret pointed to the basket of bread, then at a spare chair and then at herself.

"You want to eat breakfast with us?" Primrose said. "You'll get a better one with the mistress at ten o'clock."

"No supper," Margaret said.

"Ah..." they all said, and in no time a place was set for her and she was helped to bread and butter, some fried fish, and a bowl of porridge, which she hadn't eaten since she was in the nursery. It was delicious.

With a quick "Thank you", she scuttled back to the entrance hall, fished in her boxes for a clean chemise and gown, and went upstairs to dress properly. Then she went in search of paper and ink, for she understood now what she must do to make her wishes known. Her sisters could no longer aid her, so she must shift for herself from now on. There were no writing supplies in her room, so she went down to the hall and set off in a different direction. The first room she tried was dark, the shutters and curtains closed. There was just enough light to see that it was filled with formal furniture, stiff and unwelcoming, with no desk or writing table. The next room was larger, since it was on a corner, but it showed only a ghostly array of covered furniture. But beyond it was a delight — an enormous library, whose stained-glass windows of Biblical scenes showed it to have once been the chapel. Now, the pews and organ were gone, with only a fresco of the Risen Lord on one wall showing where the high altar would have been. However, the reading tables were covered over, and there was no writing desk, so again she went on, her soft slippers making no sound.

The next room was a drawing room with the imposing shape of a large pianoforte in one corner, then round the corner to the great hall she had seen from the gallery above, past the red baize door again and another corner. A small dining room, a room with another shrouded pianoforte, although smaller, and another sitting room. Then a larger room, showing signs of recent occupation — some sewing on a table, a partially completed screen, a box with tassels, ribbons and feathers. And finally, the room just before the entrance hall was a study.

And here at last she found a writing desk stocked with paper, pens and ink. She sat down, made a tolerable pen and began to write.

'6am - chocolate, washing water in my room.

'7am - maid to help me dress for morning walk, plate of small cakes, with fruit in them if possible.

'9am - maid to help me change into morning dress.

'10am - breakfast with Mrs Bradwell and Miss Tilford.

'1 hour before dinner - bath, and maid to help me dress.

'10pm - maid to prepare bed, lay out nightgown.

'Clothes for laundering will be left in the green basket in my dressing room.

'Clothes to be repaired will be left on the red chair beside the bedroom door.

'Thank you. Margaret Winterton.

'Also please take my boxes to my room and unpack.'

Then, after sanding it carefully, she went down the corridor to the servants' quarters and handed her list to a surprised Rose.

~~~~~

Breakfast was taken in Aunt Letty's room, at the same table where dinner had been eaten the night before. Aunt Letty wore the same loose gown and robe she had worn then, or another just the same. Aunt Pru wore another wide-skirted gown, again in black, and in the light of day she looked even more wizened and old-fashioned than before, as if she had modelled herself on the portraits in the gallery. If she had worn her hair a little fuller and a hat with wide brim, she could have stepped out of a portrait from the previous century.
~~~~~

The meal was substantial, and Aunt Letty ploughed methodically through eggs and fried ham and mounds of spiced rice, continuing long after Margaret and Aunt Pru had finished their toast and coffee. Then, with the aid of Rose and another maid — perhaps it was Daisy — Aunt Letty was assisted to a chair beside the window, her feet on a footstool and a rug covering her legs. In the daylight, the waxy sheen of illness upon her face was plain to see.

"Sister, you may run away now. I shall not need you now that I have the girl. She can write my letters for me and give me my tonic. Off you go now, for you are not wanted here."

Aunt Pru looked from Margaret to Aunt Letty and back again, then, without a word, she turned and left the room, one end of her shawl trailing. The maids piled the breakfast dishes onto a trolley and disappeared with it. Margaret was alone with her aunt.

"Letters, girl. Sit. Write." Aunt Letty pointed to a small desk positioned so that the window gave it plenty of light. "New letter. Today's date. Write this. *My dear Matthew, Your proposal interests me. That part of Dunton Woods has never been of much use to us, although we were used to lease them to Malham in the old days, and he got some logs from them and rough shooting. Come over and we will talk about it. Tell Mortimer not to worry about Lady E. It was always a little ambitious, even for your firstborn, and he is very young yet to be thinking of marriage. Did you try my receipt for curried chicken? Such a bland meat can only be improved with a little spice. Have you had much sport lately? Some pheasant would be most welcome. Yours et cetera, Letty.* There now. Let me see what you have written, child. Hmph. Not bad, not bad. You have a legible hand, at least. Very well, fold it and direct it to Viscount Delacrost, Norton Forbury Manor. Good. New letter. Today's date. *Dear Selina, You should not take any nonsense from your cook, despite her threats to quit the place. She is there to do your bidding, and if you want a salmagundy, she must make it, and no nonsense about it. As for William...”*

Margaret dipped her pen in the ink and wrote, dipped and wrote, until her fingers were cramped. Still, it was easy work, with no thinking or talking required. She was a fast writer, but even so, Aunt Letty’s rapid speech would have outrun her fingers, were it not for the want of breath which frequently overcame her aunt. Then she would pause for long moments, her ample chest heaving, until she was able to continue. In these pauses, Margaret’s pen was able to catch up again.

Six letters she scratched out to Aunt Letty’s dictation, sanded, folded, directed and sealed them. Then Aunt Letty rang a brass bell that stood on the table beside her, and a maid who had been waiting outside — Lily, Margaret thought — ran in to collect them and ran out with them.

After that, they worked on the household accounts. Aunt Letty went through a pile of bills, separating them into those to be paid and those which need not be.

“Pru will deal with the business of paying them,” she said loftily, as if money was too sordid a matter with which to involve herself. “She pays those I have approved, and only those.”

Margaret’s task was to write down the items and amounts. There were separate books for the chandler, the butcher, the greengrocer and so on, and a larger book where everything was recorded. This involved some adding up, which was easy enough. At the end, though, she had to say each total, and even though she knew exactly what the numbers were, somehow they stuck in her throat. How hard it was! Other people found it so easy to talk —

Lucy managed to rattle away constantly, and without any trouble — but Margaret's words just got stuck, somehow.

Then there was an interruption. Rose threw open the door and announced, "Mr Melville Haymer, madam."

Mr Haymer was a man of not yet thirty years, and the tallest man Margaret had ever seen. She jumped to her feet as he entered the room, but even so, he towered over her. Yet there was some diffidence in his manner, some hesitation in his approach, that rendered him not in the least threatening. He glanced at her with what she could only interpret as a conspiratorial twinkle in his eye, although she had never met him in her life. He made her want to smile, and no man, young or old, had ever before affected her thus.

"Mrs Bradwell," he said, making his bow. He was too tall to be graceful, but the gesture was slow and careful, as if, with his long arms and legs, he was trying not to bump into the furniture. "And how are you today?"

"All the worse for seeing you, Haymer. Girl, here is Dr Simpson's curate come to pray for us sinners, so you had better mind your manners, and reflect upon your wickedness. My niece, Haymer."

"Miss Winterton, a pleasure to make your acquaintance," he said, with another cautious bow, as Margaret made her curtsy. "Mrs Bradwell, I am sure your niece has no such wickedness to reflect upon."

"Unlike me, you mean," she said, laughing heartily at her own jest, although this brought on a coughing fit which required a dose of her tonic before she could compose herself.

While she followed her aunt's instructions for the tonic, Margaret cast covert glances at him, for it was a surprise to hear him described as a curate. In her experience, curates were poor creatures, with worn clothes and no style at all, always harassed. Mr Haymer, by contrast, looked every inch the gentleman. His clothes were plain, but his coat was well cut, his boots were polished to a high shine, and his buckskin breeches were spotless. Nor did he wear the Geneva bands that so many clerics preferred, sporting instead an immaculately arranged neck cloth. Only his air of reserve differentiated him from most gentlemen of Margaret's acquaintance, who veered towards the prideful and arrogant.

In this interlude, Mr Haymer pulled up a chair and sat composedly. Aunt Pru crept into the room and engaged the curate in conversation. She asked him about various acquaintances, and he answered each question with an economy of words, mingled with gentleness. Even his speech was slow and measured. "Tolerably well. No, he has taken a turn for the worse. She is to return on Tuesday next. He has obtained a new position at the Manor House. Not too well, as you may imagine." He seemed to know everyone, but then, as the curate, that was only to be expected.

While Aunt Letty was recovering, Margaret resumed her seat and Mr Haymer, seeing her mourning gown, turned to her and said gently, "You have recently lost your father, I hear, Miss Winterton. I am very sorry for it, since it causes you to leave your home in this abrupt manner. It is fortunate, however, that you have kind aunts who so generously offer you a home. I am sure it will be a great comfort to you, in your loss, to be amongst family."

Margaret was much too overcome to attempt an answer.

He went on quickly, "And it will be a comfort to you, also, to be of aid to your aunts, in providing them with companionship and fingers nimble with a pen." When she still made no answer, he went on, "You had a good journey here, I trust, Miss Winterton?"

She nodded.

Unflummoxed, he continued, "You have come from Brinshire, I understand?" Another nod. "I have never been there, but I am told it is a very pleasant county. Are you pleased with what you have seen of Shropshire?" She nodded again, and he smiled, not in the least discomposed by her lack of response. "You will not have had time yet to consider which church you will attend, I daresay. Your aunts keep no carriage and cannot walk so far, so I am pleased to hold services here whenever they require it, although that is not often. The servants walk down the valley to Heston Ford church where the rector preaches, so that they may meet their friends, but it is a long step for a lady such as yourself. Six miles, perhaps, and the same back afterwards. There is a path through the woods, however, that leads directly to Dunton Cross, where I lead my own small congregation in prayer each Sunday. It is above ten miles by road, but the path is not much above a mile in each direction and perfectly dry most of the year, being under the trees. You would be most welcome there, Miss Winterton. Services at nine each Sunday as well as on Holy days, and again at two on the first and third Sundays of each month."

She nodded, but trembled at the prospect of going to church quite on her own. How would she ever manage it?

3: A Visit from the Viscount (February)

The lowering January skies were already presaging dusk by the time Mel emerged from the track through the woods into the tiny village of Dunton Cross, where the lamps in the parsonage windows welcomed him home. He gave his horse into the care of Robert, his groom, and entered the house by the yard door.

Mel's foster parents, Dr and Mrs Simpson, were already taking tea and cakes in the library. They were a fine looking couple of above fifty years of age, and owing to the good fortune of four substantial livings, no depredations from children of their own and a modest additional income from Mrs Simpson's skill as a writer of novels, they lived a life of great ease and comfort. Dr Simpson had two curates to take care of the business of his four parishes, stirring himself only to take the services at Heston Ford, his principal church, each week. Since he chose not to live in his own parish, the rectory was leased to a retired admiral, to the great benefit of Dr Simpson's purse. The bulk of his time was spent by his own fireside, amongst his extensive collection of books.

In consequence of this interest, the library was quite the finest room in the house. When Dr Simpson had been appointed to the living, more than thirty years earlier, his first task had been to add on a large new wing to the parsonage, to provide a library for himself and a small study for his wife to write in. The locals still called it the new wing, but to the Simpsons, and to Mel also, the library with its high ceiling and uncounted books was their calm refuge from the whirl of daily life.

"You are very late," Mrs Simpson said, as she poured Mel's tea. "What delayed you?"

"I called again on Jacob Williams but found him already gone to his maker, poor man, as his daughter-in-law had predicted."

"Yet still you went all that way to Heston Ford, knowing him likely to be beyond earthly reach?"

"Mrs Williams asked it of me, and I saw no reason not to go," he said mildly. "I was able to say a prayer with the bereaved."

"She asked it, so you went, even though you had many other calls on your time, and you have missed your hour of piquet with Luke. You are too easy-going sometimes, Mel." But her twinkling eyes softened the reproof.

He smiled. "There will be more opportunities for piquet, but not for old Mr Williams. Shall you bury him, sir, or do you wish me to do it?"

"I had better do it," Dr Simpson said. "As the former leader of the parish council, he is entitled to the attention of the rector, I believe. Although not if it be a Tuesday."

"Heaven forfend that you should miss your game of chess with Mr Brackley," his wife said, laughing.

"He has not many games left to him, so I should not like to deprive him of so much as one of them," Dr Simpson said complacently. "And did you call at Pendarreth, Mel?"

"I did, sir."

"Oh, do tell!" Mrs Simpson cried. "What is she like, this niece?"

"She is a very pleasant young lady. Very quiet." He paused, but they clearly expected more, so he went on, "She is very well-mannered."

"Yes, but is she pretty?"

Mel laughed. "Now do not be thinking to play the matchmaker, madam, I beg you. Leave the poor lady in peace to find a husband for herself. She is still in mourning for her father."

"So she is, I had forgot. Poor Mr Winterton! Were Mrs Bradwell and Miss Tilford in black gloves for their brother-in-law?"

"Miss Tilford was in full black like her niece, but Mrs Bradwell bore not so much as a black ribbon."

"Well, that is very bad, but she always went her own way. So Miss Winterton may not marry for some months yet, but still, one may consider the possibilities. She is a lady, after all, so she will marry a gentleman. Now who can we think of who might be suitable? A man of the cloth — perhaps only a curate now but with prospects for something better."

Mel laughed and shook his head. "Really, Mrs Simpson, you are incorrigible. Those romantic novels you write incline you to see romance everywhere. But Miss Winterton has several Tilford cousins who are old enough to marry. Or there are two sons at the Manor."

The room was silent for a moment, as the Simpsons exchanged glances. A log shifted on the fire, sending sparks flying up the chimney.

"Edward Haymer is a pleasant boy," Mrs Simpson said eventually. "He must be of an age with this niece, I think."

Another silence. Mel understood their reluctance to discuss the matter of Lord Delacrost's sons, but for himself he felt no qualms. He had long since come to terms with his own relationship to the viscount. He bore the family name, but he had not seen the viscount above a dozen times in his life and had no wish to know him better.

The conversation moved on to other subjects, but Mel had little to contribute. His thoughts were rather more occupied than he would like with a pale face set with a pair of luminous brown eyes.

~~~~~

Margaret found the routine of Pendarreth easy to adapt to. She had her morning walk before breakfast, while her aunts were still abed, and although it was miserable to be on her own, it was comforting to have at least some part of the old Woodside habits continuing here in new surroundings. At one end of the great hall, she had found a small door which was locked and bolted, but with the key still in the lock. It was not hard to get the door open and make her escape.

At first she had not dared to venture far afield, so she walked round and round the house, exploring the outhouses, the old creamery and brewery, the glasshouses and the coach house, still containing a closed carriage and dusty barouche, although there was not a single horse left in the large stable. Gradually she became more adventurous and strayed into the sunken rose garden, and
~~~~~

then a small shrubbery. One day she found a reflecting pool, long and narrow, the water choked with fallen leaves, with stepping stones across it half way down. But gradually her steps led her to the woods that hedged the gardens and closed it off from the outside world. She had not the courage to enter yet, but it was soothing to stand under the protection of the outermost trees and draw strength from them. The silent trees calmed her and brought her tranquillity. They were so tall, so strong, so steadfast. She always felt as if she could do anything and be anyone she wanted when she was amongst them.

From ten o'clock onwards, she belonged to her aunts — first at breakfast, then writing Aunt Letty's letters. On her third such morning, her aunt handed her an opened letter.

"One of your sisters writing to you. Let me see... Lucy. She writes well enough, I dare say, although a little sentimental, and if she would write a little less and not cross her lines so much it would be easier to read. A few words I could not make out at all, but I daresay you will know what she means. Your letters are much easier to read. *'I have arrived safely. Margaret.'* Ha! Woman of few words indeed. Now do not look so outraged. I am responsible for your welfare, so I have to examine all your correspondence, you know."

Margaret was so angry at this interference that she felt she would burst. No one had ever read her letters before, and it was not as if she were conducting a clandestine correspondence with a man. Her sisters' letters were surely beyond any need for examination. Yet she was not sure what she could do. One of the maids went every day to Heston Ford to collect the mail, and Margaret could not ask her to defy Aunt Letty's orders and give her letters directly into her hand or ask her to take her own for dispatch. It was wrong of her aunt, very wrong, to intercept her private letters as if she were a green girl with no sense, but she could not argue, so she tucked the letter away in her reticule and bent her head to her work without a word.

From twelve until two each day, except Sundays, Aunt Letty was at home to callers, although there were not many. At two, she rested before dinner, so Margaret sat with Aunt Pru in the morning room for an hour helping with her endless tapestry that involved almost as many stitches to be unpicked as were made anew. Dinner was at four, after which the two aunts played cribbage and squabbled in a gentle manner until Aunt Letty was tired enough to sleep.

"Poor dear," Aunt Pru said, as they left Aunt Letty to the care of Poppy and Ivy. "She sleeps so badly at night, but Ivy will look after her. Good night, Margaret."

And so saying, she bustled off to her own room, which was on the far side of the great hall.

Margaret had no intention of going to bed at six o'clock, nor was she minded to sit in her own room. The first night, she returned to the morning room, lighting all the candles and reviving the fire. But then she remembered the pianoforte in the room next door. There was no fire laid, so the next day she took a note to Rose in the kitchen, and that night there was a fire burning merrily and the holland covers had been removed.

She played for some time, not singing, simply letting her fingers glide over the keys. One of her boxes was half full of sheet music but for tonight she played familiar pieces she could manage without thought, allowing her mind to drift away with the melody. As she played, if she closed her eyes she could almost imagine she were at home at Woodside with the others. Her memory could conjure up Lucy's constant chatter, occasionally interrupted by

Annabelle's calm comments or Fanny's softer tones. But when she stopped playing, those remembrances drifted away like smoke and she was alone in a strange house with no friends.

"Is everything to your satisfaction, miss?"

Margaret jumped. She had not heard Rose come into the room, and her strong accent was jarring. She turned on the stool, nodding. The maid stood by the door, holding a candle.

"If I may say so, miss, it's lovely to hear music in the house again. No one's used the music room for... oh, donkey's years. If you want music to play, there's some in the cabinet over there, or a bigger selection in the withdrawing room, over by the great hall. A better instrument, too. I'll get Mr Merrill to come in and tune them, if you like."

"Thank you," Margaret whispered.

"Will there be anything else, miss?"

Margaret shook her head.

"Would you like a supper tray in your room later?"

Margaret nodded eagerly.

"Aye, dinner's earlier than you're used to, I expect. If you want anything else, come through to the kitchen. Jasmine sleeps by the range, so she'll get you whatever you need." She hesitated, then said, "Sorry we left your boxes in the hall. We have to have orders, you see, and Miss Tilford never gave none. Right, then I'll leave you to it. If you could see that the candles are all blown out before you leave. Don't want the place to burn down, do we? Good night, miss."

She curtsied, and, candle flickering in the draught, she disappeared.

~~~~~
~~~~~

'My dear Margaret, I think of you often as I look out of my window upon my part of Shropshire, knowing that you look out of yours at another part, yet still in the same county, which is such a comfort, do you not think? Annabelle is in Cheshire and Fanny is far, far away in Yorkshire and Rosamund will soon be in London, quite at the other end of the country. I am so glad you are near me. However I do not think there is any possibility of us meeting. I looked up the county in the atlas in the library, and although I could not quite work it out, I do think we are too far apart. But still, I feel as if you are close. How are our aunts? Are they kind? Have you a great deal to do? And who have you met? Are you much in company? Do write and tell me all about it. Your affectionate sister, Lucy.'

~~~~~

"I called at Pendarreth today," Mrs Simpson said at dinner one day.

"And what do you think of the niece... what is her name?" Dr Simpson said.

"Winterton," Mel said, passing a plate of carved meat down the table to Mrs Simpson. "Miss Margaret Winterton."

Mrs Simpson took the plate, then looked searchingly at Mel. "You said she was quiet, Mel, but silent might be more to the point. She said nothing but *'Yes'* and *'No'* and *'Thank you'*. I gave up all attempt at conversation, and I must tell you, I am not accustomed to such rebuffs. Was she the same with you?"

"She was. In charity, she has suffered a great change in her life, losing not just her father, but her home, her prospects of marrying well and the company of her sisters," he said. "I sincerely pity her."

"As do I, naturally," she said. "The whole world must pity her. Nevertheless, some exertion in company is necessary, if only for the sake of good manners. Nor do I feel that Mrs Bradwell and Miss
~~~~~

Tilford will encourage her to make such exertion. Mrs Bradwell calls her *'girl'* and barely speaks to her, and Miss Tilford says nothing to the point and never has. Without rational company about her, it is hard to see how she may ever improve."

"Perhaps she has never been exposed to rational company?" Dr Simpson said. "What is known of her family?"

"Her mother is spoken of as the sensible one of the Tilfords," Mrs Simpson said. "Miss Anne Tilford, as she was, the youngest of them. Her husband, Mr Edmund Winterton, was a gentleman, although of no particular standing in society. The eldest daughter married well, however - her husband is heir to a barony. Lord Westerlea of Westerlea Park in Brinshire. A pretty property, apparently, and there is a house in town as well. I have not heard whether he has introduced the younger Miss Wintertons into good society, but on the whole they must be considered a respectable family, although how rational you would think them I cannot say. Your standards are high, my dear."

He chuckled and refilled his wine glass. "But I wonder why she came here. It seems an uncomfortable place for a young lady, acting as companion to two elderly ladies in that gloomy house. Do not Mrs Bradwell and Miss Tilford have a rich brother? That would be the proper place for Miss Winterton, surely."

"They do, or a half-brother, at least," Mrs Simpson said. "Mr Arthur Tilford was an attorney, but he married very well and lives as a gentleman now. He has a large fortune from his wife, and so does not need Pendarreth, which is left to Miss Tilford. Not that it is worth a great deal or so rumour has it. There is very little land attached to it now. As to why Miss Winterton came here, I cannot say, but there were four sisters to be found places, so perhaps they had to be scattered about amongst the various relations. One has become a governess, so I heard."

"That is very sad," Dr Simpson said. "Governesses are never well-regarded."

"She must have suitable accomplishments for the post," Mel said. "That speaks well of all the sisters, if one of them has sufficient quickness and learning to teach others."

"Dear Mel," Mrs Simpson said, reaching across the table to pat his hand. "You always see the best in people."

"But of course," he said, bewildered. "There is good in everyone, if one looks for it."

"If only that were so," Dr Simpson said with a smile. "More mutton, my dear? Mel? Or shall we begin the fish?"

~~~~~

FEBRUARY

One afternoon, Margaret's letter-writing for Aunt Letty was interrupted by a caller somewhat more distinguished than the usual inquisitive wives of the neighbourhood.

"Lord Delacrost, madam," Rose intoned as she threw open the door to Aunt Letty's room.

Margaret jumped to her feet and dropped into a curtsy.

The man who entered was elderly, his hair iron-grey, and tall although a little stooped, but otherwise hale. He bore the sort of unbending expression which denotes a general dissatisfaction with life, but he smiled at Aunt Letty.

"Letty, my dear girl," he said bowing over her hand. "And how are you? A little brighter than last I saw you, I do believe."
~~~~~

She simpered like a girl. "Matthew! How delightful! Rose, bring some Madeira — the best, mind. Girl, bring a chair for his lordship."

"And who is this?" he said, turning vivid blue eyes on Margaret. She curtsied again.

"My niece," Aunt Letty said. "One of Anne's brood. Her fool of a husband mortgaged the estate to the hilt and left his girls destitute when he died, so we are all obliged to offer them charity."

"What about Arthur? He is best placed to do something for them, it seems to me."

"Oh, him! He has twelve children and no room for another dependent in his house, he says, but he got one of the girls a post as chaperon. Another is gone as governess to the Earl of Brackenwood. Do you know him?"

"A little. He is rarely in town. However many sisters do you have, Miss... er...?"

"Winterton," Margaret whispered. Then, a little louder, "Winterton, my lord. Four."

"But the eldest is married, is she not?" Aunt Letty's gruff voice seemed loud in Margaret's ears. "To a baron's heir. What is his title, girl?"

"Westerlea."

"I know Lady Westerlea," the viscount said. "Lives in town. Very elegant woman. Probably know the son, too, although I can't bring him to mind. Oh, I *do* recall him — bit of a dandy, with a very pretty wife. Your sister, eh?"

He turned his gaze on Margaret, and she lowered her eyes demurely. If he were looking for any similarity to Rosamund he would be disappointed, for she was the beauty of the family, and

Margaret could not compare. None of them could compare with Rosamund, although Fanny had such a sweetness in her countenance as gave her an air of fragile prettiness that was much admired.

Rose arrived with the Madeira at this point, so Margaret and her family connections were forgotten, and she was able to creep away to a chair a little apart from Aunt Letty and her noble visitor, while the business of pouring and sipping went on. Margaret was not offered any. For a while, the talk was all of past times and old acquaintances, and Margaret could make nothing of the stream of names and places, or the references to events long gone which set them both laughing. But then, abruptly, the viscount set down his glass.

"So. Will you sell me the woods, Letty? I will give you a fair price for them, with no haggling, and you will be able to be comfortable again."

"Are you sure you would not rather lease the land?" she said. "That way gives us both time to change our minds, if circumstances alter."

"No, no dithering, Letty. I want the business settled one way or the other. Sell or not, as you please, but do it swiftly, so that those sons of mine may have some shooting there before we go to town. I have always wanted that parcel of land, you know, for it adjoins the Manor's best coverts and would enable one to walk from Elford Farm all the way past Dunford Heights to Barnston Strake, with excellent sport at every step. There are some fine trees in the deep wood as well. You have done nothing with it, nothing at all. It is ripe for felling. You never would countenance the idea before, so although I am sorry for the change in your circumstances, naturally, I shall be very glad to take it off your hands."

"Oh, do not pity me, Matthew! I am not rolled up yet." She laughed throatily. "But you know how I am situated, with everything tied up for one or other of the children. Horace has drawn against his expectations again, foolish boy, and I cannot raise the necessary any other way. I would have sold the woods to you years ago if not for Pru. She was always sentimental about the Heights. She still talks about the games we played up there as children and the hidden places — the spring and the old bridge and the tree house, you know how she is. Even when we had the money to pay the men to do the work, she never wanted anything touched up there. She is more attached to Pendarreth than is rational. Everything must be left just as it always was. But I am quite determined on this, so she will have to get used to the idea. I shall talk to Higgins about a price. He will know what is fair and can draw up the papers."

"Whatever sum he settles on, I shall pay you that amount. I would never swindle you, Letty, I hope you know that, not when we are such old friends. You may call upon me whenever you have need."

"Just as long as you get something out of the deal too, eh?" Aunt Letty said with her deep laugh.

"So much the better," he said, his face creasing into a smile. "Send Higgins to me as soon as he has something for me to sign. And now I shall bid you good day, Letty."

He rose, and Margaret jumped up too, but he said nothing to her and made no bow, his attention all on Aunt Letty. Perhaps he had forgotten Margaret was even in the room. As he left the room, she curtsied to his retreating back.

"Now, where were we?" Aunt Letty said. "Ah, yes. The letter to Mr Crawley. Let me see what you have written so far, girl. *'Crawley, Pray be so good as to increase the number—'* Very well. *'—the number of boxes supplied by four per week, of the best quality, and do not send me any more bills until Lady Day, for you will not be paid any sooner. Mrs Harold Bradwell.'"*

Margaret's pen scratched away, the letters carefully formed in her best hand, but her thoughts were far away. A tree house! Somewhere in the woods around the house was a tree house, and she was determined to find it.

4: Lemon Cakes In The Library

Within five minutes, a timid tap on the door was followed by Aunt Pru's head, wreathed in its voluminous cambric cap with long lappets that made her look like a strange sort of dog.

"Letty? What did dear Matthew want?"

Aunt Letty sighed. "You could have heard for yourself, if you had come in. It was nothing private. *Dear* Matthew came to talk about Dunton Heights."

"Dunton Heights?" Aunt Pru's voice quavered. "What is the matter with Dunton Heights?"

"Nothing is the matter! Why should there be anything the matter? He wishes to buy the whole tract, that is all."

There was a long, frozen pause. Margaret wondered if Aunt Pru had stopped breathing, she was so still.

"Buy it? How can he buy it? That land is not for sale."

For the first time, Aunt Letty looked uncomfortable. "I know you will not like it, Pru, but it must be done. I was obliged to settle some debts before Christmas, and now..."

"Oh dear," Aunt Pru said gently. "Horace again?"

"Well... yes, as it happens. There is always something, for one or other of them. Naturally one's children turn to their mother for aid in difficult times. Even you, who have never been a mother, must see how one must offer them succour."

"Oh yes, dear, of course," Aunt Pru said. "I quite see that. It must be so. One must do everything possible for one's children, that is understood. But you cannot sell Dunton Heights."

Aunt Letty huffed with annoyance, her eyes flashing. Her breathing became rapid. "But we must... no other choice... nothing else to be done... unless you wish me to... sell my... jewels... Girl! My tonic! No, not that one, the brown bottle."

"If there is no alternative, then indeed you must sell your jewels," Aunt Pru said affably.

"There *is*—" For several long, agonised moments she fought to breathe as Margaret struggled to measure the correct amount of the medicine, as she had been taught, and help her aunt to drink it. Eventually, however, her breathing eased, although her skin had taken on a sickly sheen.

"There is an alternative," Aunt Letty said hoarsely. "Dunton Heights."

"No, dear," Aunt Pru said. "You cannot sell it without my permission, and I do not give it."

"What?"

"I own Pendarreth," Aunt Pru said. "Had you forgotten, dear?"

Aunt Letty shrieked with rage, the cry abruptly terminated by loud gasps as her breathing became difficult again.

"Oh dear me," Aunt Pru said calmly, "She is having one of her turns again. Margaret, dear, tell Rose to send Daisy as fast as she can to Heston Ford to fetch Dr Harling."

By the time the physician had arrived, bled Aunt Letty and dosed her with laudanum, the day was almost gone. Margaret and

Aunt Pru ate dinner in the hastily prepared breakfast room next to the kitchens. Aunt Pru was quite her usual self.

"Now you must not be alarmed, Margaret, for your aunt has had these little turns before. In a day or two she will be quite herself again, you know. There is not much amiss with her beyond an occasional shortness of breath, which is perhaps merely the consequence of too much syllabub and too little exercise. I myself walk every day, except when there is frost or snow on the ground, or the wind is from the east, for there is nothing so injurious to the health as an east wind. Every afternoon I take the air in the woods. It is most beneficial, and you could do worse than to follow my example. Pass the claret, if you please."

~~~~~

The following day, Aunt Letty stayed in bed. This did not cause as much of an alteration to the routine as Margaret might have expected, for her aunt still ate breakfast, despite her illness. She ate less than usual, however, seeming pale and tired.

But after breakfast, she summoned Margaret and Aunt Pru nearer to the bed.

"Pru, you will write my letters today. Girl, I have a different task for you. You are to go to the library — you know where that is? Good. To the library, then, and look out all the papers you can find relating to the Pendarreth estate. There should be the deeds, and Father's will, and Grandfather's will, and the sale of the Newtonmore mill and the Woodend Farm. Start with the big desk. Rose has the keys. Then the two smaller desks and the cabinet beneath the family bible. After that... well, just search about. There is also the study, but I have no idea if there are any important papers there. Grandfather used it, but Father preferred the library. Do not return to me until you are sure that you have everything
~~~~~

relevant. We will settle this question of ownership and who may give permission once and for all."

"Letty, dear—" Aunt Pru began.

"No, say nothing," Aunt Letty said tiredly. "All the documents are here, after all. I expect Higgins has copies of everything, but the originals are here. We shall examine them all, and then we shall know what may be done."

Margaret was aware of a thrill of excitement. The library! It was a place she felt comfortable and safe. All libraries were safe places, but one that had God and the saints looking down on her was especially reassuring. And so much paper... she loved the smell of books, that leathery, dusty scent and the peculiar mouldy aroma of old paper.

Lily and Daisy had already set the fire blazing in the massive hearth, but the library was still as cold as an icehouse. When Margaret arrived, they were busy whisking away holland covers and flicking feather dusters around. Rose unlocked the massive desk against the wall at one end of the room, its multitude of cubby holes and drawers stuffed to overflowing with papers.

"Don't envy you sorting this lot out," Rose said dubiously, picking up a couple of old letters that had slithered to the floor. "Quite a job, I'd say. Anything else you need, miss?"

Margaret shook her head absently, her mind already engaged on her plan of attack. How best to find anything to the purpose in that clutter of papers? There was, she decided, only one way, and that was to remove everything from the desk to the tables and work methodically through them, sorting into piles as she went.

"Just ring the bell if you want anything," Rose said as she left, pointing to a thick bell rope.

Margaret nodded.

Bills and letters, letters and bills. There was nothing recent, but she found tailors' bills dating back fifty years, likewise for the vintner, mantua maker, milliner, boot maker, saddler, haberdasher, grocer and a score of others, all neatly inscribed *'Paid'* and a date. The letters recorded the births and marriages and lesser events of two generations of Tilfords, at least. Only one document was pertinent to her investigations — a bill from attorneys Higgins, Purdue and Williams, of King Street, Ludlow, for the drawing up of a will for Mr Alfred Tilford of Pendarreth. She made a note of the date, then set the bill aside. But of the will itself there was no sign.

Several hours of such sorting produced numerous piles of paper, neatly stacked, but no further documents relevant to her search. She had begun examining the cabinets beneath the book cases, a task requiring her to sit on the floor, but had not found anything useful, when the door opened and a face peered in.

"Ah, there you are, Miss Winterton. Mrs Bradwell told me I should find you here."

She scrambled to her feet with a smile and curtsied to Mr Haymer. Such an amiable man and not at all frightening, despite his great height.

"How are you today, Miss Winterton? I see you well, I hope?"

She nodded.

"Gracious me," he said, looking around at the heaps of paper. "What an Augean task! Or is it Sisyphean?"

She laughed and shook her head. Impulsively, she sat down at the now cleared desk and reached for the pen and a fresh sheet of paper. *'Would you like some Madeira, Mr Haymer?'* she wrote, then held the paper up where he could see it.

He beamed. "Oh, yes, please! That is a kindness indeed."

Margaret pulled the thick rope hanging near the door, causing a bell to sound a deep, echoing note in the corridor outside.

Mr Haymer jumped, then laughed at himself. "The chapel bell?"

Margaret nodded, then scuttled back to the desk to take up her pen again. *'Please bring some Madeira.'* She chewed the feathery end of the pen. *'The best quality. Also some cakes. Thank you.'*

When Rose appeared, startled but amused, Margaret thrust the paper at her. She read it, laughed, then curtsied. "Very well, Miss Margaret."

Margaret smiled at this small success, then returned to her cabinet, hauling another armful of papers to the table — it was the second table, the first being now filled — and sat down to begin sorting. Mr Haymer pulled up a chair on the opposite side of the table. Discovering he could not see her, he carefully slid the book stand further down the table. She looked up with a little smile. Such a pleasant man! She liked him, she decided.

Rose and Lily returned bearing trays, and before long both Margaret and Mr Haymer were sipping an excellent Madeira and enjoying delicious lemon cakes. He said little, merely munching his way absently through the whole plateful of cakes, all but one. His hand reached for it, then drew back as politeness reasserted itself.

Margaret laughed and pushed the plate nearer to him. With a smile, his hand shot out, and the cake disappeared in two bites.

"Ah, Primrose is an excellent woman and an even better cook," he said, licking his lips in obvious satisfaction. "There is nothing I like so well as a lemon cake. Except possibly a cherry cake. Or a raisin cake. Or seed cake. Or marzipan... I do love marzipan, Miss Winterton." He sighed.

She giggled, hand over mouth, and nodded her agreement.

The door opened again, and Aunt Pru fluttered in, shawl trailing. “Oh, Mr Haymer… well now, you are quite at home with Margaret, I see.”

He rose and made her a bow, the gentle movements of his head slow and precise. Even so, his knee bumped the table with a thud. He was such a large man and not well-coordinated. “I trust I see you well, Miss Tilford?”

“Oh… oh, *I* am perfectly well, naturally. Nothing ever ails me.”

“That is a happiness indeed, where it is so,” he said politely. “It is a pity Mrs Bradwell has not your strong constitution, but she will recover from this latest set-back, or so Mr Harling said, when I passed him on the road.”

“Oh yes, she will be quite herself again in a day or two. We shall not need your professional services just yet, Mr Haymer.”

“My professional services are available to the living as well as the dead, Miss Tilford. Should you like me to hold a service here to give thanks for Mrs Bradwell’s safe recovery?”

“Her safe recovery? Oh, I am sure we can manage to give thanks in our own way, Mr Haymer. You need not put yourself to any inconvenience on that account.”

“It is not the least inconvenience in the world, since it is my job, and it might be a comfort to you all. I can see how difficult it is for you to get to church when you have no carriage. Or perhaps I might ask Dr Simpson to send his carriage—”

“I beg you will do no such thing!” she said with asperity. “Margaret, how are you getting on? What are you doing spreading everything about in this wild way? You do not need to read every single paper, you know. Father’s will is all that is required.”

Margaret had no idea how to answer that. How could she know what a paper was, or whether it was important, without reading it?

Mr Haymer came to her rescue. "Miss Winterton must be clever indeed if she can determine the nature of a document before she has examined it," he said gently. "But I wonder you do not apply to Mr Higgins. He must have either the will itself or a copy, and even if he does not, he would be able to answer your questions on the dispositions contained therein, if there is any doubt in the matter."

"There is no doubt at all," she said, two spots of colour on her cheeks. "Pendarreth is mine, as it was always intended. Father made his will in my favour after Letty married, for it was only ever for the two of us, you know."

Despite the heat in her manner, he answered her placidly. "Your brother is not to inherit, eventually?"

"Certainly not. He has no claim at all. It was our mother who owned Pendarreth, for she was an only child, and Father changed his name to Tilford in order to marry her, as her father required. Arthur and Anne are from his second marriage, you know, so they never had the least claim to Pendarreth, not a shred of a claim. Only Letty and I had any right to it, and when she married, Father gave her a good dowry and promised Pendarreth to me. He changed his will to cut Letty out, the whole drawn up legally, and he showed it to me, so that I would never be in any doubt. Pendarreth is *mine*, Mr Haymer, and if Margaret cannot find the proper papers here, then I am certain that Mr Higgins will confirm it. And now, perhaps, you will be so good as to leave Margaret to continue her duties in peace. Good day to you, Mr Haymer."

And so saying, she swept out of the room.

Mr Haymer did not leave Margaret in peace. Instead, he resumed his seat, legs stretched out in front of him, neatly crossed at the ankles, arms folded.

"Well, how interesting, for Mrs Bradwell is equally confident that the estate is jointly owned by the two of them. Or perhaps she meant by all four children equally, I am not quite certain. Yet Miss Tilford saw the will when it was drawn up after Mrs Bradwell married."

Margaret frowned, then got up and fetched the solicitor's bill for the drawing up of a will. That was no more than seven years ago, and must have been long after Aunt Letty had married. She pushed the paper along the table so that it was immediately in front of Mr Haymer, then pointed to the date inscribed thereon.

He read it, his face alive with interest. "This must have been just before he died, but after Mrs Bradwell was widowed. So their father made a subsequent will. Well, well, well. And no one is quite sure of the contents of this later will."

She shook her head, frowning.

"You disagree with my reasoning, Miss Winterton?" he said amiably.

She shook her head again. That was not it.

"Oh. You think it is not valid? Or was not executed?"

A stronger shake. "Funeral," she said.

"Mr Tilford's funeral? But it was after this will was drawn up, so...?"

Frustrated, for it needed more words than she could manage to say, she rushed back to the desk and the pen. Quickly she scratched at a blank paper. *'There should have been a reading of the will after the funeral.'*

"Of course!" he said, when he had read it. "Naturally there should have been a public reading of the will. Well done, Miss Winterton, for remembering that, but of course..." He hesitated. "Your own circumstances are such as to put these considerations at the forefront of your mind. I beg your pardon — this subject must be distressing for you." She shook her head, with a quick smile to reassure him. He smiled back and went on thoughtfully, "I wonder why there was no reading? Perhaps because only the two ladies were here, and both thought they knew the contents. And if there were no other significant beneficiaries... Yes, I can see how it might be. The attorney would assume they were both aware... Yes, it might be so."

She watched him, fascinated by the workings of his mind as he thought it through, and the way he spoke them out loud. If only she could do that! She had never much liked the young men she had met previously, who had invariably grown impatient with her silences. No doubt they thought her brain was faulty in some way to render her almost dumb, but it was not so. Her mind was quick enough, and her tongue could shape the words of a prayer or a song perfectly well. But when she had to speak her own thoughts, somehow the words fell into a deep well in her mind and could not find their way out again.

~~~~~

After exhausting the many hiding places in the library, Margaret turned her attention to the study. Here all was tidiness and order, every surface empty. There were no ornaments, not even a clock, and the walls held but one solitary painting of indifferent quality, a rather nondescript landscape of river and trees. The desk bore only writing implements and a leather-bound book for recording the arrival of visitors. The last entry was in January — *'Niece Margaret arrived. Dinner late.'*
~~~~~

The cabinets revealed drawers stuffed with piles of bills, one drawer for those still unpaid and the others all labelled, *'Paid'*, but covering only the last few years. She guessed that Aunt Pru had taken charge of Pendarreth's affairs since her father's death, and this was her work. Aunt Letty decided what was to be paid, but it was Aunt Pru who managed the money.

One shelf was filled with more of the leather-bound books, piled up higgledy-piggledy. They recorded every visitor to arrive at Pendarreth, together with the room assigned to them, entertainments arranged and the date they left. These started almost fifty years ago and must also be Aunt Pru's work, for the same handwriting filled all of them and no one else had lived at Pendarreth for all those years.

The earlier ones were delightfully detailed — *'Outing to Comberwood Mere with the Prices, the Lutons, the Miss Templemeads, all the Woodford cousins (even Perry!) and the devilishly handsome Mr R, who entertained us all with renditions from Shakespeare the whole day. He really should be on the stage. Perry fell in the water, and the youngest Miss T was found kissing naughty Mr R behind the pavilion. The pickled eggs were bad so Tom Woodford threw them all in the lake. If the trout are all dead next year, we shall know why. Mrs Price drank too much champagne and fell asleep in the carriage, and Mr R held my hand all the way home. Such a wicked boy.'* Margaret smiled at this glimpse of a summer long ago. Later, though, the entries were more perfunctory, a mere record of names and rooms.

She flicked through the books, rearranging them into date order. So many months and even years when no one came, and Aunt Pru had been here on her own. One year, it was just Aunt Pru and someone called Selina. No wonder she was so protective of Pendarreth! She had been born here, had passed her whole life here and here she was still. Everyone else came and went as a visitor.

But of the important documents there was no sign.

Margaret went back to the library. Here, in the place where the late Mr Tilford had kept all his papers, was where the wills and deeds must be. She looked around it with careful eyes, trying to see if there was anything she had missed. She checked all the drawers of the desk again, but there was nothing new, and nothing untoward that might suggest a secret compartment.

She turned her attention to the books. Perhaps the missing papers had been hidden amongst them? And almost at once, tucked away with the tall atlases on a low shelf, she came across a carved wooden box, standing upright just like a book, the spine inscribed with the single word *'Pendarreth'*. There within were all the papers relating to the estate since it had been built almost two hundred years before. Here in some humble clerk's spidery scrawl were the deeds of this parcel of land or that, and the bills of sale and letters of administration and receipts for monies paid, and copies of the last will and testament of every Tilford who had ever owned it.

There were four by Alfred Tilford, formerly Alfred Phillips. It took some time to work out the reasons for each one and tie them to the other important family events documented by the papers in the library, but eventually Margaret had it straight in her mind and was able to write a list of them all on a sheet of paper.

The first will, shortly after his marriage, left Pendarreth to his wife, the former Miss Maria Tilford. Then, after her death, the property was left equally to his two daughters, Letitia and Prudence, and should they predecease him, to a Tilford cousin. Then, after Aunt Letty's marriage, Pendarreth was left solely to

Aunt Pru, just as she had said. But then there was the fourth will, made only a few months before his death.

'To my daughter Prudence Isobel Tilford I leave the Red Cottage, Pendarrath, and the whole of Dunton Woods, Dunton Heights and Lower Heston Woods which lie outside the perimeter wall of Pendarreth Estate, to be hers without reservation, to use and enjoy as she pleases, together with the sum of three thousand pounds, in compensation for previous expectations. To my daughter Letitia Maria Bradwell née Tilford I leave the estate of Pendarreth, being the house and surrounding demesnes, and all monies pertaining thereto, to be hers without reservation, to use and enjoy as she pleases. This I do in gratitude for the timely aid and relief afforded me in my time of trial by the late Harold Edward Bradwell of Kings Norrington, in the county of Warwickshire.'

5: Inheritance And Wills (March)

Aunt Letty shrieked in triumph at this happy news.

"I knew it! It was Uncle Roderick, of course. Always in some scrape or other, for he was the greatest trial to Papa, but that one time was a great deal worse. He was quite rolled up, and Harold helped out. Papa packed the little idiot off to India, where he promptly fell into a fever and died, and everyone breathed a sigh of relief, I can tell you. Well, fancy Papa remembering the debt after all that time. And now Pendarreth is mine! Ha!"

She gloated so much that she suffered another seizure, more severe and long lasting than the first. Dr Harling came twice every day, but even his finest leeches brought little improvement.

Aunt Pru, on the other hand, suffered no outward signs of illness, but she was grey-faced, as if grieving. Mr Higgins came once to confirm all that Margaret had discovered — that Aunt Letty was the sole owner of Pendarreth and might leave it where she chose, while Aunt Pru owned all the acres of wild woodland that surrounded the estate. "I thought you knew!" he said, wringing his hands. "I was sure you must know."

While Aunt Letty recovered, Margaret was no longer required for letter-writing duties, and Aunt Pru was so silent and withdrawn that she scarcely knew whether Margaret was there or not. Once she had tied up and labelled her bundles of papers in the library, and filed them away in the cabinets, therefore, she felt herself at liberty to fill her days as she chose.

She chose to look for the tree house that had been mentioned. There was a very good chance that it had rotted away entirely after so many years, but it would be a project for her, and she dearly loved a project. She had found a good map of the house and all the grounds in the library, so she took a fair copy and drew lines to divide it into sections. Then she began a methodical search of the woods outside the estate, marking on her map all the tracks she found, and anything of interest.

It surprised her how many tracks there were, and well enough used that they were clear to follow. None of them led anywhere, just meandering through the trees, passing dells and glades or running beside tumbling streams, their brown water rushing over mossy stones. Here and there little waterfalls splashed into pools overhung with ferns. She soon found the bridge Aunt Letty had mentioned, a little stone arch over a deeper stretch of water, but of the spring and tree house, there was no sign.

~~~~~

"I was talking to Higgins after church today, my dear," Dr Simpson said to his wife as they sat down to dinner. "There is a great upset at Pendarreth, and Mrs Bradwell taken ill again and wills spoken of."

"Oh dear," Mrs Simpson. "I always thought her illness as much indolence as anything else, but if she is truly ill, then I am heartily
~~~~~

sorry for her, and perhaps I shall take the carriage tomorrow and enquire."

"I do believe she is truly ill, by all Higgins says, but that is not the whole of it. The Pendarreth ladies have discovered that the estate has not been disposed as they thought, and there is a falling out over it. Higgins was summoned to explain it all, and is to make a new will for Mrs Bradwell as soon as she is well enough to give him instructions. He could not tell me any of the details, naturally, but it sounds rather serious."

Mel told them what he knew of the matter, although it was not very much. "It must be presumed that Miss Winterton found the later will and it was not as the ladies expected, although why they did not know of its contents long since I cannot imagine. Mr Higgins should have told them of it."

"Indeed he should," Mrs Simpson said, then added with a speculative gleam in her eye, "Poor man, to be caught up in such a storm. And his poor wife, too. She is a lady of the greatest sensibilities, and she will be quite cast down by any possible question over her husband's professional conduct. Perhaps I can offer her such comfort as a visit from a neighbour may bring."

Her husband chuckled. "Oh certainly, my dear. Do go and offer her comfort, and perhaps she will offer you the whole story in return."

His wife looked at him, all wide-eyed innocence. "Why, so she may! Just think of that!"

Mel shook his head, but he smiled all the same. "You are incorrigible, Mrs Simpson."

But that lady's stratagem was successful. At Pendarreth, she was given no news except that Mrs Bradwell was a little better, and Miss Tilford and Miss Winterton were not at home. However, the visit to Mrs Higgins was all that could be wished for, and after Mrs Simpson returned home, as soon as the gentlemen were settled in the library with their cups of tea and plate of cakes she told them all about it.

"Pendarreth was *not* left to Miss Tilford after all, although it was widely thought to be so," she said triumphantly. "Instead, she got the woods and Mrs Bradwell got the estate, in gratitude for some good deed rendered to the late Mr Tilford by Mr Bradwell years ago. Mr Higgins, poor man, went to the house after the burial to read the will, but the ladies turned him away, and there being no one else to hear it and the other bequests no more than small amounts to the servants, he did not press the point. Besides, he knew that Mrs Bradwell's will left everything to her sister, so whichever of them lived longest would have the disposal of the property, which was just as it should be, in his opinion, so he never attempted to speak again on the subject. Although now he wishes he had done so, naturally. He feels it most severely, Mrs Higgins says."

"I wonder how it came about that there was any misunderstanding in the matter," Dr Simpson said. "A sensible father would have made sure his daughters understood how his property was to be disposed of."

"But imagine, my dear Mr Simpson, how miserable his life would have been if he done so. Miss Tilford would have petitioned for her share of the inheritance, and Mrs Bradwell would have wanted to keep it all, and there would have been no peace for the poor man."

"The situation would have been awkward in other ways, too," Mel said thoughtfully. "How uncomfortable for Mrs Bradwell to know that she was the means of depriving her sister of that which she had long felt was rightfully hers. She had never herself had expectations of Pendarreth, being well provided for by her husband, by all accounts, and must have felt all her sister's hurt at the unkindness of it. She would have welcomed it for the sake of her children, while also suffering on her sister's account. No doubt she would have been very torn. Perhaps it is better that the truth be concealed until now, when there is no possibility of alteration."

Mrs Simpson laughed. "Mel, I believe you give her too much credit for sensibility. I am not sure that Mrs Bradwell is the type of person to enter into anyone else's feelings on any matter not affecting herself. Perhaps I malign her, but she has never struck me as having much sympathy for her sister's position. She gives her orders as if she were mistress of Pendarreth, and Miss Tilford, timid soul that she is, has always deferred to her on every matter."

"I do not think Miss Tilford is quite as timid as she appears," Mel said, smiling. "She is very strong-minded, when she chooses to be. Or when a matter is important to her. I should certainly not like to cross her."

Mr Simpson set down his teacup and steepled his fingers. "Now that the true situation is known, it creates an interesting dilemma for Mrs Bradwell. As the rightful owner of Pendarreth and with no entail or other constraint, how should she leave the estate after? To her sister, who has few years left to enjoy it? Or to one of her own family, who would gain a great benefit from such a bequest? And if so, which one?"

"She will leave it all to her son, surely," Mel said. "That is proper, is it not?"

"Oh yes, the delightful Mr Horace Bradwell," Mrs Simpson said, wrinkling her nose in distaste. "The man who inherited his father's vast fortune, and has managed to reduce it to a mere competence in no more than ten years."

"His investments may yet come about," Mel said. "At least he is not a gambler or one who lives high. He likes to take up these new inventions, that is all."

"Which invariably fail, taking his money with them," Dr Simpson said impatiently. "He has not his father's skill in business. He still has some property to give him consequence, which he has had the good sense to hold on to, but his liabilities are very great, by all accounts. His mother had to frank him again last year, so Higgins said, and it is rumoured that he is in difficulties again. I should not like to see Pendarreth fall into the hands of such a man."

"Pendarreth has rarely fallen into the hands of any man," Mrs Simpson said. "It has most often descended in the female line. Presumably that is why it was never entailed on the male line, as so many of these great houses are. Mrs Bradwell would be following the traditional pattern if she were to leave it now to her sister, or to one of her daughters."

"Or to her niece," Mel put in.

"To Miss Winterton? Has Mrs Bradwell developed a fondness for her?" Dr Simpson said in surprise.

"It is not Mrs Bradwell who has developed a fondness for her," Mrs Simpson said archly, with a sidelong glance at Mel.

He tried not to colour up. "I hardly know her," he protested. "You must not be matchmaking, Mrs Simpson, truly you must not. Even if I were in love with her, which I am not, and she with me, which she is not, there could be no question of marriage. I can never marry."

"So you always say, yet I have never understood it. You have a good allowance from your father, you have a home here for as long as you want it, with plenty of room for a wife, and you have excellent opportunities for preferment in your profession. Why should you not marry, when the right woman crosses your path?"

Mel said nothing, for what was there to say? He could not explain it, not even to someone as close to him as his own foster mother.

"Do not tease the boy, Aline," Mr Simpson said. "He knows his own mind. Despite what your novels say, men do not need to be harried and cajoled into marriage. We can decide the matter for ourselves."

And fortunately for Mel's peace of mind, she said nothing more on the subject. He was quite determined on the question of marriage, but on the issue of love he was not so sanguine. A man may be as determined as he likes, but a pretty face adorned with expressive eyes could still disturb his thoughts far more than he would wish. And now, with all this trouble at Pendarreth swirling around the appealing Miss Winterton, his thoughts flew there even more frequently. He was beginning to fear for his heart.

~~~~~

MARCH

Margaret quickly learnt to keep out of the way of trouble. There was no avoiding one or both of her aunts at breakfast or dinner, but otherwise she disappeared unless sent for. The library was her great joy, although it seemed that books had simply been tossed onto shelves anyhow, as they were read and abandoned. Such disorder offended her greatly, so she spent an hour or two there every day, working her way steadily through the shelves, rearranging the contents in a sensible manner. Often she found a particularly interesting one to take away and read.
~~~~~

She had made another discovery — the old schoolroom, on the upper floor. It was freezing, but she had ordered a fire to be laid every day, and if it should be too wet or cold for her walk, she could hide away there with the old globes, slates and copy books. It made her sad, for it reminded her of her sisters, but then almost everything she did reminded her of her sisters. When she got up in the morning, when she washed and dressed, when she had breakfast, when she walked through the woods, when she had dinner — all these activities had previously been carried out with one or more of her sisters. Even at night, she had always shared a room with Fanny, and sleeping alone was so painful that she could not even cry. She had cried when Mama had died, and again when news of Jeremy's drowning had reached them. She had cried when Papa had died, and they had found out that they were poor. She had cried all the way to Pendarreth. But here, alone as she usually was, she could not cry. Her grief was too deep for tears.

One advantage of the schoolroom was that it was on the same floor as Aunt Letty's room, so she could hear the little brass bell that she rang whenever she wanted something. If the bell rang twice, she knew that the maids had not heard, and she would go to find out what was wanted.

She could also hear when visitors arrived. She would hear the knocker on the front door below, and then the door creaking as Aunt Pru opened it — she always opened the door herself, for some reason. Sometimes the visitor disappeared into the morning room to talk to Aunt Pru, but sometimes it was Aunt Letty they came to see. Dr Harling, Mr Higgins, Lord Delacrost... all of them came regularly, but none stayed long. Margaret kept out of the way when they were in the house. Mr Haymer came, too, and then Margaret would creep down the corridor and into her aunt's room to listen, just as Aunt Pru often did. She liked Mr Haymer, and he generally said a prayer or two while he was there, which was a great comfort when she could not get to church.

To her great annoyance, Aunt Letty still controlled the mail, both that arriving and that leaving, even when she was ill. For two or three days, letters arrived and were placed in her room in the wicker basket used for that purpose, but they were not opened. Letters to be sent, likewise, waited for her attention in their own wicker basket. Margaret could see them, but dared not remove any addressed to her, and she would not submit her own letters for inspection.

Writing her own letters was a task she found difficult at the best of times. When Aunt Letty dictated, the words went into Margaret's ears and fell straight out again to the quill in her hand, with no need to think about them. Likewise, simple orders to the maids were no trouble to write. But forming her own words, writing interesting sentences that conveyed something more than mere platitudes, was a different matter.

What could possibly interest her sisters, caught up as they were in their own far more fascinating lives? Rosamund was preparing for the season in London, where she would mingle with the great names of English society. Annabelle was in the household of an earl, and treated as quite a member of the family. Lucy wrote at length of the balls and dinners she had been invited to, and Fanny was mingling with the Marquess of Carrbridge's family in Yorkshire. Margaret's own life was unspeakably dull by comparison.

Still, letter-writing was a necessary chore, so each week at the hour she had allotted for the task, she sat down at the small desk in her room, drew forth paper, prepared a pen and began. *'Dear Rosamund,'* her pen wrote. That part was easy. She had to start with Rosamund, as the eldest, and she knew how to begin a letter, so she could manage the first two words. Sometimes she could even write a little more. *'I am well.'* But then she became stuck. The words danced in her head — *'I am so lonely… I miss you very much… no one cares about me here… I wish we had never had to split apart… if only we were living in a little cottage with chickens, all together… I am so miserable…'* — but somehow the words stayed in her head, and could not make their way to the paper. Besides, her sisters did not want to hear such misery. So she cried a little and at the end of the hour she crumpled the paper, threw it on the fire and put away her pen for another week.

Her greatest comfort was her walks through the woods. Each day she uncovered a little more of the woodland that surrounded Pendarreth, and added her findings to her copy of the map. She worked methodically, for that was the only proper way to proceed, to ensure that she covered every inch of ground. Each time, therefore, she went to the precise point where she had left off on the previous occasion and started from there. One hundred paces due north, then five to the west, then one hundred south again and so on, back and forth, until a square the size of one hundred paces had been covered, and every object revealed could be placed precisely on the map. It was not easy, and involved a great deal of scrambling about and pushing through brambles, but she always wore her oldest gown, so the odd tear was of no moment.

Each day she learnt a little more. She had not yet found the tree house, but as she ventured into the section marked on the map as *'Dunton Heights'*, she discovered the spring, which welled up out of the ground to form one of the myriad small streams that trickled through the woodland. Beside the spring was a flat stone with a metal cup chained to it. The water was ice cold, but tangy with a slightly earthy taste that was not at all unpleasant.

One day, high on the slope that formed the centre of the Heights, she came to a thick hedge of holly, thirty feet tall or more, perhaps the remains of a boundary of some sort. It was too thick to push through, so she stepped along its length, counting the paces, until she came to the narrowest sliver of a gap. It was just wide enough for her to squeeze through without too many scratches.

It was indeed a boundary, for the holly hedge marked out a wide square of open ground, the narrow gap she had used the only entrance. The ruins of a cottage lay at one end of the square, although little of it remained now, save the chimney and a jumble of mossy stones. Beside the chimney were a couple of scythes and a whetstone, and in one corner of the square, hard up against the hedge, a heap of cut brambles testified to efforts to keep the inside of the hedge free of encroaching wilderness. It was a strange, secret place, hidden away behind the overgrown hedge, a secret that no one would come across accidentally. Only a girl with a very methodical mind would insist on finding a way through that prickly deterrent.

But the hedge hid more than a ruined cottage. In one corner, surrounded by the first green shoots of bluebells, lay a low mound of stones, with a small posy of dried flowers atop it. A grave. That in itself was interesting, but not unusual. People buried all sorts of things in woods — dogs, or unbaptised children, or even horses. There might even be a small marker of wood or stone to commemorate the dead, to demonstrate the affection in which the deceased was held. The posy and respectfully cleared brambles suggested that the deceased was not yet forgotten.

This grave was different. Amongst the numerous pebbles covering the grave were many of a different colour, so arranged as to spell words. And it was the words which shocked Margaret to her core, for they made no sense.

'Melville Matthew Haymer. Born first day of February 17—. Died third day of February 17—.'

Yet Melville Haymer was very much alive and well.

6: The Schoolroom

Margaret went straight back to the house after discovering the baby's grave, for she wanted to mark it on the map while her memory was still fresh. She kept her map in a locked cupboard in the schoolroom, and she felt more comfortable feeling the weight of the key in her reticule, knowing the map was safe. It was not that she was doing anything wrong, but she was not certain that her aunts would understand her need to record her findings so methodically.

That morning, Aunt Letty was well enough to dictate some letters, although without her usual industry. She was clearly tired and stayed in bed, her face pale and waxy.

There were three visitors, but Aunt Letty turned away Mrs Simpson, the rector's wife, without seeing her — "She is only here to see how close I am to the grave, and I shall not give her the opportunity to gloat," she said — and Dr Harling was admitted but quickly sent away. "No more leeches, for God's sake!" Aunt Letty cried, and in this matter Margaret was entirely on her side. She had only been leeched once, but she had screamed the whole time and suffered from nightmares for months afterwards, and Mama had said she should never have them again. Even now, her darkest dreams were filled with crawling, slithering things that clung to her no matter how she tried to shake them off, until they fell, sated, of their own accord.

But Mr Haymer was admitted.

"Well, Haymer, come to pray over me again, have you?"

"If you would like me to, Mrs Bradwell. I do believe you are much improved since my last visit. Your cheeks have more of their habitual colour."

"And you have more of your habitual flummery, you wicked flatterer." But she laughed all the same.

"I speak only as I find," he said. "I hear good reports of you from Dr Harling, so I have told the sexton he may put his spade away for the moment."

That made her laugh again. "I hope he may not be troubled on my account for some time."

"So do we all," he said politely. "And how are you, Miss Winterton?" He turned benign eyes on Margaret. "Are you well?"

She nodded, but Aunt Letty said, "Pfft, why bother asking her, Haymer? She never answers. Well, if you are going to pray over me, you had better get on with it. I am a little closer to my judgement than I was yesterday, so you may ask the Good Lord for mercy on my behalf, for He never listens to me."

"He always listens, Mrs Bradwell," he said in his mild way. "Is there any particular matter upon which you would like me to intercede on your behalf? Or is this a more general plea for mercy?"

She hesitated, then lifted her chin defiantly. "Ask Him to forgive me my sins, Haymer. We all have sins to be forgiven, do we not?"

"Indeed we do."

"Even you?"

"Even me," he answered composedly.

"And God will forgive everything?"

"If the sinner repents. Let us pray."

When Mr Haymer had finished his prayers, he rose to leave. Turning to Margaret, he said, "Would you accompany me to the door, Miss Winterton?"

She jumped up at once, unable to stop herself from smiling. He smiled, too, his eyes crinkling at the corners in the most attractive way.

"Ha! So that is how it is, is it?" Aunt Letty said. "The penniless curate and the penniless companion. I wish you joy of each other." And she cackled with laughter so hard that she could not catch her breath, and had to summon Holly from the dressing room to administer her tonic.

"She is more her usual self, today," he said to Margaret as she closed the door behind them. "Does she harass you? She can be thoughtlessly cruel, sometimes."

Margaret was still blushing too furiously to answer him. There was also the puzzle of Aunt Letty describing him as penniless. His clothes were those of a gentleman of some wealth, she could not be mistaken on that point, no matter what Aunt Letty said. His manner of dress was far from being ostentatious, but every garment was of excellent quality. A relative had left him a modest competence, no doubt. She wondered idly who his family were, but Haymer was a common enough name in the district. She had heard mention of several Haymers. But no other Melville Haymers, that she knew of.

As always, he calmly carried on talking, taking no notice of her embarrassment.

"I have not yet had the pleasure of seeing you at church in Dunton Cross, Miss Winterton, and Dr Simpson reports that you have not been seen at St Peter's in Heston Ford, either. Is that because you choose not to attend?"

She shook her head.

"Dunton Cross is but a mile from here, but perhaps you consider that too far to walk?"

Again she shook her head.

"Are you afraid to walk there on your own?"

How to answer that? She *was* afraid, but not of being on her own. They had reached the door to the schoolroom. She stopped and gestured to him to follow her inside.

"Oh, is this your refuge?" he said, walking around just as she had, when she had first discovered the room, touching the globes, the books, the faded lines of neat script pinned to the walls. "There is something sad about a schoolroom, I think. All those lively children confined to desks. I was never taught in one, for the parlour was where I had my lessons. Latin, Greek, numbers and the sciences with Dr Simpson, my foster father, and the works of literature with my foster mother. I greatly enjoyed all of it. Did you enjoy your lessons, Miss Winterton?"

She nodded, delighted by his reminiscences. She had not realised that Dr and Mrs Simpson had raised him, sent him off to a university and then received him back again as Dr Simpson's own curate.

"Was there something particular you wished to show me, Miss Winterton?"

She nodded, and lifted the slate she held in her hand. Sitting down, she chalked on it, *'I would love to go to church but I do not know the way. I am afraid of getting lost in the woods.'*

He let out a long breath. "Of course. I should have realised. Perhaps if Dr Simpson were to send his carriage—"

She shook her head violently. Rubbing out the previous words with a cloth, she wrote, *'I prefer to walk to church if I can.'* Then, after a pause, she added, *'I am exploring the woods slowly. One day I will find the way to the church. Then I will come every Sunday.'*

"But Dunton Woods are huge! It could take you years to find the right way through. Miss Winterton, would it be presumptuous in me to offer to come here on Sunday next and accompany you to church, and back here afterwards?"

She wiped the slate again. *'I could not possibly take you away from your duties for such a task, although I am deeply grateful for your generosity in making the offer. You are very kind.'*

"My only duty is to lead the service," he said with a smile. "It would be the greatest pleasure to me to enable you to attend church, if that be your wish. If I ride over at, shall we say, eight o'clock, then you may sit on Placid's back while I lead him, so you will not be in the least tired. Then afterwards, I shall see you safely home again."

'I should like that very much. I have so missed church, for saying my prayers each night is not at all the same, is it? There is the greatest comfort in being part of a crowd of worshippers, and saying the responses and' She pulled another slate towards her and continued, *'singing the hymns in unison. I miss that. I am used to being part of a crowd, even at home. I do not mind being alone, but I like to be part of a gathering, too, the bigger the better.'*

When she looked up at him, his grin almost split his face. "This is so exciting!" he said. She must have shown her bewilderment, for he went on, "You are talking to me, properly. We can have a real conversation. That makes me very happy, Miss Winterton."

She blushed, and, rubbing out one slate, wrote, *'All the words are inside me, but they cannot seem to escape from my throat. They do not mind my fingers writing them however.'* Then, hesitantly, she added, *'It makes me happy too, Mr Haymer.'* He could not imagine how happy she was to find words tumbling out of her like this, just like normal people. If only she could speak like this. Even writing was usually difficult, except for prosaic ones such as orders for the servants. But with the quiet curate, the words flew from her. Yes, it made her happy indeed.

He laughed, and it was such a merry laugh that she could not help joining in. Then, half embarrassed, she put her hand over her mouth.

Perhaps he realised the impropriety of their situation, alone in the schoolroom and talking with what must be seen as great intimacy, for he shifted away from her slightly and moderated his expression. "Have you explored much of the woods, Miss Winterton?"

She nodded more solemnly, for that reminded her of the strange discovery that had occupied her thoughts a great deal. She brought out her map and spread it on the table between them. He exclaimed in delight.

"This is an excellent representation, very accurate, although the woods have encroached a great deal onto the gardens of Pendarreth since this was first drawn up. This is the garden wall here, and all the way round, see? And nought but a thin strip of woodland within the wall, and all the rest pleasure grounds and parkland. So it was when I was a boy. But now, the woods have crept nearer and nearer to the house, and nothing of the formal gardens remain except a few patches here and there, and everything so overgrown and neglected. But then there is only one man and a boy from Heston Ford who still come up here to tend the garden, and most of their time is spent with the vegetables."

She rubbed out her chalk-marks and wrote, *'I like the wildness of the gardens, for that is how nature ought to be. Man's work should be all straight lines and circles and symmetry, to show his mastery over the unrestrained wilderness. It is fun to explore, for one never knows what one may find around the next corner or hidden in a patch of overgrown shrubbery.'*

"That is very true," he said gravely. "All these formal areas here are quite gone now, I believe, but I imagine that folly is still there, and the rustic shelter. Overgrown with weeds, I daresay. Now, Miss Winterton, let me show you the path to Dunton Cross."

He pored over the map, and she watched his face, alight with enthusiasm. He was such a gentle, soft-spoken man that it was a delight to hear him speak with such animation.

"This is it, do you see? This branching here about half way is the only tricky part. That track comes out by Mr Malham's farm, and the church is just at the end of that lane. But I will collect you and take you there, so you need not worry about losing your way. Now over here is the main Pendarreth drive, which becomes the road to Heston Ford, and this path here would take you up to open moorland and all the way to Barnston Hope and Trimble Whit, but that is a very long step. I do not advise that on foot although it is a wonderful summer outing on horseback. But you have already explored some of this area I see, around the track to Norton

Forbury. What is this? Your writing is so small and neat! Ah, a spring just there. And... a grave?"

She nodded, suddenly wary. Should she tell him? But perhaps he would know what it meant. She reached for her slate.

'The grave is marked with a name. Melville Matthew Haymer. And a date. Twenty nine years ago. Born the first of February. Died the third of February. It must be the grave of an unbaptised baby.'

She watched his face close up, as if he were shutting her out suddenly. "That is... interesting," he said.

Rubbing out the words, she wrote deliberately, *'It is a common name, Haymer.'*

"It is the family name of Lord Delacrost," he said quietly. "The many Haymers in this area are descendants of a long line of viscounts and the barons before them, either formally or... informally."

She understood the subtle allusion. *'So you are related to Lord Delacrost?'* she wrote. He nodded. *'I did not realise that.'*

Formally or informally. It certainly made sense. If he was an illegitimate son, acknowledged but not part of the family, permitted to take the family name and perhaps given an allowance, but otherwise left to make his own way in the world, that would explain why he had foster parents, and why he seemed so wealthy for a curate.

"It is not something ever spoken of," he said in his gentle voice. "People generally understand how it is, if one is a Haymer with only foster parents, and therefore no one enquires into one's parentage in the usual way."

After a hesitation, she wrote, *'Do you see the family very often? Or at all?'*

He smiled but answered gravely, "I do not dine at Norton Forbury Manor."

She nodded in understanding. Such an intimate subject to be discussing, especially when they were quite alone. He was a clergyman, she was no schoolroom miss and the door was wide open, but still it was not quite proper and she felt a thrill to be so daring. Alone with a man!

At Woodside, the only reason for her sisters to leave her alone would be to receive an offer of marriage. Well, there was no danger of that from Mr Haymer, or any other man. With neither beauty nor fortune nor liveliness to recommend her, she would never receive another offer of marriage, or if she did, it would be someone like Mr Pickles with the missing teeth and bad breath and the huge hooked nose, whose panting declarations of love had quite overwhelmed her, so that she had fled in tears. In another few years, she would put on a cap and accept her spinsterhood and that would be the end of it.

But in the meantime, she could dream, and this placid giant of a man, so reassuring and calm, was beginning to fill her dreams to an alarming degree. He ought to leave, or she ought to encourage him to do so, but he showed no inclination to move and she had no wish to see him go just yet.

So she cleaned a slate and wrote, *'Is there a tree-house in the woods?'*

"There is. Wait... let me see if I can find the place..." He studied the map carefully, and then, without hesitation, stabbed a finger down. "There! Just beyond that pool there is a clearing and a massive oak tree. The tree house is there."

It was a part of the woods that she had not yet visited. *'Still? It was there when Mrs Bradwell was a girl. Is it still usable?'*

He tipped his head to one side, considering. "Let me see... it was still intact when young Joe Malham took his sweetheart there to propose, or so he told me when they came to see about the banns. That must have been... oh, the summer before last. I should not imagine it has vanished since then. But take care if you go there, Miss Winterton. It may not be safe."

Somewhere a clock struck and he jumped up. "Goodness, is that the time already! I beg your pardon for detaining you so rudely."

She laughed. *'I detained you, remember?'*

That made him laugh too. "You are too good, Miss Winterton. Until Sunday, then."

He bowed, she curtsied and as he strode across to the door, she whispered, "Thank you."

~~~~~

Sunday could not come soon enough for Mel. He rode here and there about his duties, he wrote his sermon, he ate his meals as usual, but all without much attention, for his thoughts were far away.

When he told Mr and Mrs Simpson his plans, their reactions were exactly as he had expected — she smiled knowingly, and said she looked forward very much to making Miss Winterton's acquaintance, and he looked serious, and took Mel aside to question the wisdom of devoting too much attention to a young lady who was forever beyond his reach. Mel answered them both the same way, telling each that he had not the smallest intention of marriage, an answer which fully satisfied neither. She was a romantic, who longed to see him happily married, and he knew enough of Mel's history to understand his reasons for caution.
~~~~~

Sunday saw him aback his horse well before the appointed hour, but nevertheless as he arrived, she was already waiting for him, standing calmly under the carriage porch. He had not seen her before in her outdoor clothes, but she looked just as he had expected. She still wore full black, but her pelisse was well-cut, if plain, and her bonnet was elegant. He wondered how much was her own taste, or how much her sisters' hands in choosing her clothes. Probably both, he supposed. She was self-assured enough to have her own opinions on the matter.

"Miss Winterton, good morning!" he cried as he jumped to the ground.

She smiled, and then, looking at the horse, a flash of fear crossed her expressive face.

"Do not be alarmed," he said gently, smiling down at her. "Placid is very much as his name suggests and will convey you in perfect safety, but you may walk if you prefer. Will you come and meet him?"

She nodded, and he led her to the horse's head and showed her how to stroke his nose, and then offer him a lump of sugar.

"Now he will be your friend for life," he said, which brought a shy smile. "Did you never learn to ride?"

She shook her head.

"Well, you need not learn today, either. If I may lift you onto his back, you need only sit sideways and I will lead him along. May I lift you?"

With another shy smile, she nodded and within moments he had his hands at her waist and was lifting her up. She was so light! Such a tiny thing, as small and delicate in his hands as a bird. She sat still, a little apprehensive at first and then more composed, as he led the horse through the woods, up and over the low ridge that separated Pendarreth from the world and then down into Dunton Cross, and the parsonage. He talked the whole way, partly to fill the void of her silence, but partly because of his excitement at her company. If her words stuck in her throat, his rose up in an unstoppable waterfall of meaningless chatter. She did not seem to mind.

At the parsonage, he left her with Mrs Simpson, who was delighted to take charge of so interesting a person, and the two ladies proceeded to church together, sitting in the parsonage pew. Mel had the pleasure of discovering that she had not spoken false of her ability to join in the responses and sing in unison, for there her voice was, mingling with all the others, but as clear to him as if she were the only person in church.

Afterwards, the three of them went back to the parsonage for breakfast, where she took her full part in the conversation, for he had provided her with slate and chalk for the purpose.

Then he had the delight of another half hour alone with her, as the horse plodded steadily through the woods. And by the time he left her at the entrance to Pendarreth, he knew that he was three parts in love with her, and his life would never be the same again.

7: The Tree House (April)

Mel faced some searching questions that evening. Dr Simpson wanted to discover his wife's opinion of Miss Winterton, and she was more than happy to oblige. The topic consumed their gathering in the library before dinner, and most of the meal. Dr Simpson made no comment, however, until Mrs Simpson had withdrawn.

Seeing the expression on his face, Mel raised his hands in surrender. "I know what you are about to say, sir, and I confess that I have a great regard for Miss Winterton. I cannot marry her, however, and my resolve on that point is in no way weakened."

"I am sure it is not, although you will suffer for it, without a doubt. But it is not of your own happiness that I would caution you. Having heard Aline's opinions of the lady, it is clear that your regard for Miss Winterton is returned in full measure by the lady. Have a care that you do not raise expectations that you have no intention of meeting."

"Your wife is of a romantic inclination, and sees affection everywhere, even when there may be nothing more than open-hearted warmth in the case. So it is here, I am certain. Miss Winterton has been torn away from her family and her home, and left to the sole company of two elderly and quarrelsome ladies, who have not the least care for their niece's welfare. Naturally she responds with friendship towards anyone who shows her the least kindness."

"Friendship?" Dr Simpson said, with a wry smile. "What Aline described sounded like more than friendship."

Mel sighed. "Miss Winterton has a great deal of quickness. She is perfectly well aware that she has no fortune herself and that I am merely a curate. She also knows something of my circumstances regarding Lord Delacrost. She is too sensible to expect an offer of marriage from me."

"But Aline also knows *something* of your circumstances and sees no bar to marriage," Dr Simpson said pointedly. "You are too good-tempered for your own good, Mel. You see a lady who is friendless and lonely, and you can no more refuse to offer her the hand of friendship than whip your horse. Yet friendship may easily lead to something more, or the expectation of it, and I would hate you to be drawn in to a situation that can bring nothing but grief to both of you."

And Mel had no answer to that. He could not avoid seeing Miss Winterton from time to time, but he had no wish for her to form an attachment towards him when he could offer her nothing. He resolved, therefore, to see as little as possible of her in the future.

This resolve lasted precisely three days, until their next meeting. She was sitting with her two aunts in Mrs Bradwell's bedroom when Mel called, and it was clear from all their faces that he had interrupted an argument. Miss Tilford had tears on her cheeks and after a perfunctory greeting, she rushed out of the room.

"Foolish girl," Mrs Bradwell said. "You will have heard, no doubt, how we are situated here, Haymer? Father in his wisdom left Pendarreth to my sole care, and now I must decide how to leave it when I am gone. Pru, naturally, thinks she should be the recipient, but I have my own children to think of."

"It is her home," Mel said mildly. "She must be terrified at the prospect of being asked to leave it at this stage of her life."

"Well, no one would expect her to leave," she said crossly. "She was born here and has lived here all her life. Of course she will stay here."

"But if there is a new owner, then she has no *right* to live here," Mel said patiently. "She could be thrown out at a moment's notice with nowhere to go and, perhaps, very little to live upon. It must be a frightening prospect for a gently brought up lady of that age. You could alleviate those concerns by leaving Pendarreth to Miss Tilford for her lifetime, and thereafter, wherever you choose."

"Perhaps, but she plagues me so much with her tears and pleading."

He made some suitably soothing comments, but she was not minded to be soothed and her irritation soon descended into another spasm of weakness. She called fretfully for Holly to bring her tonic and waved Mel away.

He rose to leave, and Miss Winterton jumped to her feet too. He could have bowed and made her a polite farewell, but her expression arrested him. Her round face was pale, as always, her dark hair swept up into a neat coil without the fussy curls some women affected and her eyes — those eyes! So eager, alight with inner fire. She always seemed so demure and reserved, but when she looked at him that way he felt he could see a different woman inside, one who was anything but reserved, one who burned with passion and would dance under the stars in her shift if the mood took her. And by God, he would love to watch her do it!

Somehow he could not speak, the words of farewell caught in his throat. And that was just how she was, too, he realised in surprise. She could not speak the words she wanted, either.

Perhaps seeing his difficulty, she smiled and crossed the room to the door, holding it open for him. He passed through and she followed him, closing the door behind her with a soft click. They walked along the corridor side by side, unspeaking. The windows beside them gave a view over the inner courtyard, where one of the maids worked in the herb beds, picking some early leaves for the pot.

She opened the door of the schoolroom for him, and without hesitation he entered the room, all his resolution flown away, lost to a pair of glowing eyes.

Sitting down, she reached for her slate. *'I want to thank you again for your kindness on Sunday. It meant so much to me to be able to go to church again, and I very much enjoyed meeting Mrs Simpson. She is a very kind lady, and I have realised'* She began on another slate without pause. *'that she is Aline Simpson the novelist, and I have read several of her books. Pray give her my apologies for not recognising it at the time, and tell her that'* She started on a third slate. *'I enjoyed* The Lady's Dilemma *the best and I like all her heroes because however wicked they were before they met the heroine, they immediately reformed and lived blameless lives thereafter and loved her devotedly.'*

She beamed at him, and he could not help returning her smile, for such enthusiasm was infectious. "I preferred *The Mountain Lady* myself," he said. "Mr Turnbull's exploits were so stirring, do you not agree?"

'But not very believable. He was said to be very slender and he had broken his arm, yet he clung to that tree branch suspended over the crevasse and he fought the villain and won, and I do not think it very likely.'

"But very heroic," he said gravely.

'True heroism is not so ostentatious, Mr Haymer. A man may do no great deeds and slay no dragons, but if he is honourable in his dealings and quiet in his manners and civil to all, then he is a hero to me.'

"I shall remember that next time I am face to face with a dragon," he said solemnly. "I need not slay it, but so long as I am civil to it, I may yet be a hero.'

She burst out laughing, and her merriment warmed his heart. Dear Lord, but he was enchanted by her! She was everything he could wish for in a woman, not just in her face and form, but in every way. She was all that was delightful, and he wished with all his being that he could court her in a regular manner and make her his wife. But it was impossible.

She wiped the slate again. *'Mr Haymer, I am not yet familiar enough with the woods to find the way to Dunton Cross. May I hope for your help in the future to assist me to'* Another slate. *'make my way to church? Once I have memorised the landmarks I shall be able to manage by myself.'*

He picked up her hand and held it in both of his. "Miss Winterton, it would give me the greatest pleasure. Next Sunday at the same time?"

Her face lit up with excitement, and to his equal delight and embarrassment, she threw her free hand round his neck, stretched on her toes to reach him and kissed him soundly on the cheek.

~~~~~

'Dearest Margaret, I hope you are well and have none of this dreadful grippe that we have suffered from here. Half the town is abed with it, and Dr Hay so busy all day and half the night. Lady Harriet and Miss Hay has been handing out as much restorative pork jelly as the kitchen can make, and it does seem to help. The weather is a little warmer since Sunday, and Lady Harriet took Miss Hay and me for a drive in the country yesterday in her fine carriage. Margaret, you have never seen such charming vistas as we enjoyed, the moors so wild and strange, with oddly shaped rocks everywhere, and the trees wrought small and crabbed by the constant wind. But there are flowers and birds that flit about and everything that is charming. I do like Yorkshire! It is like an old uncle, seemingly fierce but with twinkly eyes. Do write and tell me what your part of Shropshire is like. Is it wild or orderly? And is the society pleasing to you? Do tell me everything you have done. Your affectionate sister, Fanny.'

~~~~~

APRIL

Margaret was dizzy with joy. She had never done anything by half measures, and so she had never been just a little in love or had a slight partiality for a man. She was either indifferent or she adored, and with most men she was indifferent. Civility and fine clothes held no interest for her, and she had found that most eligible men were so arrogant that their manners repelled her. But with Mr Haymer she was not repelled and could not be indifferent. He was kindness itself, gentle despite his great height, and always seemed so sincerely happy to see her that she could not resist him. So it was that she found herself head over ears in love, yet hardly knowing how she had reached that point. Howsoever it was, such powerful love could not be contained. She smiled constantly, and when she thought herself unobserved, she danced for the sheer exhilaration of it, her skirts swirling, her arms moving in time to the music running through her head.

Each Sunday, she waited for him impatiently and was cast down when he returned her safely to Pendarreth. Each time she looked at him expectantly, and he said, "Same time next week, Miss Winterton?" and nothing more was said on either side about her making her own way to church. Once or twice a week he came to see Aunt Letty, too, and then there would be half an hour of conversation in the schoolroom afterwards, when he told her about the people she was beginning to know at Dunton Cross, and she showed him her map and how much of the woods she had explored. She knew perfectly well that they were being talked of and a marriage anticipated, for she saw the whispers and looks after church. For herself, she cared nothing about such talk, and Mr Haymer himself treated her exactly as he always had, with courtesy and friendliness, but not a hint of anything more.

But that was all right. So long as he was willing to see her, she was happy. She expected nothing from him, but his company was the greatest delight to her and she would not willingly give it up.

One Sunday, as they were returning through the woods, and Mr Haymer was humming a tune as they walked, he stopped at a crossing of paths.

"Miss Winterton, may I show you something? It will be but a small diversion from our route."

She nodded, and he led Placid down the side path and on into a part of the woods that she did not know at all yet. Most of the woods were dark, with tall pine trees and occasional clearings dominated by bushy shrubs, but this part was open and light, shafts of sunshine peeking through the high canopy of lacy green, the ground soft and muddy in places.

After a while they came to a larger than average clearing, and there in the centre was a vast oak tree of enormous age, the trunk at least twenty feet around. And high up in the branches—

"Tree house!" she cried.

He laughed, and lifted her down from the horse's back. "The ladder is round the far side."

Excitedly, she ran across the glade, and round the base of the tree. The ladder was a solid wooden construction, angled against the tree and firmly affixed to it. After testing its solidity, she held her skirts in one hand and began to climb. After loosely tying the horse to a bush, Mr Haymer followed her. She felt the ladder creak a little as he added his greater weight to it, but it shifted hardly at all.

She soon attained the platform, where several smoothed chunks of wood made informal seats. There she found another ladder. Laughing, she went on upwards, to find a second platform, with a small shelter with a bench inside it. One final ladder led to the uppermost level, containing a large hut with a narrow fenced exterior ledge.

Inside, there were no windows, only small openings covered by latched shutters. The furniture consisted of wooden benches around the outside, a large table and several chairs. Unlike her tree house at Woodside, there were no cushions or rugs or curtains, nothing of comfort. But it was a tree house, and she flung open the shutters, breathed deeply of the moss-infused air, and laughed from sheer delight.

Mr Haymer ducked his head to enter, and immediately the room seemed smaller. "Do you like it, Miss Winterton?"

She nodded and then, because her excitement could not be expressed in any other way, spun round on the spot. "Wonderful!" she said, throwing out her arms. One day, when she had explored this part of the woods thoroughly, she would be able to find her way here again, but for now it was sufficient to know that the tree house existed.

"Miss Winterton," he said, seating himself on a bench, which looked somewhat too small for him, "I have a small gift for you, if you would permit me?"

Surprised, she took another seat and watched as he rummaged in one of the pockets in his voluminous coat. He produced a little wooden box, about the size of a small book, and set it on the table before her. It was made of polished wood, with the letter 'M' inlaid into the lid. She pulled off her gloves and ran her finger over the letter wonderingly.

"M for Margaret," he said, smiling. "It is presumptuous of me, I know."

She shook her head, her hands feeling the smoothness of the wood, and the delicate brass hinges and fastening.

"Open it," he said. "I think you will like what is inside."

Carefully she unfastened the lid. It opened like a writing box, offering a smooth surface on a slope, but instead of leather, there was slate. Beneath the thicker side she found chalks and a wiping cloth.

"It should be small enough to fit inside your reticule," he said. "Now you will always be able to talk to me. Or to anyone," he added hastily.

Scarcely believing it, Margaret ran shaking hands over the smooth slate, her heart welling with wonder that anyone should think to do such a thing for her. No one else had ever wanted to talk to her, to listen to what she wanted to say but could not. Her sisters had mostly understood her at once, or, if they did not, they guessed until they did. Everyone else either told her crossly that it was time she learnt to speak properly, or else they gave up and ignored her. But Mr Haymer wanted to converse with her, as an equal. She was overwhelmed with gratitude.

With trembling fingers, she picked up a piece of chalk. *'This is beautiful. Who made it?'*

"I did."

'You are very clever.'

"Oh, not really. I like working with my hands. It is very soothing working with wood, especially to make something that has both utilitarian and aesthetic qualities. You must feel the same way when you net a purse or sew a reticule — practical objects yet you may allow your artistic sensibilities full rein. It gave me great pleasure to make your slate box, and I am very glad you like it, Miss Winterton."

"Thank you!" she said, but it was not enough. Her emotions rose up inside her and, having no other outlet, she sprang to her feet, rushed across to him and flung her arms around his neck. And even that was not enough. As he made no move to evade her or push her away, merely sitting passively and gazing up at her with a little smile on his face, she could not stop herself. She leaned forward and kissed him full on the mouth.

And he responded. His arms went around her and he engaged in the kiss with every bit as much enthusiasm as she did. After a while, he pulled away from her a little.

"Miss Winterton, I do not think—"

Shaking her head, she put one finger on his lips to hush him. Then she sat down again, and pulled the slate box towards her.

'Do not be alarmed. I ask nothing of you, I expect nothing. My heart is full of love for you, which can be expressed no other way, but I have no wish to marry. Not even you!'

He laughed a little at that as he read her words, but said in serious tones, "Why do you not wish to marry?"

'It would be horrible to be owned by a man and have no will of my own and spend my whole life having to keep him happy at all costs. I would not be me.'

"No man who truly loved you would hold you in such subordination. He would cherish you, and adore you, and it would be his life's work to make *you* happy. A marriage of equals, two minds alike in quickness and learning, and two hearts united in tenderness, and each respecting and esteeming the other — that would not be horrible, surely?"

She smiled, but wrote, *'And where is such perfection to be found? Even if a marriage were to begin so, how can it endure for many years without falling into indifference or worse? One day one would wake up, a horde of children at one's feet, with a man who is a virtual stranger, and never there except for the dinner hour, and already drunk by then. It is safer never to marry.'*

He was silent for such a long time, his face grave, that she thought she had offended him. Her stomach somersaulted in fear. Had her honesty driven him away? Yet she could not do otherwise. Her nature compelled her to be open with him.

Reaching across the table, she took his hand, and to her relief he squeezed it in return and smiled. "I beg your pardon. I have been considering how best to answer you. Your fears of marriage are understandable, and I must assume arise from your own family's situation. Your father, perhaps, was the one already drunk by the dinner hour? But it is not always so. My own experience has been very different. I see every day the possibility of a marriage of true affection that does not fade with the years, and the happiness that results therefrom. But Miss Winterton... Margaret..." He lifted her hand to his lips. "You have honoured me with your confidence, so let me do likewise. Know that your love for me is returned a thousand fold, and if I could marry you at once and treasure you for ever, I would do so."

Joy exploded inside her. He loved her! Her own love was returned a thousand fold! But oh, how typical of a man to claim the greater part, and not acknowledge that her love could equal his own. The thought made her smile. And yet, amidst the surge of happiness that rose inside her, there was a tremor of something else — fear, perhaps. Or bemusement, for it was the strangest declaration of love she could have imagined, stranger even than her own.

"But I cannot," he went on. "My life is not my own, nor can I decide my fate, for I am not just Mel Haymer, humble curate. I am also the Honourable Melville Matthew Haymer, eldest son and legal heir to Lord Delacrost."

8: Sunday At Dunton Cross

Mel watched her face as she took it in, shock quickly replaced by understanding and then puzzlement.

"Do you want to hear the whole story?" he said quietly.

She nodded, and he patted the bench. "Come and sit beside me, then. Let me hold your hand and I will tell you all, for I would have no secrets from *you*."

Willingly, she came and nestled next to him, placing her hand trustingly in his. For a moment, his throat was so tight that he could not speak, only hold her hand and feel the soft smoothness of her skin. She was so close that he could smell her sweet scent — something made from rose petals, he thought, for she made him think of summer sunshine and gardens heavy with perfume. With a sigh, he collected his scattered thoughts.

"Lord Delacrost married a Miss Eliza Marford, a well-connected lady. However, they had no children for many years. Then, at last, a child was conceived, and great was the rejoicing. Lord Delacrost went to London well ahead of the appointed time for confinement to ensure that all was made ready and the best *accoucheur* engaged, for the lady was not in her youth and they were afraid of difficulties. And it so happened that the baby chose not to wait for the expensive *accoucheur* in London, but arrived early, with only Lady Delacrost's maids in attendance. All was well, and the baby was a boy. Melville Matthew, he was to be named, after his grandfather and father. A letter was sent to London informing his lordship of the happy news. And then, not two days later, the baby died."

Margaret's mouth was round with shock.

"But all was not lost. It so happened that there had been another birth in the neighbourhood recently, also a boy, but a bastard child to some poor woman. You can guess the rest, I daresay. The bastard child was smuggled into the Manor House, the poor dead child removed, and when Lord Delacrost arrived from London, there was his wife, smiling and holding her child in her arms. Except that it was not her child, nor his either. I am that child, Margaret, the spawn of some unknown woman by way of an unknown man, a cuckoo in the Haymer nest."

She reached up a soft hand to stroke his face, and he smiled down at her with a sigh of contentment. There was no pain in the story when his love was beside him, close enough to kiss... so close...

No... he must not. She had caught him by surprise the first time, and had been quite unable to resist the warmth of her lips, but there must be no repetition, on that he was determined.

Laughing a little, but gently removing her hand from his cheek, he went on, "Sweet Margaret! But do not distract me, for I must tell you all. None of this was known at the time. After a month or so, I was sent to a wet nurse in the village, as was usual in the Haymer family, and life went on. But after two years, Lady Delacrost lay dying and chose not to leave the mortal world without confessing to her husband what she had done. She had no idea where the baby had come from or what had become of her dead child. The latter we now know, of course, since you have discovered that grave in the woods, and it is a comfort to know that his short life is not forgotten and he is still honoured, even after all these years. But as to the former, Lord Delacrost made strenuous enquiries, to no avail. No one knew of a woman who had given birth around that time, and the maid who must have arranged it all was long gone and could not be found. Lord Delacrost took legal advice, but it is all but impossible to reject a child so long after the event, when there was nothing to prove such a switch had ever taken place."

She frowned, detached her hand and pulled the slate box towards her. *'Why could he not disown you when you were not his child?'*

"The law is very strict on such matters, otherwise heirs could be cast off every time there was a family quarrel. A man has only a short time to repudiate a child — before it is born or very shortly thereafter. If he does not do so, then the child is legally his and there is nothing he can do, unless he can provide convincing proof to the contrary. If Lady Delacrost had signed a sworn statement, or if my true mother had been found, or if a witness to the exchange had come forward — one of the maids, for instance. But there was no evidence to be found. Lord Delacrost could not excise me from the succession to the title, which goes, as most do, to the eldest legal son. Property may be inherited according to the regular laws, but the peerage works on older principles, and must abide by the terms under which the title was created. So I will be the viscount in time, there is no avoiding that. Still, Lord Delacrost could not abide the deception, so as soon as I was old enough, he arranged to have me fostered with the Simpsons. Only Dr Simpson knew the truth, but he could be depended upon to keep silence. He told me the story of my origins, of course, but no one else has ever known of it, not even Mrs Simpson, until now."

Margaret smiled at him, and pressed one finger to her own lips and then to his. The temptation was irresistible — he slipped one arm around her waist, hugged her tight and kissed her forehead.

"So matters stayed while I grew up, and for myself I regret none of it. My upbringing and education were as fine as any man could wish, my foster parents were everything a child could desire and I was perfectly happy. The viscount, meanwhile, had married again and produced two more sons, but they could not inherit while I stood between them. The title and estate were both legally bound by entail to the oldest son. When I was one and twenty, therefore, Lord Delacrost came to see me. He explained that he could not avoid me inheriting the title, there was no way around that, but the entail on the estate could be broken by the two of us acting together. If I agreed to break the entail with him, and agree never to marry and have legitimate heirs, so that the title would eventually revert to his other sons, he would make me an allowance for life and permit me to live my life untrammelled. I had no hesitation in agreeing, for I have no desire for great wealth, and had no thought of marriage at that time. Indeed, I had already decided that I would never marry, for exactly that reason. I felt I was not entitled to deprive the true heir of his inheritance. So now you understand how I am situated. The second son, Mortimer, will have his father's fortune, and the title will revert to his line after I am gone, but only if I never marry."

She shook her head.

"You disagree?"

Again she pulled the slate box towards her. *'Only if you never have legitimate sons.'*

"But that is the same thing... or almost. If I marry, then it is a matter of chance whether there will be sons or not. I dare not risk it. You do see that, do not you?"

She nodded solemnly, then wrote, *'But we can still kiss.'* Then she looked at him expectantly.

Oh, those eyes! So vivid and lustrous... so tempting... but he must not be drawn in any further. "Delightful as your kisses are, I... I am a man of God and... and we should not... It would be wrong." She shook her head. "Not wrong?" A stronger shake. Then, with a huff of frustration, she reached for her box.

'Not forbidden by law. Not God's law. Not man's law.'

"No, but... Margaret, we should not, you know it is so. We should not kiss, we should not hold hands, we should not be alone like this."

The chalk tap-tapped rapidly on the slate. *'But we <u>are</u> alone, we <u>do</u> hold hands, we <u>have</u> kissed and I cannot believe that to be wrong.'* After a pause for thought, she cleaned the slate and wrote, *'What is done with purity in our hearts and without wicked intent cannot be a sin in God's eyes. It is only man who condemns without understanding. I ask nothing more of you and never will, but when I cannot speak what I feel, then I must express it in some other way or I will burst. Do you understand?'*

He nodded, quite unable to speak.

'Mr Haymer' she began, then hastily rubbed it out with her sleeve. *'Mel, I shall never marry, never have the comfort of my own home, my own family. My destiny is to be the spinster living on the charity of my relations. One day I shall be gone from here, never to*

see you again, but I shall always have the memory of your gentle touch. All I ask is to love you and kiss you and be happy for now.'

He could not deny her. His whole life had been dedicated to obedience to the wishes of others — to his foster parents, to Lord Delacrost, to the church and his congregation, to God. Even though he questioned the rightness of her argument, in the face of her surety he could not refuse this one small comfort to the woman he loved. Whatever the cost to his own tranquillity, he trusted Margaret to know what was best for her and in that moment that was all that mattered.

He closed his eyes and yielded to her kiss.

~~~~~

There was a change at Pendarreth at this time, for Aunt Letty's elder daughter came to visit. Mrs Herbert was a sensible woman of not yet fifty, who had been concerned by the reports of her mother's health and had come to see for herself what was amiss and whether some filial care might improve the patient's spirits.

Aunt Letty, of course, was of the opinion that the visit was less nobly motivated. "You never came to see me before, so why else come now?" she grumbled. "You are just trying to wheedle Pendarreth out of me, but you will not succeed. None of you will succeed."

Aunt Pru was distressed by such talk, and wept and wrung her hands. "But *why* will you not leave the house to me, Letty? You know it is only fitting."

Mrs Herbert livened up the dinner table enormously with her tales of her two sons and several daughters and their various exploits. She also took some interest in Margaret herself. Aunt Letty tended to sleep for most of the afternoon now, so Aunt Pru, Mrs Herbert and Margaret dined in the breakfast room, and then
~~~~~

withdrew to the music room, where Margaret played and the two older women talked. Or rather, Mrs Herbert talked. Aunt Pru mostly listened, but she did seem calmer and less anxious with Mrs Herbert around.

When Aunt Pru went to bed, Margaret was obliged to leave the pianoforte and make conversation with Mrs Herbert. This was nothing like so burdensome as it would once have been, for now she had her slate box. She could tap away with her chalk, and express every thought.

Mrs Herbert examined the box with interest. "But you can talk? For I have heard you singing, and you say *'Yes'* and *'No'* and so forth, and your voice is perfectly normal."

'The words will not come out of my mouth.'

"How peculiar! And how long has this been going on?"

'I have never had much to say. One or other of my sisters always spoke for me. But it got worse when I came out.'

"Ah, yes, society," Mrs Herbert said sagely. "It can be very overwhelming. Did you have a season in London?" Margaret shook her head. "I did, and it was the most dreadful time of my life. I was quite overcome by it all. One would imagine that a life of dissipation would be easy enough, but I hated every moment of it, and the pressure to marry, and marry well, was hideous. I was quite oppressed by it, indeed, it made me positively ill, and Mama took me away early and sent me here to recover my spirits. I was quite prostrate — so afflicted that I remember nothing of that time except that I slept a great deal. Dear Aunt Pru cared for me devotedly but even so, it took me many, many months to restore me to anything like equilibrium, I assure you. After that, I lived very quiet and later I married my dear husband and have been quite comfortable ever since. Goodness, it must be thirty years ago now!

I remember very little of those days, but it was a difficult time for me, and I do feel for you, my dear, truly I do. And so you are quite destitute?"

Margaret nodded.

"We did wonder somewhat, when we heard you were coming," she said, with a little laugh. "Well, you know how it is, with a property like Pendarreth, and dear Aunt Pru is rather a dreamer, so you might have thought—" She laughed again. "But now that I have met you, I can see that you are not at all the type— And anyway, the house is in Mama's hands now and she knows what is due to the family — her *own* family, that is. Family is so important, is it not? One must do everything in one's power for one's own children."

She smiled in satisfaction, and Margaret had to clench her fists to keep from writing a strongly-worded response on her slate.

Two days later, Aunt Letty's other daughter arrived, and a day after that a letter was received from her son, informing her that he, too, would be arriving for a "visit of comfort to poor, dear Mama in her hour of darkness". The effect of this letter was immediate. The whole house, it would seem, must be thrown into turmoil by the impending visit of Mr Horace Bradwell. Mrs Herbert was obliged to move to a smaller bedroom to leave the Queen's room for the son and heir, and a great many additional dishes were ordered for dinner, the best claret and port brought up from the cellars and the finest crystal and china unearthed from their hiding places and polished until they shone.

In all this uproar, Margaret had a small matter of her own to worry about. Mr Haymer brought word that Mr Cardwell, Dr Simpson's other curate, had contracted a putrid fever of the throat, and was obliged to keep to his bed. Mr Haymer and Dr Simpson, therefore, were obliged to undertake his duties at the two small parishes of Barnston Hope and Trimble Whit.

"I shall not be able to collect you in the morning to take you to Dunton Cross," Mr Haymer said, as they hid in the schoolroom away from the scurrying housemaids one morning. "I shall be able to bring you back after breakfast, but I must ride over to Barnston Hope first thing in the morning."

'I know the way to Dunton Cross now. I shall be able to walk by myself.'

"Are you sure? I do not like to think of you alone in those woods. If you should go wrong..."

Margaret rested a hand on his arm, leaving a chalky mark there, and shook her head. *'You must not worry. I shall be fine. I know the way.'*

She was not in the least afraid. She had explored that part of Dunton Woods thoroughly now, and had no doubt of her ability to find her way without help. On Sunday, therefore, Margaret dressed with care, for this was a special day, worthy of her best clothes. It was time, too, to set aside her deep mourning and begin to wear colours again, albeit the subdued greys and mauves of half mourning. Accordingly, she put on a new gown, pelisse and bonnet, all in grey with black and white trimmings, and grey kidskin gloves. Then she hesitated. Her matching reticule was too small to hold both her psalter and her slate box. Could she leave the slate box behind? She could not. Her old black reticule held both comfortably.

The walk was not in the least arduous. Had the sun been shining it would have been very pleasant, for the trees were in almost full leaf now, and the scent of bluebells filled the air. But the sky was dark and lowering, with the threat of rain to come. She did not mind. So long as she arrived at church dry, a little shower on the walk home would not trouble her in the least, especially as Mr Haymer would be with her.

Mrs Simpson was watching for her from the parsonage window, and sent the maid out to intercept her.

"Do come in and wait here in comfort, Miss Winterton. There is no need to sit on that wooden pew until the bell rings. Besides, Mel may be late, for it is a long way from Trimble Whit. There now, do sit down. I have finished that chapter that we talked about last week, and have begun the next, although I am not at all happy with it. It is a very strong step, to attempt to elope all the way to Scotland, and the practical difficulties must be very great. What do you think?"

Margaret pulled out her slate. *'Perhaps the father could overtake them before they get very far. Then, seeing how strong their attachment is, he might relent and allow them to marry.'*

"Hmm. Possibly, although I have made him so evil already that it will be difficult to have him change now. How about if he overtakes the carriage and there is an exchange of gunshot, so that he is killed?"

'No no no! Not at Mr Wilberforce's hand! The coachman might shoot him, so that he suffers lingering illness on account of his wound, and Drusilla and Mr Wilberforce nurse him devotedly. Then with his dying breath the father gives his permission for them to wed?'

"Oh... that has possibilities. But what of Lucia Crane? How might I resolve her difficulties?"

'I hate her. Can someone shoot her too?'

Mrs Simpson laughed out loud. "You have a point, my dear. But perhaps killing people, even made-up ones, is not a suitable subject for Sunday. We should reflect upon the Scriptures, perhaps. Ah, there is the bell now. Are you ready?"

A few drops of rain were falling as they hurried into the church and took their places in the front pew. Margaret loved the services at Dunton Cross. The congregation was small, not much above one hundred souls, but they joined in the responses and lifted their voices in song with great enthusiasm. At Frickham, Matins had been a dull service, rushed through so that old Mr Proffitt could get to his breakfast, and only at the Eucharist had there been leisure for hymns and the swelling notes of the organ. But Mr Haymer liked music, so there was always singing. And then there was the pleasure of listening to his voice as he led the prayers.

Afterwards, with the rain beginning to fall more steadily, they dashed back to the parsonage and had breakfast together, the three of them. Margaret thought it rather odd that Mrs Simpson never went to Heston Ford to hear her husband preach, but perhaps the convenience of Dunton Cross church immediately next door to her home outweighed uxorial loyalty. It was just as well, however, for Margaret could never have breakfasted at the parsonage without Mrs Simpson as chaperon, never have enjoyed sitting across the small table from the man she loved, their knees almost touching, his eyes watching her with that intimate, conspiratorial gleam that made her feel cherished.

As they ate, the rain increased until it was a veritable storm.

"You cannot walk home in this downpour," Mrs Simpson said firmly to Margaret. "Wait until after the Eucharist."

But even then the weather was no better.

"When Luke returns with the carriage—" Mrs Simpson began.

"Dr Simpson must go on to Barnston Hope when he is finished at Heston Ford," Mr Haymer said. "By the time he returns, the horses will be done for."

"Then Miss Winterton must stay the night with us," she said with a smile. "I have long wanted you to have dinner with us, my dear, and here is my opportunity. Luke will be delighted to meet you at long last."

Margaret frowned, but Mr Haymer understood her concern. "John, the manservant, will go to Pendarreth to inform your aunts, and to bring back a change of clothes for you."

She pulled out her slate. *'I can walk. It is not far, only a mile. Not even half an hour.'*

"Miss Winterton, half an hour in this torrential rain?" Mrs Simpson said. "You would be half drowned, and at this time of year, there is still a wintry chill in the air. An infection on the lungs could be fatal. It is not to be thought of. John goes every morning to Heston Ford for our mail, whatever the weather, so he is quite used to it, I assure you."

"His sister works at Pendarreth, too, so he will be very happy for an excuse to go there," Mr Haymer said.

And so it was decided, and Margaret could not suppress a tremor of pure joy at the prospect. Dinner with Mel! What could be more delightful? She made no further demur.

9: Visiting (May)

Margaret took off her bonnet and gloves, trying not to grin too widely in anticipation of the pleasure of a whole night at Dunton Cross parsonage, and dinner with Mel and the Simpsons. And there were to be two full courses, she heard.

"The gentlemen like a good spread on a Sunday, after the exertions of the offices," Mrs Simpson said.

"I like a good spread on any day," Mel said plaintively, and his foster mother laughed.

"So you do, so you do. There is a lot of you to be filled with sustenance, it is true." She patted him playfully on the stomach. "You cannot imagine how much he eats when he sets his mind to it, Miss Winterton, and yet he never grows fat."

Margaret could well imagine, having seen him eat his way through plates heaped with eggs and fried meat at breakfast, and then tuck into the bread as well.

And so began the happiest evening Margaret had seen since leaving Woodside. Dr Simpson was a most amiable man, very learned but without pretension, just as happy to listen to his wife expressing her opinion as to expound his own. Margaret had never before seen a married couple who held such an even dialogue between them, each listening attentively to the other and neither claiming dominance. Mel joined in too, from time to time, but it seemed natural for his opinion to be respected, for he was a man. For a woman to be listened to with such respect was a new experience for her. She could not participate in the conversation, for she could not write on her slate box while eating, and the discussion ranged far over her head anyway. Yet she never felt excluded or looked down on because of her silence.

When Mrs Simpson and Margaret withdrew to the library, which seemed to be where they spent most of their time, they naturally fell to discussing Mrs Simpson's latest book again, until Mrs Simpson sighed.

"Well, now that we have settled poor Lucia Crane's fate, perhaps we should return to more suitable topics for a Sunday. What did you think of Mel's text for the sermon today? Galatians chapter five, verse twenty six. *'Let us not be desirous of vain glory, provoking one another, envying one another.'"*

Margaret pondered that for a moment, then wrote, *'I do not desire vain glory, but it is hard not to envy those who have everything one wants.'*

"What do you want, my dear?" Mrs Simpson said gently.

Without pausing for thought, she wrote, *'To live in a house as happy as this one.'*

"Oh, my dear Miss Winterton! I want that for you, too, and who knows, perhaps you may have your wish, one day. Perhaps you may even live in this house?"

Margaret understood the allusion, but she shook her head. With no hesitation, she wrote, *'No. I shall never live here. It is not possible.'*

She was given the parsonage's guest bedroom, a room of modest proportions but of infinite interest to her because it was the twin of Mel's own. When she looked out of her window at the church next door, she could imagine Mel gazing at the same view. When she climbed into the capacious bed, she saw him in her mind's eye climbing into one just like it. Had it not been for the attic stairs which ran between the two rooms, they would have shared a wall, and she could have rested her hand against it and visualised him doing likewise on the other side of it.

She slept well, with no bad dreams or nightly stirrings, and woke to the sound of Mrs Simpson's cockerel crowing his stout little heart out. A neat maid brought hot water for her wash and chocolate to drink, then helped her into yesterday's gown, for whoever had packed for her at Pendarreth had sent only evening clothes.

Once dressed, she wandered downstairs, but the library was deserted, the fire swept out and relaid, but not lit. Back in the hall, she encountered John, the manservant.

"They's not up yet, madam, leastwise, not Dr and Mrs Simpson. Never up afore ten. Mr Haymer's in his study, though."

He pointed the way, and she tapped tentatively on the door. He called out and she entered, rather shyly. His face lit up when he saw her. He was in his shirt sleeves, but he reached for his coat and shrugged himself into it.

"How delightful it is to see you so early in the day," he said, rather wistfully, she thought. "Did you sleep well?"

She nodded. Pulling out her slate box, she wrote, *'Are you working? I will go away if you are busy.'*

"Not busy at all. I am just scribbling a quick letter to an old friend from university days. His wife has just presented him with their third son. They have two daughters, as well."

'He has been very busy.'

He laughed. "Indeed he has, for he is exactly my age, nine and twenty, and I cannot quite imagine having such a large family so young. The house must be a nightmare, with so many children to watch over."

'They watch over each other. When there are many children, the elder look after the younger and there is always someone to talk to or go for a walk with.' She stopped, feeling tears brimming, but resolutely she blinked them away. It did no good to repine over what could not be changed. *'Do you ever visit your friend?'*

"Once, not long after his marriage, but he was very caught up with his wife, and had not much time for an old friend. But he writes regularly, and I to him. If you will forgive me, I will just finish this so that John may take it to the post office in Heston Ford. You may read any of my books if you wish, to fill in the time before breakfast. Or perhaps you have letters of your own to write?"

It was a casual remark, but Margaret realised at once that she could indeed write to her sisters from here, and be sure that no prying eyes would see her words. It was not that she had any great secrets to conceal, but she hated with a passion the thought of Aunt Letty reading everything she wrote. And a letter from the parsonage could not be bound by Aunt Letty's orders. Could she manage to write something — anything — to her sisters? She could try.

'May I write to my sisters?'

"But of course. Here, take this end of the desk, and use my quill. I can find another. There! Now write as much as you wish. John will wait."

She wrote to each of them, in order, and perhaps it was because Mel was there, or the urgency of needing to write all four letters before John went to the post office, but for once the words allowed themselves to be written. Just a few words, but it was better than nothing. *'Dear Rosamund. Thank you for your letters. I am quite well. Aunt Letty is a little better. Aunt Pru is quite well. Yesterday I walked to church by myself.'* She stopped, chewing the pen thoughtfully. Yes, they would understand the achievement in that, but she must write more... news, that was what they liked. *'Aunt Letty's son is to visit. I hope you are well. Margaret.'* Then the exact same words to each of the others, for how could she write differently to any one of them? After Rosamund it was Annabelle, then Lucy and finally Fanny.

When she raised her head, Mr Haymer was watching her, a little smile on his face. She must have looked puzzled for he said, "Forgive me, Miss Winterton, but my letter is finished and I was drawn by the intent way you write. Your concentration is so strong that I do not believe you even heard the clock strike."

Her eyes flew to the clock on the mantel. It showed ten minutes after ten o'clock.

He laughed. "Yes, it is time for breakfast. Let us get your letters sealed and handed over to John, and then we may eat."

But when her letters were folded and sealed, and she was about to leave the room, he stopped her, looking at her with such intensity that she blushed and smiled all at once. He ran one finger down her cheek, then quickly withdrew it and held his hands behind his back, as if to prevent himself from reaching out for her.

"Miss Winterton... Margaret... tell me at once... are you content with the way things stand between us? Knowing that there can never be anything more between us than... than this?" He touched one finger to his own lips and then against hers, softly, so softly, like the delicate touch of a bird's wing. "Knowing that we can never marry?"

She nodded, and then, so that there could be no misunderstanding, she pulled out her slate box and wrote, *'I am content. Very content. I want nothing more.'* Then, after a moment's hesitation, she added, *'Are you content also?'*.

"If you are, then so am I."

He smiled then, and allowed her to stretch up to him for a kiss that warmed her all the way down to her toes. Yes, she was perfectly content.

~~~~~

"You are getting in very deep with Miss Winterton," Dr Simpson said, as he and Mel lingered over their port that evening.

"I know it, sir," Mel said sombrely. "However, I am following her lead in the situation, and she is fully aware of my circumstances."

"Fully aware? She knows of your promise to Lord Delacrost?"

"She does, and she herself has no wish to marry. We are quite open about the business, and I asked her only this morning if she were content with the situation, and she assured me that she was."

Dr Simpson sighed. "That is all very well, but in my experience these things can get out of hand very easily. It is clear to me that there is a deep affection on both sides. I will not presume to tell you what you must do, for you are a grown man and an ordained clergyman, so you may order your life as seems best to you, but do
~~~~~

have a care for the lady. She is quite an innocent, I think, and you would not wish her to be drawn in inadvertently."

Mel smiled. "She may be an innocent, sir, but she is also more conversant with her own mind than most ladies of her age. It is easy to be misled by her silence, but you may be sure that it stems from no lack of rational thought or proper feeling."

"Hmm, perhaps so, but what does it stem from, in that case? Miss Winterton has a retiring nature, but there seems to be a something more to this inability to talk. Yet she can sing and say the responses in church, and she manages simple formalities."

"She says the words get stuck in her throat," Mel said. "If I had to guess, I would perhaps wonder if some unpleasant event in her childhood caused her great distress. Combined with her natural reticence, and the protectiveness of her sisters and their willingness to speak for her, that might be enough to account for it."

"It may be so," Dr Simpson said. "She told Aline her condition worsened when she came out."

"Hmm, four or five years ago. That would have been about the time that her mother died, and not long after that her brother. He was twelve, and was sent away to sea to be a midshipman, but on his first voyage the ship sank. Being the only son and heir, it devastated Mr Winterton, who consoled his grief with the bottle, seemingly, not to mention dice and cards. Hence the Miss Wintertons' present state of penury."

"Miss Winterton told you all this?"

"She did," Mel said. "Now that she knows how to talk to me, she is very confiding. It does seem likely that the two deaths so close together caused her to be even more reserved than before."

"Whatever the cause, it makes her unfit to marry a man with any position in society. She can hardly go to social engagements with her chalks and slate. Perhaps it is just as well she has no wish to marry."

"Miss Winterton must be valued for her amiability and good sense wherever she goes," Mel said, affronted on her behalf. "She is also an accomplished musician, and likes to dance, I understand."

"She may like to dance as much as she chooses, but it will do her no good if she cannot converse with her partner," Dr Simpson said repressively. "How else may a man judge her fitness to be his wife if he cannot talk to her? "

"With the right husband, society need hold no fears for her," Mel said, hands clenching around his port glass. "The *right* husband would understand and make allowances, and help her to take her place alongside him, no matter what—"

He broke off, seeing the expression on Dr Simpson's face. "Ah. You are quite right, sir. I am getting in very deep. Probably I am well on the way to a broken heart," he said bleakly. "One day, both her aunts will have left this world, and Miss Winterton will go to one or other of her sisters, and I will have nothing left to me but pleasant memories."

They were indeed pleasant memories. Her warm kisses. Her shy smile as she showed him her map, and her explorations of the woods. Her fierce intentness as she wrote her letters. The sweetness of her voice as she sang. Her charming blushes as she told him openly that she loved him.

But mostly, her kisses, showing him a passion that no one observing her could possibly expect. When she left him, he would have an emptiness inside that nothing on earth could fill.

~~~~~

'Dearest Margaret, Thank you so much for your letter. I was much relieved to hear that you are well, and that Aunt Letty is a little better. And her son to visit! You will be all excitement, dear. We have excitement of our own here, for the house is full of visitors and there is bustle everywhere. Only the schoolroom is tranquil. The strangest thing has happened. One of our guests is a sea captain, and it transpires that he actually met Jeremy just before he boarded his ship. Is that not the most marvellous coincidence, that he should be here now? He told me all that he remembered of Jeremy, but I suspect his memory is faulty, for he told me that Jeremy was a small creature, when he was half a head taller than every other boy of his age, and broader, too. Captain Hunt also said that Jeremy was greatly looking forward to a life at sea, and there he <u>must</u> be mistaken, I am persuaded, for never was a boy less enthusiastic about his career. So while it is very kind of Captain Hunt, I do not quite know what to make of his story. Do let me know what you think when next you write. Your loving sister, Annabelle.'

~~~~~

MAY

Pendarreth was a different place altogether with Mr Horace Bradwell in it. Aunt Letty's two daughters, Mrs Herbert and Mrs Fordham, had slipped effortlessly into the household with barely a ripple, and Margaret scarcely saw them except at dinner. Her son, however, seemed to fill the place. Apart from his coachman and grooms, he brought with him a valet and two manservants, who spent all day traipsing up and down the stairs, and a negro boy who sat outside his room at all times awaiting the call of *"Boy!"*, whereupon he would run in to receive orders and then dash off to fulfil them. The child never seemed to walk anywhere, and

Margaret was constantly having to leap aside as he tore past in a great rush.

Aunt Pru hated having so many men in the house. "No need for it," she muttered, fiddling with her endlessly drooping shawl. "Not designed for *men*. No room for men here. He only does it to annoy." If Mr Bradwell was in Aunt Letty's room, Aunt Pru would slink out, and not return until he had gone somewhere else. Usually the somewhere else was the woods, accompanied by two of his men, several guns and half a dozen excitable dogs, leaving Aunt Pru distraught at the desecration of her precious woodland. Primrose was delighted to have so much game to cook, but no one else was pleased to have Mr Bradwell staying, not even his own sisters.

No one else except Aunt Letty, that is. She was as excited as a girl to have her son visiting, and at first her health improved considerably. They all dined in her room again, and she was well enough to take her place at the table beside her son. The two of them chatted and laughed together as if they had not a care in the world.

"There is excellent shooting up on the Heights just now," Mr Bradwell told the assembled company as he carved the beef. "I never saw so many plump pigeons. I do love a pigeon pie."

"So do I, so do I," Aunt Letty said, beaming at him. "There is nothing so fine as a pigeon pie. Another slice of beef, if you please, Horace. Do you know, I think I could even manage one more. We have not much fish just now, but Delacrost will send some over soon, I am sure. I wrote to let him know of your arrival, and I am sure he will wait upon you before too long. I do not know why he has not come yet."

"I daresay he is in town for the season, Mama," Mrs Herbert said. "I saw his name in the lists for the opening of Parliament after Easter."

"Nonsense, he never stays for the season," Aunt Letty said brusquely. "He goes for the opening, and any matters of particular interest, but otherwise he is always at Norton Forbury. As if I would not know where he is, Selina! He is my oldest friend, or the oldest still living, that is. He hates the season — nothing but silly chits of seventeen who have no idea how to go on, he always says."

Mrs Herbert slammed her glass down, spilling a little wine. "Well, really, when he twice married girls barely out of the schoolroom himself. Silly chits, indeed!"

Aunt Letty continued as if her daughter had not spoken. "Speaking of silly chits, what are you doing to get those girls of yours married off?"

With a sigh, Mrs Herbert said, "Nothing at all, Mama, except to accompany them into local society and allow them to form their own attachments."

"Pfft, such foolishness! You should take them up to town. Delacrost would help you fire them off, with his connections. You will never get them settled without some exertion on your part. A season in London would do the trick, I make no doubt."

"I hate the season, too," Mrs Herbert said quietly.

"Letty, dear, do not *harass* poor Selina," Aunt Pru said. "She must be the best judge of what is appropriate for dear Susan and Maria."

"She can do nothing for them since they have no portions worth the mention," Mrs Fordham said acidly. She was a thin woman with a pointed nose, who, it seemed to Margaret, did nothing but complain. "Selina has no money, and nor have I, so we are depending upon you to leave Pendarreth sensibly, Mama."

"Mama knows what is proper for her family," Mr Bradwell said stiffly. "We can trust her to leave Pendarreth where it will be most appropriate."

"You mean to you, I suppose, Horace," Mrs Fordham said with a sniff of disparagement. "You got all Papa's money, so I do not see why you should have any more."

"A man has appearances to maintain," Mr Bradwell said. "You two both made your choices in life when you married, and anything left to you would just go straight to your husbands. A Bradwell inheritance should stay in the Bradwell family, is that not so, Mama?"

"But it is not!" Aunt Pru squeaked. "Pendarreth is a *Tilford* inheritance. It should stay the property of a Tilford."

"You mean yourself, I suppose?" Mrs Fordham said. "And what happens after you die, Aunt Pru? There are no Tilfords left to leave it to, apart from distant cousins, or Uncle Arthur, who is not even a proper brother, only a half."

"That does not matter," she said, her voice so high with distress. "The *name* does not matter. Pendarreth should belong to someone with a right to it, someone with the strongest connection to it. It should go to someone who was *born* here."

And, with tears running down her face, she fled the room.

10: Agreements (June)

"Honestly, Mama, Aunt Pru grows more eccentric with every year that passes," Mrs Fordham said. "Why do you put up with her?"

"She is Mama's only surviving sister," Mrs Herbert said sharply. "Sisters are often very close. Is it not so, Miss Winterton? For you have four, I understand."

Margaret nodded.

"Does the child never speak?" Mr Bradwell said, his masculine voice loud. "I swear I have never heard her speak."

"She has something wrong with her," Aunt Letty said. "She never talks."

"That is a pity," Mr Bradwell said. "She is pretty enough, I suppose, and her figure is good if she would not hunch her shoulders so much. Can she speak at all?" He turned speculative eyes on her.

"She can speak a little," Mrs Herbert said, with a smile at Margaret. "She can also write her thoughts very lucidly, so if anything... *unexpected* were to happen to her, she would certainly be able to tell of it."

"Is that so?" He gazed at Margaret once more, but she did not lower her eyes, and in the end he was the one who turned away. "Tabitha rarely says anything sensible, but I have to agree with her on one point, Mama. You really must remake your will, now that you are the rightful owner of Pendarreth. You should listen to me, for I am the head of the family now, you know."

"I never listen to aught but my own counsel," she said.

Mr Bradwell paused to refill his wine glass. "Perhaps I will go down to Heston Ford tomorrow to see Higgins, Mama, and talk to him man to man. If you will not listen to me, perhaps the opinion of your attorney will weigh with you."

"Stop plaguing me, all of you," she said, although without rancour. "I shall make my will when I am good and ready, and not before."

"Just make sure we all know what is in it," Mrs Herbert said. "That way there will be no confusion or misunderstanding."

But Aunt Letty only cackled with laughter. "Horace, pour me some claret."

"Mama, Dr Harling said—" Mrs Fordham began.

"Never mind what Harling said. Claret, Horace, and none of your miserly half glasses, either. I want to enjoy life for a change."

~~~~~

'Dear Margaret, So sorry I have not written for a while, but we are giddy with entertainments at this present, as you may imagine. The only reason I have leisure to write today is because there is a dreadful downpour and we have had to postpone our Venetian breakfast, it being too inclement to take to the river. Tonight we are at Almack's, as usual, and tomorrow our first musical evening. We were at Carlton House two evenings ago and Robin was
~~~~~

distinguished by the Royal Personage, who spoke at least twelve words to him — such an honour! Do let me know how Mr Horace Bradwell's visit went off, and whether you have had any invitations while he is with you. Cannot write more as I am to meet Lady Carrbridge. Yours in haste, Rosamund. PS Forgot to tell you that Robin saw Lord Delacrost recently and Pendarreth was mentioned, but he did not say anything about you. I think he has left town now though.'

~~~~~

Three days later, Aunt Letty had another of her seizures, and a rather more severe one this time. For several days, only Dr Harling and the maids were allowed into her room, and the other five members of the household ate their meals in near silence in the breakfast room. Then Mr Bradwell was allowed in occasionally.

One day, Lord Delacrost arrived and was closeted with Aunt Letty for several hours. Mr Bradwell was summoned once or twice, but mostly the viscount was alone with Aunt Letty. Lord Delacrost stayed for dinner that evening, which rather astonished Margaret, for he had never done so before.

This threw the staff into great turmoil, for they were to eat in the great hall in honour of the occasion, with fires hastily lit and the long table laid with six covers at the end nearest the kitchen. They gathered before the meal in the withdrawing room, the holland covers barely removed in time, and the air still full of dust.

To Margaret's even greater astonishment, Lord Delacrost came directly to her when he entered the room and sat beside her.

"Are you well, Miss Winterton?" he asked politely. Too flummoxed to find any words, she simply nodded her head, but he went on smoothly, "Are you well settled here now? It must be four months since you came into Shropshire."
~~~~~

"Yes," she managed. "Thank you."

"And are you pleased with the county?"

"Very." With a supreme effort, she added, "I like the woods." But her heart was racing, and she could hardly breathe. Oh, if only he would leave her alone! He had not addressed a word to her since the day she had been introduced to him, and she had found it a perfectly satisfactory state of affairs.

"Ah, Dunton Woods! A fine piece of land. I had thoughts of buying it, until it was discovered that Miss Tilford owned it, and she is less amenable to selling than Mrs Bradwell." He laughed in a relaxed way, not at all put out, it seemed. "But perhaps she might lease it to me, for a consideration. She is a clever lady, Miss Tilford, and she may see leasing as the most profitable option, for the woods are seldom used these days. I am glad they give you pleasure, Miss Winterton. And you have made friends in Dunton Cross, I hear. Dr and Mrs Simpson, and Mr Haymer."

She nodded, not sure what to say.

"There is great excitement amongst the common people on the subject. You know what villagers are like, Miss Winterton — they gossip about everything, and in particular they love to make matches. If there be an unattached man in the village, and an unattached lady — why, the common folk will have them paired off before one can turn round. I am sure you know how it is. You lived in a village before, as I understand."

Again she nodded, letting him say what he had clearly come to say to her. Knowing Mel's true history, she understood the viscount's concern that there might be a marriage in the offing. She listened as he went on talking.

"And if nothing is done to contradict such rumours, why, they grow and grow until they become established fact and the two persons concerned, however little they may have thought of such a thing for themselves, find all their friends in expectation of the happy day of their union. And so one or other of them may begin to consider the matter as being already settled. But sometimes a word here or there will set things straight so that no one is disappointed, and no one is obliged by the weight of expectation to do something that perhaps he may not be willing to do. Do you understand me, Miss Winterton?"

Another nod, but she could not prevent a blush from creeping over her cheeks. She brought out her slate box, and wrote, *'I am not betrothed to Mr Haymer, nor do I have any intention of being so.'*

He nodded, and abruptly rose and crossed the room. Not long after, they were called in to dinner by one of Mr Bradwell's manservants. There were only six diners, and Margaret might have supposed that they could make their own way in whatever order pleased them, but Aunt Pru, being in the rôle of hostess, would not have things so informal.

"Lord Delacrost, I suppose you should lead dear Selina to table..."

"I beg you will excuse me, aunt," Mrs Herbert said crisply. "His lordship should offer his arm to *you*, I think."

"Oh no, dear, no! A single lady take precedence over a married woman? That cannot be right."

"Then perhaps Mrs Fordham will take my arm, and Mr Bradwell should certainly accompany his aunt," the viscount said with all the authority of nobility.

Meekly, they fell into place, Margaret taking up a position at the rear with Mrs Herbert.

"There, that is better!" that lady said comfortably. "We need no man to lean upon as we walk the twenty feet to our dinner."

It was considerably more than twenty feet, which gave Margaret plenty of time to ponder the interesting idea that Mrs Herbert disliked the viscount rather strongly, and to wonder at it.

The dinner was not a great deal better than usual, for poor Primrose had had no notice of the extra guest, or time to prepare such dishes as might be supposed to tempt the appetite of a lord. In the event, he ate from every dish without discrimination, and apart from praising a ragout of veal, made no comment on the food. He and Mr Bradwell carried the conversation between them, Mrs Herbert being almost as silent as Margaret, and Mrs Fordham opening her mouth only to complain that a dish was too rich or too plain or too spicy or the meat not adequately cooked or the servants not quick enough with the removes. Aunt Pru, as always, ate like a bird and said nothing unless spoken to directly. No one said anything to Margaret, but she caught the viscount's piercing blue eyes resting on her from time to time. On each occasion, she looked away quickly and when next her eyes strayed in his direction, he was no longer looking at her.

When the ladies withdrew, Margaret was able to take advantage of the magnificent pianoforte in the withdrawing room for the first time, and there she stayed for the rest of the evening, playing softly and escaping attention while the rest of the party played cards and talked about people of whom she had never heard. She was very glad to reach the tranquillity of her bedroom at last.

The following day, the viscount came again, very early, when Margaret and Mr Bradwell were at breakfast and the other ladies were not yet dressed. This time, Lord Delacrost brought Mr Higgins, the attorney, with him, together with the attorney's clerk, and Mr Harling, the physician. The visitors went straight in to Aunt Letty, and Mr Bradwell, despite voluble protests, was excluded.

Several hours passed, during which Aunt Pru followed Margaret around the house — to the library first, and then to the withdrawing room, where Margaret had decided that the sheet music needed to be rearranged to a proper system, and her own added to the Pendarreth collection. Poor Aunt Pru said little, only wringing her hands and picking up her shawl, which repeatedly fell from one or other arm. They were joined by Mrs Herbert and Mrs Fordham as soon as they were dressed, and then Mr Bradwell, pacing back and forth, hands clasped behind his back.

In the middle of the afternoon, Rose came to find them.

"Mistress's compliments, but would you care to join her in her room."

Aunt Pru, Mr Bradwell and his two sisters immediately left the room. With a sigh, Margaret turned back to her piles of music.

"And you too, miss," Rose said, half apologetically. "She mentioned you by name."

Aunt Letty was in bed, her face grey with exhaustion. Lord Delacrost, Mr Higgins, Dr Harling and the clerk stood to one side of the bed, while Aunt Pru and Aunt Letty's children were on the other. Aunt Letty's maid, Holly, was at the foot of the bed, looking anxious. Margaret felt she had no business to stand with the immediate family, for this matter did not concern her, so she took up a position beside Holly. Rose crept into the room in her wake, and shut the door.

Mr Higgins cleared his throat. "Mrs Bradwell has instructed me to inform you all that she has this day drawn up a new will to dispose of the property of Pendarreth and other considerations.

She has given me very clear instructions, and I have written the will according to her exact wishes. Dr Harling will vouch for Mrs Bradwell's state of mind and confirm that she is not suffering from any confusion. He has graciously witnessed Mrs Bradwell's signature to this new statement of her wishes, as have I. The major part of Mrs Bradwell's wealth is held by her only for her lifetime, and will be disposed of according to the terms of her late husband's will, but for the goods and property held in her own name, I am instructed to inform you all that there are only two principal beneficiaries, Miss Prudence Tilford and Miss Margaret Winterton."

A sigh ran through the room, a little breeze of disappointed hopes.

"*Margaret?*" Mrs Fordham said, in outraged tones. "You would leave something to your niece, rather than your own children?"

Margaret felt just as shocked, and a shiver ran over her. A beneficiary? It was totally unexpected, for Aunt Letty had never shown the least sign of the kind of interest in her welfare that might lead her to make her a bequest.

Mr Higgins cleared his throat. "Mrs Bradwell feels that her own children are adequately provided for. Miss Winterton, however, has no prospect of marriage without a dowry, no matter how small."

"Oh, a *small* dowry," Mrs Fordham said with a sniff. "Not that she will think of marrying while she is still in mourning for her father. And Aunt Pru is to get Pendarreth. So that is settled, then."

Aunt Pru burst into tears of joy. "Oh, sister! Dear sister, I knew you would do the right thing in the end! How happy—"

"Yes, yes, but go away now," Aunt Letty said, her voice hoarse, her breath ragged. "All of you, go away."

~~~~~

JUNE

All was harmony at Pendarreth now. Mr Bradwell, Mrs Herbert and Mrs Fordham returned to their homes, being now convinced that their mother was not about to expire on the spot and following Dr Harling's advice that calm was the best treatment for her irritated nerves. Aunt Pru was happy and smiling, attentive to her sister and quite determined to elbow Holly aside, and tend to all Aunt Letty's needs herself. Aunt Letty's health improved under this restful regime.

Margaret was glad all was settled, and Pendarreth could return to its usual somnolence. She tried not to think of the bequest that might be hers. A few hundred pounds, perhaps, certainly no more, for she knew from Aunt Letty's letters that she had not much money in hand, only her widow's portion, which was merely an income for life. She must have contrived to save a little from it. How kind of Aunt Letty to make provision for her!

Not that she wanted to marry, not even Mel, as she had told him, although not solely for the reason she had given. She was not fit to be a wife, or to have the management of a household, or to raise children, not when she could not even talk properly. Having long ago come to terms with her inadequacy, she accepted that she was excluded from the normal ambitions of womanhood. She could not explain this to Mel, for he would argue, sweet man that he was, and tell her it did not matter a jot, and other such nonsense. But it did matter, and she was resigned to spinsterhood, and a life as the little-regarded poor relation in the household of one or other of her sisters.
~~~~~

Before they had left, Mrs Herbert and Mrs Fordham had amused themselves by listing all the eligible young men of the neighbourhood, and endeavouring to find the best match for Margaret, now that she was to have a dowry.

"It could be Arthur Malham," Mrs Fordham said. "He will inherit the farm, eventually, and a very pretty piece of land it is too. Why, his mother has her own coach *and* a barouche, and dresses very fine. That would be a good match."

Margaret bent over her sewing, trying to pretend they were not discussing her future happiness as if she were not even there.

"He must be close on forty," Mrs Herbert said, laughing. "Really, Tabitha! Try for someone a little nearer to Cousin Margaret's own age."

"Well then, Edward Haymer is much of an age with her. The son of a viscount might be aiming a little high, perhaps, although one must remember what a close interest Lord Delacrost has taken in Mama's affairs. There is no chance of Mortimer, of course. As the heir, he will need to make a great match. What do you think, Selina?"

"Edward is a pleasant boy, but I do not suppose you have ever met him, have you, Margaret dear?" She shook her head. "There, you see? And a younger son must look for an heiress, not a girl with a modest dowry, such as Margaret will have. As for Mortimer, she is a great deal better off without him. He was an unpleasant boy and I doubt he has improved much. But how about a different branch of the Haymer family? The curate from Dunton Cross is here frequently, and gets on well with her, is not it so, dear? That would be a perfectly unexceptionable match."

Margaret kept her own counsel, but she quailed as she wondered what they would say if they knew the truth — that Mel was the legal heir to Lord Delacrost, and not an illegitimate son. And she wondered uneasily if Mortimer Haymer realised. It was so odd that no one acknowledged Mel, when the birth had been properly registered, and was not a great secret. His name was even in Debrett's, together with his date of birth, for she had looked it up. It was very puzzling, but it was not a puzzle she could resolve, so she put it out of her head.

11: A Long-Expected Death

As she was not yet needed again for secretarial duties, Margaret continued her walks in the woods, methodically exploring and marking her findings on the map. Sometimes, she went to the little grave, and always now there were fresh flowers on it, pretty little woodland blooms, tied into a posy with a ribbon. Once she found that the inscription marked in coloured stones had been destroyed, the stones scattered about, but the next time it had been begun again — *'Melville Ma'* it read, and at each visit a few more letters had been added. In many weeks of such walks she had never seen another soul, apart from Aunt Pru, who did not even notice Margaret waving to her from a nearby path or clearing, but would walk on, head down, muttering to herself and stabbing at the ground with her stick. Poor Aunt Pru! She had taken the loss of Pendarreth hard.

On wet days, or during odd hours when no other occupation called, Margaret tidied and sorted and rearranged in the library and withdrawing room until every paper and book and piece of music was in its place, arranged by size and then alphabetically.

Every week, she sat at her desk and attempted to write to her sisters but still the words would not come. Even at the parsonage now she could not do it. There was so much she wanted to share with her sisters, but the words swirled in her head and refused to come out. It was frustrating to feel so much inside her and yet not be able to express it. With her slate box, it was easier and easier to say exactly what was in her mind — or her heart. But with a pen in her hand, it was impossible. What a strange, defective creature she was!

During the daytime hours, she kept herself busy enough not to brood, but at night her thoughts would crowd in on her, and she would sit by the open window listening to the wind soughing in the trees or the rain pattering down, and remember her sisters. When she was particularly restless, she would slip silently out of her room and creep through the house, listening to its night-time creaks and shufflings, smelling the sweet summer air rising from the gardens and run her fingers over the smooth wooden bannisters. She liked houses at night when their occupants were asleep, and she could feel the house like a great creature, yawning and stretching itself. At least, most of the occupants were asleep, but occasionally she glimpsed a wavering candle in a different part of the house, and once she almost bumped into Aunt Pru, just managing to fade into the shadows in time. Margaret was not the only one who wandered the house at night.

She no longer needed Mel's help to get to church each Sunday, but this was not such a great loss as it might have been, for when she set out on foot, as soon as she entered the woods she was sure to encounter him somewhere along the path, waiting for her. After the service, he walked most of the way home with her, and sometimes, before they separated, he would allow her to steal a kiss.

Once a month, she stayed on for the Eucharist too, and then she would invariably be invited to dinner at the parsonage. On those days, they would pass the whole afternoon in the parlour, with the door wide open for propriety, while he talked and she tapped away on her slate, and both of them laughed a great deal. She could not remember when she had laughed so much. Not since Jeremy had gone away, perhaps. He had always had that happy knack of making every day as sunny as summer, and even the most commonplace expressions delightfully humorous. Mel had something of the same talent for lifting her spirits.

She had tried to explain it to him, but without success. *'You always make me feel better,'* she wrote one day.

"Were you unhappy before?" he said, his soft voice filled with concern.

'No, I just felt ordinary. You make me feel different. Full of energy. As if everything is coloured more vividly, and not grey and dull and flat. I feel as if I can do anything."

And he had smiled, and accepted the compliment gracefully, but without any real understanding. It was not being in love that made her feel that way, she knew that. Love was a different feeling, a warmth that started in her heart and spilled out to fill her whole body. But this well-being was something else, and it took her a while to fully comprehend it.

Her joy came, she realised, from being loved in return.

It was not just the light in Mel's eyes when he looked at her, making her shiver. Nor was it his kisses, glorious as they were. It was his utter acceptance of her just as she was, her own queer, half-broken self, with all her paralysing shyness and inability to string a coherent sentence together. He never tried to push her to talk or to mingle in company. When she haltingly attempted speech, he never finished her sentences for her, or, if she wrote, jumped in to answer before she had half written what she wanted to say. He was infinitely kind and patient and understanding, and he made her feel utterly safe. He was her friend and protector, he loved and cherished her, and she was totally content with him.

But life could not go on in this charming state of bliss for ever, and the day came when Margaret's aunts fell out again. The irritant was once more the fate of Dunton Heights. Being unable to buy the land, Lord Delacrost now pressed Aunt Pru to lease the woods to him, on whatever terms she deemed acceptable. She refused.

"Oh no! No, no, no! The woods are sacred, they are not to be *used.* It was bad enough with Horace and his dogs rampaging through like an army on the move, devastating the undergrowth and scaring away all the songbirds, but at least he is seldom here. But I cannot permit such destruction on a regular basis. Oh no, indeed not."

So she said repeatedly. But one day when they were sitting around the dinner table in Aunt Letty's room, Aunt Letty said, "Now sister, it is time we settled the matter of Dunton Heights once and for all. I cannot keep Matthew waiting indefinitely. It is not as if the land is to be sold — it is only a lease, after all. I must have your agreement to this, and no more nonsense."

Aunt Pru dropped her soup spoon in distress. "Oh *no*, sister! I could not! It is impossible."

"Gentlemen must have their sport," Aunt Letty said brusquely. "Especially when it puts food on the table. You enjoy a partridge dish as well as any of us, I daresay, sister."

"Not when the birds come from Dunton Heights," she said with a visible shudder.

"Good Lord, Pru, you are as protective as a mother hen with those woods. Well, if they are not available, then there are some other parcels of land belonging to Pendarreth that could be made available to Matthew, for a price."

"Parcels of land?" Aunt Pru said faintly.

"There are several minor agreements subsisting between the two estates which need to be regularised," Aunt Letty said. "It is always so with these large estates which run alongside each other, that there are numerous trivial little arrangements that date back centuries, some formal and some informal. Matthew has identified a number which could sensibly be regularised so that I may leave Pendarreth in good order. Rose, remove this soup. Girl, pass me the asparagus. Lord, I love asparagus. There is nothing quite like it."

Aunt Pru paled, and, not long after, left the room.

"Pfft, she has no stomach for business dealings," Aunt Letty said. "Hard to imagine how she would manage if she were mistress here. Let the place go to rack and ruin, most likely." And she laughed heartily at this prediction, although Margaret thought Pendarreth was already on the way to rack and ruin. Aunt Letty reached for her glass, taking a sip and then pulling a face. "Damn this tasteless pap! Rose, fetch me some claret and never mind Harling's orders."

The next day, Lord Delacrost came to talk to both the sisters, a discussion which left Aunt Pru in tears. They argued all afternoon, until Aunt Letty had one of her seizures. Then Aunt Pru was stricken with remorse, and nothing would do for her but she would tend her sister herself.

"It is too late to send for Dr Harling today," she said, her voice cracked with distress. "By the time someone has gone down to Heston Ford and found him and fetched him back, it will be dark. Besides, we know what to do for her."

"Aye, the tonic in the blue bottle, one measure at once, then two more when she can manage them, then every two hours," Holly said.

Dinner was a silent affair, and as soon as she had eaten a few mouthfuls, Aunt Pru went back to Aunt Letty's side. Margaret went to the music room, as usual, but music would be inappropriate with such illness in the house, so she read for a while, rearranged the ornaments on the mantel in size order, and then went early to bed, there being nothing else to do.

The following morning, Margaret was woken before dawn by Rose, bending over her with a candle in her hand.

"Miss! Wake up, miss. You'd best come. It's your aunt — she's gone."

Gone? "Where has she gone?" Margaret said, only half awake. Then she realised, and shot upright in bed.

"Aye, she's dead," Rose said grimly. "Took sudden in the night. Ivy came to get me, but by the time I got to her room, she were gone. Poor lady. And poor Miss Prudence. She'll miss her sister something fierce."

Margaret scrambled into some clothes, and went into the room next door. There Aunt Letty was, her skin grey even by candle light, no longer propped up on her pillows as she liked to lie, but sprawled sideways onto the blankets where her last, most dramatic, spasm had hurled her. Her mouth was wide open, but her eyes, thankfully, were closed.

Aunt Pru, still in her robe and voluminous night cap, was kneeling beside the bed, weeping. Ivy, Holly and Primrose stood in a little cluster near the door, Holly sobbing noisily. One by one the other servants crept in.

Margaret crossed to the desk, pulled out paper and pen, and wrote, *'Has anyone sent for Dr Harling?'*

When she showed it to Rose, she shook her head. "No one's touched her or done anything. We was waiting for orders." She nodded towards Aunt Pru, who was muttering under her breath now, as if praying.

"I touched her," Ivy said, suddenly. "When I saw her lying there not breathing, I tried to rouse her. She fell like that, all in a heap across the bed. So I ran for Rose. Miss, may I... may I set her straight? She don't look right lying like that."

Margaret considered, then wrote, *'Put her back in exactly the position she was in when you found her. Then leave her like that for Dr Harling to examine.'* A moment's thought, and then she added. *'Someone should go at once for the doctor. And send word to the parsonage.'* She chewed the pen thoughtfully. *'The doctor may want breakfast. Also, there might be many visitors over the next few days.'*

"Cakes," Primrose said at once. "And a funeral tea to think about. Heather my girl, we have work to do."

"I'll go for the doctor," Daisy said.

"Good, and Poppy, you can run over to Dunton Cross to tell them at the parsonage," Rose said briskly. "Jasmine, go and get started on the grates, will you?" The maids began to disappear to their appointed tasks. "Will you be all right, miss?" she said to Margaret.

She nodded. *'I will look after Aunt Pru. May I have some coffee, please?'*

~~~~~

The inhabitants of the parsonage were still abed when a loud pounding on the door, accompanied by yells of, "Oy! Wake up! You's wanted at Pendarreth!" drew them protesting from their blankets. Mel and the Simpsons emerged onto the landing and stared at each other, bewildered.

"Whatever hour is it?" Mrs Simpson said.

"Four or five — no later than that," Mel said. "I will go down, and see what has happened."

The hammering ceased as soon as he began to draw back the bolts. The door creaked open, and there was Poppy's white face.

"The mistress is gone, sir. Dead as a doornail. In her sleep, like."

"Come in, Polly, and wait in the kitchen while I get dressed."

She scuttled away, just as Dr and Mrs Simpson descended the stairs. "Mrs Bradwell?"

Mel nodded. "I can deal with it. If the good lady is already gone, there is no urgency, so go back to bed. I will take Robert with me to convey messages."

It took almost an hour for him to dress, and the horses to be made ready. Leaving the groom to follow more slowly with Poppy, Mel rode along the track to Pendarreth. He stabled his horse, and entered the house by way of the kitchen.

"Where are the ladies, Primrose?"

"Still in Mrs Bradwell's room," the cook said, raising her eyes heavenwards, without ceasing to knead her dough. "Miss Prudence is that upset, sir, no one can get her to stir from her sister's side."
~~~~~

Mel made his way along the familiar passageways and up the stairs. He knocked on Mrs Bradwell's door, and Rose opened it to him, her anxious expression changing to relief when she saw him.

"Come in, sir. There now, Miss Prudence, here's Mr Haymer to see you."

Mel's eyes swept the room, taking it in at a glance — the dead woman on the bed, her sister kneeling beside it, looking up briefly at him before bowing her head again, the maids standing quietly and—

She was already in black, sitting in a corner, head down, reading what looked like the Bible. When he entered, she jumped up, set her Bible on a table, and came towards him, hands outstretched.

How could he resist her? It was inappropriate, here at this sombre scene, but he could not help it. He caught hold of the hands reaching for him, and clasped them to his chest. To his heart, he realised, the right and proper place for them.

"Miss Winterton, I cannot tell you how sorry I am. My deepest condolences." If his voice was not quite steady, it was not from want of trying. "This happened during the night, I understand?" She nodded. "Has Miss Tilford been like this ever since?" Another nod. Her eyes were huge in the pale face, looking up trustingly at him.

Reluctantly, he released her, and stepped nearer to the bed, crouching down beside Aunt Pru. "Miss Tilford? Will you not come and sit on a chair, Miss Tilford? You will be so much more comfortable."

With a sob, she shook her head.

"May I pray for your sister?"

A hesitation, but then she nodded.

He stood at the head of the bed, and began reciting the first prayer in a quiet voice. Hearing him, Holly came through from the dressing room, and knelt beside Aunt Pru, head bowed. Margaret did not kneel, but stood, head lowered, eyes closed. He thought she swayed a little, matching her movements to the cadences of the words. She had so much music in her that wanted to burst out, so much *life*. She looked like a timid little mouse, but inside was a tigress waiting to display her sinuous grace.

By the time Mel reached the Pater Noster, Aunt Pru was recovered enough to say some of the words, after which she seemed a little more herself.

"You will bury her?" she croaked, looking at Mel. "It must be you."

Mel hesitated. "Dr Simpson is the rector. It might be considered a slight if the curate takes the burial. Mrs Bradwell is one of the neighbourhood's principal inhabitants."

She drew herself up a little. "I am her sister, and my wishes must prevail."

"Perhaps her son may disagree? Burials are men's work, Miss Tilford, but I assure you that I shall be there to see your sister safely sent to her eternal rest."

After a pause, she nodded and allowed Holly and Rose to help her to her feet and lead her gently from the room. Mel gestured for Margaret to follow him out likewise.

As they stood in the passageway outside Aunt Letty's room, watching Aunt Pru slowly making her way to her own room along the gallery above the great hall, he said in a low voice, "How are you? Not overset?"

She shook her head, and gave him a little smile.

"I did not expect it, for you have too much good sense to become overwrought. Has anyone gone for Dr Harling?" A nod. "And Mr Trimfoot, the carpenter?" A shake of the head. "My groom is following, bringing Poppy, so he may ride down to Heston Ford. And word must be sent to the family. That task will fall to you, I imagine." She nodded again. "And Lord Delacrost, perhaps. He was a particular friend. Mr Higgins, also. But her son first."

She nodded, shivering, and he understood her fears. Everything had changed, and now the future was uncertain.

12: The Reading Of The Will

With Aunt Pru prostrate, all the management of the house now fell upon Margaret's shoulders. She spent the morning writing letters in the study to all those Mr Haymer had suggested, and also to her own sisters. She had to force herself, but it must be done and at least she did not have to think about the words, or find an interesting way to express them. *'Mrs Bradwell had died'* or *'Aunt Letty has died'* — nothing more was needed. Daisy was dispatched to take them at once to the post office in Heston Ford.

Rose came and went, needing orders for the kitchen or the preparations for visitors. Men came from the village, for death was a matter for men, that was understood. The knocker sounded again and again, and with Aunt Pru keeping to her room, it was Margaret's lot to attend to the visitors. Dr Harling was kindly, seeing to Aunt Letty, then spending almost an hour with Aunt Pru.

"I have given her a sedative," he said, as Margaret showed him to the door. "She is asleep now, poor lady. No doubt she will feel better in a few days, if she follows my instructions carefully and receives no further upset, but I will not vouch for her health if she receives another blow so soon after the loss of her sister. Still," he added thoughtfully, "it is not like her to be *quite* so overset. She had always a great deal of sensibility, but this is not an unforeseen circumstance, after all." He hesitated. "You are a sensible woman, Miss Winterton, so I do not scruple to tell you that Mrs Bradwell has not always shown as much consideration as one would expect from a lady towards her less fortunate sister. Miss Tilford has been quite distressed in recent months, and a few words would have made her completely easy. But now... Still, she has you, and you will take care of her, I am sure."

Margaret nodded, although his words started a dozen hares running. Take care of Aunt Pru? Her aunt had never seemed to need to be taken care of, and given their positions, with Aunt Pru now the sole mistress of Pendarreth and Margaret the very poor relation, the case would seem to be quite the reverse. Would Aunt Pru even want her to stay on at Pendarreth? Her rôle had been as companion to Aunt Letty, to ensure Aunt Pru was not tied to the sickroom. Now that she was relieved of that duty, was there any reason for her to stay? Aunt Pru had managed perfectly well on her own for years, after all. The rest of the family had come and gone, but there had been long spells when she had been alone at Pendarreth, as the guest books in the study testified.

The memory of the guest books joggled some thought in her mind, but it was ephemeral, drifting out of range before she could grasp it. Aunt Pru... alone... long spells...? No, it was gone.

Dr Harling was looking expectantly at her, as if awaiting her answer, but she had heard not a word. "Um..."

"Pray allow me to reiterate, Miss Winterton," he said in tones that suggested his time was far too valuable to concern itself with repetition for the benefit of absent minded young ladies. "My question was whether you yourself might be in need of a restorative. May I give you a tonic? Something to help you to sleep?"

She shook her head, then added, "No, thank you."

"Hmpf. You think yourself fully in command of your feelings and quite unruffled, I daresay, but come the evening, your thoughts may overcome you, and you are of an age prone to hysteria. Here..." He rummaged in his bag, and produced a small brown bottle, already neatly labelled with her name and dosage instructions. "It will be best to do as I suggest, Miss Winterton."

She had not the words to argue with him, so she accepted the bottle and made him a small curtsy.

"There, that's a good girl," he said. "I shall call again tomorrow to see how your aunt goes on, but do not hesitate to send for me if she becomes hysterical again."

Mel came to take his leave after sitting with her aunt, but assured her he would return later that day. Not half an hour after he had gone, Lord Delacrost arrived.

After he had offered his condolences, she pulled out her slate box and wrote, *'Do you wish to see my Aunt Bradwell?'*

"I will see her, yes. She was an old friend, and I must make my farewells."

The bed had been straightened and remade with an embroidered cover on top of the blankets. Aunt Letty lay flat, as she never had in life, with a single pillow beneath her head. She had been dressed in a fine silk gown, her hair tidied and her face coloured with a little powder and rouge. Margaret had never seen her wearing anything but a bed robe, and gazed at this new, stylish aunt with fascination.

"Well, Letty," the viscount said, picking up her wrinkled hand adorned with several jewelled rings, "the deed is done, and we must hope for the best, eh? I wish you good fortune, my old friend, until we meet again." His voice was perhaps a shade more subdued than normal, but still he sounded exactly as if he spoke to a living person and not a corpse.

He set Aunt Letty's hand down again and turned to look thoughtfully at Margaret. "Did your aunt talk to you about this *dowry* of yours, or who she wished you to marry?"

Margaret shook her head.

"No, she has been too ill, of course." He looked her up and down. "Now you are back in mourning for your aunt. Hmmm... did you ever leave off black for your father? I did not notice. Ah, you were in half mourning, I think."

She nodded.

"Well, that is very proper. What would you consider appropriate for your aunt? No more than three months, I daresay. Would you agree?"

She chewed her lip, then brought out her slate box. *'I will follow Aunt Tilford's lead.'*

"Ha! Then you will never leave off your blacks, for she has been wearing black ribbons for as long as I can remember — decades, and as often as not could not say who she was mourning. But you are young, and must look to the future. A month, perhaps six weeks, of full black for your aunt, but then you might start to consider the matter of a husband. It would be as well to have it settled sooner rather than later. Ah, there is the knocker again. Higgins arriving, I daresay, so I shall take my leave of you, Miss Winterton."

He accompanied her back to the front door, where she found Mr Higgins knocking in some impatience.

"You had better get some crêpe on the knocker," the viscount said in disapproving tones. "Not at all the thing to have so much noise in a house of mourning. Good day to you, Miss Winterton. Higgins."

"My lord," Mr Higgins said, bowing low, but his lordship swept past without a glance and leapt into his waiting carriage, leaving Margaret bemused. Why on earth was he interested in her marrying? And how could that possibly be relevant on such a day? Yet he had been with Aunt Letty when she had drawn up her new will, which included a bequest for Margaret. Was it possible that he had her in mind for one of his own sons? Mortimer, the elder, and rather a wild character, or Edward, the younger, a gentler soul, if rumour spoke true. No, surely a viscount could look higher for a daughter-in-law than the near-penniless niece of a neighbour.

The days passed in a whirl of activity. Aunt Pru kept to her room, taking her dinner on a tray. Mr and Mrs Bradwell arrived, and then Mr and Mrs Fordham and Mr and Mrs Herbert, and they brought all their children with them, for Aunt Letty's husband had been a very wealthy man, and all his fortune, held by Aunt Letty for her lifetime, was now to be distributed. Suddenly the house felt overfull, and Margaret could find no refuge to escape the bustle.

~~~~~

'My poor, dear sister, Such shocking news! I had no notion that poor Aunt Letty was so ill, for in your last letter you said she was better and so naturally one hopes for a sustained improvement. And now this! How dreadful for you to be back in mourning again. At least, I suppose you had set aside your blacks for Papa, for I had done so, and I know Fanny and Annabelle also, and Rosamund cannot be in
~~~~~

deep mourning when she is in London and out gallivanting every night. Although I do not see Mr Dalton as much of a gallivanter, do you? He is much too correct for that. He processes through a room, like royalty. Very imposing. But that is nothing to the point. What will happen to you now dearest? Shall you have to leave? And where will you go? I suppose you will have to throw yourself on Rosamund's mercy, and naturally she will take you in at once, but it will be awkward for you, for they cannot leave London just now and I cannot think that it will suit you to be in such a hustle-bustle place. Perhaps Fanny might be able to beg a favour from Lady Harriet, for she seems to be a very amiable lady, and not at all stiff-rumped as some of these high ranking females are. I can do nothing for you, for Mr K is not at all accommodating, and Annabelle is only the governess and not in any position to ask for help for a sister, however agreeable her earl is. You poor dear, I do feel for you! Do you have friends about you to support you? I am sure you do, for with your sweet nature you must have scores of kindly friends. Do write at once to tell me how you go on, dearest, or if you cannot manage to write to each of us, you may write just to Rosamund and she will pass on your news. Or it might be better to write to Annabelle, for then there will be nothing to pay on the letters. Do write soon, dear Margaret. Your worried sister, Lucy.'

~~~~~

The day of the funeral arrived. The women wept over the coffin as it was removed, and watched the doleful procession of carriages depart. Then they withdrew to the library to drink Madeira and eat bonbons and reminisce over the deceased until the men should return. Aunt Pru disappeared to her room, and Margaret sat quietly in a corner, trying not to think about Papa's funeral only a few months earlier, or the dreadful reading of the will afterwards when Mr Plumphett — poor Mr Plumphett, so distressed he could barely
~~~~~

speak — had had the unhappy task of informing the Woodside sisters that they were destitute, and would soon be homeless. At least this will contained nothing to distress her, just a small legacy as a dowry.

The Miss Bradwells, Miss Herberts and Miss Fordhams clustered in a far corner to whisper together, their black-feathered fans held up to hide their faces from their mamas. The older ladies gathered in a rustle of bombazine around the cold fireplace, its massive tapestry screen of once vibrantly coloured peacocks faded to grey outlines. Mrs Fordham soon tired of talking about her mama, and began to prowl about the room, opening the book cases and removing books at random, then walking away from them. Such acts of disorder greatly agitated Margaret, but she tried very hard not to fidget. She would be able to tidy them away into their proper places later.

"Lord, that is a monstrous ugly ormolu clock on the mantel," Mrs Fordham said. "Do you not think so, Selina? Has it just recently been put out?"

"It has been there for ever," Mrs Herbert said. "It used to have a chime, but something cracked inside so Vickers stopped it."

"Vickers? Who is Vickers?"

"The handyman from Heston Ford who was here when we were children," Mrs Herbert said. "Little, stooped man."

"No, it was Davidson who used to see to the clocks. The head footman with the cadaverous head. So ugly, although he could not help that, poor man. Every Monday morning he would go right round the house winding up all the clocks. I do not remember anyone called Vickers. He must have come later after Aunt Pru had her funny turn."

"Her funny turn?" Mrs Herbert said.

"Yes, surely you remember? It was when you were exiled here after you made a mull of your season. More than half the staff were let go and Mama was so angry about it, for she could not see why anyone would turn off a perfectly good butler. Aunt Pru just said she wanted no more men in the house, for they made her feel uncomfortable, and since there were only the two of you living here at the time, having more than a skeleton staff was an unnecessary extravagance. She even got rid of the cook, and kept only those two peculiar old women who lived over the stables. And yet you had this Vickers fellow here. How very odd. Why were all the others let go, and then he was taken on?"

Mrs Herbert looked at her blankly, her fingers playing with the fringe of her reticule. "I am sure I have no idea. You know Aunt Pru — always a little eccentric."

"But you were here, Selina. You must have known why she did it!"

She lifted one shoulder indifferently. "It was a very long time ago, Tabitha. All I recall of that time was spending a great deal of it in bed with all the curtains drawn. I hardly left my room for months and... everything is hazy. By the time I was myself again, most of the servants had already left, and if Aunt Pru ever gave a reason, I do not remember it. But I believe you are right about Davidson , so Vickers must have been later." She frowned, as if struggling to remember. "Well well, it is all in the distant past now. Ah, do I hear carriages approaching? Are they back at last? Margaret, will you go and look, dear, and fetch Aunt Pru if it is the gentlemen."

The viscount led the procession from the carriages into the library, a long line of men in black coats. Mel was there, half a head taller even than the viscount. Margaret recognised Dr Simpson, Dr

Harling, Mr Higgins and his clerk, and the apothecary. After she had let them in, she hastened upstairs to fetch Aunt Pru.

Her aunt was sitting quietly in a chair in her room, quite composed. As Margaret entered, she gave a smile that made her look ten years younger. "Are they all assembled? Then let us go down, for this time, we will hear the will read. Today begins the next stage of Pendarreth's future."

Sedately she walked along the passageway to the gallery, then down the stairs. Margaret followed, bemused by the change in her aunt. Gone was the fluttering little old lady, replaced by a serene matron, one who knew her place in the world and embraced it. Regally, she entered the library, passing composedly through the crowds of black to take her chair at the very front, like a queen.

Margaret would have scuttled away to a dark corner, but Mr Higgins sent his clerk after her. "This way, *if* you please, madam," he said, leading her determinedly to the very front, beside Aunt Pru. Her aunt smiled benignly at her. The viscount took the seat next to her, and with great rustlings and whisperings everyone else sat and Mr Higgins began.

The will was very long. After a lengthy preamble, there were small bequests for any number of servants and former servants, agents and managers, charitable gifts. Then Aunt Letty's own children — money or businesses or property to the men, jewellery to the women. Aunt Letty had held only a life interest in most of it, but her husband had left only vague instructions for how it was to be disposed of, so the recipients had not known what good fortune might come their way. There were smiles and gasps and a squeak of delight from one lady. Margaret was relieved that she would not receive anything so handsome. A modest dowry, that was all. A few hundred pounds, perhaps, scraped together from Aunt Letty's widow's portion.

Eventually, Mr Higgins came to the point.

"To my sister, Prudence Isobel Tilford of Pendarreth in the county of Shropshire, I leave all my remaining jewellery, including the Phillips tiara, the Tilford diamonds and the Haringay sapphires." He paused, but the smile on Aunt Pru's face never wavered. *"To my niece, Margaret Anne Winterton, formerly of Woodside in the county of Brinshire and presently residing at Pendarreth in the county of Shropshire, I leave the said Pendarreth in its entirety being the house and surrounding demesnes, and all monies pertaining thereto, to be hers without reservation, to use and enjoy as she pleases, provided that she shall continue to reside therein and not sell, lease or otherwise dispose of the said Pendarreth, and provided also that she marry one or other of my grandsons within a reasonable time of my decease. If she should marry elsewhere, or otherwise fail to comply with this requirement, as determined by the executors of this will, then ownership of Pendarreth shall transfer without condition to the Right Honourable the Viscount Delacrost. I nominate constitute and appoint Henry Aloysius Higgins and John Harling both of Heston Ford in the county of Shropshire executors of this my last will and testament in witness whereof I the said testator Letitia Jane Bradwell née Tilford have hereunto set my hand and seal the day and year above written."*

The silence in the room was absolute.

Margaret felt as if time had slowed, so that every breath, every beat of her heart saw minutes elapse. Yet the clock on the mantel ticked on relentlessly, its slow, sonorous beat reverberating through her head like a church bell. There was a humming, like the drone of bees, but far away, as if she were under water. Voices, but far, far away. A thin sound, like a distant scream.

Humming, humming... roaring... far away...

Something hit her face...

Falling...

13: A Change In Circumstances

Mel stood at the back, with the servants. His height gave him a clear view over the heads of those seated before the desk where Mr Higgins sat, and he had edged himself forwards a little so that he could see something of Margaret's face. It was not a good view, just a little of her profile, her expression solemn and her cheeks pale as alabaster. He wished he could see her eyes, those huge, luminous eyes that haunted his dreams. She looked so small and lost in the ornate library chair, of the type that was too large for any normal person. To one side, Lord Delacrost towered over her, and on her other side, Miss Tilford sat ramrod straight, an odd smile on her face.

Then the bequests, most of it having been held in trust by Mrs Bradwell for her children. Small smiles of satisfaction from each person named. Gleeful congratulatory glances from one to another. Then Miss Tilford was mentioned, and at last, Margaret...

Dear God, what had she done? Left Pendarreth to *Margaret?* And only if she should marry one of her cousins? What an abomination! Miss Tilford's face drained of all colour, her smile fading to incredulity. The room was so still, the ticking of the clock was audible. Margaret sat immobile, her hands folded neatly in her lap, but her face—!

He started forward, just as the room erupted in a babble of excited chatter. Half the listeners jumped to their feet, and Mel lost sight of Margaret for a moment. A male voice was shouting, "Impossible! Impossible!"

A shriek rent the air. Miss Tilford was on her feet, screaming and raining blows on—

"Margaret!" Mel gasped, hastening forwards.

Just as he got a clear sight of her again, she slid sideways off her chair, eyes closed. Mel battered his way forwards through the excited crowd, but could not reach her in time. It was the viscount who pushed her assailant back, and bent over Margaret. Scanning the room, his eyes fell on Mel's.

"Haymer! Here."

Mel reached Margaret's crumpled form and scooped her into his arms.

"Where to?" the viscount said.

"Outside," Mel said, nodding towards a door. He was finding it hard to catch his breath. Was she injured? Dead? No, even now her eyes were fluttering, and there was no blood.

"Stand aside!" the viscount said peremptorily, and miraculously a gap appeared in the crowds, those aware pulling aside those still too busy exclaiming in wonder to notice what else was going on. Mel strode through the opening, Margaret in his arms, as the viscount rushed ahead to open the door. Behind them, screams and shouts filled the air, but Mel paid them no attention. Let others deal with Miss Tilford.

He thought quickly — where to go? Not towards the great hall, where refreshments had been left out for the mourners.

"This way," he said, leading the way down the corridor to the entrance hall and then into the study next door. A fire burned low in the grate, and the tall windows spilt light into the room.

"Here, lay her down here," the viscount said, pointing to a chaise longue.

Gently Mel set her down. She was so pale, but her chest rose and fell steadily.

"We must find someone with smelling salts," Lord Delacrost said. "And... burnt feathers. Is that not what women use in such cases?"

Mel had not even had time to turn towards the door before Mrs Herbert and her daughters burst in. Somewhere in the distance, faint screams could still be heard.

"Dear heaven!" Mrs Herbert said. "What an uproar! Lord Delacrost, pray let us attend to Margaret. Susan, take my reticule and retrieve the smelling salts. Maria, find some brandy, dear. Mr Haymer, chafe her hands, like so."

Mel needed no urging to do so, kneeling down beside her with alacrity. Her fingers were as cold as ice, but almost as soon as he touched her, she opened her eyes and gazed up at him.

"Mel?"

"There now, dearest," he said. "Do not fret. You are quite safe."

Mrs Herbert waved the sal volatile under Margaret's nose, and she spluttered and sat bolt upright. "Ugh!" She pushed the bottle away. "Please, no more of that horrid stuff. I am perfectly all right, I assure you."

Mel sat back on his heels, chuckling.

"Whatever is the matter?" she said, tipping her head to one side. "Do share the jest."

"You are talking," he said simply. "How wonderful it is to hear your voice properly."

"Oh." She looked at him ruefully. "Yes. When I... first wake. But..." Helplessly she shrugged, the words drying up as she became aware of them.

"Now see what you have done," Mrs Herbert said to him crossly. "Ah, well done, Maria. Now, Margaret, have a sip of brandy, dear, and you will soon be just the thing."

Obediently she sipped, and Miss Susan Herbert, a well-grown young lady of twenty, sat beside her and wrapped a sisterly arm around her. "Poor, poor Cousin Margaret! Such a shock! I do not wonder you should be quite overset. We had no notion Grandmama meant to do anything so totty-headed."

"Really, Susan, where do you get such language?" her mother said.

"Why, Papa said—"

"That is quite enough!"

"But it is the *oddest* thing to do, Mama, you must own it. I am sure everyone expected Pendarreth to go to Great-aunt Pru, but to leave it to Cousin Margaret, and with the most peculiar conditions, why, what could she possibly mean by it?"

Mrs Herbert, who had been kneeling on the floor beside the chaise longue, now stood and pulled a footstool across to sit more comfortably. "It *is* odd, I will own. Margaret, had you the least idea?" She shook her head. "And clearly Aunt Pru had none, or she would not have set about you in quite that... that *violent* way, shrieking like a harridan, and slapping you, dear! So dreadful. Lord Delacrost, you were privy to Mama's mind when she was drawing up her will — do you know why she arranged matters so awkwardly?"

"No doubt she had her reasons," he said smoothly.

"Yes, yes, but what were they?"

"I cannot say."

"Cannot or will not? Oh, you are hopeless! Keep your own counsel then, if you must. You were always buttoned up. Why are you still here, anyway? A fainting female is women's work, my lord. Begone."

"Certainly, Mrs Herbert," he said, making her an ironic bow. "Mr Haymer, it appears our services are no longer required."

Mel had no choice but to release Margaret's hand. Her huge eyes followed him as he rose. Smiling down at her, he said, "You will go on well enough now, dearest. Mrs Herbert will take care of you. I shall call tomorrow to see how you do."

She nodded, but made no attempt to detain him, so he followed Lord Delacrost out of the door, where they almost bumped into Dr Simpson. "Ah, there you are, Mel. How is she?"

"Recovering."

"Good, good, but she cannot stay here. Miss Tilford is in a very excitable state, wildly hysterical. If she should attack Margaret again, who knows what the outcome may be? Let us take her to the parsonage."

"Nonsense," Lord Delacrost said brusquely. "She is perfectly safe here. Harling will be dealing with Pru, and once she has had a rest she will be quite herself again."

"My dear sir, you cannot possibly be certain of that," Dr Simpson said. "Miss Tilford hit Miss Winterton hard enough to render her unconscious, and had to be dragged away from her. It was the greatest good fortune that there were so many people present to intervene, and that there was no knife to hand."

"You exaggerate, Simpson. I saw a very elderly woman flailing her arms about in distress, that is all, and a young woman who fainted, as highly-strung young women are apt to do in a crisis. You make a piece of work about nothing."

"A piece of work—! Great heavens, man, if you are wrong, Miss Winterton could be murdered in her bed! It is unthinkable for her to continue here as if nothing had happened."

"Then she can come to the Manor," the viscount said. "Just until we can be sure of Pru's state of mind."

"The Manor? A young woman of one and twenty living at an establishment consisting only of three gentlemen? I hardly think so. She will come to the parsonage, where Mrs Simpson will be delighted to look after her."

"And *him*, I suppose," Lord Delacrost spat, glaring at Mel. "*He* will look after her, too, I make no doubt. Pah!"

He spun on his heel and stalked away towards the library, whence small knots of people were drifting, whispering in shocked voices.

"Hmm," Dr Simpson said, looking at Mel speculatively. "But we can consider his lordship's behaviour later. Do you go and see if Margaret wishes to come back to the parsonage with us, and I shall order the carriage brought round."

~~~~~

Margaret felt curiously light-headed, as if she had been cut free from the prosaic everyday world and left to float about, drifting in the wind with nothing to disturb her. The last time she had been in a carriage had been five long months earlier, in January, when Mr Robin Dalton had brought her to Pendarreth. Now she sat beside Dr Simpson with Mel opposite her, travelling away from the house, past the two stone gateposts and on down the narrow valley with its woodlands pressing close on either side. For a long time there were no habitations at all, then a lone house of red stone with pretty gardens all around it. *'Red Cottage'* was etched on the gate. Aunt Pru's house, left to her with the woods.

After another mile, they came to the outskirts of Heston Ford, all bustle and cheerful liveliness, with a market going on in the main street and hawkers shouting for custom and sheep bleating. A group of men, farmers by their clothes, were sitting outside an inn with tankards, singing lustily. They cheered as the carriage went by. "Hoy there, vicar!" one of them called out, but one of his friends shushed him, perhaps reminding him that the vicar had that day conducted a funeral service.

Margaret wondered what they would make of the news, when they heard it. Would they care? Some of them must farm Pendarreth land and owe allegiance to the family, but perhaps not so many now. She had seen the plans and the bills of sale, and knew what a great estate it had once been, and knew also how many parcels of land had been sold off over the years. Not large amounts, just a field or two here and there, and odd strips of land, but gradually Pendarreth had been nibbled away until little remained except the house and the valley and the woods. Even the woods had now been dispersed, for they belonged to Aunt Pru, while Pendarreth would soon belong to Lord Delacrost.
~~~~~

She could not bring herself to think of it as hers. Even though for a little while the law said it was so, it depended on her marrying one of Aunt Letty's grandsons, and that she would not do. She would never marry anyone, not Mel and certainly not one of the indistinguishable young men who had been introduced to her barely two days ago. It was monstrous of Aunt Letty to expect it of her.

They turned onto the main road, but before the town was quite left behind, they made another turn into a high-hedged lane between farmland heavy with corn on one side and pasture on the other. The lane meandered about past cottages and over small streams and eventually, after several miles, into the village of Dunton Cross, and the familiar parsonage beside the church.

John, the manservant, emerged from the house to greet them, trying to suppress his surprise at seeing Margaret handed down from the carriage by Dr Simpson, and a couple of boxes strapped to the back of it.

"Please find your mistress, John, and inform her that we have a guest staying for a few days. Put the boxes in the guest room. Oh, you had better advise Mrs Milligan, but tell her that Miss Winterton knows to expect pot luck."

Then there was a little bustle, with the maids coming out to help with the boxes, and a couple of grooms, and then Mrs Simpson hurrying out to greet her.

"Oh, my dear Margaret! But whatever has happened? Wait — is that a bruise beside your eye?"

"We will tell you all directly, my dear," Dr Simpson said, " but do you take Miss Winterton upstairs to remove her bonnet and rest a little. She has had a trying morning. There will be tea and cakes in the library, Miss Winterton, whenever you feel like company."

Mrs Simpson looked from one to the other, then wisely suppressed the questions that she clearly wished to ask. She whisked Margaret straight up to what she now thought of as her very own bedroom. Only one night had she passed there, but still it felt homely and reassuring. She removed her bonnet and gloves, and Mrs Simpson unbuttoned her spencer for her. That lady said nothing, for there was nothing to be said without knowing the whole story. Still, Margaret could see that she was agog with curiosity, although far too well-bred to ask. She sat down on the bed and pulled out her slate box.

'Aunt Letty left Pendarreth to me, but only if I marry one of her grandsons which I have no intention of doing. If I do not, then it goes to Lord Delacrost. Aunt Pru was bequeathed Aunt Letty's jewels."

Mrs Simpson's jaw dropped open and she flopped down on the bed beside Margaret.

"Well, of all the idiotic and thoughtless things to do! I have no patience with that woman, none at all. I should like to slap her, truly I should."

Margaret chuckled. *'You will have to dig her up first.'*

Mrs Simpson gave a bark of laughter, and then, somehow, they were both laughing until tears rolled down their cheeks. It seemed at the time quite in keeping with the rest of the day.

~~~~~

Mel sat in his study, pretending to deal with his correspondence but in reality listening to the faint notes of the pianoforte drifting through from the library. He had never heard Margaret play before, since she had only ever been there on a Sunday previously, but she was most accomplished at the instrument, and he had a little smile on his face as he listened to her performance.
~~~~~

She was happy, he could tell. All yesterday evening she had smiled, listening to the Simpsons' bantering as they argued back and forth about the meaning of the will, and at breakfast she had smiled again. Now she was playing a rousing air that made his feet tap. Ah, how he would love to dance with her! She played so well that he was sure that she would be an excellent dancer, too. Perhaps this evening Mrs Simpson would play for them, and he could dance with her, if she did not mind his lumbering incompetence.

No, that would be inappropriate. She was newly in mourning for her aunt, and besides, her position in the household was precarious. Mrs Simpson's presence protected her, but they must be careful not to give rise to undue speculation. There was already talk, as he was uncomfortably aware. In recent weeks, more than one of his more forward parishioners had smirked knowingly, and enquired how Miss Winterton was. One or two had even asked him directly when they might wish him happy. Oh, if only they knew how such enquiries pierced him to his very soul!

His study was at the front of the house, the window overlooking the drive, so he was the first to see Lord Delacrost arrive on his spirited black horse, accompanied as always by his two grooms. Mel heard the knocker sound, heard John open the door, heard the low murmur of voices. He went out into the hall.

"Good morning, my lord. Will you step inside?" He indicated the open door of his study.

"My business is not with you, Haymer. This fellow says Miss Winterton is not at home but—"

"I am sure she will see *you*, my lord, but I should like a word first, if you would be so good."

The viscount grunted, but entered the study. Mel closed the door firmly on the interested John.

"Will you sit, my lord? Some Madeira, perhaps?"

"This is not a polite morning call, Haymer, and my time is valuable. Say what you have to say, and be quick about it." He paced restlessly about, so that Mel was obliged to stand, too.

"Very well. I will speak plainly, then," Mel said, taking up a position behind the desk, out of the way of the viscount's prowling. "You should know that Mrs Simpson as yet knows nothing of my precise connection to you. She believes, as half the world does, no doubt, that I am your bastard son."

"Would that you were!"

"You will find no disagreement from me there," Mel said. "It would have been infinitely easier for both of us. However, she knows nothing, so have a care what you say before her. Miss Winterton, however, knows all."

"Oh yes, I can well believe you have no secrets from *her*," the viscount sneered.

"It was necessary that she know my circumstances so that she would understand why I could never marry her. But when we talked, she made it very clear that she has no wish to marry. *'Not even you,'* as she said to me." He smiled as he remembered. "So you see, you need not be concerned about the matter. I have given my word to you, and I shall not break it."

"You may not intend to, but I see how things are between you," Lord Delacrost said. "Men are weak, Haymer, and driven by their lusts to behave in ways which are quite against their better instincts. Good intentions are not enough. You will see."

Another length of the room paced off, his fisted hand punching the back of each chair he passed.

"That is a sad reflection on your own sex," Mel said mildly. "I cannot speak for men in general, only for myself, and I know that my word binds me. I trust in God to give me the strength to keep that bond. I do not know by what arts you persuaded Mrs Bradwell to write her will in such a way, but you have wasted your efforts and distressed Miss Tilford to no purpose. Margaret will not marry any of her cousins, and no fortune of any size would induce her to do so, where her affections are not engaged."

"No, because she wants *you*."

"She does not, and you were quite wrong to interfere. Had you left well alone, Miss Tilford would have inherited, and Margaret would doubtless have gone off to live with one or other of her sisters. As it is, you have cruelly deprived Miss Tilford of her expected inheritance and made her Margaret's enemy, and you have also made it impossible for Margaret to leave Pendarreth for some time — years, perhaps. She has no means of escape."

"Escape? Why should she wish to escape? Pendarreth is a fine house, and she will live like a lady there. She is a woman of property now."

"Not so. The house is not hers. She cannot sell it, or lease it out. If she marries one of the grandsons, it will be his. If she marries anyone else or does not marry at all or simply chooses to live elsewhere, then it will be yours. In any such case, Miss Tilford will be homeless."

"She is not homeless," Lord Delacrost said. "She has the Red Cottage, a perfectly adequate property for a woman in her position."

"It is cruel to expect a lady of her years to leave the only home she has ever known," Mel said firmly. "Margaret certainly will not, which means that she is tied to the house for as long as Miss Tilford lives. Yet you have made it impossible for the two of them to be under the same roof. How is Margaret to solve this conundrum, hedged about with constraints as she is? She is not a bird to be caged at your whim, my lord. She needs — she *deserves* to be free."

"Free to marry you, of course."

Mel exhaled in exasperation. "How much more strongly must I express myself? I shall never marry Miss Winterton, never. I have given you my word. Have I not always done as you wished? Have I not kept the secret of my birth all these years? Did I not break the entail willingly? Have I not earned a modicum of trust from you?"

"I trust no one," Lord Delacrost said. "Pah! This is ridiculous!"

And so saying, with another thump of the nearest chair back, he stormed out of the house, whatever he had to say to Margaret quite forgotten.

14: Mistress Of Pendarreth

Two days later, Mrs Simpson planned a visit to Heston Ford.

"Should you like to go with me, dear?" she said to Margaret over breakfast. "I am only going to Parry's to remonstrate with Mr Parry about the sultanas he supplied, for I never saw such a quantity of caterpillars. We have plenty of our own caterpillars without paying him by the pound for extra. Perhaps I shall look in at Mrs Brighton's, in case they have any gloves to replace my tan ones, although I daresay I shall have to go to Ludlow in the end. I might call on Mrs Higgins, too, if you do not dislike the idea."

Margaret had been nowhere and visited no one since her arrival at Pendarreth five months before, so the novelty of the excursion appealed to her. She knew Mrs Higgins, too, for she was one of the few ladies who occasionally called at Pendarreth. To Heston Ford, therefore, they were to go.

If the expedition had been, as promised, visits to two shops and a morning call on an old acquaintance, it would have been tolerable, and Margaret might even have enjoyed it as a change from the house and her routine occupations. However, in walking merely the length of the high street, they encountered seemingly half the genteel population of the town, all of whom stopped to speak to Mrs Simpson and must therefore be introduced to Margaret. She saw their faces change abruptly from polite smiles to avid curiosity as they realised who she was. It was of all things the kind of attention she hated most. She imagined them watching as she walked on down the street and then turning to their friends. *'So that is Miss Winterton, who inherited Pendarreth. I wonder how she wheedled Mrs Bradwell into leaving her everything. How meek she looks, and yet how slyly she must have worked on a sick old lady to cut out poor Miss Tilford. What a shameful thing!'*

Mrs Simpson sailed serenely on, but Margaret scuttled along in her wake, red-cheeked with mortification. She had never drawn so much notice in her life. It was the utmost relief to reach the attorney's modest house.

Mrs Higgins was a thin little woman, rather fashionably attired for an attorney's wife in her middle years, Margaret thought. Her gown was made of the flimsiest sprig muslin, and pale like a young girl's, decorated all over with tiny orange flowers, and trimmed with orange flounces. She wore black ribbons on her sleeves, however, in honour of Aunt Letty.

"Oh, my dear Miss Winterton! How dreadful to lose your aunt so soon after your father. How distraught you must be! I declare, I am quite prostrate with grief myself for poor, poor Mrs Bradwell. Despite her illness, we all thought she would go on for years. And yet it is an ill wind, is it not? For now you are mistress of Pendarreth, and what a fine thing for you! Not but what it is the most appalling calamity for poor, poor Miss Prudence, of course, for we all expected... and Mr Higgins did think she might reconsider but... Still," she went on brightly, "it is a fine thing for you, Miss Winterton. Some tea?"

"It is the strangest will imaginable," Mrs Simpson. "It is hard to know what was in Mrs Bradwell's mind when she laid out such bizarre provisions."

"Oh, indeed, but Mr Higgins said... Of course, he mentioned this in the strictest confidence, so perhaps..."

"We will not breathe a word, my dear Elvira," Mrs Simpson said smoothly. "Besides, Margaret is intimately concerned with the business."

"Oh, yes, indeed, she has a right... Mr Higgins would be the first to agree, I am persuaded... Although, to be sure, he does not really know himself what the purpose was, except to make provision for her poor, orphaned niece and yet also keep Pendarreth in the family, do you see? Mr Higgins can see no deeper reason, although he did rather wonder at Miss Prudence being overlooked in favour of Miss Winterton. He did suggest to Mrs Bradwell that perhaps she might wish to leave Pendarreth to Miss Prudence for her lifetime, and then afterwards to Miss Winterton, for she could have done that, you know. It is quite a regular thing, and perfectly unexceptionable. But no, she would have it so."

"But to Lord Delacrost, if Margaret fails to comply? That is not keeping the house in the family."

"No, and Mr Higgins was quite incensed about it, I do not scruple to say, Mrs Simpson. Incensed, he was. Of course, his lordship helped Mrs Bradwell's son not long ago — some debts settled, so perhaps it was felt— But to leave the house outside the family! Mr Higgins thought it most improper, and then—" She lowered her voice to a whisper, although no one else was in the room. "His lordship was there, you see, before the will was drawn up, and so Mr Higgins wondered if there were any undue *pressure* brought to bear. But that could not be so, could it? His lordship is a *viscount* and a peer of the realm and a man of honour, and he would never do such a thing. Would he? No, I am certain he would not."

Margaret sipped her tea and said nothing. The viscount's interest in her future was less puzzling when one knew of Mel's circumstances. His lordship had already warned her away from Mel, and this, surely, was another attempt to make sure she did not marry him. How foolish! As if she would rush to marry a stranger, in order to keep Pendarreth.

~~~~~

The calm atmosphere at the parsonage did much to restore Margaret's spirits. However frightful the contents of Aunt Letty's will, there was nothing at all to be done about it. Mr Higgins came to talk to her about the situation, and reassure her that the executors would be liberal in their interpretation of the terms.

"We are quite agreed, Miss Winterton, that you may take as much time as you need to get to know your cousins and choose between them, if you are so minded."

'I am not so minded,' she wrote in furious haste on her slate, the chalk stabbing with staccato raps. *'I do not wish to marry any of them. I do not wish to marry at all.'*

The attorney beamed at her genially, resting his hands on his ample stomach. "Well now, who can say whether you might not change your mind on that subject? We shall allow you time to consider your future very carefully, you may be sure of that. As for the requirement that you live at Pendarreth, occasional short absences will not induce us to invoke that element of the will, so you may be easy on that head."

'What do you mean by occasional?'

"Oh, once or twice a year, something of that nature."
~~~~~

'How short is a short absence?'

"Oh, you want it all set out precisely, do you? Hmm, two or three weeks, you know. A month, perhaps."

'What if I should wish to go to London for the season? A month would not be adequate.'

"No, indeed," he said. "Two or three months in town — we should not object to that, you know. Perfectly unexceptionable."

'And if I should be invited to stay with a friend?'

"A friend?"

'The Marchioness of Carrbridge, for example.' Margaret plucked all her aristocratic acquaintances and tossed them under Mr Higgin's nose. *'The Earl of Brackenwood? Lord Westerlea, my sister's father-in-law?'*

"Well, yes, one could hardly refuse the nobility, if a peer of the realm should so far condescend as to invite one to his home. The executors would certainly look favourably on such an invitation."

'Then you and Dr Harling are to decide where I go, and who I may visit, and for how long? You are to order my life for me?'

Mr Higgins removed his spectacles and polished them vigorously. "Well now, Miss Winterton, well now." He replaced the glasses carefully on his nose. "Dr Harling and I will have to consider most carefully the conditions under which we might regard the terms of the will to be violated, but you will not find us restrictive. We would not interfere in those activities appropriate for your station. However, absenting yourself for long periods would hardly be in keeping with the *spirit* of your aunt's generous bequest, now would it? She left Pendarreth to you on the understanding that you would take the greatest care of it, did she not?"

'Did she? I do not know why she left Pendarreth to me. It had much better have gone to Aunt Pru who loves it.'

"And you do not love it?" he asked.

'Not as much as Aunt Pru does. I like it well enough, but it is not my home. If I were to live there for sixty years, and come to know every path and tree and bush, I would love Pendarreth as much as Aunt Pru and would be devastated to be uprooted from it, just as she would be. Pendarreth is Aunt Pru's home, not mine.'

"You are ungrateful," he said, brows snapping together. "Nevertheless, Pendarreth has been put into your hands, for better or for worse, whether you like it or not. It is an undeniable truth, however, that ladies are unfit to have the management of property, which is why you need a husband to assume control of the property. Everything you have said this morning reinforces the correctness of that assessment. You are too young, too ignorant of business matters to have charge of a great estate. You should marry as soon as you may, Miss Winterton, out of duty to your aunt."

At this, Margaret was so cross that she snapped her slate box shut and refused to say a word until Mr Higgins went away in bewilderment.

~~~~~

Margaret was in daily expectation of Lord Delacrost calling again, and this time, perhaps, he would not be distracted by Mel, but would insist on seeing her. She could not imagine what Mel had said to drive him away with his object not attained, but nor could she imagine what the viscount had to say to her. His very interest in her was unsettling, and she could only assume that it related to his fears that she might marry Mel and threaten the inheritance of his other sons. But that was foolish. Had she not told him already
~~~~~

that she had no intention of marrying Mel? And it was no more than the truth, after all.

But when Margaret had been at the parsonage for almost a week, he came again. This time, she was in Mrs Simpson's tiny study, helping her with a particularly tricky moment in the book she was currently engaged in writing. The heroine had been kidnapped by her wicked uncle, but had made good her escape even as her handsome admirer rode to her rescue. Now the two were on opposite sides of a raging torrent of a river, and the only bridge had been tampered with by the wicked uncle. It was a tricky problem to resolve, and had occupied the two ladies ever since breakfast.

Their heads lifted when they heard the distant echo of the door knocker. A murmur of male voices, low at first, then louder. The door of the study opened and John came into the room.

"Madam, are you at home to—"

"Of course they are at home," Lord Delacrost said crossly, pushing past the hapless manservant, who melted away quickly, before he could be held responsible for this high-handed intrusion.

"Lord Delacrost, what an unexpected pleasure," Mrs Simpson said calmly. "Will you come through to the library, where we may be comfortable?"

Mel loomed in the doorway behind the viscount, and suddenly the room, already small, felt tiny, with two such large men in it.

"This will not take a moment," Lord Delacrost said. "I have dealt with your problem at Pendarreth, Miss Winterton. Pru will be out of the house within the hour. She has a perfectly good house of her own in the Red Cottage, and I have at last been able to persuade her of it. Those women of hers are packing as we speak. You may return there in time for dinner, and have no fear that you will meet her, or that she may attack you again."

Margaret was so shocked she could neither move nor speak.

"My lord, I do not think—" Mel began.

"That is all," Lord Delacrost said. "Good day."

He turned and would have gone, but Margaret burst out, "No!"

Half turning back, he raised one imperious eyebrow. "No?"

Margaret thought she might explode. She wanted to wipe the supercilious sneer off his arrogant, autocratic face. "How dare you interfere!" she cried. "Aunt Pru *belongs* at Pendarreth. It is her home, and you have no right to hound her out of it, no right at all!"

He drew himself up to his full height, which was considerable, and said haughtily, "You dare to speak so to *me?*"

"I do not care who you are! If you do wrong then I must and will speak. Pendarreth is *mine*, and it is for me to say who lives there, not you. When it is yours you may do with it as you please, but until then, *I* shall say what happens under its roof. Oh, of all the arrogant, presumptuous men, you are the worst!" She stamped her foot. "I must go there at once! Poor, poor Aunt Pru, to be thrown out of her own home! She will be quite overset."

She set off for the door, but the viscount stood immovably before her. "You will do no such thing," he growled.

Lifting her chin, she said, "Stand aside, if you please."

He glared at her, and if there were any power in looks alone, she would have curled up and burst into flames on the spot, there was so much anger in his eyes. But she glared right back at him, and with an exclamation of disgust, he turned, pushed past Mel and stomped loudly out of the house.

Margaret would have run straight out and up the stairs to fetch her bonnet, but a bark of laughter from Mel stopped her, his face alive with merriment. "Dearest, you were magnificent," he said, raising her hand to his lips for a kiss. Instantly all her rage fizzled away, replaced by the most delightful warmth.

"So anger unleashes the words," Mrs Simpson said musingly. "How fascinating. And his lordship makes *such* an excellent villain. What a pity I already have one in that rôle for this book. But that black look… I can do something with that. Oh, but Margaret, of course you must go to your aunt at once, poor lady. Let me send for the carriage, dear."

When she could tear herself away from Mel's embrace, Margaret shook her head. "Too slow. Walk."

"Then I shall walk with you," Mel said.

"And I," Mrs Simpson said. Then, when they turned puzzled faces towards her, she added unconvincingly, "For propriety."

The three marched at speed through the Pendarreth woods, Margaret's fury setting a rapid pace. Mel's long legs were easily able to keep up, but Mrs Simpson soon lagged behind and Margaret was forced to moderate her haste. Even so, it seemed no time before they passed the crumbling stone wall that marked the boundary of the pleasure grounds, and crossed the lawn. Not wanting to wait until someone came to open the front door, Margaret went directly to the kitchen door. There she found Primrose sobbing over her mixing bowl, and Jasmine and Heather whispering together in a corner.

"Oh, Miss Margaret, right glad I am to see you," Primrose said, setting down her bowl and wiping floury fingers on her apron. "You don't mean it, surely? You won't send her away?"

Margaret shook her head violently. She reached for the words, but none would come, so that her mouth moved without a sound. Helplessly, she turned to Mel.

He understood. "Where is Miss Tilford?"

"In her room, packing, poor lady. She's that upset, I never saw—"

Margaret could not wait to hear what Primrose had never seen. She tore out of the kitchen, through the baize door, along the passage and up the stairs, then along the upper corridor to Aunt Pru's room. It was the twin of Aunt Letty's, one of the larger, corner rooms. Between them lay the great hall, with the gallery above it allowing an easy conduit between the two rooms.

When she knocked, there was no answer, but Margaret was not minded to wait for permission to enter. Pushing open the door, she went in. The room looked as if a whirlwind had torn through, emptying every cupboard and drawer and box, and hurling the contents about with abandon. Rose and Lily were on their knees before a battered old travelling box, froths of lace and tissue paper foaming around them. Holly sat on the bed beside Aunt Pru, who was sobbing wildly.

Margaret ran across the room, weaving as best she could around the heaps of clothes, and knelt at her aunt's feet, taking her hands. But again she could not find the words.

"Mel," she said, looking across the room at him in entreaty.

He was beside her in a few strides, and he too knelt at Aunt Pru's feet. "Margaret wishes you to stay here. This is your home."

"Always!" Margaret said. "Always."

"She wants you to know that this will *always* be your home, that she does not want you to leave. She tore into Lord Delacrost something fierce," he added, with a wide grin. "You should have seen her! *'I do not care who you are,'* she said to him. *'Aunt Pru belongs to Pendarreth. You have no right to hound her out of her home.'* You should have seen his face! It was beyond price."

Aunt Pru looked from one to the other, bewildered.

"No one will make you leave your own home," Mel went on gently. "Margaret is quite determined on that."

Aunt Pru fell on her neck and wept even more, and it was some time before she could be restored to some semblance of serenity. Mel explained it to her over and over, and the maids set about returning every gown and fichu and shift and bonnet to its rightful place, but still she wept, although as much for joy now as for grief. She could not quite be convinced that Lord Delacrost would not return, nor that, if he did so, Margaret was more than a match for him, but she accepted that, for the moment, she was safe.

"He told me I had to go, so that you would come back to Pendarreth," she said, when she was calm enough to speak. "He said you were afraid of me, but that cannot be true. As if I would ever hurt you! My own niece, afraid of me — but he said if I stayed here, you would not come back and he would get Pendarreth, and I do not want that, not at all! You will not let him have it, will you, dear?"

Margaret shook her head.

"And I may stay here with you, and we will go on comfortably, just as we did before?"

She nodded, and Aunt Pru sighed in satisfaction.

"That is all right, then," she said, beaming happily.

After a while, Dr Simpson arrived in the carriage, bearing Margaret's boxes, and by then it was almost time for dinner, so the Simpsons and Mel stayed to eat their pot luck with them.

"It will not be much," Aunt Pru said, wringing her hands. "Oh dear! I do not believe there is any fish in the house, and with all the visitors gone—"

"Not to worry," Mel said cheerfully. "We will eat a second dinner back at the parsonage, so we shall not starve."

Margaret ate very little. It was enough to have her friends at her table, to listen to their wit and learning, to gaze at Mel's beloved face and to know that she was on amicable terms with Aunt Pru again.

"Will you be all right?" Mel said quietly to Margaret, as the parsonage party prepared to leave.

Margaret nodded.

"You are sure she will not—"

She shook her head vehemently. Aunt Pru was a strange creature, but her attack had been the work of sudden, violent emotion. Now that she had calmed down and accepted her fate, she was her usual placid self.

After the parsonage party had left, Aunt Pru said, "Well, niece, so you are mistress of Pendarreth now. Come with me."

She led the way to the study, lighting a candelabra, for the room was in its dusk gloom.

"Now, child, here are the keys, you see?" She pulled open a drawer of the desk. "This one is for this drawer here, that for the cabinet, this for the safe, where the money is."

"Safe?"

"Behind the picture of the river. The river *bank*, do you see? Papa's little joke, that the money was in the bank."

"Money?"

"Yes, dear, money," she said with a hint of sharpness. "You need not fret about household matters, for what need is there for change? No, we shall go on as we always have. But the money — you are good with numbers, Letty said. Now, Mr Poole comes out from Ludlow every quarter with the rents and so forth, and nowadays he settles with the merchants and shops for us, to save us the bother. An excellent man, and Papa trusted him completely so you need not fear that he will cozen you, you know. The unpaid bills are here awaiting Mr Poole, and the paid ones here. The household record books are here — oh, Lily must have been tidying, for these are most orderly. You must keep a note of everyone who arrives and leaves — oh, you will get the idea. Just ask if you are not sure. Well, this is delightful! Such a *burden*, all this money business and record-keeping, so worrisome, and dear Letty not the least bit helpful, for she left it all to me, and so I left it all to Mr Poole. *So* much better that way. So happy that you are here to take care of it, and I need not worry about it any more. Good night, dear."

And so saying, she tripped away, one end of her shawl trailing, leaving Margaret, rather bemused, in command of the room.

15: Of Letters (July-August)

Margaret soon found that she was not so much mistress of Pendarreth as all that. Aunt Pru still ordered meals, and gave the servants their instructions, who referred to her as *'the mistress'*. Letters left on the hall table to be taken to Heston Ford still disappeared to be scrutinised, and the incoming ones were read, although unlike Aunt Letty, Aunt Pru never commented on the contents. Margaret tried just once to tell Rose that she wanted her own letters brought directly to her, but nothing changed and so she gave it up.

She was not deterred. If she had had the use of a carriage, she could go herself to Heston Ford, delivering her letters to the mailing office there and collecting those addressed to her. There was a carriage in the coach house, but it might need repairs, and then she would need horses and a coachman, and probably a groom as well, all of which would be expensive. Could the estate afford it? She had no idea, but she was determined to find out.

Accordingly, her first task was to set the accounts in order. The late Mr Tilford had pursued one system, and Aunt Letty another. However, all the bills were there, together with neatly arrayed statements from the bank and the industrious Mr Poole.

All that was needed was to organise the papers into a proper order, and tabulate the results into her own account books. For comparison, she had all the old account books, going back for fifty years. Excitement buzzed inside her at the prospect. She had already made a beginning in her search for the will, so she brought all the papers from the library desk and cabinets into the study and settled down to find out just how much Pendarreth was worth.

~~~~~

'Dear Margaret, It is a very long time since we have heard from you, and we are beginning to grow concerned. Do let us know how you are, and what is happening at Pendarreth since Aunt Letty's demise. It is very worrying to hear nothing from you. Please do make an effort to write. Rosamund.'

~~~~~

JULY AND AUGUST

The weeks passed pleasantly, if one did not count the never-ending grief of being separated from one's sisters. Margaret had begun to accustom herself to the loss, but that meant only that the fiery pain had reduced to a deep-seated ache that never went away. A dozen times a day something would remind her of one or other of them, and renew her sadness.

At least she had her weekly visits to Dunton Cross to sustain her, and that happy half hour when Mel walked home with her. Sometimes they walked in silence, holding hands, their gloves removed so that they could feel the tingle of bare skin against bare skin. Sometimes they sang hymns as they strode along. And always the walk ended with a hug, his strong arms around her pulling her so close she could hear his heart thrumming. Or was that her own pulse thundering? And then with a sigh he would set her free again, and bid her farewell for another week, his face wreathed in a sorrow that mirrored her own.

Often she would see him between Sundays if he called to see Aunt Pru. Her aunt was always happy to see him. She never wanted him to pray over her, but she gave him tea and cake and heard all the news from Dunton Cross and Heston Ford, and further afield if he knew of it, and giggled like an ingenue at his small attempts at jokes. Margaret sat quietly at these meetings, content to listen and to watch, noticing the way Mel's right hand gestured as he spoke, while his left rested on his knee, delighting in the low melodious timbre of his voice, watching his expressive eyebrows jump up and down. They were rigidly polite to each other at these public meetings, for there was no point inviting censure, but neither of them was adept at subterfuge. His voice softened when he spoke to her, and that invariably made Margaret blush. Fortunately, Aunt Pru never seemed to notice, or if she did, she never commented.

She at least seemed unreservedly happy during these summer weeks. She hummed as she went about the house, smiled benevolently at Margaret when their paths crossed and acted as if she had not a care in the world. Margaret was no longer in fear of a physical attack from her aunt, but she wondered whether she truly comprehended the situation. Did she understand that Margaret's hold on Pendarreth was tenuous? Did she realise that one day in the future the house would belong, not to Margaret, but to Lord Delacrost? She gave no sign of it. Whenever Margaret attempted to talk about Pendarreth, even to ask a simple question about the management of the house or estate, Aunt Pru would give her beatific smile and say, "Pendarreth is yours now, dear. You must do as you think best." Naturally, this dispensation did not extend to making any real changes, as Margaret soon discovered, and any orders she gave the servants were referred to Aunt Pru for authorisation.

One of her earliest undertakings was to open the safe, wherein she found almost thirty small purses, each containing a quantity of money — coins of all denominations, and small rolls of banknotes as well. Each purse contained a sum close to one hundred pounds, so that, after sorting, almost three thousand pounds lay spread out on the desk in heaps of increasing value. Margaret had never seen so much money in her life before, and shivered with excitement. When that did not sufficiently relieve her feelings, she danced around the room twice, and then curtsied very respectfully to the safe which had provided such largesse.

But now she need have no concern about one matter dear to her heart. Her confinement at Pendarreth chafed, but if she could set up her carriage she would be free. She could go shopping, or pay calls occasionally. She could send her letters from the office in Heston Ford. She tidied away the money, each type of coin into its own bag, locked them away in the safe again and sat down to write a note to Mr Williams, the coach-maker of Heston Ford. A business letter — that was so much easier to write than anything about herself.

That afternoon, Margaret and Aunt Pru sat down for their dinner, still at the unfashionably early hour of four o'clock. Margaret had argued for a later time, but Aunt Pru had said serenely, "Oh no, dear. Dinner is at four at Pendarreth." And that had been the end of the matter.

Her aunt chattered away about her walk through the woods that day, how she had seen a cuckoo and how well the apples in the orchard were growing, but then she reached into her reticule and pulled out a letter, the seal broken and the sheet unfolded.

Margaret immediately recognised her own handwriting on the direction.

"Mine!" she said at once. She reached for her slate box, but Aunt Pru answered before she could write anything.

"Oh yes, dear, it is your letter to Mr Williams. Whatever are you doing writing to him? We have no need of his services."

"Yes, we do," Margaret said, anger propelling her words for once. "I want a carriage."

"A carriage?" Aunt Pru tittered. "Oh no, dear, no. Whatever do you want a carriage for?"

"Visiting. Shopping."

"What nonsense! Who would you visit? You know no one. And as for shopping, the servants will fetch anything you want, you know."

"I want a carriage," Margaret said, snatching the letter out of Aunt Pru's fingers.

"Gracious me! Such temper! But it is impossible, dear. A carriage needs horses and horses need grooms and we have neither. We cannot have *male* servants here, you know, not when there is no gentleman in residence. Most inappropriate. But there — you are very young and unfamiliar with the world. You did not know, so we shall say no more about it." She snatched the letter back, and crumpled it in her hand. "Will you pass the raspberry creams, dear? I could manage another spoonful, I believe."

Margaret said no more, her brief spurt of anger useless against her aunt's intransigence. Against the viscount, she had succeeded triumphantly, but her aunt was a worthier opponent. No, that was unfair. Aunt Pru was not even aware of a fight. She simply saw no good reason why anything should ever change. She herself had no need of a carriage, so she could not understand the restriction that so fretted Margaret.

And yet once she had been different. Where now was the Aunt Pru who had held hands with the naughty Mr R one summer's day long ago? Once there had been horses in the stables and footmen to answer the doorbell and a normal household, with gardeners and grooms and people for dinner. There were even balls in the great hall, and grand entertainments, and roses twining around the drain pipes in the courtyard to fill the air with perfume. Now the stables were empty and only plain herbs grew in the courtyard.

But why had it changed? Something had happened, and Aunt Pru had let almost all the servants go, and after that everything had been different, but who could say after all these years what had caused the change? Most likely one of the manservants had been presumptuous, and she had decided to dispense with all of them. Her father had been away at the time, so no doubt she had felt vulnerable. He had been away a great deal, and Pendarreth was a big, empty house for a woman on her own.

Whatever the cause, there was no moving her aunt on the subject, and Margaret was not minded to distress her by fighting openly for a carriage. She still had her walks to Dunton Cross each Sunday, and the whole of Pendarreth land and beyond to explore. In addition, she still had her letters from her sisters to give her a glimpse of the outside world. How remote it seemed now, that world that they described. Rosamund's life in London was a whirl of balls and routs and dinners and the nobility. They were full of *'His Royal Highness said to me…'* and *'I told the duchess…'* Margaret could not quite imagine such a life. Annabelle talked happily of her earl, who sounded delightfully normal for a nobleman, and Lucy of Mr Audley, who was perfection personified, it seemed, and Fanny

— dear Fanny! — had her intriguing neighbour who had been smitten at the first sight of her.

Yet what could she write to them? She could not explain the nature of her understanding with Mel, or Aunt Pru's peculiarities, nor the grave of the poor baby up in the woods. She could not describe her joy at bringing the accounts into order, knowing how much money sat in the safe, nor her frustration at not being able to have a carriage and escape once in a while. It was all too complicated for her to put into words, and so when she sat down each week to pen a missive to each of her sisters, she could write nothing that mattered and so she wrote nothing at all.

Each week she determined that this time she would manage it. Or perhaps she would ask Mel to help her — she could tap away on her chalk box and he could write the words for her, and then post the letters. But there was so much to tell, so many words, and when she thought about it, the task daunted her. Where could she even begin? It was impossible for her orderly mind even to contemplate such a huge undertaking.

And so the summer drifted away, and the only change was that Lord Delacrost's sisters came to stay at the Manor, bringing their various children with them, and every few days a fine carriage would roll up the Pendarreth drive, disgorging a gaggle of women in silk and lace and feathers. This was clearly expected, for Aunt Pru had ordered the receiving room opened up, its holland covers whisked away and the antiquated formal furniture dusted and polished to the highest degree. Here the viscount's grand relations sat stiffly, sipping tea from fingernail-thin china cups that Margaret had never seen before, eating one of half a dozen varieties of cake and talking boastfully about people she had never heard of and the many entertainments of the London season.

Clearly they had been told of her affliction, for apart from a brief greeting, they made no attempt to talk to her. Margaret sat quietly and watched them. She was heartily glad that she had not been born to a titled family, and therefore need not be as arrogant and vain and empty-headed as these foolish women. Her own life was dull, perhaps, compared to theirs, but she would not trade it for all their silks and jewels and soirées at Carlton House.

~~~~~

In August, a letter arrived from Mrs Fordham. It was addressed to Margaret, but Aunt Pru read it first and came into the study in high distress, hands fluttering.

"Look, dear, look! See what a disaster sister has brought upon us. Oh, this is just as I feared! But you must write at once and tell them we cannot undertake to receive visitors. It is quite impossible! It was one thing when poor, dear Letty was so ill, and then, later… well, one must make allowances, but I had hoped that all such foolishness might be behind us now. All we want is a quiet life, do you not agree, dear? We cannot be expected to entertain, and there will be the boys' valets and grooms and all manner of nonsense. But you must write and tell them to go away, dear. You must."

Margaret could make nothing of this stream of woe, but eventually she managed to extract the letter from her aunt's waving hands.

'Upper Ford Lodge, Hertfordshire. 18th August 18— My very dear Cousin Margaret, I know you to be a sensible girl, so you will fully appreciate the delicacy of your situation, still in mourning and yet with the future so uncertain. Given the peculiar nature of Mama's will and especially the provisions made in regard to you, it seems to me that matters are best settled sooner rather than later,
~~~~~

a sentiment which I make no doubt at all aligns with your own view of the matter. I have consulted with Mr Higgins and Dr Harling, in their position as executors of the will, and they have graciously given permission for your male cousins to submit themselves to you over the summer, with the purpose of allowing you to become better acquainted with them and thus make a speedy choice from amongst them. To this end, I propose to bring Daniel and David to Pendarreth on Wednesday next, to stay for a month. You will find them both to be amiable and good-natured young men, with excellent education and manners, entirely suited to take the onerous charge of Pendarreth from your shoulders. I should be happy to see either of them as your husband. Naturally, I have apprised my brother and sister of this plan, and expect that they too will wish to avail themselves of the opportunity. Yours in anticipation of a swift conclusion to this outlandish business, Tabitha Fordham.'

"You must write at once, dear, to put them off," Aunt Pru said.

Margaret shook her head, and pointed to the words *'Wednesday next'*. "Tomorrow," she said.

"Ohhhhhhh!" Aunt Pru wailed. "It is too late! It is too late!"

It was very much too late. She had hoped for a few months of tranquillity, or perhaps a full year, but it was not to be. Now all the peace of Pendarreth was cut up. From tomorrow Margaret would be hounded and harassed, and how would she ever endure it?

16: Invitations (August)

The house was full of young men. Harold and Lucius Bradwell. Daniel and David Fordham. William and Walter Herbert. At first she could not distinguish one from another, for they were all expensively dressed in an array of fashionable styles, and lolled about the place in a languid manner, filling each room with their deep, male voices and masculine presence. After dinner, they lingered over their port and then played cards noisily for half crowns, winning and losing with equal good-humour.

They said little to Margaret beyond the dictates of civility, asking how she did but not waiting for her to answer, and thereafter ignoring her, as if they had no more interest in her than in any other young lady in England. But from time to time, when they thought themselves unobserved, they gazed at her with avaricious eyes, making her shiver.

Their mothers came with them, too, and a sister or two apiece, far too many for the breakfast parlour, so they dined in the echoing vastness of the great hall, with the valets acting as footmen, and not one of the female servants to be seen. Afterwards they all sat in the splendour of the withdrawing room, and Margaret was able to hide behind the pianoforte, and wonder, as her fingers danced about over the keys, what on earth they were to do with so many people for a whole month. Aunt Pru was no use, for she hid herself away, only emerging to eat her dinner, and then scuttle away again. What entertaining was to be done fell to Margaret, or to the guests themselves.

Gradually, it became easier to tell one of her suitors from another. The dandy. The one with political aspirations. The shy, bookish one. The arrogant one. The greedy one. The energetic one. And slowly, imperceptibly, it became clear to her that they had come to some arrangement amongst themselves and that only one of them was to be offered to her. Then he began to court her in earnest.

Mr William Herbert was a man of so much energy that he was perpetually engaged on some active enterprise, involving horses or dogs or guns, or, more usually, all three. And if he suspected that she planned a walk, there he would be, waiting to pounce as soon as she left the house, and insisting on walking with her, his riding crop, which never seemed to leave his hand, constantly a-swish and his booming voice destroying all tranquillity for several square miles around him.

Even indoors there was no refuge. Finding her in the library one day reading the newspaper which one of the visitors had left there, he plumped himself down on the next chair to hers, his long legs sprawling too close to her for comfort, and said, "Anything to be read in the newspaper, eh, cousin?" One foot tapped repeatedly, as if sitting still were too great a test of his patience.

Pulling her slate nearer, she wrote, *'No, nothing at all,'* and then bent her head to carry on reading.

For a moment there was silence, then he gruffly acknowledged the jest. "Ah, there is wit behind that pretty face, then. Very good, coz. I deserved that, I suppose."

She smiled. *'It was not the most sensible question in the world.'*

"Hmpf. So let me ask a more sensible one. How do you like Shropshire?"

'I like it very well, especially the woods.'

"And are there any entertainments to be had in the area just now? I suppose a lot of people are still in town, or at Brighton or some such, but it is devilish dull out here in the middle of nowhere, if you do not mind my saying so. I had thought a young lady of your age could introduce us into local society a bit, but not an invitation to be seen. Are there no balls to be held soon?"

'I do not know of any.' Then she added punctiliously, *'You would not wish to dance so soon after your Grandmama's death, surely?'*

"It is two months now," he said in pained tones, and she realised for the first time that he bore not even a black armband. Two months! She could leave off her blacks if she wished. He went on, "I hardly knew her, anyway. Do you never entertain? Dinners, and so on?"

For an instant she had a vision of Woodside, the dining room crammed with guests, the table laden with wonderful delicacies and the air humming with laughter and conversation. Or the few times she had dined in the elegance of Westerlea Park, or in Lady Elizabeth Drake's opulent dining room. Then there would be the delight of listening to other young ladies performing on the instrument for a change. Sometimes, there was even impromptu dancing.

She was swept with a longing to dance again, to feel the music flowing through her whole body, not just her fingers. Oh, to be able to lose herself in the rhythm of the dance, to jump and twirl and stamp her feet and *laugh*. It was one of the few times when she did not mind at all being noticed. She liked all big gatherings, the sort with so many people that she could hide herself away in a corner and watch everyone else, but dancing was different. When she danced, she could stand proudly at the head of the set, or wind her way down it, and not care at all that everyone was looking at her. Music made her bold.

But she could put none of this into words, so she contented herself only with, *'Aunt Pru likes to live quietly.'*

"Oh dear! What a trial she must find us, then." He chuckled as he spoke, not at all discomfited.

He got up and walked around the room for a while, rapping his knuckles on every table as he passed by, until Margaret wanted to scream. His clothes were well-made, but his cuffs were dirty, and his waistcoat had a button missing. With an audible sigh, he took his seat again, drumming his fingers on the table where she was reading. His fingers were thick, and the nails were dirty and torn, as if left to their own devices, with no attention from their owner. He tried a new topic. "I daresay you do not often get into Ludlow, but what think you of Heston Ford? It is a fine town, is it not, as small, nondescript market towns go?"

That made her smile. Without the other young men around him, he would be almost companionable, if he were not so surly and unkempt. Margaret was so fastidious herself, that the least untidiness repelled her. *'I hardly know it. I have passed through it twice, and visited it once. We have no carriage here.'*

"There is a carriage in the coach house, surely?"

'It has not been used for years, and we keep no horses.'

"Ah. But that is dreadful, coz!" he said, seeming sincerely distressed by this lamentable state of affairs. "We must remedy this deficiency at once. Let me take you there in my curricle. You can do a little shopping, or pay calls, or just walk about the town on my arm, you know. I should like it of all things. What do you say?"

She hesitated, for although a curricle ride with a gentleman with his groom perched behind them was unexceptionable, she could not be entirely comfortable spending several hours in the company of a man she knew so little about. It would look rather too particular, to her mind. But he was gentlemanly enough to see the difficulty.

"Or we could make up a party. Daniel has his curricle, too, and he could take Susan. That would be fun, would it not?"

She agreed to it, and it was arranged that they would meet again in one hour. An hour! It was not long, but it would be long enough to write some hasty letters. Not to her sisters, but she had another plan in mind, a plan that made her laugh for joy. Soon, very soon, she would be able to dance again. She sped to her room for paper and ink, and her quill flew, the words spilling onto the page almost without thought. Urgency and her own need gave her pen wings.

In the end, six of them went to Heston Ford, for David Fordham and Lucius Bradwell rode alongside the two curricles. They shopped, visited the circulating library, and then enjoyed a cold collation at the inn before returning to Pendarreth in the afternoon. As they went about, they met several of Margaret's acquaintances, introduced to her by Mrs Simpson. Perhaps they were deterred by the fashionable company she was keeping, for they merely bowed or curtsied or bade her a good day, before passing on, leaving her thankful she had not been called upon to make introductions.

"Thank you very much," Margaret said to William as he deposited her at the front door. "I... enjoyed it."

"So did I," he said. "Thank you very much for the pleasure of your company. What was the best part of the day, coz?"

She chuckled. "Post office!" she said, laughing at his bemused expression, before scampering into the house.

Finally, finally — she had managed to post her own letters.

She could not, however, wait until her little scheme was discovered by means of the replies. So the next morning, she went to see Primrose in the kitchen, one of the household record books under her arm.

"Dinner for *how many?"* the cook said, appalled.

Margaret pointed to the slate.

"Forty? Maybe more? Lor' love us, that'll stretch us, Miss Margaret."

'You can hire help from Heston Ford. Send to Ludlow for whatever you need. The menu is here in this book and even the receipts for unusual dishes. Does it not sound delicious?'

"Oh... what book is this?"

'The household record from years ago.'

"Goodness — so much champagne and brandy! Lobsters and turtles... And we can afford this?" she said dubiously.

'Yes. There is plenty of money. Tell the merchants to send the bills to me. If you have any questions, ask Miss Tilford. This plan was hers.'

Primrose just goggled at her.

Margaret's next step was to tell Aunt Pru, and so she followed Poppy upstairs as she carried the breakfast tray. To say she was nervous would be an understatement. She wondered how much of it showed, or whether her habitual public demeanour, head lowered and hands neatly clasped in front of her, hid all signs of her churning stomach and racing heart. Once, Aunt Pru had loved large parties and had organised them enthusiastically, as the record books in the study demonstrated. However, the scale and number of entertainments had dwindled in recent years, and had died away altogether when Aunt Letty had become ill, some five years ago. Could Aunt Pru's interest be revived, or had she gone too far into eccentricity to return? Or would she feel it was still too soon after Aunt Letty's death?

Poppy knocked on the door briskly, then strode in without waiting for an answer. Setting the tray on a table, she opened the shutters and then the bed curtains.

"Good morning, madam. Another lovely day, and no sign of rain, and here's Miss Margaret to talk to you."

Aunt Pru looked even smaller and more wizened in her frilled night gown and cap, still half asleep in the middle of the vast bed. She wriggled herself upright, and Poppy propped the tray on the bed in front of her.

"Margaret, dear?" Aunt Pru said, blinking at her. "Is anything amiss?"

She shook her head, then wrote hastily, *'I have invited some people to join us for dinner ten days from now.'* She placed the slate where her aunt could read it, and waited.

"People? How many people?"

'About thirty extra.'

"Who? Tell me who you have invited."

'Everyone from Norton Forbury Manor. The Simpsons and Mr Haymer. The Higginses. The Harlings. The Malhams.' She hesitated, but there was no explosion of anger, so she went on, *'We can invite more if you would like. You know best. I told Primrose to follow your plan from thirty years ago.'*

Aunt Pru clapped her hands together excitedly. "How thrilling! But only ten days — so little time. Quick, fetch Poppy back. I must get up at once, and talk to Primrose. Someone will have to go to Ludlow… and if I drop a line to Matthew, I am sure he will send some fish from his lakes. Goodness, what work there will be!"

~~~~~

Margaret found all the planning for the dinner taken out of her hands. Aunt Pru was energised and happy, as she had never seen her before. She had been too worn down to contemplate such a scheme on her own account, but now that Margaret had set the hare running, she would have charge of the whole enterprise.

Two women from Heston Ford moved in to help with the extra work, although they seemed a bit bemused to find themselves addressed as Pansy and Buttercup.

"*Buttercup?*" one of them said. "I got a perfectly good name already. Peggy I bin since parson splashed my face, and Peggy I'll be when he plants me in the ground. Buttercup, indeed."

But Buttercup she became, in Aunt Pru's imperious manner of getting her own way by the simple expedient of ignoring all objections.

Margaret kept out of the way, and the guests, after some early offers of help were serenely disregarded, learnt to do likewise. A succession of visitors came to express their happiness at receiving an invitation and to assure Margaret of their pleasure in
~~~~~

accepting. "How lovely it will be to see the great hall in all its glory once more," they twittered. "Shall you have dancing after dinner?"

Margaret smiled and nodded and said that she hoped so, for that was, after all, the whole point. She would willingly sit through an interminable dinner and the polite nothings that went with it, if she could have just an hour of dancing afterwards.

Lord Delacrost came with two of his sisters and various of their children to accept their invitations. Since Aunt Pru sent word that she was indisposed, as she often was when gentlemen came to call, and the other ladies of the house were out, Margaret was forced to receive them alone.

The viscount also brought with him two personages of the utmost interest to Margaret — his two acknowledged sons. Mortimer was a solid young man with a haughty manner, of rather undistinguished appearance and sneering features that would, one day, be as harsh as his father's. Clearly he had been informed of her affliction, for after a couple of polite remarks to her, he moved away and thereafter ignored her. The younger son, Edward, had far more pleasing manners, sitting beside Margaret and demonstrating his kind nature by framing all his civil enquiries in such a way as to require her only to nod or shake her head. When she responded by writing a longer answer on her slate box, he seized it up and exclaimed, "Such an ingenious device, and it allows you to conduct a conversation just as well as anyone else, I vow. This is a charming piece of workmanship! Where did you find it?"

'It was made for me by Mr Haymer, the curate at Dunton Cross.'

"He is very clever, then, this Mr Haymer. I thought I knew all the Haymers hereabout, but I had no idea we had a clergyman in the family. Father, how are we related to the curate at Dunton

Cross? For he is a Haymer, so he must be some relation, I am sure. A distant cousin, I daresay."

Margaret caught Lord Delacrost's eye. His expression was a curious mixture of anger and confusion, and she realised with surprise that he had never planned for this eventuality, and had no falsehood ready to slip glibly from his lips. He had never even mentioned Mel to his sons, nor to the rest of his family, judging by the unconcerned conversations around the room. She and Lord Delacrost were the only two there who knew the truth.

Quickly, she reached for the slate, hoping to distract Edward's enquiring eyes away from his father, and wrote, in perfect truth, *'The relationship is unacknowledged.'*

He looked a little conscious, understanding the allusion, and instantly changed the subject. Soon afterwards, he moved away and struck up a conversation with two or three of Aunt Letty's grandsons. Despite the fact that the Manor House and Pendarreth were only a few miles apart, and the only houses of any size in the neighbourhood, it so happened that the young men had never met before. Mortimer and Edward spent most of their time with their maternal relations, and Aunt Letty had never encouraged any of her family to visit her, so their paths had never previously crossed. Now that they had met, and found that they were of similar age and shared an interest in the sort of outdoor activities of all such young men of wealth and no occupation, it took no time at all for a friendship to be struck up and an arrangement made for a shooting party.

"Margaret, what do you think," William Herbert called out from across the room. "The Haymers have not been invited to this dinner of yours, by some oversight."

"Miss Winterton had not been introduced to us," Edward said, laughing. "Why, we were not even in the county until yesterday. Unless she can tell the future, she could hardly have invited us, you know, Herbert."

"No, but she can invite you now."

Margaret looked at Lord Delacrost, who lifted one shoulder in an almost imperceptible shrug, so she nodded and smiled. It promised to be an interesting evening. She could only hope that no awkward questions were asked. On the other hand, it would be the ideal opportunity for Lord Delacrost to tell his sons the true state of affairs.

~~~~~

With the maids busy polishing and rearranging furniture in most of the public rooms, Margaret found her study routinely invaded by the visitors. She learnt to dread the knock on the door, followed by a cheerful face and the dispiriting words, "Are you busy? Am I interrupting you?"

She could only smile and shake her head, and in they would come, to pace idly about the room, picking up this or that and putting it down in the wrong place, and generally making her want to scream. But even if she had had full use of her voice, she could hardly be so unmannerly as to throw them out.

"What are you doing with all these papers, Margaret?" said William Herbert to her one day. He was a most restless young man, riding his horse hard for an hour or two every morning, or striding about the grounds, hands waving energetically as he debated some point of discussion with one or other of his cousins. He had always been an attentive suitor, but lately he had taken to following Margaret around, and she guessed that his mother was encouraging him to press his suit a little harder.
~~~~~

"Accounts," she said.

He picked up one of the piles of bills and scanned through them. "These are from years ago," he said in astonished tones. "Why are you bothering with bills that were paid... let me see... good grief, seven, no, eight years ago. You do not need to concern yourself with these. Let me deal with them for you."

With a couple of strides, he crossed the room to the fireplace and tossed the bills into the grate. She squeaked with alarm and tore across the room to retrieve them. It was fortunate that no fire was lit, so no harm was done, except for a little soot here and there.

"Stop it!" she said. "Do not *touch* anything."

"Only trying to help," he said huffily. "You being so new to household management, and so forth. Besides, no need for you to worry about bills, for your husband will relieve you of that chore, and you can concentrate on your embroidery, like a lady should."

She just glared at him, and not long after that, he made his excuses and went away.

But the next morning, when she set off early for her walk through the woods, he emerged from the house at the same time. Was it planned? He was dressed for riding and carried his crop, but he seemed suspiciously unsurprised to see her.

"Taking the air, cousin? May I join you?"

And so instead of the pleasure of thinking her own thoughts and uncovering the secrets of the next unexplored square of woodland, she had all the misery that arises from the company of a disagreeable companion. He talked when she would rather have listened to tiny scuffles in the undergrowth. He strode about so heedlessly that he flattened the stems of bugle and foxglove and campion. He thrashed the bushes with his whip so that birds fled. When he found a badger's sett, he poked into it enthusiastically with sticks, and wished he had his dogs with him for a bit of sport. Margaret led him on the shortest possible route and made an early escape back to the house.

From a locked drawer in her study, she drew out a sheet of paper, which listed a series of dates. Carefully, she counted the days. Nine days. Just nine days to go, and then her abominable suitors would have been at Pendarreth a full month, and would go home. Just three days after the dinner, she would be free again. She put her head in her hands, and wondered if she could last so long without running quite mad.

17: Dinner At Pendarreth (September)

SEPTEMBER

Mel could not remember the last time he had worn full evening dress. Cambridge, perhaps. Certainly there had been little enough call for it at Dunton Cross. There were assemblies at Heston Ford occasionally, but being no dancer and not in the market for a wife, he had never attended one. His social life had consisted of gentle card parties or quiet evenings at home.

But now he looked at his reflection in the mirror and wondered at himself, to be attending a formal dinner at Pendarreth, hosted by the woman who held his heart in her hands, yet to whom he must appear in public as a mere acquaintance. For tonight, he was her parish clergyman, and nothing more.

He was the first downstairs, followed soon after by Dr Simpson. His wife took rather longer to appear, having dithered back and forth between two gowns for some time, and then deciding at the last minute to modify her hair.

"Are you sure you wish to do this?" Dr Simpson said to Mel as they waited. "There is still time for you to cry off. We can make your apologies."

"Why should I wish to cry off? I am looking forward to the evening."

"That much is obvious," Dr Simpson said with a rueful smile. "You have been humming to yourself all day. But Mel, I am perfectly serious. It is a dangerous business you are engaged on with Miss Winterton."

"Dangerous? If you mean that my heart will be broken—"

"That is *not* what I mean, or at least, not entirely. Love is a powerful force, and sometimes good intentions are not sufficient to keep a man out of trouble."

"Now you sound like Lord Delacrost, although he expressed himself more crudely," Mel said, smiling.

Dr Simpson did not return the smile. "You should give the matter some consideration," he said shortly. "You think yourself perfectly in control, and no doubt on the Sabbath, when you accompany the young lady back to Pendarreth, your mind is sufficiently elevated to protect you. But an evening party, with good food and wine, lively company and the lady in full dress, the air warm and the doors wide open to the terrace... your defences will be lowered, and it would be fatally easy to take a misstep. No, do not shake your head in that disbelieving way, Mel, for it can happen to the best of us. It is all too easy for a simple kiss to turn to blazing passion. I speak with authority on the subject, for that is exactly how Aline and I came to marry, because of just such a summer evening. Neither of us wished it in the least, but love makes fools of the most sensible of us."

"You were forced to marry?" Mel said, shocked. "Yet you are so happy!"

"Oh yes, and no doubt we would have married anyway, when my circumstances improved, but our own foolishness propelled us into it in some haste for fear of consequences. We were quite uncomfortably situated for a while, and learnt a great deal about managing on a small income. In your position... do have a care what you do this evening. Ah, here is Aline at last."

"So sorry to keep you waiting, gentlemen," she said, as she glided down the stairs. "Goodness me, Mel, you look very fine tonight. You need a pin or some such in that cravat, though. Let me fetch one—"

"No more delays, my love," her husband said, asserting his authority for once. "The carriage is outside."

She argued no further, and without more ado they mounted the steps to the carriage and were away, the older couple chatting about the delights to come, and Mel silent, pondering his foster-father's words. He could see why there might be concern, although for his part he thought such fears groundless. He and Margaret understood each other, and neither wanted more than to enjoy each other's company sometimes, and perhaps to share a kiss now and then. But to others, it must seem odd, this restraint. Unnatural, even, and perhaps it was, stepping beyond the normal bounds of propriety and yet not progressing to matrimony. But he was bound by his promise to Lord Delacrost and she was bound by her own nature, and thus the arrangement worked satisfactorily. Still, it would be as well to keep his distance that evening, if only not to attract comment.

It was no short drive to Pendarreth. By the track through the woods it was no more than a mile, but the road wound about for five miles to Heston Ford, and then another six slow miles through the gloomy woods to the house. Once they passed the stone gateway, the carriage drive was lit with lanterns and footmen rushed out to assist them up the steps and into the house.

Mel had never seen Pendarreth wearing its party finery. A hundred candles blazed in every room as they processed from the hall to the receiving room, where they left their cloaks, then through the King's room and into the glory of the library, where the reading tables had been swept away and replaced with small tables for cards later.

And there she was, hovering unobtrusively near the door, allowing Miss Tilford to play the rôle of hostess. Mel was not fooled. He knew that this was all her doing. He made his greeting to the aunt before turning to the lovely upturned face, her huge eyes shining.

How beautiful she looked! Evening dress became her well, for she had a pleasing figure — far too pleasing to be hidden away beneath the high-necked bodices she usually wore. She had set aside her blacks, too, wearing a pale lavender instead, which suited her pale complexion and dark hair to admiration.

"Miss Winterton," he murmured, bowing over her hand, as she curtsied gracefully. "How splendid everything looks! I trust I see you well?"

"Yes," she said, nodding vigorously. "Thank you." Then, with an effort, "And you?"

"I am perfectly well, as always."

"Good," she said, beaming at him.

They were the last to arrive, the room a sea of waving feathers, twinkling jewels and an overpowering mingling of perfumes. He looked about him, recognising many of the faces, although he was not at all certain he could attach names to them. There were some he did not know, however.

"Who are the expensively-dressed ladies over there? The Manor House family?"

She nodded.

"Lord Delacrost's sisters, I collect, and some of his nephews and nieces."

She nodded again, then added, "Sons, too."

He threw her a quick glance, and found her looking anxiously at him. "Mortimer and Edward?" he said in a low voice, and she nodded again. "Good heavens. I did not know they were back here, still less that they would be invited. Or that their father would permit them to come. Did he know I was invited, also?" Another nod. "Well..." He was not sure what to make of that. Did Lord Delacrost intend them to meet? Or was he simply hoping no one would ask any questions? If so, he took a great risk. Or perhaps — Mel was aware of a thrill as the thought occurred to him — was it possible that he had told his sons the truth, and now *wished* them to meet? That would be a great change, and very much for the better. Secrecy did no one any good.

But there was no time to consider the matter further, for one of the footmen now announced dinner and the guests began to arrange themselves for the procession to the great hall. The viscount was first, naturally, but he chose to take Margaret in, not Miss Tilford. Well, Margaret was Miss Winterton of Pendarreth now, the mistress and owner, so perhaps that was correct. Then a younger man stepped forward to claim Miss Tilford — that must be the elder son, Mortimer. For just an instant, Mel found amusement in imagining himself in that lofty position, walking two paces behind Lord Delacrost wherever he went. No, he was much better off as he was. Besides, there was a grave in the woods that proved he was no son of the viscount's. And that was an interesting thought...

The Manor House party now broke into neat pairs and filed through, and then Dr Simpson, as the younger son of the younger son of an earl. Mrs Bradwell's family fell in behind, then the attorney and the doctor. Finally came the Malhams, farmers dressed in their very best for the occasion, disputing the right to be last with Mel. He waved them through with a smile, for as the parentless bastard, he came even lower than respectable farmers. There being more men than women, he walked out of the library quite alone, the last and least of the guests.

As he walked into the great hall and waited patiently to take whatever seat remained when all had settled, he saw the viscount lead Margaret to the head of the table. She demurred with a blushing shake of the head, but he insisted and, after ordering a few others to seats nearby, he himself took the place of honour beside her. At the foot of the table, Mr Horace Bradwell appropriated the rôle of host, with Miss Tilford beside him. Gradually the seats were filled, and Mel took one of the last vacant chairs. Dr Simpson was called upon for the blessing, which, being a practical man, he made short so as not to keep the company from its victuals a moment longer than necessary.

The soup was served and Mel was grateful for the respite. For a little while he could sup and be silent, and cast covert glances up the table. He was situated far away from Margaret, but her position in the hostess's chair made her clearly visible to him. She ate composedly, he observed, and only two spots of colour in her cheeks betrayed her discomfort at her elevation. She would have preferred to be lower, he knew, and he would have preferred it too, for then they might have sat together and—

No, that would never do. He must keep his distance from her tonight, and draw no attention to either of them.

"I have quite forgot your name," said the buxom young lady beside him. He had scarcely noticed her as he sat down, but now he recognised her — one of the Miss Herberts. Susan, that was it. "I remember you, of course," she went on, "for no one could forget a man as tall as a tree, but I cannot bring your name to mind."

"Haymer, Miss Herbert," he said gravely. "Melville Haymer. I am the curate at Dunton Cross."

"Dunton Cross? Then you are not staying at Norton Forbury Manor?"

"No. I have nothing to do with Lord Delacrost. Haymer is a very common name in these parts."

"But you must be related somehow. Who is your father?"

"I have no idea. Miss Herbert, may I pass you anything? The buttered mushrooms, perhaps? Or this... I am not sure what it is precisely, but I suspect crabs were involved at some point."

She looked askance at him, but whether she realised the import of his words or merely understood that he did not wish to talk about it, she allowed herself to be diverted to the subject of food. But across the table, a young man Mel had never seen before was staring at him, open mouthed, his soup spoon suspended in mid air. Mel had a sinking feeling it was one of the Manor House party.

The meal passed pleasantly enough. There were enough removes and courses and delicacies to please the most discerning palate, and for the less discerning the claret flowed freely. Mel soon found Miss Herbert losing interest in him, but on his other side he had the entertaining company of Mrs Malham.

"Well, this is most agreeable, Mr Haymer," she said to him as soon as she could spare any attention from the formidable amount of food heaped on her plate. "Everything of the finest, and no expense spared, I'll be bound. Look at all these candles, and those in the library were a full eight hours, I vow. *Most* agreeable, although there are those looking sideways at us and wondering why they are expected to shake hands with farmers."

"Mr Malham is not really a farmer, though, is he?" Mel said, smiling at her. "He handed over the reins to Joe long ago."

"Aye, that's true enough, but he's not properly a gentleman, either. He still dabbles in this and that, for all the money he's salted away. He likes Arthur to play the gentleman, mind you, after that expensive education, but Joe is happy as a mere farmer. Now I, on the other hand, am very much a lady, for I sit at my leisure all day, my needlepoint to hand, my embroidered slippers resting on a footstool." She chuckled throatily, her multiple chins wobbling. "You would never think it to look at me now, but I was somebody to be looked up to in my day, for the Penfolds are a very old family and have been in Shropshire longer than the Haymers. Why, I was courted by Lord Delacrost's brother for a while."

"Really?" Mel said. "What was Lord Delacrost like in those days?"

"Oh, you want all the scandals, do you? No, don't shake your head, for of course you do. Well, he was wild, as all these idle, spoilt young men are. The three Haymer brothers, they were all wild — Matthew, Elliott and Julius. We all went around together, me, and Pru and Letty Tilford, and Jane Callander and Lucy Whitehouse. Oh, and the two Pinkerton boys. Julius Haymer turned out all right, because he married Jane, in the teeth of opposition from both sides, I might add, and went off to be a lawyer in London. Did very well for himself, too, so I heard. Elliott wanted to marry *me*, but a Miss Penfold from Ludlow with only ten thousand pounds was not quite good enough for the Haymers, so he was packed off to the army, and never came back, poor boy. And Matthew —" She stopped. "Ah, it is all old history, now."

"Then you need say no more about it," Mel said politely. "There is a little more of the salmon, if you would like it."

"I could perhaps manage a little more. Thank you. And just another spoonful again, for it is quite delicious, is it not?"

For a while she was silent, concentrating on her plate, but when she eventually pushed it away with a sigh of satisfaction, she said, "Aye, that was a strange summer. We had been so close, and then... everything fell apart. Because of Matthew, mainly. You see, Pru was head over heels in love with him, but *he* wanted Letty, and the girls fell out over it. Pru somehow managed to persuade Letty to marry Harold Bradwell instead, but Matthew never did marry Pru. Although," she added in a lower voice, "rumour suggested that he should have done, by rights. After that, he went off and married Eliza Marford, and Pru never married anyone. Very sad, the whole business. Poor Pru! She was very cut up about it. She quite disappeared from society for a while. Went to stay with an aunt, I believe. And then there was poor Eliza, too! A rotten time of it, she had, and all those years without a babe to show for it."

She paused, waving a footman to replenish her wine glass. Mel said nothing, reluctant to interrupt the flow of secrets. Miss Tilford and Lord Delacrost — he would never have guessed at that coupling. The viscount had wanted to marry the older sister, and somehow Miss Tilford had persuaded her to marry Mr Bradwell instead. It was hard to credit that meek Miss Tilford had had any sway over her domineering sister.

After a fortifying draught of wine, Mrs Malham went on, "At least Eliza and Pru became close, so they had that comfort, anyway, with Matthew away so much, and neither of them with a child to raise. Although perhaps Eliza had her revenge on him in the end, a very pretty revenge for all *his* indiscretions. Or maybe not, for that story is not yet finished." She chuckled, the chins wobbling again. "You have no idea what I am talking about, do you? Probably just as well, although *you* of all people—" She threw him a sideways glance, then looked furtively around the room, perhaps to see if anyone might overhear. When she was satisfied, she leaned towards him conspiratorially and said in low tones, "Matthew thinks everyone has forgotten, but it is not so. It was in the papers, and everything. And it is in Debrett's, of course. These things are never forgotten, not for a nobleman. So however Eliza may have deceived him, there is no escaping his fate. Or yours. Ah, the ladies are withdrawing. Enjoy your port, Mr Haymer."

Mel rose while the ladies left, then allowed the other gentlemen to rearrange themselves around Mr Horace Bradwell, before taking the furthest unoccupied seat. However, he paid little attention. He could think only of Mrs Malham's words. Clearly she knew perfectly well who Mel was. *'It was in the papers, and everything. And it is in Debrett's, of course.'* His birth, she had meant — for two years, he had been the acknowledged heir.

But then Lady Delacrost had confessed her deception and promptly died, and Lord Delacrost had banished his heir, and even his own family were now unaware of who Mel was. What had the viscount told them? That his eldest son had died? Or perhaps nothing at all. Yet the local people had not forgotten. Of course not. Such a thing would not be talked about openly, but it was known. Not all the details, perhaps, but they would have worked out the essential elements. They would have strung the sparse evidence together to make a coherent story — a wife, barren for many years, takes a lover and has a son; on her deathbed, she confesses and the husband banishes the child. Yes, it made sense. It was not the full story, not the correct story, but it made a great deal of sense.

"Come on, Edward, wake up!" a strident voice boomed. "Pass the port, like a good fellow."

Opposite Mel, the young man he had noticed before jumped, and hastened the decanter on its way. Then he returned to staring transfixed at Mel.

But at least he had a name for him now. Edward. Mr Edward Haymer, the youngest son of Lord Delacrost, and legally Mel's brother.

18: An Evening Party

The ladies were at the instrument when Mel entered the withdrawing room. One of the Viscount's nieces was playing and singing with perhaps more ebullience than talent. There was a smattering of applause. Then Miss Maria Herbert played, to rather more enthusiasm. Mel was no expert, but he found both performances pleasing. Then, to his delight, someone asked Margaret to perform.

"Will she sing?" one of the viscount's sisters said to another lady, and they both sniggered.

They did not snigger for long. Margaret took her seat, declined the offer of music and performed from memory the most enchanting Italian air. She played and sang like an angel, and it was not his own partiality that declared it so, but the opinion of several of the assembled audience, who cheered and clapped afterwards, and begged her to play again.

Blushing, she demurred and rose from the stool, but Susan Herbert said loudly, to much laughter, "You had better stay there, Margaret, for I am sure no one could better your performance. I shall certainly not attempt it!"

With several of the others likewise pressing her to continue, she sat down again, smiling shyly, and played on for half an hour or so, before the company permitted her to leave the instrument.

After that, Mrs Herbert agreed good-naturedly to play for the young people to dance, and the carpets were rolled up. The viscount's elder son, Mortimer, led Margaret to the head of the set that instantly formed, and Mel watched in the greatest delight as she demonstrated her graceful steps in the cotillion. How lightly she jumped and turned! How gracefully she positioned her feet and held her arms, and how radiant she looked.

As soon as that dance ended and her partner led her off the floor, several more surrounded her, begging for the honour of her hand. It was as well that Mel recognised his own inability to dance at this point, for had he not been possessed of two left feet, he would indubitably have been a part of her cloud of admirers, hoping for the favour of twenty minutes of her undivided attention. As it was, all he could do was look on in delight. His heart swelled with pride to watch her, as if she were truly his own, instead of merely a friend.

He had to remind himself sharply that she would never be his own, and not just because of his promise to Lord Delacrost. Watching her dance, seeing her ease in such company, was like meeting her for the first time. She was still painfully shy, she still found words troublesome, but she was used to such social engagements and had found ways to cope. Conversation would always be a struggle for her, but she could play and sing and dance, she could move through the company with practised ease, her demureness an attraction for these wealthy, assured men. Mel was the one out of place here, the curate who would never be more than a country clergyman. Even were he free to wed, what could he possibly offer a woman like Miss Margaret Winterton of Woodside?

It was borne in on him, as he watched her happy smiles as she danced, that he did her the gravest disservice by encouraging her friendship. If he could sever that tie, she would be free to fall in love properly with a man of her own class, free to marry one of her cousins and remain mistress of Pendarreth. For that was her destiny, surely. She would marry and settle here in this house, gradually making it her own. Her children would be raised here, their laughter echoing through the corridors and up and down the stairwells. They, too, would explore the woods and climb up to the tree house.

And in this charming vision, Mel played no part. She was not for him. He would always be an outsider in her life, and that was as it should be. He would remain single, keep his promise to Lord Delacrost and hide his grief behind a smile.

For an instant, he shook like a leaf, closing his eyes until the ice-cold wave of sorrow had washed over him and away until he was merely empty and drained. That emptiness would never leave him. His life was over. These few weeks when he had enjoyed her trust and her kisses — oh God, her kisses! — were finished. He would never be more now than the man standing at the side of the room, admiring her from afar. He was in the shadows and she was a butterfly, her exuberant colours lit by brilliant sunshine. All that was left to him was to watch her dance in the sun.

After the cotillion, followed by a country dance and a reel, he could watch no longer. It seemed to him that every young buck in the county was fluttering around and fighting over her. Margaret's dancing, so light and elegant, he could watch for ever, but the ogling young men angered him so much that he withdrew to the library, where several card games were in progress.

"Haymer!" a voice called out. "Will you join us? We can cut you in on the game, if you wish."

"You are too kind, Harling, but my brain is too addled for card play tonight. I shall examine the books, I think."

"Aye, well, if it's books you're wanting, you are in the right place," Dr Harling said, and his companions roared with laughter at his astounding wit, and called for more brandy.

The library was large enough that, by wandering to the far end of it, Mel could escape the increasingly raucous mirth of the card tables, and enjoy some peaceful solitude at the book cases. Not for long, however, for after a very few minutes, Lord Delacrost sidled up to him.

"You are not dancing, Haymer?"

"I have no wish to embarrass a lady by displaying my ineptitude to the world, my lord," he said.

He grunted. "And one might guess which lady you do not wish to embarrass."

"Any of them," Mel said lightly, but the scowl on the viscount's face did not soften. He set down the heavy volume he was holding, his fingers running over the leather and gilt binding. Books... so many books here, so little valued. Only Margaret and the housemaids ever came here.

Margaret... He sighed, tired of the mistrust, tired of being hedged about by secrecy and lies. But there was yet one possibility. "There is a grave in the woods," he said.

"A grave?" The viscount lowered his eyebrows suspiciously.

"The well-concealed grave of a baby, who died at the age of two days some nine and twenty years ago. And there is a name, too, written out in coloured stones."

"Good God! The name and dates? The real name? Melville?"

"Yes."

"Two days old?"

"Yes. Might it make a difference? In getting things changed, I mean?"

"It might. It very well might." He looked at Mel speculatively. "But why would you tell me this?"

Mel leaned back against a pillar. "Has it never occurred to you that I want to be free of this hideous injustice every bit as much as you do?" he said. "I am more grateful than I can say for your generosity over the years, ensuring that I was educated and raised as a gentleman, and in providing me with an allowance, but I had a thousand times sooner be free of any connection with you, even if it rendered me poor."

"Which it would," he said gruffly. "I'd not support you if I could cut the knot, make no mistake about that. God, if only I could cut the knot!"

"You cannot wish for it more than I do."

"Hmpf. I doubt that. But this grave... you described it as well-concealed, yet you managed to find it."

"Miss Winterton discovered it. She has been exploring the woods systematically—"

"Pah! Then it is useless!" Lord Delacrost said in disgusted tones. "Any lawyer worthy of the name would point out that she — and you! — had an interest in the matter. You wish to free yourself from constraint so that you may marry the girl, and so she conveniently discovers this grave. No, that will never fly, my boy."

Mel was floored by this argument. His fist thumped the book in frustration. "Devil take it! Then what *would* set us free?"

"The truth," Lord Delacrost said. "Sworn affidavits from those who knew what really happened in February twenty nine years ago. Nothing less will do. But all my enquiries have yielded nothing. We are stuck with each other, I fear, Haymer."

~~~~~

Two days later, Mel was in his small workshop, appended in lopsided fashion to the side of the coach house, busy making a card table. The base was already complete, and he was occupied in making a backgammon board to fit into it, when John, the manservant, came in.

"Beg pardon, sir, but there are two gentlemen to see you. I've taken the liberty of showing them into the parlour."

"The parlour, eh? Should I run upstairs for my best coat, do you think?"

"I couldn't say, sir," John said, with a glimmer of a smile. "Although best coats are to impress ladies, in my book, not gentlemen, and I doubt these two will be impressed whatever you wear."

"You terrify me, John. Who am I to have the pleasure of entertaining?"

"Mr Mortimer Haymer and Mr Edward Haymer, sir."

This news was so startling that Mel had nothing at all to say to it. He washed his hands and donned his everyday coat in silence, and then made his way without haste into the house.
~~~~~

When Mel had been a boy, the parlour had been his schoolroom, filled with globes and copybooks and a chart on the wall showing all the kings of England since the Norman Conquest. It had long since become the characterless room where parish business was conducted — nervous couples come about the banns, or the bereaved discussing a burial. Once a month, the parish elders met to discuss arcane matters of tithes and glebe lands, or mundane matters of candles or cracked windows. Nevertheless, something about it still reduced him to his twelve year old self, facing the uncertain world with fortitude and terror in equal parts.

So he entered with trepidation. "Good day, gentlemen."

They turned and looked at him, Mortimer with scornful disdain and Edward blank-faced. "Daresay you know why we have come," Mortimer said belligerently. His brother touched his arm gently, and he subsided.

Mel could guess the reason, but before he could frame a response, Edward burst out, "Is it true? Are you Melville?"

"That is my name," Mel said cautiously.

"You are Melville Matthew Haymer, born on the first of February?"

How to answer that? Mel could not be sure of any of it.

To his surprise, Edward burst out laughing. "I beg your pardon, Mr Haymer. We have put you in a difficult position. May we sit down?"

"Of course, of course. May I offer you anything? Tea? Madeira?"

Edward accepted a glass of Madeira and sat composedly sipping, while Mortimer prowled about the room. Mel was not minded to stand on ceremony, so he poured a glass for himself and sat opposite Edward, waiting.

"Let me tell you a story," Edward said. His brother, with a sigh, plumped himself down on a window seat and folded his arms. "Several years ago," Edward went on, "I went to stay with a school friend one Easter. He was the grandson of an earl, so one day he showed me his family history recorded in Debrett's Peerage. I had never seen the book before, for we had no copy at home, so we looked up my family history, too. And that was how I discovered that I was not the second son, but the third. There was an older brother I knew nothing of, a Melville Matthew Haymer, some eight years older than I. That was curious, but no one had ever mentioned this mysterious brother, so I thought nothing of it. Perhaps the child had died, and the event had not been transmitted to the compilers of the book."

He took another mouthful of Madeira, then carefully set the glass down again. "It seemed to me that if this brother were important, my father would have told us of him. Since he had not, I set the matter out of my head. Until the other night. And there you were, Mr Haymer, bearing the name of my older brother, being of exactly the right age, and bearing also, it has to be said, a striking resemblance to the portrait of our grandfather that hangs in the library."

"Is that so?" Mel said, amused by the ability of the human eye to discern a family likeness just where one was expected to be. How many babies had he baptised who were said to look exactly like their father? Yet he had never seen one which did.

"So why is it that the eldest son of a viscount is pretending to be a simple curate in a rural parish? What is the meaning of it, Mr Haymer?"

"I am not pretending to be anything," Mel said mildly. "I truly am a simple curate. As for the rest of it, you must ask your father."

Edward folded his arms with a huff of annoyance. "He will say nothing about you. Said we should mind our own business. We hoped *you*—"

"If your father will not talk about, then neither can I, as I am sure you will appreciate," Mel said.

"But we must know!" Edward burst out. "Mortimer may not be the heir at all. That is a damnable position to be in."

"I agree," Mel said. "Nevertheless, the only person who can explain it is your father."

"We are entitled to know how we stand!"

"Again, I agree, but I cannot help you."

Mortimer jumped to his feet. "This is a waste of time. The fellow is too stupid to understand anything."

"No, not that," Edward said thoughtfully. "But I do not see the need for secrecy. It makes no sense."

"Yet again, I agree," Mel said, with a tight smile. "Secrecy leads to rumour and uninformed speculation and mistrust. It is deeply unpleasant for everyone. Nevertheless, it is your father's will."

"But—" Edward began, but Mortimer growled in displeasure.

"This is useless! The idiot knows nothing, and tries to pretend he does. Melville Haymer, indeed! I daresay that is not his name at all, and this is nothing but a hum. Leave him be, Edward. He is nobody, after all, just an ignorant rustic. When I am viscount, I shall have him turned off for insolence."

Mel kept his face impassive, but it was a relief when Mortimer stormed out, and his brother, with an apologetic shrug, followed him. How much damage had been done by the viscount's unconscionable secrecy? Mel had an uncomfortable feeling that, through no fault of his own, Mr Mortimer Haymer was now his enemy.

~~~~~

Margaret was exhausted and her head ached abominably. She had slept for no more than two hours, but now she was awake again, thirsty and heavy-eyed. But for the first time since the evening party, she felt energetic and looked forward to the day. It was Sunday. Today she would walk through the woods to Dunton Cross and Mel would be there. She would be able to hear his voice resounding from the pulpit or raised in song, she would be able to shake his hand after the service and she would be invited back to the parsonage for breakfast. Then she could talk to him, touch his hand and perhaps steal a kiss. And then, at last, she would feel better.

The day was dreary and damp, but her spirits rose with every step that brought her nearer to Dunton Cross. There was the familiar church, and faces who greeted her with warmth, for she was a part of the congregation now. She slipped into the pew, and Mrs Simpson smiled and patted her hand. The service began and he was there, a little serious, but then that was his working face.

He did not catch her eye. Not once. Slowly, like water seeping out of a leaky bucket, all her happiness in the day drained away. It was no surprise, therefore, when he made some excuse after the service not to come in for breakfast. There was something he had to do — could not be avoided — no need to wait, he would get a bite to eat somewhere else. She could not misunderstand him, and although Mrs Simpson exclaimed at it, and spent the whole of the breakfast hour puzzling over it, Margaret understood.
~~~~~

She had not mistaken his aloofness at Pendarreth, then. At first he had watched her, his eyes filled with warmth as they always were when he looked at her, the clear reflection of her own love shining back at her. But after the third dance, something had changed. His expression had grown darker, and he had turned and left the room. He had only returned to take his leave at the end of the evening, bending over her hand with stiff formality. Something had changed — she had offended him somehow and now he had abandoned her. It was as if the sun had been snuffed out.

19: Suitor

The weather grew very sultry, with torrential downpours in the afternoons, and the roads reduced to shining rivers of mud. When the sun emerged again, every tree and bush sparkled as if hung with diamonds, and the heaviest heads of the roses bent over almost to the ground.

At first, Margaret thought that the poor condition of the roads was keeping the visitors at Pendarreth, for the end of their appointed month came and went and yet they lingered on. But after a few more days, she began to be aware that her suitor was pressing her rather more closely. What was worse, two or three of the others were beginning to take an interest in her, perhaps seeing that William Herbert's suit was not making progress. She began to fear that they would not leave until she had reached a decision to marry one or other of them.

That was not at all to her liking. Accordingly, at the end of dinner one evening, before the ladies rose to leave, she summoned the most senior of the footmen and pushed a piece of paper into his hand.

"Please read," she said. "Aloud." Then, in case he still did not understand, she added, "Announcement."

He nodded, taking the point. "Ladies and gentlemen," he intoned. Then, as they quietened, he went on, "Miss Winterton wishes to make the following announcement." Then he read the paper.

'I thank you all for coming to Pendarreth, and allowing me the opportunity to fulfil the terms of my aunt's will. However, I have no wish to marry anyone, now or in the future, and therefore you may return to your homes as soon as you wish. I shall inform the executors of the will of my decision, and put in train the necessary proceedings to transfer ownership of Pendarreth to Viscount Delacrost. Thank you.'

Rising smoothly to her feet, she indicated that the ladies should now withdraw. In silence, they did so.

Oh, if only she could run away to her room! It was hard to know how her legs could carry her to the withdrawing room, for they seemed turned to jelly, and she trembled from head to toe. She wobbled away into a corner, and found her work basket, where she applied herself with intensity to a piece of plain embroidery that scarce deserved such attention. And at first, she was left alone, the ladies whispering together at the other side of the room. But she knew her peace would not last long. Oh, if only Mel were there! She could bear anything if he were with her.

It was Mrs Herbert who was the first to come and sit beside her. "You poor thing, I know just how you feel."

Resolutely, Margaret kept her eyes firmly on her stitchery.

"Naturally you feel overwhelmed. Inheriting the house, and then having to choose a husband—"

Margaret's head shot up. If that was what she thought, she was fair and far out.

"So many personable young men swarming about you. It is enough to make anyone dizzy, who is unused to such attention. And you are piqued, of course, because you think they only want Pendarreth and not you. Such sentiments are perfectly natural, and do you great credit, my dear. Modesty is very becoming in a girl of your age. But you should also be aware of your own charms, for you are perfectly capable of attracting the regard of a man of good family. It is merely that your lack of dowry must have deterred a prudent man of modest means. Now that you have added Pendarreth to all your other attractions, a man who had, perhaps, admired you from afar but had been unable to speak may now dare to approach you openly. Do you see?"

Still Margaret said nothing. She turned her eyes back to her embroidery, hoping that Mrs Herbert would take the hint and go away.

"I confess that when William first mentioned you, when we were here for Mama's funeral, I was a little concerned. You are such a quiet little thing, that I could not at all see how you could ever run a household without a great deal of help. But now that I have got to know you, and have seen for myself how capable you are in every way, I have not scrupled to encourage William to allow his fancy a free rein." She lowered her voice and leaned closer to whisper in Margaret's ear. "You may not guess it, for he is very shy, but he is in a fair way to being very much in love with you. There," she said, in normal tones. "What do you think of that, eh?"

Margaret thought very little of it. She wanted to say that if William were in love with her, then she was the Queen of Sheba. He had only danced with her once at the evening party, and after that all his attentions had been bent towards the young ladies of the Manor House party. Nor was his shyness much in evidence, for when no better entertainment offered, he flirted outrageously with his cousins. She nurtured hopes that he might, in time, lose interest in her altogether.

His mother, however, was made of sterner stuff, and talked for half an hour of her son's virtues, until Margaret pleaded a headache and escaped to bed. The headache was true enough, and she spent another near-sleepless night trying not to think about Mel and wondering what on earth she could do to convince her supposed suitors that their cause was hopeless.

As if all this were not enough, her suitors were rarely seen without one or two, or sometimes a whole gaggle, of their female cousins, and they in their turn were trailed by one or more of their mamas, so that Margaret felt that the house was Bedlam and there was no respite anywhere. It was fortunate for her sanity that the young men had formed an affinity with the two sons of Lord Delacrost, and that the frequent invitations that resulted drew them away from her orbit for hours at a time. Sometimes she might have as much as a whole afternoon with nothing more to trouble her than Aunt Pru's endless string of minor complaints — "But I say nothing about it, Margaret dear, for Pendarreth is yours now, and you must do as you see fit, and my wishes have nothing to do with it" — or Mrs Herbert and Mrs Fordham gently chaffing each other about the respective merits of their offspring, or the more raucous squabbles of the young ladies.

And then Lord Delacrost came to call.

There was just one benefit to his visit, in that he chased everyone else out of the study, and it was a symptom of how low Margaret's spirits had sunk that even this small advantage cheered her greatly. But that was the only boon to be had.

"What is this nonsense I hear, that you will not have any of your cousins, miss?" he boomed, his eyebrows threateningly lowered. "You are an ungrateful child, when I have gone to so much trouble on your behalf."

"You?" she cried involuntarily, for although she had suspected his hand in recent events, she had not expected him to own it.

"Naturally. Who else?" he said abruptly. "What, did you think Letty loved you so much that she passed over her own sister to see you installed as mistress here? It was no such thing, I assure you. That foolish son of hers was worrying her to death with his debts, so I took the chance to straighten out his affairs, and she repaid the favour by arranging for you to marry well. And now you throw that kindness back in my face."

Margaret reached for her slate. *'Thank you, but I cannot marry. I shall never marry anyone.'*

"Nonsense!" he said, the eyebrows lowering again.

How many times had she said it, yet no one believed her? Except Mel. He alone accepted her as she was.

'It is the truth.' He still looked disbelieving, so she added, *'I am not fit to be anyone's wife. I am broken.'*

To her astonishment, he merely laughed. "My dear girl, you refine too much upon it. You are not, perhaps, suited to society in London, but you need not go there, you know. Marry one of your cousins, provide him with a son or two, and nothing more would be expected of you, nothing at all. You could bury yourself here, just as Pru has done all these years. Your husband would not wish you to hang on his coat tails, you know. That is how it is done, living separate lives. Good Lord, did you think you would have to be presented at court and all that folderol? Not a bit of it. Your husband would uphold the family honour in London, and you would live secluded and peaceful here, and need not see him above two or three times a year. Now that would not be so bad, would it?"

She stared at him, appalled by this extraordinary vision of married life. Was that how he had managed his own life? How dreary. She thought of her own parents, discontented and out of sorts with each other sometimes, and occasionally flaring into quarrels, but mostly they had walked through life side by side, in a tolerable degree of harmony. Papa had been so distraught by Mama's death that he had gone quite to pieces. What about Mr and Mrs Simpson, living in perfect charity with each other, as the very best of friends? And Mel—

She had to break off that line of thinking. Mel and marriage were not thoughts that should ever jostle against each other in her mind. He could no more marry than she could. It was as well she remembered this before she was carried away into a vision of perfect domestic bliss.

'I can never marry,' she wrote firmly.

He grunted, staring at her, and she could not tell whether there was more of anger or disgust in his expression. Eventually, he said, "I thought to give a dinner at Norton Forbury, in return for your invitation the other night. You and your aunts and cousins. Would Saturday suit you? It will not be so splendid an affair as yours, naturally, the day before the Sabbath, but—"

"No!" she said, and then wrote, *'Thank you very much, but I must beg to be excused. My aunts and cousins may like to go.'*

He grunted and finally went away.

She slumped down at her desk, head in hands. Perhaps she would have a few minutes' peace before—

William was there so quickly that he must have been waiting outside the door.

She could not bear it. Jumping to her feet, she made a run for the door.

"Cousin?" he said. "No need to run away. I thought we might play a game of—"

"Sorry," she muttered. "Headache."

And then she fled to her room. Not ten minutes later, there was a knock on the door, and Susan's head peeped round it.

"May we come in? William said you were feeling out of sorts, and of course you are, with him around. He has not a drop of tact. But we will bear you company, dear cousin. Just think what a comfortable coze we may have. Come on in, Maria. You see, it is as I said, she is not in bed, and merely wanted to escape from boring William. Is he not tedious, Margaret? Now David is much more the thing — so deliciously attired!" The two girls giggled. "Yes, pull that chair forward Maria. What do you have here? Oh, just Madeira. Well, that will do. Maria, pour three glasses. Now, Margaret, I have the most exciting news to impart, for who do you think came over for tea last evening after you had gone to bed? Mortimer Haymer! What do you think of that? He *said* he came to talk to William, and I own they were closeted together for some time, but that cannot be the whole reason, can it? And he was most agreeable and stayed for more than an hour, not playing cards or anything dull, but talking to Maria and me. Oh, and Elinor, as well, but she don't signify. What do you think of that? And guess what he said to me? He said..."

Margaret had not the energy to interrupt her, and as for chasing her away, it was inconceivable. Any person of true sensibility would have been perfectly aware that she wanted no company, but Susan and Maria Herbert were not such persons. Like their mother, they were boisterous, cheerful souls, who could not imagine a greater reviver of spirits than to be surrounded by chatterers.

Eventually they left and Margaret scrambled into her nightgown and climbed into bed, lest any other helpful person sought to elevate her spirits by constant noise.

If only she could lock her door! Like many other aspects of Pendarreth, the locks were so old and neglected that they rarely worked, even if a key could be found. Margaret had petitioned Aunt Pru to be allowed to send for the locksmith, but her aunt could see no need for any such attention. "Why would you want a lock to your room, niece?" she had said, in bewilderment. Even the bell pulls, so necessary to a well-ordered house, could not be replaced. "Ivy sits in the gallery all night awaiting a summons from anyone who might need anything," Aunt Pru said complacently. "Much more efficient than ringing bells in the basement, and waiting for ever for the scullery maid to fetch someone. The old ways are best, Margaret dear." And there was no moving her on the subject.

Margaret had reached the limits of her endurance. She could not face another day of relentless pursuit, not when her feelings had been made perfectly plain on the matter. Why would they not believe her protestations? Why would they not listen? Why, oh why, would they not leave her alone? It was more than she could bear. If her sisters had been there, they would have formed a protective shield around her, and deflected the worst of the attention to themselves. And if Mel had been there—

She could not pursue that line of thought without hot tears of anguish. Why had he abandoned her, just when she needed him so much? When he was with her, she could be strong and whole and face any adversity with courage. She could even contemplate marriage, perhaps, with Mel by her side. Her dreadful suitors did not entice her, but Mel was different. Mel would not turn into Papa, huddled away in his book room with a bottle, or off doing who knew what in the town. But alone, she had not the strength to fight, and the constant buzz of people around her wore her down, bit by bit, just as a tiny, tinkling little stream will eventually cut through solid stone, or so the books said. And she was not solid stone, just a very sad and lonely girl, who missed her home and her sisters and her bright, shining love. She could take no more.

After another sleepless night, therefore, she rose at first light, dressed herself and gathered a few possessions into a knotted scarf. Then she went down the service stair to the kitchens and raided the pantry. She could not escape through the kitchen door without waking Jasmine, fast asleep in front of the range, so she crept into the great hall, to the little side door that still had a working lock and a key. With slow, careful hands, she turned the key, wincing at every squeak and scrape. But it turned, and the door opened, and she was free. She closed the door behind her and locked it, pocketing the key, and then set off across the dew-laden grass for the woods.

20: Searching

Mel had been dreading Sunday. The previous Sabbath had been hideous, with Margaret's reproachful eyes gazing up at him, and even though he had studiously avoided looking in her direction, he had been acutely aware of her, watching him, not understanding.

Why should she, after all? He had not explained his withdrawal, or even told her of it. He had seen her arrive at church, happy and excited, and gradually lose all her sparkle. Afterwards, he had not even trusted himself to go back to the parsonage with her. He knew how it would be if he did — she would turn those expressive eyes on him, rest one hand on his arm and look at him in her guileless way, making him feel like the pond slime he was for so neglecting her.

In all his imaginings of the day, however, he had not suspected that there was one eventuality even worse than seeing her unhappiness. He had not dreamt that she would not come at all.

Yet so it was. There was the empty place in the pew where she always sat. Mrs Simpson sat alone, one eyebrow raised in decorous surprise.

He hardly knew how he got through the service that day, for his mind was far away. He guessed how it was, though. She was so upset with him that she would come no more, the rift between them unbreachable. Half way through the sermon he had an even worse thought — he had distressed her so badly that she was ill, and perhaps even now lay on the brink of death. This awful prospect so overpowered him that he faltered and fell silent, and only the whispers of the congregation brought him back to his duty and allowed him to continue.

Mrs Simpson smiled and shook her head when he tried to convey some part of these horrors to her over breakfast. "Ten to one it is nothing at all," she said. "A mild indisposition, perhaps, such as all ladies suffer from time to time. Or she may be a little tired from all the excursions and pleasures arising from the entertainment of her cousins and aunts."

"You only say such things to make me feel less wretched," Mel said despairingly.

"No, indeed. I say such things because they are very likely. The other possibility is that she has gone to the services at Heston Ford. Luke said there were three carriages from Pendarreth there last week. What more natural than that Margaret should wish to attend church with her relations? That is where the Pendarreth pews are, after all."

This was a happier thought, although Mel was aware that, if it were so, it was most likely because his coldness towards her had driven Margaret away. Was that not exactly the outcome he was attempting to achieve — to push her, very gently, away from him and towards her cousins? So why did the idea make him so miserable?

"Should I go to Pendarreth to enquire?" he said. "If she is ill—"

"Then she has her aunt and her cousins there, and they will send for Dr Harling if there is any concern."

"Yes, yes, but perhaps no one has noticed! I could just walk through the woods and be back well before Evensong, you know."

She shook her head. "Mel, think how particular it would look if you go haring about the countryside just because Margaret was not at church today. There is already far too much talk, especially since she stayed here for a full week after Mrs Bradwell's will was read, which made it seem as if there were a family feud." She went on more gently, "You have said you wish to maintain a greater distance from Margaret from now on, and although I am sorry for it, your feelings do you credit. It is her welfare that you consider first, before your own happiness, which is exactly as it should be. So have the courage to keep to your resolve. If you are not willing to marry her, then it is better by far to stay away and give her the opportunity to make a match elsewhere."

He could find nothing to say in response. Much as his mind was convinced that Margaret ought to marry one of her cousins and thereby keep Pendarreth, his heart was in violent disagreement with the notion, and he could not reconcile these conflicting emotions.

"Would you like me to pay a morning call at Pendarreth this week?" she said. "I wrote to thank Margaret for the splendid dinner we enjoyed, but I have not yet called on her. That would be unexceptionable, would it not? And I shall be able to set your mind at ease."

"Thank you!" he said. "You are very good. It *would* be a relief to know that she is well. Might you go tomorrow? Please?"

She laughed. "I very well might."

Mel was a prey to every nervous disorder that night. He slept fitfully, dreamt of vivid terrors, and when he woke, prowled restlessly around his room assailed by every kind of fear. He knew, in the quarter of his brain where reason still dwelt, that Margaret was almost certainly perfectly well, and merely avoiding him because he was no longer a friend. Had that been all, he would have been quite content, or so he told himself in his sterner moments. As content as a man could be who had lost the only woman he had ever loved, and thus all hope of happiness. But he could not shake off the apprehension that some mishap had befallen her.

Consequently, he was awake and dressed long before Mrs Simpson could possibly go out, and then paced about the breakfast room, eating nothing, and asking every five minutes if she had not finished yet and was it not time to send for the carriage.

"I have a better idea," she said, spreading marmalade on her toast. "I shall walk to Pendarreth, and you shall come with me to ensure I do not get lost. You need not come into the house, but may wait in the woods for me, and I shall be able to give you the earliest intelligence of Margaret's wellbeing."

They did not reach the house. Within five minutes of starting up the track to Pendarreth, the sound of rapid hoof beats ahead was followed almost instantly by the sight of a fine black horse, ridden at speed, bearing down on them. Mel pulled Mrs Simpson off the path, but the horse reared dramatically at the sight of them. The rider almost at once brought his mount under control, and held him with great skill, even as the beast danced about in its urge to be off.

"Mr Haymer! Well met!" he called, as cheerfully as if he were on foot and not wrestling with his irate mount. "Just the person I need. Am I correct in thinking that Miss Winterton is at the parsonage?"

Then she was not at Pendarreth? Mel felt a frisson of fear ripple through him. But who was the horseman? He had to scratch around in his memory to put a name to the man. One of the Herbert brothers, he thought. Yes, William, the older of the two.

"Good day to you, Mr Herbert. No, Miss Winterton is not at the parsonage, and was not at church yesterday. Mrs Simpson and I were just on our way to enquire after her. Is... is anything amiss?"

Mr Herbert noticed Mrs Simpson for the first time, and politely dismounted, his horse skittering nervously as he did so. "Beg pardon, ma'am. I trust my horse did not alarm you? I was not in expectation of meeting anyone on this track."

"Not at all, but now I am in some alarm for Miss Winterton. Do you mean to say that she is not at Pendarreth?"

"She is not, and the house has been scoured from top to bottom, even the attics. No one thought anything of it at first, for on Saturday night everyone dined at Norton Forbury, and as she had never intended to go there, she was not missed. And yesterday, it was assumed that she was at church. But now it has been discovered that her bed has not been slept in for two nights and—"

"Two nights!" Mel burst out. "Then she disappeared on Saturday? And no one looked for her until now? Good God, she might be lying insensible in a ditch, for all anyone knows!"

"As I say, she was not missed because—" Mr Herbert began huffily. Then, perhaps realising the seriousness of the case, he went on more temperately, "Well, no matter why, but now everything is being done to find her. The maid who attends her confirms that she has taken a few things with her — some clothes, and so forth. So she has not merely gone out for a walk and fallen into a ditch, Haymer. She has gone to stay with someone. Our hopes were with *you* but..."

Mel knew not how to answer him, for guilt assailed him. If only he had maintained his friendship with her, she would indeed have come to him and been safe.

Fortunately, Mrs Simpson cut in smoothly. "There are one or two people in Dunton Cross to whom she might have turned. Mr Haymer, let us go back there now, and make enquiries."

"No," he said thoughtfully. "Not I. Do you go, Mrs Simpson, and if no one there knows anything, Miss Winterton has friends in Heston Ford also. I shall go on to Pendarreth, for I wish to talk to the maid myself."

"You will not find out anything new," Mr Herbert said. "Well, have it your own way. I shall ride over to Norton Forbury to apprise his lordship of events, and see if they have seen anything of the lady there. Good day to you both."

And with a quick leap into the saddle, he wheeled his horse and was off at a gallop again.

"What a tiring young man," Mrs Simpson said. "And those boots need a good polish. Mel, do you really think there is more information to be had from the maid?"

"Perhaps. I should also like to know what led to this state of affairs, and why Margaret was so desperate that she was obliged to run away. But I shall walk you back to the village first."

"By no means," she said. "Do not delay on my account. It is barely a hundred yards to Malham's Farm from here, and even I can hardly get lost in so short a distance. Oh... do you think Margaret may have got lost in the woods? For these paths are very confusing."

Mel smiled in affectionate memory of Margaret's carefully drawn map, and her systematic exploration of it. "No, she knows parts of the woods very well, and she is too sensible to venture beyond her own knowledge. Send John to Pendarreth with word if you find her."

And with that, they parted. Mel's long legs soon brought him to the edge of the lawn, but he no longer burned with fear for Margaret. He knew now that she had left of her own will, and he could perhaps guess both the reason for her precipitate departure, and her hiding place. But first, he needed more information.

The kitchen door stood wide open, shrill voices issuing from it. Mel found Mrs Herbert and Mrs Fordham haranguing Primrose.

"I don't know nothing more, madam, honestly," Primrose was saying as Mel entered. "Oh, Mr Haymer! I'm right glad to see you, sir. You'll know where she's hiding, I'll be bound."

"Ah, Mr Haymer," Mrs Herbert said. "Margaret is at the parsonage, I take it. Silly girl, causing so much trouble!"

"She is not at the parsonage, and she is not in the least a silly girl," he said, more sharply than he intended, so that the two ladies raised their eyebrows in surprise. "Whatever happened here to make her take off in this way?"

"Nothing happened," Mrs Fordham said disdainfully. "Whatever makes you think that something happened? I am sure no one has ever shown her anything but kindness and understanding, despite her... peculiarities."

Mel took a deep breath, and forced himself to speak calmly. "Margaret is not one to run away, not unless she is provoked or frightened. Did any of the young gentlemen offer her insult?"

"You forget yourself, Mr Haymer," Mrs Fordham said coldly. "You are accorded the respect due to a gentleman on account of your profession, but were you not a man of the cloth, we should not even be speaking to you. Kindly remember your place when addressing your betters."

"Oh, stop being so pompous, Tabitha," said Mrs Herbert impatiently. "Who knows what Mr Haymer's place is, anyway? I am sure I do not. Besides, it was a sensible question. Margaret has been suffering a great deal these last weeks, and those boys are not the most sensitive persons in the world. I know what it is like to be hounded by persistent suitors. I feel for her greatly, you may be sure."

"Oh, you had to throw that in my face again! Just because you had a season in London and were supposedly overwhelmed by the passions of all your numerous admirers, you think you are so much better than me. I had admirers, too, you know, but I made less fuss about them than you did. Honestly, Selina, it is the outside of enough! Can you never let me forget—"

Mel edged out of the room, as Primrose shook her head and turned back to her pastry. A quick investigation of the offices found Rose and Lily in one of the pantries, whispering in low voices, faces serious. They both smiled with relief when they saw Mel, and again he had to explain that he had no more idea of Margaret's whereabouts than they did.

"She took some clothes with her, I understand," he said. Rose nodded. "Did she also take any food?"

"Aye, she did, sir," Rose said eagerly. "Some cold chicken and bread and apples, and half a pie went overnight. But that means she's off on her own somewhere, maybe sleeping out in the open."

"Not in the open, I suspect," Mel said, smiling.

"She's not in the hayloft or any of the outhouses," Lily said. "Those were the first places we looked. The young gentlemen searched the attics, but there's nought up there but spiders. Miss Margaret's too fastidious to be sleeping in all that dust. Why, she even took a plate and bowl with the pie."

"Did she indeed?" That made Mel laugh. "Have you anything I might take to her? Some of those curranty little cakes, maybe?"

"Oh, yes!" Rose said. "Her favourites! Primrose made them special, in case she came back. Lily, run and fetch some. Wrap them in a cloth, so Mr Haymer can carry them. So you know where she'll be, sir?"

"I have an idea. I may be wrong, though, so say nothing to anyone just yet."

He made his way across the gardens, past the waving stems of overgrown roses and penstemons, under a bank of towering rhododendrons and through the encroaching woods to the perimeter wall. An arch which had once held a gate gave access to the wilderness that was Dunton Woods. One path hugged the wall, but he took the broad path leading up the hill, which was the direct route to Norton Forbury, and much churned by horses of late. Once there had been little traffic between the Manor House and Pendarreth, but recent events had seen far more riders passing in both directions. Today, though, nobody passed by, and the woods were silent under a lowering grey sky, full of rain.

Mel soon turned aside onto a smaller track, and now he was in new territory, for he had never travelled the route in this direction before. Twice he went wrong and had to double back, but he was not foolish enough to attempt a shortcut. Whenever he looked at the almost impenetrable mass of briars and bushes that sprouted everywhere, he thought of Margaret quietly and methodically walking up and down each square, and then recording her findings. He had never fully appreciated before just how great an undertaking that must have been.

Eventually, he found the right way through the maze, and came to the clearing where the tree house stood. There were no signs of life, and for the first time, he doubted himself. If he were wrong... But he would not abandon hope yet.

At the foot of the tree he stopped. He could hardly terrify her by climbing up unannounced, so he called out, "Margaret?" Then, louder, *"Margaret!"*

There was no answer, and then his heart quailed.

"Margaret, it is Mel. Are you all right? Please answer me, dearest."

Silence.

Dear God, was she ill? Or dead? No, he must not be foolish. Perhaps she had stepped out for a moment... or perhaps she had never been here at all, and he was utterly wrong. Whichever it was, he had to know.

In terror, he set his foot to the lowest rung of the ladder and began to climb.

21: Currant Cakes And Kisses

Mel had to climb all the way to the top of the tree house before he found signs of occupation. The door of the hut stood open and on the table lay the plate and bowl, with the pie on the plate and a couple of apples in the bowl. Neatly folded on the bench were a few items of clothing. He had to go all the way into the hut to find his object, however, for she was hidden by the open door.

There on the other bench she lay, eyes closed, her face as pale as death, her head resting on a folded cloak, one arm stretched out to the side, the delicate fingers motionless.

For one appalled moment, he thought she was dead, and terror roared through him so fast that he could not breathe. But then he saw the slow rise of her chest, and realised that her pale skin still had the pink tinge of life. She was asleep.

Scarcely knowing what he was doing, he slumped onto the opposite bench beside the piles of clothes, where he could watch her sweet face while he composed himself after his shock. But all was well — she was alive, and found, and in that moment he had nothing else to wish for. So he sat, noticing now her tear-stained face and the signs of puffiness about her eyes that betokened much weeping. And although she slept, it was not a calm, restful kind of repose, for she shifted about regularly, and murmured words in a low voice, and once moaned piteously. His poor Margaret! So unhappy, and perhaps it was his fault, in part at least, for turning away from her just when she needed him most.

Her eyes opened.

For a moment, she looked at him, uncomprehending. Then, with a cry, she sat up. "Mel! Oh, Mel!"

Jumping up, she hurled herself at him with a sob. He opened his arms to her and tilted his face up as, with tears and laughter mingled, she pressed her lips to his.

The world melted away into nothingness. There was only Margaret and her love and joy and need, wrapped in his arms, safe again. He lifted her onto his knee, tasting the salty tears on her lips, feeling the softness of her body against his, the rightness of her closeness, the glorious wonder of his overwhelming love for her. She sobbed and laughed and kissed him over and over again, until his lips tingled and he was dizzy with joy.

"Darling Mel," she murmured.

"Sweetheart," he said. "I am—"

"But why did you abandon me, and—"

"—so sorry. It seemed—"

"—leave me to face them all alone, when—"

"—the best thing for you, but I—"

"—I needed you so much. You must—"

"—did not mean to hurt you. I shall—"

"—never leave me again."

"—never leave you again."

She pulled away from him a little, laughing. "Oh, Mel! I can bear anything if you are with me, anything at all. When you were not there, I was so unhappy. It was as if you did not love me any more."

"I shall always love you," he said, with utter certainty. He had never consciously considered the matter, but in some unfathomable way, he knew it to be the truth. "But it seemed to me that my presence was keeping you away from the chance of your own home and a husband and children — all those things I cannot offer you."

"Which I do not want," she said. "All I want is this — your friendship, and the knowledge that you will be here with me always."

"Nothing more?" he said. "Not Pendarreth?"

"Pendarreth is Aunt Pru's," she said firmly. "She is the one who cares most about it."

He kissed her nose softly, making her giggle. "But what about you, my love? Do you truly not care for the place at all? It is a fine house, and the woods—"

"I love the woods!" she cried. "The woods are wonderful, and when I can escape from Mr William Herbert, their peacefulness lifts my spirits marvellously. As for the house — yes, it *is* very fine, but it needs so much money spending on it. Nothing works, not even the bells or the locks on the doors. Half the windows will not open and the other half will not close, and all the chimneys smoke terribly. The house is broken. It would give me the greatest pleasure to make it whole again, and the money is there, but it is not *my* house. One day soon it will belong to Lord Delacrost, and he will do with it as he pleases, but it is not for me to mend it. Poor Aunt Pru! She loves it so much, yet she has neglected it shamefully.

I do not know what is to become of her when Lord Delacrost owns it, for it would distress her beyond measure to leave Pendarreth now, when she has lived there every day of her life."

"Aunt Pru is not your responsibility," Mel said gently. "You cannot help her, except by staying in Pendarreth for as long as possible, and it seems to me that you must be strong and send all the cousins away for a while."

"I have tried! I made an announcement at dinner — at least, I made the footman say the words — telling everyone that I had no wish to marry and they should all go away, but they will *not* go! They harass me so!"

"They have not... mistreated you in any way?"

"Oh no. Only bored me to death, and given me no peace at all. I could not escape from them. Susan and Maria even came to my bedroom when I said I had the headache, can you believe it? I could not bear it, and so I ran away. If only they would leave me alone, and go away! What more can I do? Can *you* make them leave?"

"If only I could," he said. "But I have no right to protect you, dearest. Only a husband or brother or father may do that. So long as they think there is a possibility of winning your hand, they will stay."

"But there is *no* possibility, as they have been told, but no one believes a single word from me. Except you, dearest Mel," she added, smiling at him.

For a while, they kissed again and then there were the currant cakes to be eaten, so for some time nothing more was said about Pendarreth. After a while, when the last cake had vanished, and Mel had picked up every stray crumb, he turned his mind to the problem again.

"It is not at all clear that there is anything to be done about Pendarreth," he said slowly. "If you are quite certain that you will never marry any of the cousins, then perhaps the best way out of this is to leave the house altogether. Notify Mr Higgins and Dr Harling of your intentions and let the house pass swiftly to Lord Delacrost. Miss Tilford must then throw herself on his mercy if she wishes to remain in the house. Once he is convinced that you have given it up, he will not press her to leave, I am sure."

"I have already written to Mr Higgins and Dr Harling," she said. "They have not yet replied. But I do not wish to abandon Aunt Pru if it can be prevented. All I want is for the cousins to leave me alone. Perhaps if I make myself so unattractive— Oh! I know! I shall become your mistress, then I shall be ruined and no one will ever want to marry me!"

He jumped to his feet. He could not be angry with her, but he could not hide his distress. "No! No, no, no! It is unthinkable!" He paced back and forth across the tiny hut, running his hands through his hair. "My *mistress?* Good God, Margaret, do not say such things. You have no idea what that would mean."

"But I do, and it would be perfect, for any children would not be legitimate, you see, so you would not be breaking your promise to Lord Delacrost."

"Margaret... are you truly saying that you would be content to be a mistress, but not a wife?"

"Oh... as to that... being a wife... I always imagined that it would be horrid to be meek and submissive, and to someone who was bosky half the time, too, or was a gambler, and to have to accept it and not be able to *talk* about anything important. But I can talk to you. I never feel meek and submissive when you are with me, for you make me strong and capable of anything. And I do not think you would get bosky, would you, or gamble, or anything of that nature? So I would marry *you,* if it were possible. But it is not possible, so if you are to protect me, I shall have to be your mistress, do you not see? I am quite sure I should be content."

She smiled up at him happily, and he despaired of explaining how impossible it was. Yet it must be attempted. Forcing himself to sit down again and be calm, he took her hands in his. "Margaret — dearest Margaret — you are an innocent, and you hardly know what you say, but believe me when I tell you it is impossible. Such an action would dishonour both of us, and set us beyond all bounds of propriety, even if I were not a clergyman."

"Oh… that is true. You dress so fine that it is easy to forget your profession. No, you could hardly stand up on Sundays and preach against fornication and so forth, when—"

"Margaret!" he said, half shocked and half amused. "You are not supposed to know about such things, and you are *certainly* not supposed to talk about them!"

"But it is in the *Bible!* Besides, I have had the run of Papa's library since I was seven or eight years old and there was a great deal of forn— er, that sort of thing in some of his books. Oh dear, have I put you to the blush, Mel dear?"

He laughed, and shook his head. "No, but it will not answer, I fear. We shall have to think of some other ruse to evade your admirers. Tell me, would you like to come down to the parsonage for a day or two? We can bring the minds of Dr and Mrs Simpson to bear on the problem."

"Oh, yes please! And I promise to stay in my own bedroom, if you truly dislike the idea."

She beamed up at him with such glee in her eyes that he could not help but laugh. "You are incorrigible, Miss Winterton."

But the whole way down the track to Dunton Cross, he was tormented by the idea of Margaret creeping into his bedroom at night. How badly he wished that he were not bound by his promise to Lord Delacrost, and could resolve their difficulties by the most simple and natural expedient in the world, of making her his wife. But it was impossible. He was bound and could not marry anyone. He had never felt so forlorn.

When they arrived at the parsonage, half the servants rushed out to greet them, and flap excitedly around Margaret like so many sparrows. They loved her too, he realised with delight. Everyone who saw her true nature loved her. It was only the gentry who saw no further than her difficulties with words, and lost interest. Unless she had a house to bestow on them, of course. Then, suddenly, she was endlessly beguiling.

Dr Simpson came out of his library to meet them in the hall.

"Miss Winterton! You are safe! I thank God for it. Aline came home in such a tearing hurry, and is gone to Heston Ford to look for you, but she will be back directly. Come into the library, my dear, and let me look at you." He shooed the servants away and closed the door firmly on their interested faces. "Ah, you are so pale! Robert must go for Dr Harling at once."

"No, no!" she protested. "I am perfectly well, I assure you. I am a little tired, for I have not been sleeping much, but nothing worse, truly."

Dr Simpson rocked back on his heels, astonishment written on his face. "My dear! You are talking! But how wonderful! What has caused this dramatic change?"

"I... not sure. Mel, I think. Relief..."

"You were not... harmed?"

Margaret shook her head, and Mel sighed. "Ah, now the words have got stuck again."

She nodded, and hung her head. "Sorry."

"Dearest Margaret," Mel said, taking her hand and kissing it, so that she turned huge eyes on his face. "You must never apologise for what you are. Your habitual silence only makes the pleasure greater when you speak."

She blushed and lowered her head again, and with the utmost reluctance he released her hand. He yearned to be back in the tree house, their own secret place where he could hold her tight and kiss her and murmur his love into her ears, and not have to consider the proprieties.

Dr Simpson's calm tones broke into this pleasant reverie. "Mel, Miss Winterton would like something to eat, I am sure. And tell Carys to light the fire in the guest room, if you would be so good. And even though Miss Winterton says she is quite well, it would reassure my anxieties if Dr Harling were to look at her. You will not mind that, my dear? Just to satisfy the worries of a friend? Are you cold? Do come and sit by the fire."

Being so politely dismissed, Mel went off obediently to attend to the domestic practicalities. John was dispatched to Pendarreth to tell them that Margaret was found, Carys to attend to the guest bedroom, Robert to Dr Harling and Mrs Millington to provide hot soup and some freshly baked cakes, for in the cook's opinion there were few crises so desperate that they could not be relieved by soup and cakes.

By this time, the carriage had returned bearing Mrs Simpson, to shed tears of joy over Margaret and wrap her in hugs so tight it was a wonder she could breathe. They sat around a small table so that Margaret could pretend to eat the unwanted soup, for Mrs

Millington would be offended if she did not, while Mel ploughed his way through the cakes. Meanwhile, Mrs Simpson sat in restless silence, clearly brimming with questions she was too polite to ask.

Eventually, Margaret pushed away the soup and refused the last remaining cake. “Thank you,” she said, with a shy smile.

“Do you feel well enough to tell us what happened to drive you away from Pendarreth?” Mrs Simpson said.

“There is no need to talk about any of it if you had rather not,” Mel said hastily.

“No, indeed,” Mrs Simpson said. “But perhaps we can help. If nothing else, we can listen and perhaps that alone will be some comfort to you. Let us have some Madeira, and you may tell us whatever you wish to.” A hesitation, and then she said, “Do you want your slate and chalks, dear?”

Margaret shook her head, then, very deliberately, reached for Mel, and slipped her hand into his. “I can talk, like this. Try, anyway.”

And so she talked, telling them everything that she had already told Mel of the way her cousins had hounded her, and their mothers and sisters just as much, until she felt that all the air was being drawn away and she was suffocating.

Mel held her hand and wondered that he had such power over her, that his mere touch could restore her ability to speak. He cradled her hand, gently stroking the back of it, as she told her tale.

“Then Lord Delacrost came to try to persuade me to marry one of the cousins,” she said. “He was very angry with me for saying I should not, after he had gone to the trouble of arranging for Aunt Letty to leave me Pendarreth.”

"Lord Delacrost did that?" Mrs Simpson said, in astonished tones. "But why? What is it to him?"

"Oh, because of Mel," Margaret said. "He does not want us to— Oh! You did not know." She turned stricken eyes on Mel. "Sorry," she whispered. "So sorry."

He squeezed her hand, and smiled, not at all displeased. It was time that his foster mother learnt the truth about him.

"I do not *know* anything," Mrs Simpson said, smiling ruefully. "I have always wondered about Mel, but nothing was ever said about him. Not to me, or not officially, anyway. One hears rumours, of course. That Mel is Lord Delacrost's illegitimate son, or that he is not Lord Delacrost's son at all, but the result of some liaison of Lady Delacrost's. There had to be some reason for the generous allowance."

"I am not the son of either of them," Mel said quietly. "I am some hedge-born bastard, foisted on Lord Delacrost after his legitimate heir died. Yet in law, I will be viscount after him and there is nothing either of us can do about it. But we have done what we can, for we have broken the entail, so that Mortimer will inherit the estate, and I have promised his lordship that I will never marry, in order for the title to revert to Mortimer's line in future. In return, his lordship pays me an allowance. But he sees, as the whole world must, my regard for Margaret and believes that I will break my sworn word. For that reason, he has put Margaret in this abominable position, and made her life a misery."

"That is very bad," Mrs Simpson said. "Yet if you are his legal heir, he should acknowledge you as such, or else pursue some recourse in law to cast you off. His behaviour is very underhanded. And to allow the world to think you illegitimate, when you will be viscount one day — it is not the act of a sensible man."

"There is no recourse in law unless my true parents can be identified," Mel said. "Lord Delacrost has expended every effort in that regard, without the slightest success, so we continue in this strange limbo. And his lordship and I are not the ones in the worst position. So far as I know, he has as yet told his sons nothing about me, so they know almost nothing of the true state of affairs and are left to speculate like everyone else."

"That is perfectly despicable," Mrs Simpson said sharply. "What a dreadful man! I dislike him excessively. But at least now I understand why you have always said you will never marry, Mel. Your words made me wonder greatly, yet it all makes perfect sense now."

"Let us not concern ourselves with Lord Delacrost," Dr Simpson said. "The question before us is what should Miss Winterton do to extricate herself from this difficult situation. Are you quite certain, my dear, that you do not wish to marry one of your cousins and fulfil the terms of the will?"

"Quite, quite certain," she said. "Even if there were no Mel for comparison, I should not have wished to marry any of them. I do not like to speak ill of my own cousins, but they are none of them men of much education or good sense, such as I could ever esteem as a wife should esteem her husband, nor do they exhibit any regard for me. Besides, how could anyone respect a man who marries only for financial gain, and for no other reason?"

"That is very clear," Dr Simpson said. "In that case, perhaps the best course is to notify Higgins and Harling of your intentions and leave Pendarreth altogether, so that it may be transferred to Lord Delacrost as soon as may be."

"What about Aunt Pru?" she said quietly. "He has already tried to force her out once."

"That is not your concern," Dr Simpson said. "Miss Tilford must come to terms with her future, whatever it may be. Do you have someone you could go to? One of your sisters? The married one, perhaps."

She nodded, but it was as if all the life had gone out of her. She drooped like a flower out of water. "That would be sensible," she whispered.

"No, no, no, that will never do," Mrs Simpson said briskly. "Send her away from Mel? Heartless! She must come and live here."

"Aline," her husband said, "there has already been talk. We cannot expose Miss Winterton to the world's censure by inviting her to stay here indefinitely, agreeable as it would be to all of us. A single man and a single woman living under the same roof, in a house as small as this one? It would never do. We could only do it if Mel were to move out."

"Then would you sooner see her back at Pendarreth, to be the object of every fortune hunter in the family?" Mrs Simpson said. "No, there is a very simple solution. Mel and Margaret must marry, and that is all there is to it, and do not say that it cannot be done, for *I* say that indeed it can, and furthermore, it must and shall be done."

22: A Proposal

There was no time to consider Mrs Simpson's outrageous proposal, for Dr Harling arrived at that point, and Margaret and Mrs Simpson disappeared upstairs with him.

Mel was left alone with Dr Simpson, trying to suppress the surge of hope that overcame him. Oh, if only a way could be found for him to marry Margaret that would not break his promise to Lord Delacrost! But he could not conceive of such a way.

Nor could Dr Simpson, for he shook his head sadly. "Aline gets these romantic fancies sometimes, I regret to say. She sees your affection for Margaret, and wishes for a happy resolution, and by wishing it, imagines that it can be so, just as in one of her novels. But we shall prevail upon her to see reason, I daresay."

Mel merely nodded, not trusting himself to speak. He swallowed the last of his Madeira, and busied himself with refilling his glass, but he could not prevent his hands from shaking as he did so. To marry her... to be with her always... to protect her from every hurt and misfortune... could it be possible? No, it was madness even to think of it, for if he married Margaret, then Lord Delacrost would revoke his allowance and they would have nothing but his stipend to live upon. He would be a pauper, unable to afford decent clothes, or his horse and groom, and certainly not a wife.

It was as well that he remembered this, for it enabled him to turn back to Dr Simpson and say with tolerable composure, "Mrs Simpson is always amenable to reason. She will see that it is a ridiculous idea."

Dr Simpson eyed him thoughtfully, but said nothing more on the subject.

When Dr Harling descended the stairs, he professed himself pleased with Margaret. "She has taken no physical hurt, none at all," he said. "It is only that her mind has been overwhelmed with all the changes in her life. She is a frail, timid creature, not at all used to being the focus of attention from young gentlemen. With better care from the ladies at Pendarreth, she might have managed well enough, but Miss Tilford, it seems, takes little notice of her, and Mrs Herbert and Mrs Fordham no doubt had their sons' prospects at heart, and could spare but little consideration for Miss Winterton. It is a pity that matters should have been left so. Property should not be in the hands of ladies, in my opinion. They are not capable of making rational business decisions."

"Mrs Bradwell managed all her husband's many properties and businesses," Mel said waspishly, annoyed that Harling should so readily dismiss Margaret as frail and timid.

"Ah yes, but Mrs Bradwell was a woman of strong character," the physician said complacently. "She would not have let her mind be overset by such a situation as Miss Winterton now finds herself in. She would have— Well, no matter. I have given Miss Winterton something to help her to sleep. Mrs Simpson is settling her now. She will, I trust, sleep through the night and wake much restored."

"And very hungry, since she will miss dinner," Mel snapped, too cross at the doctor's easy dismissal of Margaret to mind his words.

"Tell me, Harling, if you can," Dr Simpson cut in quickly, "how soon you will proceed to transfer the estate to Lord Delacrost, now that you are aware of Miss Winterton's intentions not to marry one of her cousins."

"But I am not aware of it," Harling said. "I have heard rumours, of course, but that is not sufficient. She must write to us — to Higgins and to me — declaring her rejection of the terms of her aunt's will. Once we have that, and have determined that the lady is serious, then we may consider the next steps."

"Then you did not receive a letter from Miss Winterton, stating exactly this?" Mel said. "It would have been sent a week or more ago."

He looked startled. "No, I have received nothing, and nor has Higgins, for we dined together only last night and had some discussion on the case. She must write again, and we shall consider the matter. However, I have to tell you that we have already agreed that we will take no precipitate action. Whatever Miss Winterton says now, she may change her mind next week or next month or even next year. Ladies are flighty creatures, who do not know their own minds. We will not hand Pendarreth to Lord Delacrost until it is seen beyond all doubt that Miss Winterton can never comply with the terms of the will."

Dr Simpson frowned. "There can never be complete certainty, Harling. There must come a point, surely, when you will declare that she is not likely to comply. If she moves away, or... or marries elsewhere... surely that would be enough?"

"A wife may easily be widowed, Simpson," the physician said. "The lady may move away, but return later. If there is any possibility that she may yet marry one of her cousins, then we cannot proceed to transfer the property. Imagine if we were to do so, and then Miss Winterton were to marry one of these gentlemen? Why, it could happen years from now, and it would be quite unjust if the property were no longer in the lady's possession."

"Was there not some clause about a reasonable time after Mrs Bradwell's decease?" Mel said. "Surely some limit must be set?"

"Indeed, so it was," Harling said. "The interpretation of that term is entirely a matter for the executors, however, and we are minded to be generous. Higgins and I are quite of one mind on this point. To be absolutely sure, nothing can be done until either Miss Winterton or all her male cousins have departed from this world."

This threw Mel into gloom. Was Margaret never to be free of her cousins' harassment? Even if she were to quit Shropshire entirely, and remove to the home of one of her sisters, there was no knowing but one or two of the gentlemen might be persistent enough to follow her. Only death, it seemed, could relieve her of the prospect. It was a hideous thought.

By the time Harling had fortified himself for the arduous journey back to Heston Ford with a glass or two of Madeira, and Mrs Simpson had left the sleeping Margaret and been informed of Harling's opinions, it was time to dress for dinner. There was only one course, since it was not a Sunday, but there were several removes, so it was some time before the servants had withdrawn and it was safe to return to the interesting topic of Margaret.

Dr Simpson's eyes twinkled with amusement as he gazed affectionately at his wife. "Now, my dear, you may tell us precisely how you envisage Mel and Margaret marrying, when Mel has promised Lord Delacrost he will do no such thing."

"Nothing could be easier," she said airily. "One must needs examine the *intent* of the promise, for it is not the act of marrying nor the having of a wife that is at issue. What Mel has sworn to do is to sire no sons who might inherit the title ahead of Mortimer Haymer. So… they marry but have no children."

"Aline…" Dr Simpson began, but Mel laughed.

"And how is that to be achieved? Such matters are in God's hands."

"Not entirely," she said crisply.

"Aline," her husband said again. "I do not think—"

"Nonsense," she said. "Mel must have some inkling that our childless state is no mere accident. We have chosen this, and it has worked out very satisfactorily."

Mel leaned back in his chair, dumbfounded. "But that is what marriage is *for*, the procreation of children."

"And also the mutual society, help, and comfort, that the one ought to have of the other, both in prosperity and adversity," Dr Simpson said quietly. "You know the words of the marriage service as well as I do. For us, that was the most important aspect. Children would have disturbed the perfect harmony of our union. Besides, we were desperately poor, just at first, so it seemed prudent to exercise restraint."

"And I wanted to be free to write my novels," Mrs Simpson said. "God put all these *people* in my head, so He cannot object if I share them with the world. Children would have been too great a distraction."

"Yet you took me in," Mel said, puzzled. "Was I not a distraction? Did I not disturb the perfect harmony of your union?"

"No, you were the most delightful child," Mrs Simpson said at once. "You satisfied all my maternal urges without any of the inconvenience and dangers normally associated with the business. And just one of you... one treasured child, and no more. It has worked out admirably." Dr Simpson coughed discreetly, and his wife, gazing studiedly at her plate, continued, "Of course, Lord Delacrost paid us handsomely for our charity, too. You had the best of everything, Mel, and the finest tutors money could buy. We were very glad of that money in the early days, when we had only this one living to provide for us, but I think within a six-month, you had found your way unerringly to our hearts. No parents could ever have been fonder than we were, and are, of you. We would have fought like tigers to keep you, if he had chosen to remove you from our care. "

"Did he visit often?" Mel said in wonder, for the subject had never been spoken of openly before. "Did he suggest tutors or subjects for study?"

"Nothing like that, except that you were not to attend Oxford university where the Haymer name might attract unwanted attention," Dr Simpson said. "In fact, we neither saw nor heard from him again until you turned one and twenty, and he came here to see you. But this is old history, and aids us not at all in our present dilemma. Aline, my dear, it is not clear to me that what you propose will be acceptable to Lord Delacrost."

"He is a sensible man, and will understand," Mrs Simpson said. "But there is a further possibility. If we can discover Mel's true parentage, then Lord Delacrost will have a legal means to cut him out of the inheritance, and he will be free."

"Free to be penniless," Mel said with a smile. "Free to be a pauper curate with barely the means to support myself, let alone a wife. It is a kindly scheme, but it will not answer, I fear."

"Then what else is Margaret to do?" Mrs Simpson said in sudden passion. "Is she to be hounded all her days, her life made miserable by these heedless people? She cannot stay at Pendarreth without protection, nor can she go away, for they can easily follow. Must she sail to Australia to escape them?"

"But how does it help for her to marry Mel?" Dr Simpson said. "Harling said—"

"It matters not what he said," she cried. "Margaret's suitors cannot persist if she already has a husband. They will not wait around in the hope that Mel will die. Whatever the executors may say or do, a husband is Margaret's best protection against her cousins' ambitions. If she had a father or a brother to protect her... but a brother-in-law is *not* the same."

"Yes... I can see that," her husband said. "As for being penniless, my cousin has several more livings at his disposal, and the bishop is a distant cousin, too. If you have some savings, Mel, you might buy yourself a very snug living or two, and be no worse off than you are now."

Mel was silent. They had an answer to every objection, it seemed. "Suppose we were to marry," he said slowly, "what then? Where would we live? Here?"

"At Pendarreth," Mrs Simpson said at once. "Margaret must stay there to protect Miss Tilford, at least until the day Lord Delacrost takes possession of the house, which may be a very long time. Indeed, she must go back there as soon as may be, to send these dreadful cousins to the right about and make sure nothing untoward is going on. The house is hers, after all, at least for a while, and she must take care of it."

"She may not agree to it," he said cautiously, for although she had told him only that afternoon that she would willingly marry him, if it were possible, she had firmly believed at that time that it was *not* possible. He also recalled her previous words on the subject. *'It would be horrible to be owned by a man and have no will of my own and spend my whole life having to keep him happy at all costs. I would not be me.'* Who could say which view would prevail if he were to offer her a watered-down form of marriage?

"Of course she will agree to it," Mrs Simpson said with a confident smile. "She loves you, and fully appreciates your worth. Now she needs you more than ever."

"But suppose she were to agree to it because she is feeling hounded and miserable, then in six months or a year, she were to feel trapped and regret what she has done. What if I make her miserable, too?"

"Impossible," Mrs Simpson said, with a little laugh. "She is always happy when she is with you. Let the banns be read, Mel. You know that is what you want."

He was silent for a long time, as his longing for Margaret warred with his common sense. It was madness to think of marrying, he knew that. He could see his own concerns reflected in Dr Simpson's serious expression. Mrs Simpson was eager, excited almost, but that was the result of her romantic sensibilities, and the decision before him was too complicated to be driven by emotion. He must be practical, and consider Margaret's needs before his own.

"I will discuss it with her," he said finally.

Mrs Simpson clapped her hands in glee, but Dr Simpson sighed heavily and shook his head. "I hope you will not come to rue this day, Mel," he said gloomily.

"Nothing is decided yet," he said. "But on one matter I can be certain — there must be no banns. Can you imagine how these cousins would react if given notice that Margaret is to wed? They would redouble their efforts to secure her. If her existence is made miserable now, just think how much worse it would be if there is only a short time to change her mind. No, if there is to be a marriage, it must be done by licence, so that Margaret is secure before anyone knows about it."

Yet still he could not be certain that he was setting his feet on the right path.

~~~~~

Margaret woke to comfortable warmth. Beneath her, the bed was soft and the linen sheets smooth. Heavy wool blankets wrapped her in their cosy embrace. The room was still dark, but flickering firelight danced through gaps in the bed hangings.

The parsonage. She was tucked up in bed in the guest room at the parsonage, with Mel next door, and Dr and Mrs Simpson just down the landing. She was safe. Nothing could worry her here. Even if William Herbert or the others came here, Mel would send them away. She was safe at last.

Yet it was so shaming to have run away. If only she had been able to express herself robustly, as any of her sisters would have done. Even Fanny, dear, gentle Fanny, would have been able to explain her feelings and would have been listened to. Yet no one took the least notice of Margaret. Aunt Pru told her she was mistress of Pendarreth, but her actions belied the words. Her guests listened calmly when they were told to leave, and stayed
~~~~~

exactly where they were. Lord Delacrost barged about, interfering — although there, at least, she had been angry enough to be firm with him. With her unwanted suitors, unless they stepped across the bounds of propriety, she could not be rude to them, or even angry.

But now she was with Mel, the one person who always listened to her and believed everything she said and never treated her like an ignorant, foolish child.

She pushed aside the bed curtains, to find Carys fast asleep in the chair by the fire, her head lolling and her mouth hanging open. It was still early, but Margaret padded across to the window and threw open the one casement that worked, breathing deeply of the damp morning air.

"You up, miss?" Carys murmured, stirring to life. "You feel better? Wait, I'll fetch some water and your chocolate."

"Thank you," Margaret said, and when Carys had gone, she hugged herself in delight, and then danced around the room. Even while she slept, she had been watched over and cherished, as she had never been at Pendarreth. She was safe!

Breakfast was just as she remembered, with Dr and Mrs Simpson chaffing each other good-naturedly, and Mel — dearest Mel! — watching her in silence, with a little smile on his face, jumping up to fetch anything she might want almost before she had looked about for it. She was ravenous, and wolfed down eggs and ham and toast and half a plate of currant cakes.

When the Simpsons had gone off to attend to their morning duties and only Mel remained, he said, "Dearest, there is a matter we must discuss. Will you come into my study?"

Willingly she followed him. He settled her on a sofa, and then pulled across a chair to sit facing her. Taking her hand, he began,

"While you slept last night, the Simpsons and I had much discussion regarding your situation. We are agreed that you cannot go back to Pendarreth unsupported, nor can your sisters protect you adequately. We feel... we all feel... that the best means of protection is for you to marry... to... to marry me, I mean. So if—"

Marry him? Was it truly possible? Joy radiated through with such intensity that she sprang to her feet, and spun round twice. He jumped up, alarm written all over his face.

"Margaret, dearest..."

She took a deep breath. Then another. Did he really mean it? *Please* let him mean it! Oh, if only...

"Mel," she said breathlessly, "are you making me an offer of marriage?"

"I... yes, I believe I am."

"Then *please* will you do it properly? Because I shall never have another offer, and I should hate Mr Pickles to be the only man who ever proposed to me. Please?"

And she sat down, looking up at him expectantly.

He laughed, but shook his head. "I doubt I can do the thing as it ought to be done — as you deserve — but I shall do my best." He dropped to one knee so that his head was level with hers, taking both her hands in his much larger ones. "Miss Winterton, you cannot be unaware of my growing admiration for you over these past few months. Your beauty, your gentle demeanour, your quickness and good sense, your many accomplishments and your good humour are..." He sighed a little. "...quite delightful. Allow me to tell you that I love you more than my foolish tongue can find the words for." He lifted one of her hands to his cheek, and held it there, eyes closed. "Oh, Margaret..." Another sigh, and then, to her great delight, he turned his head a little and kissed her palm, the touch of his lips so gentle, so intimate that she shivered with joy. "Margaret, dearest, most adored Margaret, will you do me the incalculable honour of becoming my wife?"

"Oh, yes *please*," she cried, almost bouncing in her seat. "That was quite lovely. Thank you, thank you, darling Mel. Of course I will marry you, but now you must tell me, if you please, how you intend to reconcile this with your promise to Lord Delacrost? Has he given his permission? Or is this to be a very, very long engagement?"

He kissed her hand again, and then heaved a greater sigh. "No, he has not given his permission," he said heavily. "And no, it will not be a long engagement, for we dare not wait for the wind to turn. We must be married soon, so that I can protect you from your importuning suitors. And then we will abide by the spirit of my promise, and conceive no children. Do you understand what that means, dearest? We must be... no more than friends, even though we shall be husband and wife."

She gently withdrew her hands. "You are going to break your promise to him."

"I am going to explain the circumstances to him, and reassure him that I will do nothing to cut his son's line out of the title. I must hope he will understand."

"No," she whispered, as the first tears fell. "No. Must not... do this."

"I must," he said, raising his blue eyes to her in mute appeal. "Margaret, I love you more than life itself, and I cannot, I *will* not, stand aside while all your tranquillity is destroyed, even if that means changing the terms of the promise I made years ago. I have been passive all my life, hiding away, doing whatever was asked of me without complaint, surrendering my life because I was an impostor, a cuckoo in the Haymer nest. Well, that may be acceptable for me, but not for you, my dearest love. If you are in trouble, then I must and will act, even if it sets me at odds with Lord Delacrost. Even if it means breaking my word to him."

He sat beside her on the sofa, his strong arms holding her tight, while she cried on his shoulder, wondering whether it was worse to marry, knowing Mel had broken his word, or not to marry at all.

23: To Hereford

The following day, Margaret returned to Pendarreth in the Simpsons' carriage, with Mrs Simpson in attendance to bear her company for a day or two.

"You may send me home whenever you wish, my dear," she said, "but just at first, since Mel cannot be with you until he has obtained a licence and so forth, it may be helpful to have a friend with you, someone who is unequivocally on your side. Not that there should be sides, not within a family," she added. "Yet somehow there always are. Luke's family has so many sides it is a wonder there is not a war breaking out when they all get together. You are very lucky that your sisters are so united. They sound delightful, and I hope I shall meet them one day."

They found that the Pendarreth residents were all on the same side, for once. Whatever the rivalry between the various suitors and their mamas, such differences were forgotten for once, and they united to berate Margaret with one voice for her selfishness and stupidity in running away and setting them all by the ears. Anyone listening to them might have supposed that she had done it on purpose to vex them.

She bowed her head under the onslaught, and only the thought that she would very soon be Mel's wife sustained her. His wife! And he would be her husband. They would be together always, and as for the rest of it, the not having babies part of the arrangement, she did not mind just so long as her beloved Mel could be with her. So there were no tears, and, it must be confessed, she did not listen to above half of their recriminations.

Mrs Simpson, however, was of a stronger constitution. "What nonsense!" she said robustly, when they had all expended the first flood of outrage. "Poor Margaret has been hounded to distraction by you all. Did you not listen when she told you that she had no intention of marrying any of her cousins? And if so, why are you still here? For you are not at all wanted, I assure you, and Dr Harling will be here directly to explain to you just how insensitive you have been to poor Margaret, who is far too good-natured to gainsay you, even when you make her ill with your oppressive attentions. Go away, now. Shoo! Begone!"

And so, with much affronted muttering, they dispersed from the hall, where they had gathered in a great crowd under the interested eyes of the servants. Mrs Simpson whisked Margaret up to her room, ordered the fire made up at once and hot water brought up for a bath, and insisted that a truckle bed be brought in for her so that she might sleep in a corner of the room. It reminded Margaret of the time she was ill with the scarlet fever, and Mama had slept in her room, and every time she woke from some terrifyingly realistic fevered nightmare, there she was with the lavender water and soothing words to gentle her back to sleep. How comforting it would be to have the motherly figure of Mrs Simpson with her in the dark hours of the night.

That evening they dined in Margaret's bedroom, with no fewer than ten dishes and a joint of beef, which Mrs Simpson carved, and decanters of claret and burgundy. They were very merry, for Mrs Simpson had all the gossip about her neighbours and her acquaintances in Heston Ford, and even further afield than that. Margaret was astonished and a little shocked to discover the secret lives of people she had thought entirely respectable.

'That is very bad of Mrs Crawley,' she wrote. *'She must have been very unhappy to take such a step. But I wonder how it is that such a private thing is widely known.'*

"Everything is known," Mrs Simpson said. "Amongst the common labouring class, perhaps a secret may be buried. But amongst people of our class, surrounded by servants? They see everything, and hear a great deal, too. They see when we are happy and unhappy. They know when we leave the house, and when we return. Other servants know where we go, and who we visit, and who else is there at the same time. They know perfectly well if a married woman visits a gentleman, and stays for the whole afternoon, and neither of them is to be found in the drawing room. There are no secrets for us, my dear."

But Margaret thought of Mel and the secret of his parentage that no enquiries of Lord Delacrost's had managed to uncover, and wondered. Who had given birth to him? Why had she surrendered him to Lady Delacrost? And who had buried the real Melville Haymer in the woods and made a monument to his brief life, and all these years later still put flowers on the grave? No, there were some secrets that even the servants did not know.

For half the night she sat by the window, listening to rain pattering against the glass and gurgling through the drain pipes, and wondered about the events of twenty nine, almost thirty, years ago, and whether Mel would ever know the truth. And even if he uncovered the secret, could it be proved to the satisfaction of the law, so that Mel could finally be free? But free or not, very soon now he would be *her* Mel. She sighed and climbed into bed, closing her eyes and lying still, allowing her mind to fill with thoughts of him. Soon, very soon, she would be his wife and then she would be completely safe for ever.

~~~~~

Mel chose to ride to Hereford to see the bishop. It might have been a more comfortable journey by public stage, but it was no quicker and he was minded to make his way by the quiet country lanes where he could think his own thoughts more easily. His mind was in some turmoil, for he was about to take the one step he had sworn never to take. He had given his word, and although Margaret's need overrode such a vow and he would keep to the spirit of his promise, still it distressed him to break his given word. Lord Delacrost would see it as dishonourable, in any event.

So his thoughts ran as he jogged through the autumn-tinged Shropshire countryside, the silent Robert in his wake.

They arrived at the cathedral a little after noon, and found that the bishop was, as expected, engaged for the rest of the day. An appointment was made for the following day, and Mel was found accommodation with a young canon, who was delighted to have a guest. He willingly bore Mel company as he toured around the close and the cathedral itself, admiring both the soaring architecture and the odd little map of the world from centuries ago, so different from modern maps. He smiled to himself, remembering Margaret's intricately detailed and accurate map. Everything reminded him of Margaret. Even when he attended evensong he thought of her, determining to bring her here sometime so that she, too, might be awed by the swelling notes of
~~~~~

the organ and humbled by the many beauteous voices raised in song.

The bishop was a stern-faced man, new to the position since Mel's ordination, but he was not unfriendly, listening sympathetically to Mel's story and shaking his head sorrowfully at some aspects of it.

"These great men think they may order all as they please," the bishop said. "Earthly power is given to them for the better rule of the country, but it is not for them to say who may marry and who not, or to prefer one heir above another. Lord Delacrost should have taken his case to law, if he had cause, or should have accepted what could not be mended with good grace. To ignore you for all these years is not Christian behaviour, and so I shall tell him when next I see him. Do not scruple to marry this young lady as soon as you may, and without any restraint in intimate relations. That is what marriage is for, after all, and ours is not a celibate order. A clergyman must set the example of matrimony to his parishioners. I shall authorise the licence myself. Do you wish for an early preferment? There will be no difficulty in finding something suitable."

Mel left satisfied that he had done all he could to find himself a living in the very near future, so that when his allowance was cut off by Lord Delacrost, as it undoubtedly would be, he would not need to depend for too long on the charity of his friends. Mrs Malham and Dr Simpson would also spread the word, he knew, and perhaps from one of those connections something might emerge before too long, and then he and Margaret could settle in their own home and be happy on very little money.

Mel stayed in Hereford for one more night, having obtained his licence and a wedding ring for Margaret, and then set off early for home in optimistic mood. The next day he would go to Norton Forbury to inform Viscount Delacrost of his plans, and on Sunday Margaret would come to Dunton Cross to be married. After that, they would not be apart again. He could not be quite easy in disregarding his promise to the viscount, despite the bishop's glib words — *'Do not scruple to marry this young lady, and without any restraint in intimate relations.'* He would need to consider that carefully. Still, Margaret would be his wife and that was something! He smiled as he thought of her, that sweet face with its ready smile and those luminous eyes that had haunted his dreams from the first moment he had seen them. And now he would see them every day.

~~~~~

Margaret spent the last days of her spinster life looking through her few possessions. Her clothes, she decided, were adequate. She had no need of wedding clothes, for she would be the wife of a country curate and not going into society much. Indeed, some of her gowns were rather too fine for such a station in life. She would remove some of the trimming, she decided, and dye the paler, debutante gowns to darker colours. They would do very well.

As she went through her wardrobes and drawers, she came across her collection of letters from her sisters. She drew them out now to reread, and at once realised that she had received nothing from them for some time. The last was dated ten weeks earlier. That was puzzling. The one constant of her life had always been the stream of letters from her sisters — Rosamund's practical and Annabelle's descriptive, Lucy's many pages of trivialities, and dear, optimistic Fanny's, always so idealistic. But she had been so distracted by her own affairs that she had not even noticed the lack.

But she knew the reason. With anger in her heart, she went to find Aunt Pru.
~~~~~

"Where are my letters?" she said, when she had tracked her to earth in the linen cupboard with Rose.

"Letters, dear?"

"The letters from my sisters. They write every week, at least, sometimes oftener, and I have had none for weeks. You have kept them from me."

"Well," Aunt Pru said, looking her up and down disdainfully. "You can talk well enough when you want to."

"I can talk when I am *angry*," Margaret hissed. "I can talk when someone treats me dishonourably and deceitfully. You have no business to withhold my letters from me. They are mine, and private, and you will give them to me *now*."

"Well now, dear, it was done for the best, you know. You had not written to them and so—"

"And you should not open my private correspondence! I am a grown woman, and I will *not* have my letters kept from me. I expect them to be in my room within the hour. Rose, from now on you will place every letter addressed to me directly into my hand. If you do not, you will be turned off without a reference. *I* am mistress of Pendarreth, and you will obey my orders. Is that clear?"

"Y-yes, ma'am," Rose said, white-faced, with a deep curtsy.

And with that, Margaret turned and swept away down the corridor.

It was one hour and seven minutes later by the clock when there was a timid knock on the door. Rose crept in, a sheaf of letters in her hand.

"Beg pardon, ma'am, and *please* don't turn me off, but it took her a while to find them all."

"Thank you," Margaret said. Rose's terrified face instantly evaporated all her anger, and the words dried up in her mouth. Reaching for her slate box, she wrote, *'I do not blame you for Aunt Pru's misdeeds.'*

"Thank you, ma'am. She means well, you know."

Margaret made no answer. Means well! She wondered about that. Was such interference well-intentioned or malevolent? It was hard to say. Aunt Pru presented such a sweet, timid face to the world, and yet there was a hardness at her core, and a ruthless selfishness.

As soon as the door had closed behind Rose, she settled down to read all her letters. So much had happened! So many terrible things had gone on, but they were safe, as she was too. And despite the descriptions of deaths and daggers and attempted drownings, there were certain names that were mentioned again and again — Annabelle's pleasant earl, and Lucy's charming Mr Audley, and Fanny's besotted neighbour. Margaret was not the only one who was on the brink of matrimony, it seemed.

She laughed out loud as she reached the latest missives, full of joy and anticipation of the future. And then sighed, as she read the last line of each. *'Do write soon, Margaret. We are worried about you.' 'Are you all right, Margaret dear? Please please please let me know if you are well.' 'Dearest, I am so worried about you. Write soon, even if it is only a line or two.'*

Guilt assailed her. She *must* write to them, even if it was only a few lines. At once she pulled out paper and ink, and started to write. *'Dear Rosamund, I am well. The weather is very'*

She stopped with a sigh of frustration. How idiotic! What was the point of sending such nonsense? That was not what her sisters wanted to hear, what they *deserved* to hear. She wanted to tell them about Mel, and how his strength made her feel secure and allowed her to talk sometimes, and his gentleness made her feel both loved and lovable, and how his kisses warmed her to the very tips of her toes. She wanted to tell them that she had been asleep for all these years, but Mel's love had woken her at last and she had found that the living world was good. And as soon as the question of Pendarreth was settled, she would do that. When she was Mrs Melville Haymer, and living at the parsonage, and away from the suffocating presence of Aunt Pru and had Mel with her all the time, she would write long, detailed letters to her sisters, telling them everything that was in her heart, just as they did.

But not yet.

Scooping the unfinished letter into her hands, with quick steps she crossed to the fireplace and cast it into the flames.

~~~~~

Mel arrived back at the parsonage late on Friday night, battered from many hours of riding in the rain.

"You look quite done in," Mrs Simpson said, as he entered the welcome warmth of the library. "We did not wait dinner, in case you stayed overnight somewhere, but Carys will put up a tray for you."

"Thank you, I am famished. I have eaten little since leaving Hereford this morning. We went wrong twice, and then Robert's horse cast a shoe. A long, wet day. But I did not expect to see you here. I thought you would be still with Margaret at Pendarreth."

Mrs Simpson laughed. "She sent me away. After Luke sent his third message in a day enquiring as to the whereabouts of some trivial item, I think she felt I was more greatly needed at home. She assured me that she is perfectly comfortable there now, and after I ranted at her relations at some length they are treating her more
~~~~~

civilly, so I had no concerns in leaving her. John has been going there twice a day to enquire after her, so she can get word to us in a moment if need be. She is quite safe, Mel. Did you get the licence?"

"I did."

"Then you can be married tomorrow, perhaps, if we can get Margaret here. Excellent."

He shook his head. "No, I must see Lord Delacrost first."

"Do you have to?" she said. "Why not tell him afterwards?"

Mel huffed a breath. Was that possible? Or was it just postponing the inevitable confrontation? Because Lord Delacrost was not going to like it one bit, there was no denying it.

"I feel I owe it to him," he said slowly, although he was not entirely convinced of the debt himself. Lord Delacrost had certainly financed him, but Mel had surrendered any right to the estate in exchange. Still, he was officially his father. "He is entitled to the courtesy of being informed of my plans. It will also give him time to explain it to his sons, so that they will be prepared when it becomes public knowledge. There is also the possibility — albeit a remote one, I concede — that he will use his influence to remove the guests from Pendarreth and allow Margaret peaceful occupation, so that we do not have to marry."

"Not have to marry! My dear Mel, what can you mean? This is exactly what you want."

"What I *want* is to be free of Lord Delacrost altogether," he hissed, "so that I may marry Margaret in the proper way, as God intended men to marry, and not this half-hearted version of it where we smile to the world and only *pretend* to be husband and wife." Mrs Simpson's surprised face shamed him, and he rubbed his face tiredly. "I beg your pardon, that was insufferably rude of me."

"Nonsense. You are exhausted, and when you have eaten and enjoyed some rest you will feel much more yourself. And some time when you have a spare hour or two, you must get Luke to tell you all about the many ways in which a man and wife may have a proper marriage, and yet contrive not to have children, for I assure you our marriage is not at all half-hearted, not in any aspect of it. Ah, here is John with your supper."

It was not until Mel had eaten a little and drunk some wine that Mrs Simpson said, "I should perhaps mention that Lord Delacrost is not at Norton Forbury at the moment."

Mel said down his glass with a sigh. "Not there? He has not gone off to London for months has he?"

"Oh, no, nothing like that. He has gone to his sister's in Worcestershire for a ball of unusual magnificence, according to reports. He will be home again on Monday."

Mel set down his glass with a sigh. "Another delay. Poor Margaret! Every day she remains unwed is a day when she is vulnerable to her cousins. I cannot bear her to be so importuned."

"Then marry her tomorrow, and never mind about Lord Delacrost," Mrs Simpson said.

"No," Mel said slowly. "Let us keep to the original plan. She will come here on Sunday just as usual, which will attract no attention, and then—" He huffed a breath. "Then I shall let Margaret decide. She will know what to do for the best."

"Yes, dear," Mrs Simpson said, with a smile. "A lady always knows best."

Her husband raised an eyebrow, but only smiled fondly at her.

24: A Ride To Norton Forbury

Sunday began in the manner of every Sunday for years — with a brisk walk to the church to ensure all was in readiness for the day, then back to the parsonage to read through his sermon one last time. Then Matins, with the delight of Margaret's dear face in the parsonage pew, a little shy, not quite catching his eye, but the gentle smile that hung about her lips told of her anticipation in the day.

Then back to the parsonage, and here the usual routine fell to pieces, for instead of breakfast, they sat in the library while Mel explained the difficulty to Margaret.

"Dearest, I have the licence and the ring, just as we planned, but I will not be able to talk to Lord Delacrost until tomorrow. If we marry today and I take you back to Pendarreth as my wife, he will hear that his legal heir has married after the event, and perhaps the news will reach him even before I do. Yet I cannot bear to send you away unwed."

She pulled off her gloves, and slipped her hand into his. "Then let us marry today, but I will go back to Pendarreth as usual, saying nothing. Tomorrow you will go to Norton Forbury, and then you will come to me at Pendarreth and send everyone away, and I shall have some peace."

"Marry today but not tell anyone?" he said dubiously.

"I do not want to wait any longer," she said firmly. "Nor do I want you to tell everyone at Pendarreth that we are married and then leave me alone with them. Let us marry today, tomorrow you go to Lord Delacrost and by tomorrow evening we shall be together and you will not leave me ever again."

"Margaret, will you be all right at Pendarreth tonight?" Mrs Simpson said. "To marry and then pretend that this is just a normal Sunday... and if those people harass you..."

"Then I shall go to my room and put a chair against the handle," she said firmly. "I shall do perfectly well. It is only for one more day, and then Mel will be there to protect me. Nothing terrible can happen in one day."

In the face of her certainty, Mel yielded. Mrs Simpson had always said he was too easy-going, but sometimes it was better to put aside his own doubts and bow to the judgement of others. Margaret may seem like a shy, timid creature, like a deer in the forest, but there was strong woman inside who knew her own mind. If ever she truly found her voice and learnt to speak authoritatively, she would be formidable indeed. Until then, Mel would be her voice and her loving servant.

They waited then for Dr Simpson to drive back from Heston Ford. Normally, he stayed there for the day, taking his breakfast or an early dinner with whichever of his parishioners invited him, and hearing all the news of the town, returning only in time for dinner. Today, he was needed at home, for he had another service to perform.

There in the church of Dunton Cross, Melville Matthew Haymer took Margaret Anne Winterton as his lawful wife, with Dr Simpson to officiate, John and Robert as witnesses, and Mrs Simpson and the rest of the household to weep with happiness over the blushing bride. The marriage was recorded in the parish register, and Dr Simpson handed Margaret her marriage lines with a bow.

"The paper is too large to fit into my reticule without folding," she said. "Mel, will you keep this for me? You have deep pockets."

He nodded and tucked the paper away. "It will be safe in there."

After which, Mr and Mrs Haymer and Dr and Mrs Simpson sat down for breakfast to celebrate the nuptials.

Dr Simpson soon rose to take his leave. "Forgive me, Mrs Haymer," he said, making Margaret blush, "but I must return to Heston Ford for the Eucharist. Are you quite sure you will return to Pendarreth tonight?"

"Now, Luke, it is all agreed," his wife said. "Margaret is to keep to her usual schedule until Mel has seen Lord Delacrost. When he returns, he will go to Pendarreth to claim his bride, and make the marriage public. It is best this way. You would not wish Margaret to make the announcement alone, after all."

"No, but—"

"And if Margaret stays here, everyone will be in a spin, thinking she has disappeared again."

"Yes, but—"

"Mel will be back as soon as he has seen the viscount."

"I know but—"

"Well, then, there is nothing more to be said."

Dr Simpson looked as if there were a great deal more that might be said, if he were so minded, but he chose not to and soon went away to Heston Ford.

After the Eucharist, Mel walked Margaret back to Pendarreth. They walked slowly, hand in hand, saying nothing, although occasionally Margaret would give a little shiver of excitement and pull him into her arms for a kiss. He was not at all disinclined to oblige her, so the journey took them some time, and it was already growing dark under the trees when they reached the perimeter wall, their usual parting point.

"Will you be all right?" he said, holding her upturned face in both hands. She nodded. "I shall be at Norton Forbury by noon tomorrow, but then I shall have to wait for Lord Delacrost to return. It might be late in the day, perhaps evening, before I can get away, so do not despair. I shall come for you, my dearest, I promise." She nodded again. "Then we shall be together always, and I shall take the greatest care of you."

Again her whole body quivered against his. Her huge eyes shone, fixed so trustingly on his. "And I shall take care of you," she said, smiling up at him, her hands resting on his chest. "Oh, but I cannot wear my wedding ring, or everyone will know. Will you keep it for me? Until tomorrow? After that, I shall never remove it."

"You could keep it in your reticule," he said gently.

"I should like you to hold it for me, as you hold my heart also," she said, gazing up at him with shining eyes.

He slipped it into a waistcoat pocket, then pulled her more tightly into his arms for one last, lingering kiss. Smiling, she turned away and began to walk along the track that edged the wall. He watched until she was out of sight, then, with a sigh, started for home.

It was almost dark when he reached the parsonage, the windows welcomingly aglow. Less welcome, to his mind, was Mrs Malham's carriage at the front door, the horses being walked up and down.

"What does she want on a Sunday evening?" Mel whispered to John, as he handed over his hat and gloves.

"Couldn't say, sir. They are in the library."

They were sitting around one of the fireplaces sipping Madeira, Dr and Mrs Simpson with rueful smiles, and Mrs Malham with a knowing expression on her face.

"Well, well, here comes the happy bridegroom now! May I be the first to wish you joy, Mr Haymer."

"Ah. There are no secrets in this village," he murmured as he made his bow.

She laughed merrily. "None at all, not when my chamber maid is sister to your kitchen maid, and your gardener is son to my head gardener. But you need not worry — everyone in Dunton Cross understands your need for secrecy."

"Indeed?" he said, bemused.

"Naturally you want to keep things quiet, when your father is so keen for Miss Winterton — Mrs Haymer, I should say — to marry one of those boys staying at Pendarreth. He does not want you to marry at all, I dare say, for that way it will all go to Mortimer, in time, and a less worthy recipient is hard to imagine. He was an unpleasant child and he is an unpleasant man, worse than Lord Delacrost for intemperance and wanting his own way, if you ask me. Which you did not," she said, laughing ruefully. "I beg your pardon, my tongue runs on so. I should not disparage your father."

"He is not my father," Mel said quietly.

Mrs Malham paused, the glass of Madeira suspended half way to her lips. "Oh?"

"Mel, is this wise?" Dr Simpson said, his expression alarmed.

"Wise? I cannot say, but let us have no more secrecy. The more people hear of this, the greater the chance of finding someone who knows what happened nine and twenty years ago. Mrs Malham was here then, and there may be others. *Someone* must know who my mother was. If the mystery of my birth can be resolved, then Lord Delacrost and I may both be free of this unwanted entanglement, and I can live my life as I wish to, walking in the sunshine with my wife and not perpetually hiding in the shadows. So let me tell the truth at last, and let the dice fall how they may."

So he talked, and Mrs Malham listened, nodding from time to time. At the end of it, she set down her empty glass, and said, "Matthew — Lord Delacrost — searched for your mother, you say?"

"Yes. This was two years after the event, but recent enough that people should have remembered the birth of a male child who later vanished. No one knew anything. Or perhaps if they did, they chose not to tell him of it."

"But *someone* would have spoken. Someone would have said, *'Oh yes, Maisie the dairymaid had a baby that year, but it disappeared, and no one spoke of it.'* Especially if there were silver to be earned by it. But then I dare say he only asked around the cottages and farms, and in those places an unexpected baby would not ruffle the waters unduly. There would be no need for secrecy, or a desire to give the baby up. No, a secret baby that no one ever speaks of — for that you should look at the gentry."

"Good grief — truly? But where? There are few such families within reach of Norton Forbury."

"Have you thought of Pendarreth?" Mrs Malham said thoughtfully. "That is where I should look."

"Pendarreth? But then—?"

"Yes. Prudence Tilford. She would have been... let me see, five and thirty or a little more, and there were rumours that she had had a liaison years before. With Matthew — Lord Delacrost — in fact. She was very keen on him at one time, for all she dislikes him so much now. She was a lively woman in her youth, you know, and not at all as averse to the male sex as she is now. But around that time she changed, becoming very reclusive. She threw out all the male servants and stopped going into society. Yes, now that I consider the matter, it seems very likely to me that your mother is Prudence Tilford."

~~~~~

In all the nine and twenty years of his existence, Mel had never yet visited Norton Forbury Manor House, home for many generations to the Haymer family. He had lived there for a month or two as a baby, and had many times viewed it from a distance, its imposing solidity a proud testament to the exalted rank of its owner. Since infancy, however, he had never crossed the threshold. Yet today he must. Today, he would call upon the man recognised in law as his father, and dutifully tell him of his marriage. He must hope to weather the storm of the viscount's displeasure with all his limbs intact.

He could have taken the road from Dunton Cross, a distance of some eight miles, or a shorter way across Malham's farm, fording the river and then up through the pasture beyond. He chose, instead, to ride up through the woods to Pendarreth and then take
~~~~~

the track up to Dunton Heights. There was no reason he could formulate for this decision, except that it would bring him a little closer to Margaret. He doubted he would catch a glimpse of her, not at this time of day. She liked to walk before breakfast, or else late in the afternoon when everyone else was gathering in the house awaiting the dressing gong. His thoughts brought her vividly to his mind, her skirts swirling as she walked, her great eyes alight with enthusiasm for some passing interest — a thrush singing, the unfurling petals of a flower, a colourful toadstool. He smiled at the memories. Everything set her eyes alight. She was so full of life, his Margaret, and although her vivacity was hidden from the rest of the world, it had been revealed to him. With him, she could be her true self, and dance in the moonlight, if the mood should take her. How he longed to see her dance in the moonlight.

The woods were damp and dripping, but the storm had spent itself and the sun was trying to break through the clouds. Mel rode slowly along the track outside the perimeter wall of Pendarreth, pretending he was not watching for a glimpse of a certain bonnet and trying not to be disappointed when he caught no sign of it, before turning up the well-churned track to Norton Forbury. The way drove straight up the hill through the woods, not deviating despite the steepness. To either side was jungle, densely overgrown with brambles and saplings and waist-high ferns, with deep gloom under the trees beyond. Here and there a deer track threaded through the wilderness, but the riding track was wide and clear and his horse walked on, ears flicking. Behind him, his groom Robert silently followed, knowing him well enough to understand when conversation was not wanted.

Near the top of the rise Mel stopped, gazing off to the left. Somewhere in that morass of greenery was a high hedge hiding a secret grave. Someone had walked from Norton Forbury all those years ago carrying a dead baby in his arms, and had dug a grave in the frigid February earth to bury the child. Someone still came, perhaps once a week, bearing a posy of flowers — fresh and sweet-smelling in summer, or dried to paper-thin delicacy in winter. Someone still remembered. Someone knew the truth. Once everything was settled and Margaret was safe, he would try to find that someone, the person who could set him free.

Urging his horse into motion again, he crested the summit of Dunton Heights, where the trees gave way to tussocky heather and bracken and scrawny wind-blown saplings, and a few stands of overgrown coverts. The track ran straight across to where the land dropped away, and here Mel halted again.

"Big, ain't it?" Robert murmured.

There below them in a vast bowl of green lawns and parkland lay the Manor House, its golden stone dull on this grey day. Where Pendarreth hid its charms in a cloak of greenery, Norton Forbury Manor House laid out its wares as if on a platter, clearly visible from miles around. On a summer evening, when the setting sun added a magical glow and set the hundreds of mullioned windows afire, it looked like a fairy-tale castle, all towers and high chimneys and grand symmetry. Today, without the sun's enhancement, it was merely imposing. To the sides were extensive stables and outhouses, and amidst the formal gardens sat a pavilion styled like a Greek temple, an ornamental fountain and a slender tower half-hidden by an overgrown shrubbery. If he had grown up here, Mel would have walked the gravel paths, played in the temple and climbed the tower to admire the view. Instead, he viewed it only as an outsider, and today an unwelcome visitor.

Robert said nothing more, but Mel knew he would be wondering what business took him to the Manor House. Now that he saw the house in all its majesty, he wondered himself at his temerity. He could write a letter just as easily, after all. Surely that would be a better way, less of a direct affront to his lordship?

No, he had to tell him face to face, one gentleman to another.

But first, he had to wait until the viscount returned home. Finding a sheltered spot between low bushes, Mel left Robert to watch the horses and cast himself down in the heather. For a while his mind was on Margaret, as he wondered what she was doing and whether she was being left in peace by her cousins. Was she thinking of him at the exact moment that he was thinking of her? Dear Margaret!

But then his thoughts drifted to Mrs Malham's astonishing suggestion. Was it possible that Mel was Miss Tilford's son? Was it she who had walked along the track from Norton Forbury carrying Lady Delacrost's dead baby, and buried him deep in the woods? Was she the one who, even now, left flowers on the grave? It made a queer kind of sense, for the woods were very much her domain, and she protected them fiercely.

She had always treated him kindly, too. One might almost say that she was fond of him. He recalled now the way she always giggled girlishly at his feeble jokes, and seemed pleased to see him, alone of all the men who visited Pendarreth. Indeed, she did her best to deny entry to any men, but not Mel. For him the door had always stood open, as it would for a mother's son.

If it were so, could she be persuaded to swear it before a magistrate, or sign an affidavit, or whatever needed to be done? It would be the most awkward conversation imaginable, to ask her such a thing. But if she would do it, if she could be made to see the benefit to everyone, just think how glorious it would be! He would be free at last.

"Carriages, sir," Robert called.

A procession of four vehicles was making its way slowly along the long drive, seeming to crawl like beetles from Mel's vantage point. The viscount was home again. Mel waited another hour to allow him time to shake the dust of travel from his boots, then he and Robert mounted their horses. Riding down the hill and across the park to the carriage drive, he arrived at the massive front doors of the Manor House, towering above any hapless visitor who was not already sufficiently impressed with the power of the Haymer family.

His family, according to the law, he reminded himself, as he handed the reins of his horse to Robert, and made his way without haste up the numerous steps. He did not have to ring the bell, for two bewigged footmen tugged the doors open at his approach, so that he strode unimpeded through the entrance. The hall was a vast circular space, the floors and walls of pale green marble, the glass roof supported by matching pillars, so that Mel felt queasily as if he were under water. Around the walls, white marble busts of men with stern faces gazed disapprovingly at him.

Another footman waited with a silver salver to receive his card.

"Mr Melville Haymer of Dunton Cross Parsonage to see Lord Delacrost," he said.

A stout butler materialised from behind a pillar. "Is your call social, sir, or a matter of business?"

"Business," he said, relieved that he had anticipated the question, and need not dither over the issue of whether a family matter of some delicacy qualified as a social call. He had decided not to risk being shown into the drawing room, where the ladies might be found.

The butler disappeared in one direction with the salver bearing his card, and the footman bowed low and pointed in another. "This way, sir, if you please."

He led Mel to a small anteroom just off the hall, cold and empty, with the fusty air of a place seldom used. And here, with a bow, he left him, the door shutting with a soft snick.

The anteroom was not as large or imposing as the entrance hall, but it was designed to impress, all the same. Here would be left the lower levels of society with whom the viscount occasionally did business — his land agents, his vintner, the better sort of farmer who might have some coverts for him to use, or a neighbour with a horse to sell. And the impudent curate who happened to be his heir.

Mel looked around at the paintings on the walls of bewigged ancestors in their ornate gilt frames, the cabinets of guns and swords and fragments of battle standards, and all the rich trappings of a family long established in the power of the kingdom. In glass-topped tables lay collections of exquisitely decorated snuff boxes and opera glasses. On a side table sat a silver tray with decanters of Madeira and Canary, glasses standing ready alongside covered dishes of some sugary confection or other. A bookcase held nothing but sermons. He pulled one out at random and sat down to read, for he had no expectation that Lord Delacrost would see him soon, even supposing he deigned to receive him at all. No, he would keep him waiting as long as possible, to punish him for his unmitigated presumption in daring to present himself at the family home.

But the viscount was not a patient man. Before the long case clock had struck the quarter hour, the door burst open and there was Lord Delacrost's glowering visage.

"*You!* What the devil are *you* doing here?"

"Good morning, my lord," Mel said, executing his most polished bow and trying not to bump the furniture. "I apologise for disturbing you, but there is a matter upon which I must speak to you."

"I have nothing to say to you, nothing at all," the viscount growled.

"But I have something to say to you. In private," he added, with a glance at the footman loitering beside the door.

For an instant, outrage warred with discretion, but fortunately for Mel's peace of mind, discretion won. The footman was dismissed with a curt nod and the door closed. In slightly more temperate tones, the viscount said, "Very well. Say what you have to say, damn you."

Mel licked his lips and took a deep breath. No need to be nervous about it, surely. "I have come to inform you that I have entered into marriage with—"

The viscount exploded. There was no other word that adequately described the sudden profuse reddening of the complexion, the lowered brows, the tirade of abuse that spewed forth from his mouth at such volume that Mel wondered if the tiles on the roof rattled. He waited calmly for the deluge to subside a little.

"I assure you that—" he began, but it was useless. He had never heard quite so much invective from one person, and one, moreover, from whom greater control might have been expected.

The viscount threw open the door. "Out!" he yelled, heedless of the footmen waiting in the entrance hall. "Get out of my sight, you deceitful worm, and never let me clap eyes on you again."

"As you wish, my lord," Mel said resignedly. "But be assured that—"

"Get out! I always knew you would betray me in the end. I never should have trusted you."

That was too much for Mel to stomach. "You never did," he said, coldly. "Maybe you should have tried it."

"How dare you!" The viscount's voice rose to a pitch that would have brought on a seizure in a lesser man. He came at Mel at a run, his fists raised as if to strike him.

Mel said nothing, and made no move to respond, except to draw himself up to his full height. The viscount was tall, but Mel was half a head taller, and imposing enough for Lord Delacrost to reconsider his aggression.

"Get out, you scum! I shall not forget your perfidy, you may be sure."

"When you consider my perfidy," Mel said quietly, "you might remember that you brought all of this upon yourself. If you had not interfered at Pendarreth, none of this would be necessary." Conscious of the footmen standing just feet away, he added, "Be assured, however, that this does not *materially* change our previous agreement. Good day, my lord."

25: The Old Library

It was the best he could do, and he could only hope that, once he had calmed down, Lord Delacrost would remember his words and understand their meaning. He collected his hat, gloves and riding crop from the wooden-faced footman who held them out to him, and swept out of the door, Lord Delacrost's abuse following him as he marched down the steps.

There he stopped, for Robert and the horses had disappeared, presumably gone off to the stables, and no orders had been given to bring them round again. He stood irresolute, cursing himself for not anticipating this situation and telling Robert to remain on the drive. Now he had to decide whether it was worse to go back into the house to send a footman to the stables, or try to find them himself. He had no idea where the stable block might be.

"Mr Haymer!"

He turned, expecting to see a footman chasing after him, but could see nothing. The great doors were slowly closing, cutting off the still voluble complaints of the viscount. The doors clunked shut and silence fell.

"Mr Haymer! Over here."

A few yards to the left of the entrance steps, a face peered round a bush. Mr Edward Haymer. He grinned at the surprised expression on Mel's face.

"Do come in! I daresay Father neglected to offer you any refreshment. Will you not have a glass of Madeira with me? Or brandy? I daresay you need something of the sort."

His face was so full of mischief that Mel laughed, and walked towards him. "I take it you heard all that?"

"I should imagine the entire village heard most of it, and will hear the whole just as soon as the footmen can get to The Cock Pheasant," Edward said. "Will you come in and talk to me? We are brothers, after all."

"Are we?" Mel said, too despondent to mind his words. "I should have liked to grow up with a brother."

Edward laughed. "It is not so wonderful as you might imagine. This way."

When he drew nearer to the bush, Mel saw that it concealed a small side door, useful no doubt for those returning home late at night or when the house was closed up for a season. Or for smuggling a baby in or out unseen, he realised. He followed Edward through the door, and along a short corridor to the entrance hall, now returned to silence, and past the immobile footmen. From there, they passed through a series of stately saloons, each grander than the one before, and thence to an older part of the house, all dark wood panelling and gloomy paintings on the walls. Eventually, Edward threw open a heavy oak door and ushered Mel through.

"A book room," Mel said, pleased, as he gazed around at the bookcases lining the walls, and the solid leather chairs placed around the fire and in little groups around tables.

"It is known as the old library," Edward said. "There is a new library, much grander than this, with books purchased by the yard to fill the endless shelves, but this is *my* library. Now, what will you have — Madeira? Canary? Brandy? Or shall I send for tea?"

"Brandy," Mel said with decision. "A large one. It has been a brandyish sort of morning."

Edward laughed, and poured two glasses. "There. Drink that, and celebrate your victory."

"Victory? I did not say half of all that I came to say. I would call it an abject failure."

"Not so," Edward said. "You stood up to him and did not back down or lose your temper. Few men have such courage."

"I wonder whether I should try again," Mel said. "If only I could make him understand—"

Edward shook his head. "He never listens when he gets like this. It is a waste of time even to try to talk to him. Talk to me instead! I will listen and try to understand, and tell Father of it when he is calmer."

Mel was silent, staring into the amber liquid in his glass. If only he could! This pleasant young man was so different from his father, the one calm and rational, the other erratic and ill-tempered.

Seeing his hesitation, Edward waved him to a seat and went on, "Mr Haymer, after our last conversation, I went to see Pruett, our lawyer in Ludlow, to enquire about you. He was very reticent, but your name is in Debrett's, after all, and therefore your existence cannot be denied. He would not answer my questions directly, but he hinted that there was some doubt as to your true parentage, that you are the heir in law but may not be Father's son. That is nonsense, of course—"

"Whatever makes you say that?" Mel burst out. "Such things happen, even in the best regulated families."

"Look behind you," Edward said, with a grin.

Mel turned, and there on the wall was a portrait of a man in powder and lace, wearing an embroidered golden coat. "Oh," he said, bemused. "It *does* look like me. Your grandfather?"

"And yours, surely. You are a Haymer to the marrow."

With a laugh, Mel said, "There are many, many Haymer descendants in the district. It is not surprising if a striking likeness appears in a cottage-born brat." He hesitated to say more, but what did it matter now? In time, everyone would know the truth, and Edward and his brother, of all people, were fully entitled to know it. He had defied Lord Delacrost already, and was not minded to retreat again into secrecy and prevarication. So he added slowly, "Do you imagine that if I were truly your father's blood, he would exile me so thoroughly as to pretend that I do not exist? I am no son of his and no brother of yours, and only one of those is a matter of regret to me."

Edward regarded him gravely. "Then who are you?"

"No one knows. Your father's first wife gave birth to a son who died within days. To avoid disappointing her husband, she had a replacement smuggled in. Had she not confessed on her deathbed, no one would have been any the wiser, and I would have been raised here as the acknowledged heir, and I should have had the pleasure of knowing you all my life."

"That... makes sense," Edward said, his eyes unfocused as he considered. "Yet he raised you as a gentleman. He has not cast you off."

"He would have done, had he been able to prove the matter. As things stand, I am still his legal heir and will inherit the title.

When I came of age, I helped him to break the entail on the estate, so that at least will go to your brother, as it should, and I promised that I would never marry, so that the title will eventually revert to Mortimer's line. But now… I *have* married, it was entirely necessary, and that is what I came here to tell him."

Edward was quick of mind, and grasped the essentials of the situation. He asked an occasional question, but mostly he listened as Mel explained it all, the words, so long suppressed, tumbling out of him. There was something about Edward, his serious demeanour which broke now and then into a mischievous grin, which Mel liked very much. He spoke no less than the truth when he said that he regretted not knowing him as a brother.

"This marriage," Edward said, as he replenished their brandy glasses. "Your undertaking is not entirely a matter of duty, I think."

Mel smiled, as he always did when he thought of Margaret. "Not in the least, but I should not have contemplated such a step if your father had not put Miss Winterton in such an intolerable situation. To persuade Mrs Bradwell to leave Pendarreth in that irregular way—"

"Indeed, it is unconscionable," Edward said at once. "But Father is used to having his own way, and will allow no one to gainsay him. Poor Miss Winterton! No, I believe you are correct in thinking that only marriage would resolve the situation."

Mel sighed. "Indeed it is so, but I shall still keep to the spirit of my agreement with your father. When he is a little calmer, will you be so good as to tell him that the marriage will be platonic? Tell Mortimer, if you please, that he has nothing to fear from me, and that the title will still pass to him, or to his son, in time."

"But that is all nonsense!" Edward cried. "How can any man be held to such inhumane restrictions? To agree not to marry, not to sire sons — no one should be required to give such an undertaking. You should have the same right as any man, whether he be a prince or a pauper, to marry where he pleases and father as many sons as he can."

Mel could only smile and shake his head. "It is given to few of us to marry where we please. Neither the prince nor the pauper have that choice. I am a lucky man, for my profession enables me to support a wife, and I shall have the woman of my heart always at my side. Even without sons, I shall have no cause to repine."

It was, perhaps, the first time he had expressed his feelings about his proposed marriage so openly. Even without Lord Delacrost's allowance, he had an income, which would increase with time. His needs were modest, and he knew Margaret to be a practical woman, not given to extravagance. And if they had no children, their income would not be stretched a little thinner each year. A modest living, or perhaps two, would see them very comfortably situated. And, most glorious of all, they would be together always, the best of friends, growing old in joyful harmony.

As he rode home after this conversation, Mel was, for the first time, entirely content with his decision. Later that day, he would go to Pendarreth for Margaret and after that, they would not be apart again. First, however, he must go to the parsonage to collect a few things, and to write some letters. It was necessary to inform the executors of Mrs Bradwell's will of the marriage, but how they would respond to that information was anyone's guess. He must also write to Lord Delacrost to explain all the things he had not been allowed to say to his face. He would tell him of his hopes of an early living which would take him, it seemed likely, out of the neighbourhood altogether. He would reiterate his promise to bring no sons into the world to supplant Mortimer, and express his gratitude for Lord Delacrost's generosity over the years.

Nevertheless, he must assert in the firmest manner that he could have done nothing else but rescue Margaret from a situation intolerable to her. He could only hope that the viscount would not harass Margaret.

Sweet Margaret — his bride! His heart jumped in delight at the thought of it. His lovely Margaret... his wife. He was almost unbearably happy, urging his horse to a faster pace, the sooner to be with her.

As soon as he passed the gates of the parsonage, the front door flew open and Mrs Simpson raced down the drive.

"Mel! Oh, Mel! Something dreadful has happened!"

Instantly, his blood froze. "Margaret?" he croaked, barely able to form the word, as he slid from his horse.

"She is gone!"

"Gone?" he repeated, stupidly, his heart pounding, shaking his head as if to clear the fog of befuddlement that choked it. "What do you mean, gone?"

"She has vanished again, and is nowhere to be found."

His heart slowed a little. Vanished again — yes, she would do that if she were terrified. "What has happened? Who has upset her?"

"No, you do not understand. No one has upset her, for no one saw her. When she left here yesterday, she did not arrive at Pendarreth at all. She disappeared somewhere along the way."

He almost laughed at that, for it was ridiculous. "Impossible," he said. "I walked with her all the way to the perimeter wall, and she was perfectly safe and well at that point. She was no more than... oh, two or three hundred yards from the house. She cannot possibly have vanished in that short distance."

"But she has."

Mel stood irresolute, not quite believing it. How was it possible? Nothing untoward had happened on the walk to Pendarreth, they had seen and heard no one, although perhaps they had been more than usually absorbed in each other. Had something happened to her? Or had she changed her mind about returning to Pendarreth, and gone to the tree house instead? Not directly, that much was certain. When she had run away to the tree house before, she had taken spare clothes with her, and food. Yesterday she had carried nothing but her slate box and her psalter, and perhaps a spare handkerchief. She would have had to return to the house first, yet no one had seen her do so.

Still, it was worth a try. "I shall go and look for her," he said.

"No, no, no, do nothing precipitate," she said. "You have been out for hours. We already have someone out looking for her. Come inside, do."

By this time, Dr Simpson had emerged to add his voice to his wife's, and so Mel allowed himself to be drawn into the house. He washed and changed, and the time this afforded for reflection brought him to more sanguine thoughts. Perhaps, after all, she had changed her mind about returning to Pendarreth. Even in such a short distance, between the time they had parted and the time she reached the edge of the lawn and could be seen from the house, she might have thought better of it. Or perhaps she had encountered someone. If so, she would certainly have gone to the tree house to hide. She could easily have crept back to the house at night to get food. Yes, that must be it. She would be at the tree house, as before.

As he emerged from his room, he heard the knocker sounding, and then voices in the hall. Descending, he saw Dr and Mrs Simpson in anxious conversation with a man he had never seen before, a man who would attract attention even in London. He was dressed in the first style of fashion, not ostentatiously but with no expense spared, and had the sort of pleasing features and manners that, he imagined, would make him popular with ladies.

"Ah, Mel, there you are," Mrs Simpson said. "Come and meet the gentleman who is helping to search for Margaret. Mr Audley, may I make you known to our foster son, Mr Melville Haymer. Mel, this is Mr Audley of Stoneleigh Hall in Shropshire, and of Bath."

The two made their bows.

"Delighted to meet you at last, Haymer," Mr Audley said.

"How do you do, sir," Mel said. Then, puzzled, he added, "Audley?" The name was familiar, but he could not say why.

"I am a friend of Mrs Price's," Mr Audley said, smiling, his eyes gleaming with amusement. He had the most extraordinary eyes, golden, like a cat.

"Mrs Price?" Mel said, befuddled.

Mrs Simpson laughed. "Mrs Price is Margaret's sister, Lucy."

"Oh, *Lucy*. The one who became a chaperon to two young ladies. Mr Audley. Of course. My wife has mentioned you. Let me see... you are brother to the mother of the young ladies."

"Step-mother," Mr Audley said. "Mrs Kingsley of Longmere Priory is my sister, yes. I do beg your pardon, Mr Haymer. I can see why you might be confused when I appear out of nowhere, and especially when you are in the midst of a crisis. Dr and Mrs Simpson were of the opinion that I might be of some small service to you, but if you are wishing me at Jericho, you have only to say the word and I shall disappear at once. I should like to help, however."

"You are very kind," Mel said, his head spinning as he tried to take it all in. "But… whatever are you doing here?"

"Lucy — Mrs Price, I mean — was concerned that she had heard nothing from her sister. She was afraid that she might be ill, or unhappy, or something of the sort. By coming here to see the lady for myself, I had hoped to give her reassuring news. But now I find that she has disappeared."

"Come into the library, and we can discuss this in comfort, instead of standing about in the hall," Mrs Simpson said.

But Mel could not wait even that short time for more news, and continued to question Mr Audley even as they walked into the library. "But when did you arrive, sir? And what has been done to discover my wife?"

"I reached Ludlow on Saturday evening," Mr Audley said. "I stayed at an inn overnight and for Sunday, then made my way to Pendarreth this morning, expecting to see Miss Winterton — Mrs Haymer, I should say — and be on my way again within the hour. It was not my intent to disturb her, or inflict myself on the household, you understand, only to satisfy myself that she was well. I found, instead, that she was not there at all, and the occupants of the house very cross about it."

"Cross?" Mel said, astonished. "They were angry because she had disappeared?"

"I was given to understand that she had done something similar before. The ladies I spoke to described it as *'setting everyone by the ears, and for no good reason'*. Mrs Herbert and Mrs Fordham? Do I have that right? Yes, they were very cross indeed, but they directed me here, where I learnt that Mrs Haymer's disappearance is unexpected, and worrying. With John's help, therefore, I returned to Pendarreth by the shortcut and talked to the servants, and found them in the utmost distress, convinced that something untoward had occurred. Mrs Haymer had not returned from church on Sunday, and neither clothes nor any food had been taken."

"Nothing since then?" Mel said sharply. "She knows a secret way into the kitchens, so she might have—"

"No. The servants had expected that, and checked for anything missing. There was nothing. And she has no cloak or anything warm, beyond her pelisse, and the nights are chilly now for anyone sleeping in the woods. They have had no orders about the matter, but they themselves undertook to search every part of the house and the outbuildings, and found nothing. I have been checking the paths around the house that she might have taken for any sign of her."

Mel's heart froze as he listed everything that had been done, without success. "And did you find anything?"

He shook his head. "Not the least indication. It is as if Mrs Haymer has vanished into the air."

For the first time, Mel was assailed with fear.

26: Missing

"Now, Mel, you must not despair," Mrs Simpson said. "Undoubtedly Margaret is simply hiding somewhere safe, too timid to face that dreadful crowd at Pendarreth. She will be found very soon, you may depend upon it."

"This is not one of your novels," Dr Simpson said tersely. "Everything does *not* always come right in the third volume in real life."

She flushed at the rebuke, but said composedly, "I do not mean to make light of it, I assure you, but let us not fear the worst until all other avenues have been explored. Mel found Margaret before, so perhaps he can find her again."

"The tree house," he muttered. "I shall go at once. That is where she will be, if anywhere."

"May I come with you?" Mr Audley said. "And if perchance she is not there, you may show me exactly where you left her on Sunday and we can work from there."

As they walked, Mel considered the matter again and convinced himself that Margaret must indeed be at the tree house. Where else could she be hidden? When they reached the clearing, he eagerly climbed the ladder, up and up, calling as he went. Surely she must be here? Surely she must... but she was not. The little room at the top of the tree was empty, with no sign that anyone had been there for some time.

He ran one hand tiredly over his face. "I was certain she would be here."

Mr Audley patted his shoulder. "I am so sorry. It is hard to imagine your distress just now. But we still have avenues unexplored. Show me where you parted, and we will follow the exact route your wife would have taken. There may be some sign of—"

"She should have stayed at the parsonage!" Mel burst out. "At least she would have been safe. But she did not want the Pendarreth ladies to be alarmed, or ask awkward questions. Ha! It seems she need not have worried about that. But this is my fault. If I had not gone to the Manor—"

"It is *not* your fault," Mr Audley said firmly. "Whatever has befallen Mrs Haymer, whether through her own choice or accident or... or... well, it is not *your* fault. To repeat Mrs Simpson's words, do not give way to despair."

"But she could be lying dead somewhere even now!"

"Then we will find her soon enough, but until that dreadful end is upon us, I for one shall never give up hope of finding her safe and well. Courage, Haymer! The sooner we begin a proper search the better, for if she has fallen and twisted her ankle, say—"

"Yes, yes! That could be it!"

In better spirits, Mel led the way to the exact spot where he had taken his last kiss of Margaret and watched her walk away from him.

"Ah," Audley said. "I have already examined the ground around this spot, and all the paths close to this wall. We shall have to look further afield. Which direction seems to you to be the most likely?"

While they were debating the question, voices could be heard, and two of the maids appeared, along with two of the visiting grooms.

"Oh, Mr Haymer, sir! Now everything will be all right!" Lily exclaimed. "You'll find her, sir, won't you?"

"I hope so, Lily. I certainly hope so."

"We was just checking down the path to Barnston Hope, in case—"

"Did you find anything?" he asked eagerly.

"No, sir, nothing, but we didn't dare go off the track, sir. Too easy to get lost in those woods! Do you think Miss Margaret may have got lost, sir?"

"No, she knows these woods as well as anyone."

"Not as well as Miss Tilford, I'll wager!" the girl said. "Always out in those woods, she is. Hates anyone else going through them. Sorry, sir, I have to get back to work now, but maybe tomorrow I'll get an hour off. We'll keep looking, you may be sure."

"No, you have your work to do," Mel said. "Thank you for all you have done, but it is for others to continue the search."

"But they don't, sir!" she burst out. "The upstairs folk, they just think Miss Margaret's run away, like before. But she *hasn't*, sir! She's took nothing, not clothing nor any food. There's something wrong, we're all sure of that. Us below stairs, that is."

Audley's calm voice cut in. "Is anyone else missing from the house?"

That was a good question! It was possible Margaret had left with some other of the Pendarreth guests. But no, for she had not even reached the house on Sunday night. It was impossible. Mel's spirits, lifted for an instant, again plummeted.

"Are any of the servants gone?" Audley persisted.

"No, sir, not a one, except the valets and grooms to the Mr Bradwells and Mr Fordhams. They left on Wednesday last, to stay with friends. Oh, and Mr William Herbert went off on Friday to stay with Mr Mortimer at the Manor House. They's quite cronies now, sir. It's only Mr Walter Herbert still here, of the young gentlemen."

The servants returned to the house, while Mel stood irresolute, quite unable to decide how to proceed.

"Haymer?" Audley said gently. "It seems to me that the track towards Norton Forbury could usefully be investigated."

"But why would she have gone that way?" Mel said dejectedly. "It is hopeless."

"*Not* hopeless," Audley said firmly. "Let us fetch the horses and try the route to Norton Forbury, and if we find nothing, well then, perhaps it will be time to send for the constables."

They rode in near silence, the only words spoken being the occasional question from Audley regarding their direction, and what habitations they might pass along the way. "In case the lady may have looked for shelter," he added. But Mel could give him no cause for optimism. In this direction there were no habitations at all between Pendarreth and the Manor House, not so much as a shepherd's hut. Still, it was a comfort to have Audley's calm good sense focused on the matter. Being only distantly connected to Margaret through his friendship with her sister, he could approach the problem with dispassionate clarity of mind, and Mel was grateful for it.

They reached the place near the grave, and here Mel once again stopped, pondering. There was a ruined cottage there, Margaret had told him, so perhaps she had taken shelter there? He explained it to his companion.

"The idea has merit, and I do not wish to discourage you," Audley said. "However, a secret place is necessarily difficult to find, and if you have not been there yourself, we might be thrashing through the undergrowth for days."

"I have never been there, but I have seen it marked on Margaret's map, and there is a deer track that leads most of the way there."

"The map marks deer tracks?" Audley said, raising one delicately shaped eyebrow.

"Margaret's map does," Mel said, with a sad smile. "She is very thorough. Just beyond that oak tree with the ivy is the start of the deer track, according to the map."

They left their horses loosely tied, and followed the deer track for some hundred yards deep into the forest. By then, the great holly hedge was in sight to one side, separated from them by impenetrable mounds of bramble.

"Did Miss Margaret's map show a route less damaging to one's breeches?" Audley said. "I am quite prepared to sacrifice them to the enterprise, if not, but from what you have told me of the frequency with which flowers have been placed, I suspect there is an easier way."

Mel laughed, and somehow Audley's light tone lifted his spirits. How grim a task this would have been without his stalwart companion! Now he pointed a little further down the deer path, to where another track branched off in the direction of the hedge. It led directly to a narrow opening, and by squeezing through, at the cost of some tearing to their coats, found themselves inside the hedge.

"That gap was intended for smaller people than you and me," Audley said, looking ruefully at his torn sleeve. "Female, I should say. Ah, I see the grave over there."

Mel was more interested in the ruins of the small cottage, and made his way eagerly in that direction. Only when he had ascertained that Margaret was not hidden away there did he turn to the grave.

"No luck?" Audley said sympathetically.

"No sign anyone has been in there for years, and the walls are too tumbled about to provide any shelter."

"Someone has been here, however," Audley said, pointing to the grave. "No more than two or three days ago, too." On top of the mound of stones lay a small bunch of Michaelmas daisies, a little wilted but not yet brown. "There are plenty of those in the gardens around Pendarreth."

"Yes, almost certainly they came from there."

Mel gazed at the grave, just as Margaret had described it, except that now the stones of different colours were muddled and mixed, so that no words could be read.

"Someone has destroyed the inscription," he said thoughtfully. "It used to read, *'Melville Matthew Haymer. Born first day of February 17—. Died third day of February 17—.'* But the words are gone now. Perhaps whoever placed the stones realised that the grave had been discovered."

"Or feared that it might be," Audley said thoughtfully. "The inscription would be very revealing. As it is, this is merely a pile of stones and the flowers might only commemorate a dog, or someone who used to live in the cottage. The third of February," he mused. "A bad time of year for making a grave in the woods. The ground would have been like iron. No wonder whoever buried the child raised a cairn instead."

"Raised a—? Oh, you mean the child is not buried in the ground, merely covered with stones? That makes sense. And if, as seems likely, it was Miss Tilford who constructed this, then this arrangement would have been much easier for a lady than digging a grave."

"And do you think this Miss Tilford was the lady whose baby was substituted for this one?" Audley said, with a delicate cough.

"Was my mother, you mean?" Mel said, amused by his circumlocution. "Again, it seems likely. Who else could it have been?"

"One of the servants? Such things do happen."

"Hmm, perhaps. But all the evidence points to Miss Tilford. I doubt a servant would have placed those stones so carefully to make a name and dates, and you heard what Lily said — no servants come deep into the woods now. The main tracks are well travelled, and a few still know of the tree house, but this part is little used, except by Miss Tilford. I think we must consider her the most likely person."

"Yet it is odd," Audley said. "Let us suppose that all of this is the work of Miss Tilford — the grave, the stones, the inscription, the flowers, and the never ending work of keeping down the undergrowth all about. That seems an excessive amount of grief for a child who was *not* her own, who was merely the unbaptised infant of a friend."

Mel thought about that, but could see no explanation other than the obvious one. "I daresay it is an expression of guilt for her part in the enterprise. The child's death could not be acknowledged any other way, after all."

"Is there anyone else who might know of the circumstances and might take an interest?"

"I do not know of anyone. Miss Tilford has been something of a recluse for many years past. She has no close friends in the neighbourhood." Yet he thought of the household record books that Margaret had described to him, filled with parties and excursions and gaiety, and Miss Tilford in the very heart of it. She had had friends enough in those days. And then, abruptly, she had changed all the servants and turned against men and hidden herself away at Pendarreth. It could only be because of some importunate seduction, and an unwanted baby.

And he was that baby.

While he was considering this, Audley was prowling round the perimeter of the grave, where the brambles and bracken had been cleared away and only the summer's growth surrounded the mound like a crown. With an exclamation, he tripped and almost fell. Bending down, he called out, "Look at this, Haymer."

It was a stone, half hidden by grass and the remains of bluebells, and green with moss.

"Do you know, I think there is some lettering upon it." He began to rub at the moss.

"No, no! Let me!" Mel cried, looking at Audley's pale gloves and imagining the green stains upon them, and the reaction of his valet. "My gloves will sustain the damage far more readily than yours."

Audley merely laughed, and murmured that he could well afford new gloves. Between them they scraped away the moss covering the stone. The letters had been carved inexpertly, and it was hard to make them out, but after some discussion, they agreed on *'Matthew Philip'*.

"Or perhaps *'Phillips'*," Audley said. "And the date... forty or more years ago."

"Poor Miss Tilford," Mel said, in no doubt of the meaning of the stone. "This, I think, must be her child too, who also died at two days of age. This surely resolves the mystery of her devotion to her friend's dead child — beneath the stones also lies her own babe. *'Matthew'*... then Mrs Malham is right, Lord Delacrost should have married her."

"Oh? You mean Delacrost fathered a child on her and abandoned her? Good God! What a vile fellow! Was he married then?"

"I think not."

"Then surely—" Audley stopped and looked sideways at Mel. "Is it possible, Haymer, that he repeated the offence fifteen years later?"

"Repeated the—? Oh." And suddenly his likeness to the portrait in the old library at the Manor House made perfect sense. Perhaps Lord Delacrost truly was his father. "Only one person can answer that question," he said grimly. "Miss Tilford. Everything comes back to her — to my birth and to Pendarreth. And Margaret was almost within the grounds when she disappeared, and not of her own will, for she took nothing with her. Whatever has become of her, we will not find it out by tramping endlessly through the woods. All the answers are at Pendarreth, so let us go there and ask some questions."

~~~~~

When the two men reached Pendarreth, the residents were already gathered in the withdrawing room before dinner, since only an
~~~~~

earthquake, seemingly, could change the early dining hour Miss Tilford preferred. Mel waved aside the pompous footmen who would have barred his entry, and strode into the room, not the least discomfited by his riding attire in the midst of so much evening finery.

Indeed, the sight of lace and silk and jewels and bare flesh irritated him beyond endurance. There they were, standing around sipping sherry, twittering away like so many exotic birds, smiling and laughing — *laughing!* How dared they, when his beloved Margaret was missing, and in who knew what distress?

"What do you think you are doing?" he said, his voice loud in his own ears. "Why are you here, why do you even *think* about dressing for dinner when Margaret may be injured or dead, or... or held prisoner somewhere?"

They stared at him open-mouthed. Mrs Herbert and her daughters. Mrs Fordham. Mr Walter Herbert, chewing a lip, hands tucked under his arms. And looking anxious in a corner, her shawl drooping from one arm, Prudence Tilford.

Before Mel could speak to her, Mrs Fordham stepped forward. "How dare you come in here in all your dirt, Mr Haymer, hurling abuse at us like a peasant? You are offensive, sir. Boulder, Ferrill, remove him from the house at once."

"I think not," Mel said, with icy calm, straightening to make himself a little taller. He rarely used his imposing height to advantage, but it was an effective deterrent even against the two sizeable footmen called upon to act. They hovered, just out of reach, twitching nervously. Audley was, like most men, shorter than Mel, but he moved ostentatiously to Mel's side, to make it clear that the two of them stood together. Turning to the footmen, he said, "Go away, do." And they went, scuttling out as fast as they could.

"Now, ma'am, you will treat this matter seriously," Mel said.

"I say," said Walter Herbert, lifting his chin pompously. "That is no way to speak to a lady, sir."

"Hush, Walter," Mrs Herbert said in conciliatory tones, rushing forward in a flurry of rustling silk to rest a hand on Mel's arm. "Mr Haymer, we are all agreed that Margaret has merely run away, as she has done before. She is a very sensitive girl, easily over-wrought, and—"

"Nonsense," Mel said. "I beg your pardon for speaking forcefully, but I must make you see the urgency of the situation. Margaret was within sight of the house on Sunday afternoon, yet never reached it. She has taken no clothes or food, and she is not lodged with friends. Do you not see? Someone in this house knows what happened to her."

"The servants—" began Mrs Fordham.

"They have all been questioned," Audley put in. "They are so anxious for the missing lady's welfare that they are spending their precious free time searching for her."

"Unlike any of you," Mel said disdainfully. "One of you must have seen or heard something. Perhaps something amiss on Sunday. You must tell me anything that might help."

"This is ridiculous," Mrs Fordham said, her pointed nose quivering with indignation. "Who are you to come barging in here looking as if you have been dragged through a hedge backwards, and tell us what we *must* do? We accord you a degree of civility on account of your profession, but who are you really, Mr Haymer? Some cottage girl's bastard babe."

Mel smiled equably at this thrust, more impolite than anything he had said. Now that the subject of his birth had arisen, he need not scruple to say more. "If you can prove that, ma'am, you will make several people very happy, me included. But unless and until that happens, I am in law the eldest son and heir to Lord Delacrost, and you may accord me a degree of civility on *that* account. And you need not look so disbelieving. It is all in Debrett's."

"No!" Mrs Fordham said, wide-eyed. "It cannot be so."

"It is quite true, dear," Miss Tilford said, smiling happily. "He *is* the heir to the viscountcy."

"But... but how?" Mrs Herbert said.

"The first Lady Delacrost gave birth to a son," Mel said. "When he died, she substituted... um, how was it expressed? Some cottage girl's bastard babe. Although I doubt that my mother came from a cottage."

Mrs Herbert gave a gasp, and sat down abruptly in a chair. Elsewhere, Mel could see shocked faces, and glances exchanged.

He went on relentlessly, "There is a secret grave in the woods where the real Melville Haymer is buried, and someone from Pendarreth tends it and places flowers there regularly. I do not suppose that is the work of any cottage girl, do you, Miss Tilford?"

"Me?" she said, her face ashen. "What is it to do with me?"

"Who else knows these woods so well?"

She said nothing, looking at him with stricken eyes, as every person in the room turned to face her. Mel took a deep breath, knowing full well the enormity of the step he was about to take, and the insult he was proffering. But he could not draw back now, for here, he was certain, was the heart of the mystery surrounding his birth. And if he could solve that, perhaps he would be nearer to knowing who had taken Margaret, and why.

"Well, Miss Tilford?" Mel went on relentlessly. "Are you my mother?"

He knew at once that he had mistaken the matter. She exhaled, and then uttered a sound that was almost a laugh. "Oh no! No, no, no! I am not your mother. What an idea! Good heavens, no!"

She tittered, and he could see relief in her eyes. He was close, but that was not the secret she held. Still, she knew *something* and—

Audley coughed delicately. "Perhaps we should now go directly to the magistrate? And to Lord Delacrost, for he should be informed of events here, all things considered. He may wish to assist in the search."

"He will not help you," Miss Tilford said.

"No, indeed, and why should he send his men tramping about for a foolish runaway girl anyway?" Mrs Fordham said. "And really, Mr Haymer, although we all know your infatuation for poor Margaret, it is none of your business what she does or where she goes. It is for her relations to determine what is best to be done — her aunt, and her cousins. It is no concern of yours."

"It is very much my concern," he said calmly. "Margaret is my wife."

There was such a long silence that the low sounds of the servants chinking cutlery in the great hall next door could be clearly heard.

"Your *wife?*" Mrs Fordham said.

Walter Herbert stepped forward, his face filled with terror. "Then... there is something you should know, sir. Margaret was... was *taken* by Mortimer Haymer and my brother William. They are holding her at Norton Forbury Manor House, with the object of persuading her to marry William."

27: A Dusty Room

Margaret's imprisonment was not as bad as it could have been. The room was large, and furnished with a bed, several chairs, a table, a wash stand and a wardrobe, where she carefully placed her pelisse and bonnet. There was a close-stool in a closet, a couple of oil lamps, the sheets and blankets on the bed were clean, if a little damp, and she had enough wood for a fire in the evenings. The windows commanded a fine view over the countryside, when they were opened.

But the room had clearly not seen the attentions of a housemaid for years. A thick film of dust lay over every surface, the windows were thoroughly grimed and the rugs on the floor, though of good quality, needed a good beating. Such disorder offended Margaret's housewifely standards, but she had only a handkerchief, a spare handkerchief and the little wiping cloth from her slate box, and it offended her even more to use such things for rough cleaning.

Accordingly, therefore, when Mortimer Haymer and William Herbert brought her a tray of food on her first evening as a prisoner, they were greeted by her slate. *'Please bring me a bucket, a scrubbing brush, several cloths, a dustpan and a brush.'*

William stared at her. "What the devil—?"

'I want to do some cleaning.'

"Why, whatever is amiss here? No worse than an inn room."

'This place is a pigsty. If you expect me to stay here, then it will have to be cleaned.'

William laughed. "You have to admit it, Haymer, the girl has spirit."

"Dicked in the nob, that is what she is, just like that aunt of hers," Mortimer said. "You would never be able to set her loose in town. But she will do well enough for you if you leave her at Pendarreth. Come on, leave her now, or we shall be late for dinner."

And so saying, they had left her alone to consider her predicament. She was calm now that she knew their intent. For a few terrifying moments, when they had leapt out of the bushes to grab her, she had thought they were going to hurt her, or even kill her. But their faces were uncovered, so they were not attempting to conceal their identity, and when Mortimer had hauled her roughly by one arm, William had protested, "Hey, careful there! She must not be injured!"

So she had decided not to fight against two grown men, especially as one of them, Mortimer, was large like his father. That could only end badly for her. She allowed them to lead her away up the track, and then sat unprotesting before William on his horse as they rode in leisurely fashion up the hill through the woods, over the rise and then down into the Manor House parkland. They soon entered trees again, or perhaps an overgrown shrubbery, walking the horses slowly and carefully. They stopped, dismounted, lifted her down, and taking an arm each, marched her across a short strip of lawn and into a door at the base of a tower. Then up a spiral staircase, up and up and up, one in front of her and one behind, and into this room.

"Now then, my dear," Mortimer had said, leering at her, "here you are and here you stay until you do the sensible thing, and agree to marry William here. He is not a bad sort of chap, and a better match than you would have got any other way, you may be sure."

William smiled, watching her wordlessly.

"No," she said, then, with an enormous effort, "Already... married."

Mortimer roared with laughter. "A good effort, my dear, but I hardly think so. Can you produce your marriage lines? No, I did not think so."

Then they left, locking the door behind them. She heard them laughing all the way down the stairs.

How frustrating that she had given her marriage lines to Mel for safe-keeping! It would have given her the greatest satisfaction to have waved the paper under the noses of these foolish men, and thus foiled their wicked plan. But at least she had been offered no violence, so all she had to do was to wait until she could effect an escape, or Mel rescued her.

A quick survey had shown her that, although the windows opened wide, they were too high for her to jump to the ground, nor was there a convenient vine to climb down. The sheets and blankets on the bed were too few to knot together to make a rope. With a sigh, she withdrew a hairpin, but, as she had expected, it was too flimsy to have any impact on the sturdy lock. How disappointing that real life was not so obliging as a novel.

So since she could not, it seemed, find a way out of her prison, she could at least make it clean. Her captors obviously approved of her domesticity, for the next morning they arrived with her breakfast, and also a mop and bucket, with an array of cleaning implements obviously stolen at random from the housemaid's cupboard. So when she had eaten the bread, cheese and cold chicken they had supplied, she set to work heating water on the fire, and scrubbing the room from top to bottom. In between times, she read her psalter, the only other item in her reticule beside her slate box, and prayed, and thought longingly of Mel. But she was not down-hearted. She was alive and unharmed, and she would surely be looked for before long.

Mortimer and William visited twice a day, bringing food and fresh water, and to allow William to spend time alone with her, offering inducements, should she choose to marry him. She never spoke, so he paced about the room talking more or less to himself, mostly about his horses and his dogs and his guns. He had a pair of Mantons, which were apparently something quite special in the way of guns, judging by his lovingly detailed description of them. He was such an energetic man, striding up and down the room, waving his arms about and talking so loudly that her head ached. She was always relieved when he went away, although the contrast made her weep for Mel and his quiet voice and gentle manners.

The meals displayed a monotony of character — bread, cheese, a piece of meat or pie, and an apple, morning and afternoon alike — but there was enough that she had no fear of starving. Still, she wondered how long they would tamely keep her there, at risk of discovery. She knew where she was — the old tower near Norton Forbury Manor House. She could just see the chimneys of the big house from one of the windows. There were a good number of guests still staying with the viscount as well as dozens of servants, and any one of them could stray in this direction at any time. The lower door of the tower had not been locked, she remembered, so surely someone would wander this way and decide to investigate? And then she would be rescued.

Of Mel finding her, she was less sanguine. She could not doubt that he was searching desperately for her, and she imagined him going hopefully to the tree house and then not knowing where to turn. Poor Mel! If only there were some way she could communicate with him that she was safe, at least.

Safe for the moment, at any rate, but perhaps that happy state would not last for long. Mortimer grew increasingly anxious and abusive as the days passed by and still she would not agree to marry William. By Wednesday, his haranguing took a darker tone.

"You are a stupid woman, not to see what is good for you," he yelled, his face inches from hers. "You will have to be forced to do what is right. It would give me the greatest pleasure to do it myself, but that is a husband's prerogative."

She reached for her slate box to respond.

"And you can put that away!" he shrieked. "Talk or be silent, but do not test my patience with that scratching. Will you or will you not marry William?"

She shook her head, staring at William on the other side of the room. Mortimer, she could see, was an ill-tempered man, and no gentleman. William, however, was gnawing his knuckle, and seemed uncomfortable with this abrupt change of strategy.

"Pah!" Mortimer said. "You leave us no choice. Do it, Herbert, and let us get this over with."

"No!" Margaret said.

Mortimer leaned close to her again, so that she could smell the wine on his breath. "You are a simpleton and a dullard and you need a man to show you the right way to behave. William is going to be your husband, so it is his *right* to do this, do you understand?"

"No," she said again, and picked up the slate box.

Mortimer screeched. "Put that *down!*" And with one swipe of his arm, he knocked the box from her hand and sent it flying across the room, where it hit the wall with a sickening crunch, and smashed into fragments of polished wood and slate.

With a cry, Margaret pushed him aside and raced across the room to the ruins of her box, her gift from Mel, lovingly made with his own hands. And then she cried, as she had not cried before, deep gulping sobs that racked her whole body. She lay down on the floor amidst the ruins of her box, a fragment of slate cool against her cheek, and wept with all the force of the unexpressed grief inside her.

"This is ridiculous!" Mortimer's voice. Then, as she squeaked in alarm, he picked her up and almost threw her onto the bed. "Get on with it, Herbert. This has been a prime rig, but I will not be played for a fool! So do what has to be done. You have half an hour, and if you do not get the business done, I will do it for you."

The door slammed, and his feet slapped away down the stone stairs.

Margaret eyed William warily, her tears still flowing but silently. She dashed them away, for this was no time for weeping. She needed all her wits about her now.

Slowly she sat up, never taking her eyes from William. He chewed his lip, watching her. Then, with a shrug, he said, "He has a point, Meg. I mean, it is not doing any good, you being shut up here. All you have to do is... is not make a fuss, and we can all be comfortable again."

She shook her head. "Cannot."

If only she had some way to prove her marriage, but without her marriage lines there was no hope. Her marriage could not protect her. She would have to find another way to convince him that the case was hopeless, that she could never marry a man who would treat her in such a way. But she could not. The words stuck in her throat, and she was too afraid to be able to talk. She could only do it when she was angry. Or when Mel was with her.

"It was not my idea," he went on. "It is all Haymer's doing, so that you won't marry that parson chap. Seems to think it will cut him out of the inheritance if you do that, and his father said you were on the brink, so you see... we had to step in, don't you see? But we can get this over with right now. Just lie down, like a good girl and—"

He was moving across the room towards her. She jumped to her feet, but how could she stop him when she could not speak? If only she had Mel with her! Mel's presence would let the words float out of her mouth. Well, she did not have Mel but she had her imagination. She pictured him standing by the door, almost as tall as the lintel, his eyes gazing warmly at her, and a lazy little smile on his lips, listening to her, waiting for her to speak...

"William, I have no intention of marrying you," she said, her voice strong. "Even if I had considered the question, I cannot respect a man who kidnaps me."

He started, then laughed. "Oh, you can talk when you want to, you little baggage."

Slowly, so as not to alarm him, she reached across to where her psalter lay on the bed, then cradled it to her stomach. That, too, might give her strength. He eyed the book warily, and it seemed to her that his face lost something of its assurance.

"I do not think you are a bad person," she said, "but what you are doing here is contemptible. Also very foolish. Do you really imagine I would marry you after this? So what have you achieved?"

"Mortimer says..." he began, then hesitated, as if wondering whether Mortimer was, after all, the best authority on such matters.

"Who cares what Mortimer says?" she said scornfully. "He is looking after his own interests first, not yours."

"Our interests coincide in this instance," he said. "He wants you married to anyone but the curate, and I want Pendarreth."

"Then you will both fail in your objectives. This cannot do any good, William. Your best plan is to release me unharmed and pretend this never happened."

"No," he said, looking at her speculatively. "Even if you will not marry me, I can do Mortimer a good turn by ruining you so that your prim curate will not want you."

"You are even sillier than I had suspected," she said. "I shall be glad to watch you hang, William."

For the first time, his insouciance was punctured. She could see him thinking it through, and realising that the enterprise rested on a knife edge. Success would see him married and master of Pendarreth, with Mortimer a grateful neighbour. But failure might carry a cost too high to contemplate. He glanced at her face, then down at the psalter, visibly wrestling with his conscience.

"I need to discuss this with Mortimer," he said, and dashed out of the room. To Margaret's sorrow, he remembered to lock the door.

Abruptly, her legs gave way, and she sank to the bed, shaking. For a long time, she sat motionless, straining to hear the least sound that might suggest that Mortimer was returning to make good his foul promise. *'If you do not get the business done, I will do it for you'*, he had said. But the silence was absolute, and eventually her heart beat less frantically and her breathing returned to normal. They had gone. For the moment, she had escaped a dreadful fate, but she was still a prisoner, and William could still decide to risk the gallows. Or Mortimer could, for as the son of a viscount, he might feel able to defy the law with a degree of impunity.

In the corner of the room, the shards of her slate box still lay. Sadly, she began to gather them together. As she did so, she realised that the metal binding around the slate was thick and straight and much, much stronger than a hair pin...

~~~~~

Anger drove Mel at a gallop up the hill to Dunton Heights and then down to Norton Forbury. With him were Audley, Walter Herbert and an array of grooms.

Dinner at the Manor House was served fashionably late, so for the second time that day, Mel strode dishevelled into a roomful of people in evening dress, a train of agitated footmen in his wake. And for the second time, the gathering turned pale faces towards him, in varying degrees of disinterest, curiosity or outrage.

It was Lord Delacrost, immaculate in silk breeches, who stepped out of the throng, his face suffused with rage. "Haymer, what do you—?"

"Your pardon for intruding," Mel said, with a cursory bow, "but I have reason to believe that my wife is being held prisoner on these premises."

There were gasps of surprise, murmurs of "His *wife!*" and "Prisoner?", and some tittering.
~~~~~

"You are insane!" Lord Delacrost hissed in a low voice. "If you imagine that girl is anywhere here—"

"No time for this," Mel said tersely. "Where is Mr Mortimer Haymer? He is responsible for this outrage against my wife's person. There you are... where is she, Haymer? Where have you hidden her?"

Mortimer ambled across the room, an amused grin on his face. "What, bosky already, Parson? What ridiculous notion have you got in your head now?"

"I am not drunk," Mel said. "I am reliably informed that you and Mr William Herbert kidnapped my wife on Sunday, and have been keeping her prisoner ever since. Where is she?"

Mortimer grinned, and looked around the room, hands spread wide. "See? See what nonsense we have to put up with from the peasants in these parts? Begone, Parson, and ply your untruths elsewhere."

"Wait..." Lord Delacrost said. "Mr Haymer is not a man of deceit. I have had my differences with him, God knows, but he has never played me false. What is your reliable information, Haymer?"

Mel turned and looked directly at Walter Herbert. To his credit, he stepped forward gamely, although he was chalk-white, and visibly shaking like a leaf.

"And who are you, sir?"

Walter..." he began, his voice as high as a girl. With an effort, he tried again. "Walter H-H-Herbert, my lord. William is... m-m-my... b-b-brother. He told me—"

"Walter, you *imbecile!"* William materialised from a far corner of the room, red-faced. "Shut *up!"*

"No, h-h-have to speak, Will," he said. "She is *married* to him. All a waste of time."

"You… you…" William was so bereft of words that he launched himself at his brother, and only Mel's quick thinking in pulling Walter aside prevented immediate bloodshed.

"Ladies present," Mel said sharply. "No fists in the drawing room, if you please."

"For once we agree," Mortimer sneered. "Come outside, Herbert, so that we may point out to you the error of your ways." He and William each grabbed an arm and would have whisked Walter away out of sight, no doubt to be beaten to a pulp, but Audley stepped in front to prevent them leaving.

"We will have none of that," Lord Delacrost said, his louder voice cutting across the tenseness in the air. "Let him go, both of you. Mortimer, show us where you have Miss Winterton… Mrs Haymer."

"If you believe this *buffoon* instead of your own son—" Mortimer began, but his father quelled him with a single glance from under his stern brows.

Another voice cut in more quietly. "She will be in the old tower, Father." Edward Haymer.

"Then let us go there," Lord Delacrost said. "Milford, put dinner back by one hour."

He made no apology to the ladies, watching the altercation with astonished faces. He simply marched out of the room, expecting everyone to follow, and even in the midst of his own anxiety, Mel could be both amused and impressed by such careless power. In the viscount's wake trailed Mel, Audley, Walter and Edward, then, whispering furiously, Mortimer and William, and a handful of other guests, although whether from curiosity or anticipation of bloodshed was impossible to say.

Lighting the way with lamps, they followed a gravel path away from the main house, and plunged into a tangle of overgrown shrubs. After a short time, they emerged in a grassy clearing, and there was the tower, a simple round affair of three or four stories, a folly, most likely, large enough to use as guest accommodation when the main house was full, or to make a secret refuge for the children of the house.

When they arrived, there was a single wavering light showing about half way down, but even as they watched it slowly descended, window by window. And then, to Mel's astonishment, the door at the bottom opened, and out came an immaculately clad figure in her Sunday best pelisse, bonnet and gloves, carrying her reticule.

Margaret.

He laughed for joy, and held out his arms to her.

28: Supper At The Manor House

As soon as Margaret opened the door at the bottom of the tower, the wind snatched at her candle flame, plunging her into darkness. Leaving it on the floor, she tentatively stepped outside and looked about her.

Lights, flickering lights in a big group just a few yards away. Dimly, she could make out pale faces and dark silhouettes, and one that was taller than the others. One who smiled and opened his arms to her.

She ran straight into them, and then miraculously, inexplicably, she was safe and Mel was there and her ordeal was over. His arms wrapped tight around her, holding her securely, and she was pressed against his solid chest, her cheek resting on the smooth wool of his coat.

A sharp stab.

"Ow! What is so prickly?" she said, looking up at him in alarm.

He laughed. "A holly leaf, I expect. Dearest, are you… unharmed? They have not hurt you?"

"I am perfectly well, now that you are here."

Somewhere nearby, an altercation was going on. Lord Delacrost was yelling, and Mortimer was yelling back that it was only funning — just a little joke — not the least harm in it — had he not done much worse himself? He was only following his father's example. Then a cracking sound, some gasps and silence. When Margaret turned to look, she saw Mortimer lying insensible on the ground.

"Get him out of here," Lord Delacrost, pointing at his son's crumpled form. He turned to William, "And you are no longer welcome here, Herbert. Haymer, bring Miss... your wife into the house out of this cold wind. Edward, get rid of all these people."

Everyone jumped to do his bidding, and in very short order Margaret found herself in a warm parlour, a good fire blazing, with only Mel, Lord Delacrost and another man, rather splendidly attired, although his coat, like Mel's, was torn and sported odd twigs and sharp leaves.

"And who are you, sir?" Lord Delacrost said to the stranger.

"Leonard Audley, my lord, of Stoneleigh Hall and Bath, aiding Mr Haymer's search."

"Well, I have no— What? What is it?" he barked at the hapless butler standing at the door.

"The ladies would like to know what is occurring, my lord. And... about dinner."

With an exclamation of disgust, he said, "Oh, for heaven's sake! Very well, I shall come and explain. Bring some supper in here, will you, Milford. Haymer, there is brandy and so forth on the sideboard there. I shall be back directly."

He strode out, the butler followed, and Margaret was left alone with Mel and Mr Audley.

"Mr Audley?" she said, in a burst of delight. "Of Stoneleigh Hall? Can you possibly be Lucy's Mr Audley?"

A brief flash of pain crossed his face. "I wish with all my heart that I were Lucy's Mr Audley," he said, smiling sadly at her. "However, she holds me in contempt, and will not have me."

"Oh, *no!* She holds you in the greatest esteem, Mr Audley. Her letters are full of your kindness, your generosity. I think she is very much in love with you. If you are patient, she will come round, I am certain."

His expression lifted. "Do you think so? Oh, if only I could be sure! I keep telling myself I ought to leave her alone, and tease her no more, but... but I cannot bring myself— Oh, I beg your pardon. How thoughtless of me to be talking about my own concerns. What may I get for you, Mrs Haymer? There is brandy or sherry or Madeira... or shall I send for tea?"

"Oh, never mind that! How do you come to be here? It is of all things the most astonishing. Did you have business here?"

He laughed. "In a way. Lucy — Mrs Price — was concerned about you, having had no word from you for many weeks, so I offered to find out if you were well. I confess, I had not anticipated finding anything more exciting than a lady with a diary full of engagements and no time to write letters. A kidnapping is quite beyond my expectations. And you are a married lady, too, which is also a surprise. What a story I shall have to tell her when I return."

"Oh, pray do not! She will be so alarmed — all my sisters will be alarmed if they hear the tale from you. I... I have not been very good about writing letters... I... I could not find the words... and there were difficulties at Pendarreth... all our letters were... intercepted."

"Good God!" Mr Audley said. "Oh, I beg your pardon, Mrs Haymer, but that is abominable. But I daresay Mr Haymer would have posted letters for you, and collected them too, if asked."

"Yes, but..." She stopped. This was the point she could never describe to anyone. For who would understand about words that did not want to be written? "I could not write anything. At first, I was too unhappy and then it was so *complicated*. I could not explain it, even to my sisters. I have never had to before, you see. They always understood me without me saying a word, so when I tried to write to them... the words would not come."

Mel's face softened into a smile. "Except for that first time you stayed overnight at the parsonage, remember? I was writing letters, and you wrote to your sisters at the same time."

"I was happy," she said. "And there was no time to think about it, so I just sat and wrote and the words came."

"Does that make it easier, when there is no time to think?"

She nodded. "Oh yes! Like the evening party, when I invited everyone to dinner so that I could dance. I had just an hour to write all the invitations. But those sorts of letters are easier — the words are there, waiting to be written down."

The butler came in just then with a train of footmen to lay the table and place dishes and platters and tureens, from which emanated the most delicious aromas. Margaret inhaled appreciatively.

The viscount returned just as they were sitting down to eat. Margaret had the soup spoon half way to her mouth, her first hot food for days, and was most reluctant to set it down.

To her surprise, the viscount ordered another place set, and sat down to eat with them. As they ate, Margaret told all that had happened to her. They asked few questions, for she was holding Mel's hand and so it was easy to talk fluently. Only once Mel intervened, when she described how she had talked to William and persuaded him not to violate her.

"And you managed to say all that with your slate box?" Mel said.

"No, that got broken. I do not think it can be mended," she added sadly.

He squeezed her hand. "I will make you another one, dearest, although you hardly seem to need it now."

"I can talk when you are with me," she said, smiling at him. "When I was talking to William, I imagined you there with me, standing in the corner of the room. Then I could talk."

Margaret told what little more there was to tell, and then Mel told his side of events, while Lord Delacrost said little, but listened and nodded thoughtfully. She thought he looked old and tired, but it was the first time she had seen him without his habitual bluster and brow-beating, all the arrogance stripped away, and she liked him the better for it.

When everyone had told their story, and Mr Audley had explained his part in the business, the viscount sighed. "Well, I am sorry for all that has happened to you these past days, Mrs Haymer. It is a mercy you have suffered no worse hurt than imprisonment." He sighed again. "Do you wish to lay a charge against my son?"

She shook her head.

"You could do so, and I will not prevent you."

That made her smile! His assumption that he could stop her was amusing, although she recognised the truth in it. He was a viscount, a peer of the realm, who knew all the men of power. Naturally he could protect his son if he wished it.

"It would do no good," Margaret said.

"Perhaps, perhaps not. It is a relief to hear you say so, in any event. There is a degree of wildness in most families, but this would create a great scandal if it were to become widely known."

"I shall not speak of it."

"Thank you." His hands twirled his wine glass absently, his eyes unfocused.

He was so subdued that Margaret almost felt sorry for him. "It was not your fault," she said.

With a wry smile, he said, "Now that is where you are quite wrong. Who should take the blame but myself? He has all the defects of my own character, untempered by any regard for principle or even good sense. What did he hope to achieve by such behaviour? Only distress and grief and his own downfall. Yet he said he was following my example, that is the worst of it. All my own youthful folly thrown back in my face as inspiration for my son's. I was wild enough for two, it is true, but I expected something different from my sons. But bad blood will out."

"That is not entirely true, my lord," Mel said politely. "You have two sons, and the younger is very different from the elder."

Lord Delacrost's expression lifted a little. "That is true. I have one son at least of whom any father would be proud. Mortimer's disgrace is shown the more clearly by Edward's good example. But his is not the only point of contrast. You may not be my son, Haymer, but your behaviour in every particular has been exemplary. You have dealt honourably with me, and complied with my every request, however difficult. You have my esteem, sir, despite the lowly blood in your veins."

Mel's eyebrows lifted a fraction, but he answered as composedly as ever. "I am honoured by your words, my lord, although I have wondered at times whether my blood is quite so lowly as we have always supposed. Mr Edward Haymer imagines a family resemblance in my features."

The viscount uttered a bark of laughter. "Indeed! It is possible, I suppose, for women were always my greatest weakness. Not that I ever resorted to force, or to kidnapping either. Never needed to. Even so, no cottager or farmer or craftsman has ever admitted to an unwanted birth in the family at the time. Generally these people are quick enough to claim a purse from me in such cases. No, I do not think it likely."

"I did wonder if I might be Miss Tilford's but—"

"Pru? No, definitely not. At least, not by me, in any event. What made you think of her?"

"The grave in the woods, near Pendarreth and also near the track to Norton Forbury. And..." Mel hesitated, then looked Lord Delacrost straight in the eye. "There is some history there, I understand."

"Now, look here—"

"The grave in the woods shows signs of an earlier burial, a Matthew Philip or Phillips, from forty or more years ago."

The viscount opened his mouth and closed it again with a snap. "Dear God! There was a child, then? I never knew... she said nothing... poor Pru! If I had known..."

He lapsed into silence, and no one else spoke, perhaps too polite to suggest that a gentleman who left a lady exposed to such an eventuality should not wait for her to tell him of it, but should have married her at once.

"Damnation!" he exclaimed, then, with a quick glance at Margaret, "Your pardon, ma'am. But it is unaccountable! Why did she never tell me! Yet the child died, you say?"

"Two days after the birth, if the engravings on the stone be true. Audley, that is your opinion too, is it not?"

Mr Audley agreed to it, and added, "There are still flowers left on the grave, and since no one but Miss Tilford is said to venture into that part of the woods—"

"Aye, true enough!" the viscount said, with a grunt that might have been amusement. "No wonder she was so keen to keep everyone away from those precious woods of hers. Good Lord, Letty always said she protected them as fiercely as a mother protects her child. But I see why you might have thought... but no, I had no dealings with Pru after that first time. Little minx, she was, setting out quite deliberately to—" Again he glanced at Margaret. "Hmpf, you are such a quiet little thing, one forgets you are there, sometimes. Pass the decanter, Audley, will you?"

As the viscount poured himself a good measure, Audley said, "Forgive an outsider for being a trifle confused, but what happens now to the house? Pendarreth, I mean? It falls to you, my lord, I believe?"

"Depends on those chuckle-headed executors of Letty's will. If they get a move on and decide Miss Winterton — I mean Mrs Haymer — has abdicated her claim to the property, then it will come to me. If they delay and I am in my grave, then... why, then it comes to you, Haymer," he said with a short laugh. "How amusing. *'To Viscount Delacrost'* the will said, and that will be you. In any event, Mrs Haymer has the right to live there until ownership has been transferred. So I suppose you will be moving in there, Haymer."

"We have not yet settled our domestic arrangements," Mel said equably. "We may continue to live separately for now, being mindful of my promise to you."

"Ah, that," Lord Delacrost said. "We must talk about that. Why is this decanter empty? Audley, may I trouble you for the port?"

After the port had been found and passed round, and Lord Delacrost had taken a long draught, he set his glass down and placed both hands palm down on the table before him.

"Now, Haymer, this is what I intend to do. Mortimer cannot be permitted to live as he pleases after this. I am minded to buy him his colours and see if Wellesley and Bonaparte between them can knock some sense into his skull. As for you..." He leaned back, folding his arms, and looked speculatively at Mel, who gazed steadily back at him. "You are legally my heir, and it seems there is no possibility of overturning that. That no longer matters. You have proved to me in every way that you are worthy to be my heir, both to the title and the estate. You have all the principles, the sense of honour and duty, that Mortimer has so signally failed to display. I propose, therefore, to acknowledge you openly as my heir, set up the entail on the estate again, and begin training you to take over after my death. Present you at court and so forth. And since you are already married, I shall look forward to seeing my first grandson before my eyes close for ever."

Mel's face registered all the incredulity that Margaret felt. It was impossible! After all these years pretending that Mel did not even exist, to change his mind now and turn everything upside down was the outside of enough. She had looked forward to being the wife of a country clergyman, but she could not imagine herself as a viscountess one day.

"No," she said. "No. You cannot simply wipe out twenty-nine years of neglect as if they never happened."

The viscount turned his gaze on her. "To be sure, I cannot make amends for what has happened, but I do not think Haymer bears any grudge."

"No, indeed. I was never aware of any deficiency in my upbringing."

"Delicately worded," the viscount said. "You did better with the parson and his wife than you would have done with me, I daresay, what with having a step-mother to contend with, and Mortimer would have resented you, without doubt. No, I cannot repair my past omissions, but I can treat you properly in the future. Your wife is not what I would have chosen, but I am sure she will improve in time."

"Oh pray do not improve her, my lord," Mel said. "I like her just the way she is. My lord, we are all tired. Let me take Mrs Haymer back to Dutton Cross, and we can talk about this another time."

And after the briefest of arguments from the viscount, the carriage was sent for.

Lord Delacrost's carriage was well sprung and exceedingly comfortable. Margaret rested her cheek on Mel's broad shoulders, drifting almost at once into a half doze. Above her head, Mel and Mr Audley murmured together.

"This is a change for the better, is it not?" Mr Audley said.

"I cannot say. It means my chosen career and a great deal of my comfort given up. I have never wanted to be a viscount, or a man of property."

"At least you have your wife to share the burden, and now you are relieved of the constraints arising from your promise to Delacrost. You have his permission to enter the marital bed."

Mel's chuckle was a low rumble that Margaret felt rather than heard, as one hand rested against his chest. "True, but I shall not take advantage of that licence until it is more certain that he means it. He is upset about Mortimer tonight, but tomorrow he may regret his words."

29: Breakfast At The Parsonage

"Dearest? I have brought you some chocolate."

Margaret woke to the inexpressible joy of Mel's face bending over her. The sight of him, unshaven but resplendent in his dressing robe, made her so happy that just at first she forgot all the horrors that had befallen her in the last few days and could only smile her widest smile.

"Shall I adjust your pillows for you, dear?"

"No, I can manage for myself." She shuffled and plumped and got herself settled sitting upright, while he placed two cups of chocolate on a table beside the bed, and pulled a chair nearer.

"There!" he said in satisfaction. "Is this not cosy? And perfectly proper, for we are married, after all. Oh, which reminds me..."

From a pocket in his robe, he produced a neatly folded paper. "Your marriage lines, Mrs Haymer. And this, which is also yours."

"My wedding ring," she breathed.

Nodding, he gently slipped it onto her finger. "There! Now I feel we are properly married."

She giggled, and then, because her happiness was too great to be contained, wriggled from head to toe. Never had chocolate tasted so good! He laughed, and then she laughed too, and for a while they could do nothing but grin at each other and chuckle and sip their chocolate.

But after a little, his smile faded and he said, "I suppose we shall have to go back to Pendarreth today."

"Must we?" she said, with a shiver of alarm. "It is so pleasant here, and it will occasion no comment, now that we are married."

"We must decide, I suppose, whether we wish to live together at all, just at first."

Abruptly, all her happiness in the day drained away, and her stomach felt as if it were full of ice. "You are going to send me away?" she whispered.

He sighed. "I do not know what to do for the best."

"It cannot be for the best for us to be apart!" she cried.

That brought a smile back to his face. "No. No, you are quite right, of course, but perhaps Lord Delacrost will want us to live at Norton Forbury and—"

"We do not have to do so just because he wishes it, however."

"As my legal father, he is owed the respect and duty of a son," Mel said cautiously. "That does not mean we have to follow his every whim, however. We could live at Pendarreth, I suppose. Or here, although Dr Simpson will want to get another curate, if I must give up my career."

"But why must you give it up?" she said, setting down her cup and sitting up in bed abruptly. "Why may you not still be a clergyman? Then we could have a house of our own, a country living somewhere, just as you have always wanted."

"Because I shall be viscount one day," he said patiently. "Lord Delacrost wants—"

"Lord Delacrost wants, Lord Delacrost wants! What do *you* want, Mel?"

Carefully, he set his chocolate cup beside hers, and leaned forward to take her hand. "Dearest Margaret, I already have the only thing in the world I ever truly wanted, for I have your love. Beside that, nothing else is of the slightest importance to me. I have never minded where I live, or what career I take up, or whether I sit in the House of Lords one day. It is immaterial to me. At no time have I ever wanted to ruffle the waters of anyone else's life by being disobliging. But I *do* want you to be happy, dearest, so if you tell me what *you* want, then I shall want that too. Even if it means disobliging Lord Delacrost," he added in surprised tones, as if he had never thought to hear himself speak so.

She could not help but laugh at his astonishment. "There, now, you are coming along nicely," she said. "You have taken the first step away from sainthood and towards mortal behaviour. Before you know it, you will be shouting at the servants, and striding about the country with a face like thunder, looking just like Lord Delacrost." She hesitated, then added, "You *do* look like him, you know. It is quite uncanny, in certain situations, with the light just so."

He frowned. "Do you think so? I wonder... he *might* be my father, after all, but then who is my mother? I was so sure it was Miss Tilford, but she denied it, and he also. But who else could it be? Perhaps I shall talk to Mrs Malham again, for she was here at that time."

"So was Aunt Pru," Margaret said. "If she did not birth you herself, she may know who did."

"Then I shall ask her," Mel said, with sudden decision. "I must go to Pendarreth to see her today anyway."

"To see Aunt Pru? Whatever for?"

"To apologise," he said ruefully. "I insulted her in the most unspeakable manner, by accusing her of having a child out of wedlock. What a thing to say of a respectable lady! But then I was half out of my mind with worry over you, and it seemed to me that all these things were connected somehow. If only we could be free of Lord Delacrost! If I can find my mother, we will be able to leave him behind and have that country living, with a snug little parsonage." He sighed. "Just think how delightful it would be."

She could not disagree.

~~~~~

They had barely settled down to breakfast, and Mr Audley had not yet arrived from the Malhams' house, where he was staying, when Lord Delacrost's carriage pulled up outside.

"Well!" Mrs Simpson said. "We are honoured indeed."

Margaret did not feel honoured. Last night she had been so buoyed by her escape and finding Mel again that she had not minded Lord Delacrost's bluff ways, but in the morning light, as he strode in without waiting to be announced and with the barest of greetings, he seemed like an overweening bully. She shivered.

The viscount said, "Well, Haymer, I have been considering how to go on, and I have decided to hand Pendarreth over to you at once. No point waiting for those two loobies to transfer the title to me. Your wife has the right to live there until they bestir themselves, and it will be mine as soon as they do — or possibly
~~~~~

yours, if they delay for long enough. In any event, you may as well make a start now and take charge there immediately. The only troubling aspect—"

"I beg your pardon, my lord," Mel said. "I am not quite clear about this. You are expecting us to live at Pendarreth?"

"Of course, where else?"

"Why, here," Mel said. "Or perhaps a snug little parsonage of my own. The bishop is tolerably sure he can find me something suitable soon."

"What the—? Parsonage? Bishop? What the devil are you talking about?"

"My wife and I are by no means certain that we wish to live at Pendarreth," Mel said in his placid way. "Dr and Mrs Simpson have very generously agreed that we may stay here until a living of my own is found."

"Living? Good God, man, you will drop all that clergyman nonsense now."

"Will I?" His tone was mild, but Mel folded his arms and met Lord Delacrost's gaze steadily.

The viscount glared at him, and then, to Margaret's intense relief, he chuckled. "Aye, I like a man with some mettle, Haymer. What are you drinking — coffee? Pah! How anyone drinks that nasty stuff I cannot guess. Where is that boy?" He strode to the door, hurled it open and yelled, "Boy! Ah, there you are — lurking about the keyhole, I daresay. Fetch me some claret."

He pulled up a chair and sat himself down at the table to await his wine. Margaret slid a bowl of bread towards him. He laughed. "You are a quiet one, but I would wager you see and hear everything, eh?"

She nodded. She would have said more, about how she liked to sit in a corner and watch and listen, and how people forgot she was there when she never spoke, and talked quite freely, and how much more interesting that was than the silly commonplace remarks that filled most conversations, but she could not. The words had trickled away under the viscount's loud manner, and her slate box was broken. So she nodded and said nothing.

"Well, Haymer," the viscount said when his claret had arrived, and he had taken his first draught. Then he stopped. "I cannot go on calling you Haymer, like some paltry acquaintance. You are my son, after all. I shall call you Melville."

"My friends call me Mel."

"Ha! But a father is not quite a friend, so I shall still call you Melville."

"Then what would you like me to call you, my lord?" Mel asked politely.

"You will call me Father, as Mortimer and Edward do. Now, Melville, let us be serious. You have made your point, but it will not do to have my heir buried in some rural parish like a nobody. You have a position in society to maintain now. I shall expect you to go up to London with me when I attend Parliament and so forth. There are social events at the Manor House which you will attend... which I should *like* you to attend. Now your wife will not enjoy such affairs, so she may stay at home while you are with me, and what could be more suitable than Pendarreth? It is a fair size, perfectly suitable for the heir to a title. I do not expect you to move to Norton Forbury, Melville. Give me credit for *some* delicacy towards Mrs Haymer's... um, unusual ways."

Margaret watched the two of them carefully, and now that she was aware of the likeness between them, she saw it everywhere — in the shape of the chin, or the length of the eyelashes, or the strength in their hands. But where Mel's features were enhanced by an amiable nature and a ready smile, the viscount's were spoilt by his perpetual glower. He had not, as so many wealthy men did, run to corpulence, and apart from a slight stoop appeared hale, but his countenance proclaimed him to be generally displeased with the world, and not given to being well disposed towards it.

"Dearest, what do you think?" Mel said, in his calm way. "Should you mind living at Pendarreth? For if so—"

She shook her head quickly. "If..." she began, but Lord Delacrost was a powerful disincentive to speech.

"Do you want the slate, Margaret?" Mrs Simpson put in gently. She had brought an old slate and chalks through from the parlour, but so far Margaret had managed without it.

Again she shook her head. "If... you..." In frustration, she pointed at herself, then the viscount, then Mel. "You own it," she managed.

The viscount rolled his eyes, but Mel said, "You mean it would be acceptable to you if I own it? If it transfers from you to Lord... um, to Father and then at once to me?"

She nodded, pleased. Mel always understood her. His affectionate smile warmed her inside, and began to untangle the knots of apprehension in her stomach.

The viscount grunted. "You mean you trust *him* to manage the place but not me, is that it, young lady?"

They all turned to look at her, and she blushed. This was not a situation that she could address with a few words and a gesture. She reached for the slate.

'It is not a question of management. If Mel owns Pendarreth, then I know he will always take my wishes into account regarding the property.'

"And I would not, eh?"

'You are accustomed to making decisions instantly, like a General. Mel likes to talk the matter through with everyone concerned, like a diplomat.'

The viscount chuckled. "A General, am I?"

'If you had had charge of the army, you would have seen Bonaparte off in no time.'

He laughed uproariously at that, patting her hand in avuncular fashion, highly pleased with what he took to be a compliment. "Well then, my dear, so you are content to live at Pendarreth, but there is a small difficulty. The estate has been in financial straits for many years now, and half the tenant farms sold off to keep the place afloat, and now it will need a great sum to— And why are you shaking your head, little lady?"

"Not in... financial straits."

He laughed. "Now, what would you know about it? Letty told me all about it, and the income from the rents and so forth is no more than a few hundred pounds a year."

"Eight hundred and seventy six pounds and fifteen shillings," she said.

The bushy eyebrows lifted a little. "Oh. Still, it is not much to run a place of that size, and there will be repairs needed. Trust me, you need a great deal more than eight hundred a year to live in the style appropriate for my heir. Where is that boy? My glass is empty."

Mrs Simpson jumped up to fetch the decanter. They were still sitting amidst the detritus of breakfast, the viscount absently crumbling bread, Mel working his way stolidly through a basket of bath cakes. The Simpsons sipped their coffee and said nothing, perhaps bemused by this odd discussion at their table.

Margaret took a deep breath, and reminded herself that Mel was there and the viscount, for all his bluff manners, was not angry with her.

"Five thousand," she said.

"Five thousand?" the viscount said. "Five thousand what, my dear?"

"Pounds. Per annum. Pendarreth's income."

He chuckled, then took a sip of claret. "Nonsense, child. Even in its heyday, the place was never worth more than a couple of thousand. Two and a half, maybe, in a good year. You should not listen to idle gossip."

She shook her head. "Accounts," she said. Then, to loosen her tongue, she reached for Mel's hand. "I... keep the accounts. I have seen the... the reckonings from the bank and... and from the agent. When land was sold off in the past, it was not because the estate was short of money. The late Mr Tilford invested the cash raised into various projects — mills, machinery, canals and such like enterprises. The profits were returned to a special account so that they might be used to buy land again in the future, but they never were. There is a lot of money there now, invested at four percent."

"How much?" the viscount said, his eyes narrowed.

"One hundred and seventeen thousand, four hundred and sixty two pounds, four shillings and sixpence three farthings, last Lady Day. The income from the account last year was four thousand one hundred and seven pounds six shillings and fourpence. With the rent from the tenants, the total income to the estate last year was four thousand nine hundred and eighty four pounds one shilling and fourpence."

There was a long, stunned silence. Then Mel began to laugh. "Are you minded to retain Pendarreth for yourself, now that you see how valuable it is?"

"Ha! No, I have given my word that it will be yours, but... you can prove this, Mrs Haymer?"

She nodded. "I have all the papers in the study at Pendarreth — the bills of sale, the details of the investments, the record of the profits, the letters from the bank showing the numbers."

The viscount refilled his glass. "I raise my glass to the late Mr Tilford, who was so clever with his investments. Mind you, he was only one step away from trade as it was, so I suppose he had extensive knowledge of these canals and machinery and so forth. But Letty knew nothing of this, nothing at all."

"Aunt Pru had charge of the money," Margaret said, "but I suspect she did not understand it. She left the management of it to Mr Poole."

"Who could do nothing without her approval, poor man. Well, let us go to Pendarreth at once, and Mel can settle himself in as master there, and you can show me all the financial papers, Margaret. What a surprising girl you are."

~~~~~

There were four of them in Lord Delacrost's carriage, for Mr Audley had arrived just as they were about to set off. When they reached Pendarreth, Mel and Mr Audley went off to find the ladies, Mel to make his apology and Mr Audley to make his farewells, for he had now satisfied himself that Margaret was safe and well, and wished to apprise Lucy of it as soon as may be.
~~~~~

Margaret led the viscount into the study. The curtains were still closed, but that was not unusual. She often worked at her desk before breakfast, so the room was only cleaned late in the morning. She whisked the curtains open, and began to pull out the most recent accounts and bank reckonings from the desk drawers to show Lord Delacrost. He sat down in her chair, and ran a finger up and down the columns.

"This here," he said, stabbing a finger. "Where did this amount come from?"

"I have the papers filed over here," she said, moving towards a cabinet in the corner. Something odd caught her eye — a lady's silk slipper, elaborately embroidered, lying on the floor. Bewildered, she bent to pick it up. Only then did she see what lay beyond it — a bare stockinged foot, and then a leg, and a silk-clad crumpled form. And further beyond that, a great pool of blood.

Margaret screamed.

30: The Study

It was Mrs Herbert. Her head, particularly the face, had been hit so hard and so many times over that she was not directly identifiable, but Lord Delacrost recognised the rest of her, and Margaret, when she could think coherently, knew the bracelets she wore.

The viscount took command, and for once his barked orders were fitting for the situation. He chased everyone but Mr Audley out of the study, dispatched grooms to fetch the local magistrate and constables, and told everyone else to stay in the library. Margaret sat in a window alcove, Mel beside her, one arm around her shoulders. At the other end of the library, William and Walter Herbert paced about, their hissed whispers clearly audible, while Mrs Fordham joined Susan and Maria Herbert in spirited bouts of hysteria.

Margaret felt like falling into hysteria herself. Only Mel's presence and the soothing monologue he maintained kept her agitation under control. She had no idea what he said, and perhaps neither did he, but the sound of his voice, and the warmth of his arm around her, were infinitely reassuring.

At one point, Susan and Maria came tearfully to say that they were glad to see her returned safe and well, and was it true she was married now? And when she showed them her ring, they wished her joy. Then, not knowing what else to say, they crept away again.

Later, after a low-voiced argument, William and Walter came over to see her. Walter wished her joy with apparent sincerity, but William grunted and huffed and looked at his feet, until his brother elbowed him sharply.

"Yes, yes, I know! Wish you joy and so forth, cousin. All's well that ends well, eh? No hard feelings, I trust?"

She stared at him in astonishment, the memory of their last meeting, when he had been on the brink of the most unspeakable action, vivid in her mind.

When she made no answer, he went on, "We are friends again, are not we?"

"No," she said sharply. "Not friends. Not with you."

He flushed angrily, spun on one heel and stalked off.

"Sorry," murmured Walter, and scuttled after him.

"Well done," Mel said, squeezing her shoulder. "Perhaps I should not say so, given my profession, but some acts are unforgivable."

"He stepped back from the unforgivable," she said slowly, "but he can never be a *friend*."

The maids crept in with tea and coffee and cakes, those reliable refuges in times of trouble. What adversity could not be alleviated by a cup of tea and a pound cake? Murder, apparently, for even Mel was not tempted. It was too horrible even for brandy. Even though Mel had poured her a glass, Margaret's hands had shaken so badly that he had given up the attempt. So she sat, quaking, her insides roiling, wishing with all her heart that she could go back to that moment when she had entered the study, and *not* walk towards the corner cabinet and *not* bend down to retrieve that slipper and *not* see…

She gave a gasp as the memory flooded over her again, and Mel's arm tightened around her. "Hush now, my love. Do not think about it."

Horses crunching on the gravel drive. Male voices in the hall, and booted feet. A door opening and closing, then silence again. William and Walter, with angry voices, agreed that sitting about was intolerable and orders from the viscount not to be borne, when this was a matter which concerned their own mother. They stormed away to the study. Five minutes later, rather subdued, they crept back into the library again, to fresh bursts of weeping from their sisters and aunt.

Into this scene floated Aunt Pru, her shawl dangling, her expression benign. "Good morning, everyone! Ah, Margaret, there you are, dear! I knew you would turn up again, sooner or later. Mr Haymer, how good to see you. Why, Susan, Maria, whatever is the matter? Tabitha?"

"Selina is dead," Mrs Fordham wailed. "Murdered!"

"Oh dear," Aunt Pru said. Then, perhaps feeling this to be inadequate to the circumstances, "Oh dear, oh dear."

"Bludgeoned to death," William Herbert said loudly. "In this very house. It is coming to something when one is not safe to walk about at night. I daresay it was one of the servants."

"Oh no, dear," Aunt Pru said. "*Our* servants are very reliable. I would not employ a murderer, you know. But yours—"

"It was not any of our people," Walter Herbert said stiffly. "It must have been a burglar."

"Yes, dear, I am sure it was," Aunt Pru said. "Is that lemon cake on the table beside you, do you think, Mr Haymer? I might just manage a slice."

Mel cut some for her, and she nibbled delicately at it, sitting beside Margaret on the window seat where she noticed Margaret's wedding ring. "Married, dear?" She giggled girlishly. "To Mr Haymer? How charming! I wish you joy, dear, and you too, Mr Haymer."

"Miss Tilford," Mel began, "I must apologise in the humblest terms for my words of yesterday. I meant no insult—"

"Oh, think nothing of it, dear Mr Haymer," she trilled. "I did not, I assure you."

"You are too generous, madam, but—"

"Say no more," she said. "We must not quarrel, you know, for you are my nephew now, are not you?" She giggled, and took another bite of cake. "I wish you joy, nephew, or may I call you Mel? You will not take Margaret away from Pendarreth, will you? She must stay here, of course. It is hers, now, and yours, as her husband. You are master of Pendarreth, Mel, as you should be. This cake is delicious. Will you cut me another slice, if you please?"

Mel did so, pondering her words. *'Master of Pendarreth, as you should be'*. What on earth did she mean by that? He could make no sense of it, so instead, he asked a different question.

"But may I ask — do you have any idea what Mrs Herbert was doing in the study last night?" Mel said.

"I? How should I know what goes on here at night? I always go to bed early." She rose, and drifted away, plate in hand, to sit with Mrs Fordham and the Miss Herberts.

More sounds from the hall, more voices, more booted feet, not disappearing so quickly this time. Margaret reached for the brandy glass, but Mel was there before her, holding it, helping her to drink.

"That will do you good," he murmured.

"I believe it will," she said. "I do feel... a little more myself."

"Would you mind terribly if I go and talk to Mrs Fordham and the Herberts for a little while?" he said. "They may not need me, but it may be that a prayer or two will give them comfort in this dark hour."

She agreed to it, and he went, but he soon returned. Their grief was beyond the reach of religion, it seemed.

Another hour went by, and then Mr Audley came into the library. The Herbert brothers jumped to their feet eagerly, but Mr Audley came straight to Margaret.

"How are you, Mrs Haymer?" he said. "Ah, I see that you are not overset by the dreadful discovery, but that is like you. Lucy told me you were quiet and shy, but you have a strength in you that is much to be admired."

"Thank you, sir. I take my strength from my husband."

"I am glad to hear it. But there is a task I am charged to request of you, if it be within your powers and would not cause you too much distress. The study is your domain, I understand, and ordered to your design. You alone, therefore, may be able to determine if any item, be it ever so small, is missing or misplaced in any way. Do not be alarmed that there may be a repetition of that sight which was so distressing to you, for all has been... dealt with, and there is nothing remaining now. Do you think you might be able to look about the room?"

She nodded. "If… if Mel…"

"Of course Mr Haymer may accompany you."

Unsteadily she rose, but with Mel to support her, she made her way slowly to the study.

The room was full of men, talking in loud voices. They quietened as she entered, turning as one to look at her expectantly.

"Ah, here she is now," Lord Delacrost said, in uncommonly gentle tones. "Come in, my dear, come in. Do you know Squire Wells, our local magistrate? And Mr Poole, of course. Mr Fordyce is the coroner. These gentlemen are constables. Here is Mr Lark, my agent. You remember my son, Edward, of course. And this is…"

Margaret gazed at them in horror, instinctively shrinking towards Mel, as if his mere presence would make a room full of men tolerable.

"I believe my wife would be more comfortable without so many people," Mel said, in his quiet way.

"Of course, of course," the viscount barked. "Out, all of you. Yes, yes, but later. Out you go. Squire, Fordyce, this might be a good moment to talk to those who were here last night. They are gathered in the library. Lark, talk to the servants, see if anything untoward occurred. Edward, see if Harling has arrived yet. Poole, organise some refreshments for everyone, will you. There now, my dear, is that better?"

It had not occurred to him that she might wish him to go, too. If there had to be another man besides Mel in the room, she would have preferred Mr Audley, Lucy's Mr Audley, whom she had met less than twenty four hours ago but knew intimately from Lucy's long, chatty letters. In all the tales of her employer and his family, and their multitude of social engagements and acquaintances, Mr Audley's name had woven through the whole almost from the start.

And he was just as Lucy had described, such a *comforting* presence. It was almost as good as having Lucy herself there.

The viscount's presence was not comforting at all, but he was not shouting and seemed to understand her distress. Besides, he was her father-in-law, she supposed, and therefore a person she would have to grow accustomed to. So she made no protest and looked carefully about the room.

"Take your time, my dear," Lord Delacrost said. "Point out anything that is not as you expect, anything at all."

"The door stop is missing," she said.

"Door stop?"

"A large metal device shaped like a lion, with a handle. Heavy, to prop open the door."

"Oh. Door stop. Yes." The viscount looked uncomfortable.

"I imagine it was... taken away," Mel said. "Probably it was the implement which..."

"Oh!" She shuddered, understanding him. Then, taking a deep breath, and taking hold of Mel's hand for support, she said, "It was used to kill her, I suppose you mean." Another deep breath. "Of course."

She moved on round the room, checking the safe, and automatically straightening one or two of the papers on the desk that she had been showing the viscount when the dreadful discovery had been made. Nothing was missing, nothing misaligned. But eventually she had to approach the corner where Mrs Herbert's inert form had lain. There was nothing there now except a damp mark on the bare floorboards, almost undetectable. She imagined one of the maids on her knees, scrubbing away at that great pool of blood, and shivered again. Daisy, most likely. Or possibly Poppy. Poor girl, whichever of them it was.

She dragged her eyes away from the floor to the shelves above.

"Oh. These are out of order." The household record books, all in a line on the shelf.

"How can you tell?" Lord Delacrost said. "They are not numbered or marked in any way."

"Margaret knows," Mel said, in amused tones.

"This is the earliest," Margaret said, pointing. "Then this at the end, then the one with the torn leather. Then the three red ones, then this, this, these three and this. Finally the two black ones that are a different size. May I set them straight?"

He shrugged, not much interested in the books, but Margaret was. She knew that these had been arranged in order when she had last been in the room a few days ago, so someone had looked at them since then. One of them had even been put back upside down. And it did not surprise her, when she pulled one book out, to find crumpled pages with a red stain across them.

"Blood," she said, holding it out to the viscount.

He snatched the book eagerly from her hand, and took it to the window to examine more closely.

Silently, Margaret rearranged the rest of the books into their correct order, and then scanned the rest of the bookshelves. At once, her eye saw a book that should not be there. There was a row of very old books that had probably been there since the house was built, not valuable enough to be kept behind glass in the library. Stuffed on top was another book. Debrett's Peerage.

That was the moment when Margaret understood. "Oh! *Debrett's*. So that was why she was here."

The viscount's head shot up. "You know something?"

Margaret turned to Mel. "What did you say when you were here yesterday? Was she there? Mrs Herbert, I mean?"

"She was. Everyone was there, gathered before dinner. I accused Miss Tilford of being my mother."

"Yes!" she cried triumphantly. "And no one knew, until that moment, that you were not just some little accident, given the Haymer name by courtesy, but were someone of unknown birth, substituted for the real heir." She paused. "How melodramatic that sounds. Just like one of Mrs Simpson's novels. Well, no matter. So Mrs Herbert hears that for the first time, and so she looks you up in Debrett's."

"So she finds me in Debrett's," Mel said. "I do not quite see..."

"She finds the date of your birth," Margaret said. "Do you not understand? And then she begins to wonder, and comes through here to find the household record book for that year. She was very ill when she was here and remembers little of that time. So she came in here to check."

"To find out who else was here then?" Mel said.

"No! To confirm that it was the year she thought it was. Because there was no one else here that year. No one else but Mrs Herbert herself."

She let the words hang in the air, and saw Mel's face change as he understood.

The viscount gave a strangled cry, and collapsed into a chair. *"Selina!"* he said, in a hoarse voice. "Oh dear God, *Selina*, and she never told me. Why do they never tell me?"

"Then Mrs Herbert was my mother?" Mel said, bewildered. "Is it possible?"

The viscount groaned, and buried his head in his hands. "It is very possible, Melville, and if so, then I truly am your father. May God forgive me all my transgressions, for He knows how sincerely I have repented of them, but that was my worst moment. Poor, poor Selina!"

"Mrs Herbert was your mistress?" Mel said, sounding even more bewildered. "But you are—"

"Old enough to be her father, yes, I am aware. And she was not my mistress. I am not quite so lost to all honour as that. It was a moment of madness, no more than that, and she was not at all unwilling. I have never yet taken pleasure from an unwilling woman. But I was old enough to know better, to show some restraint and... I did not. I was ashamed of myself at the time, and now I am even more ashamed. Is there any brandy in here?"

Margaret went to the cupboard where she kept decanters and glasses, and poured him a large measure. He drank it in one gulp, and silently she refilled it.

He drank again, then leaned back in his chair. "You will think me the worst of rakes if I tell you what happened, but perhaps you *should* know the worst of me. It is fitting, I believe. Come, my dear, sit down and I will tell you all."

She and Mel sat side by side on the sofa. Lord Delacrost drank again, then set the glass down on a table. "You know about Pru, that there was... a liaison when we were both young and foolish. She was the seducer, not I, but I did not turn her away, so I must bear my share of the blame, I do not deny. They were both lively girls, Letty and Pru, up to every rig. My preference was for Letty, and I would have married her, but she kept me dangling. She wanted my title, but she wanted Bradwell's money and she never could choose. Then… there was the business with Pru, and a great cap-pulling between the sisters, and after that Letty married Bradwell. I never wanted Pru, not as a wife. There was always something sly and underhanded about her. So I married Eliza, and that was the end of it. I never saw them from one year's end to the next. But the year that Selina came out…"

He took another mouthful of brandy, cupping the glass in his hands.

"She was so like her mother, it was as if time had stopped, and Letty was a young girl again. And the same liveliness… wildness, almost. Something in me responded to that, as it always had to her mother. Letty was unwell, even then — she was never right after Horace was born — so Selina was left to distant cousins to bring out, and they had not an ounce of sense between them. Selina was left to run wild, and she did, of course. She took up with Wally Herbert, who had not two sovereigns to his name, and she was into all sorts of foolishness. There were rumours about her, almost from the start. I worried about her, so I took her under my wing rather, but…"

He stopped, staring unseeingly into his glass, his eyes focused far in the past. Margaret slipped her hand into Mel's larger one. She could never regret coming to Pendarreth, for otherwise she would never have known Mel and experienced the incomparable rightness of being with him, but sometimes she wished life were less complicated.

"There was an evening when we were at some insipid party or other — a masked ball. Such nonsense! Of course, I knew her at once, and she knew me. We were both bored and tired of the whole society game, and I suppose that must be our excuse. We ended up in one of the gaming rooms, playing piquet. She had no money, so we played the drinking version — one drink for each lost partie, and a full glass for the game. You can imagine how foxed we were. I decided to walk her home, for she was situated in the very next street, and then, since she was unsteady on her feet and I feared for her on the stairs, to help her to her room. Whereupon— "

He paused for a long time, then, with a sudden sweep of the hand, raised the glass and drained the contents at a swallow.

"Whereupon she became amorous and I, weak as I am, had no power to resist her. If I could but turn back the clock! But it is useless to repine. What is done is done, and can never be undone, and you are the result of it, Melville, and for that part of it at least I cannot be regretful, not now. I left town the next day, to keep myself away from her, and a few weeks later Selina herself left town, bound for Scotland with the worthless Herbert. She must have known her condition by then. Luckily, the cousins caught up with the pair, for they ran out of funds within fifty miles, and the whole business was hushed up. She came here to rusticate, presumably, although I was not aware of it. I spent little time here, then. And a year or two later, she married Herbert anyway, so they might just as well have gone to Scotland after all. In which case you would have been raised as a Herbert, God help you."

There was a long silence. Then Mel laughed. "All these years I have wondered who my parents might be, but that is not an answer I ever suspected. At least now we know why Mrs Herbert came to the study — she was attempting to confirm her suspicion that I was the son she bore all those years ago. But it does not answer the important question — who killed her, and why?"

31: Books And Proofs

"It seems to me," the viscount said, "that the whole business might have been an accident. Selina was wandering about the house late at night, first to the library to find a copy of Debrett's, and then here to check the household record to confirm the dates that she stayed at Pendarreth. Someone could easily have seen her candle moving hither and thither, thought her a burglar, and hit her over the head."

"No," Margaret said, and the viscount turned to face her, looking surprised, as if he had forgotten she was there. "She was in full evening dress, a pink silk gown, and those garnet bracelets on her arms. No one could possibly mistake her for a burglar. She was killed purposefully."

"It could not have had anything to do with... well, the matter we have been discussing," Lord Delacrost said. "There is no need for Squire Wells or the constables to know about it, or about Debrett's Peerage. I shall give them this bloodstained book, and leave them to complete their investigations without distraction. And there is one good come from all of this, Melville. We now know that you are, in fact, my son, if by an unorthodox manner. We know who your mother was, and, with Selina's demise, there is now no possibility of proving it. So we shall proceed as before. With a death in your wife's family, it would not be seemly to celebrate your return to the Haymer fold immediately, but I shall send an announcement of your marriage to the usual newspapers. That will suffice for now. Excellent. I shall go and see how Wells is getting on."

And so saying he swept out of the room.

"Well," Mel said, eyebrows raised. "I am not sure what Bonaparte would make of him, but he terrifies me."

~~~~~

Mel agreed reluctantly that they must stay at Pendarreth, at least for the moment. It would have been heartless indeed to have abandoned the bereaved Herbert children and their aunt in their time of trouble. There was also Miss Tilford to consider, and Margaret was determined to be there to protect her from any more attempts by the viscount to move her out of Pendarreth.

"Do you have a bedroom for me?" he said to Margaret, after the viscount had left them alone in the study. "Or shall I find a bunk over the stables?"

"You do not wish to share with me?" she said, the hint of a smile making it more a tease than a reproach.

"You know my wish, I think," he said, smiling back. "But with matters so unsettled, let us go on as before, for now. Do you mind so very much?"

"Not as long as you are nearby, under the same roof. I need to be close to you, always."

"Ah, dearest Margaret." He pulled her into his arms, and for a long time no words were spoken. Only a knock on the door drew them apart.
~~~~~

Audley's head peered round the door. "A thousand pardons for the intrusion, but your man has arrived with your boxes and wishes to know where they may be taken."

"We were just considering the same question," Mel said. "Well, Mrs Haymer?"

"There is only one unoccupied bedroom at the moment, and that is Aunt Letty's," she said. "However, the servants will not enter it until it is refurbished, so that will not do. There is a bed in the little room off the old schoolroom. Probably it was the governess's room, at one time. That might suit you, until all these visitors have gone away."

"And then we shall redecorate every bedroom and you shall choose your favourite for your own," he said.

"Oh, the Queen's room is the best room in the house," she said. "But... Mrs Herbert is — *was* — in there. So many rooms with sad histories. Even this room. The study was my sanctuary, but now even this room is tainted."

"Not tainted, perhaps, but every room holds memories, happy as well as sad," Mel said. "One must not allow the sad to outweigh the happy, however shocking they may be at the time. One sees things — hears things — experiences things that are very distressing, but one must not refine upon them to such an extent that the evil seeps out and corrodes the goodness in life. You have an affectionate and generous heart, Margaret. Regard Mrs Herbert's death with sorrow, to be sure, but then put it behind you."

"That is wise," she said, looking up at him with wide eyes. "Yet I cannot forget the sight of her — her face gone! And so much blood!"

"None of us will ever forget it," Audley said quietly. "Yet we must all go on with our lives."

"How does one go on?" she whispered. "If one sees something terrible, how can one just… set it aside?"

"For myself," Mel said, "I find prayer is the greatest help. That and the acceptance of evil in the world, about which I can do nothing, so I take solace in the good. There is far more of good to be found than evil."

She nodded solemnly. "True, and this was not my fault, was it? Nothing I did, or omitted to do, caused her death."

"Of course not!" Mel said, surprised that such a thought had ever entered her mind. "No blame attaches to any person, other than the one who struck the fatal blow." But he wondered whether there was some terrible sight in Margaret's past where she *had* blamed herself, and the guilt had caused her words to stick in her throat. But he could not force a confidence. One day, perhaps, she would tell him her secret, but for now he was glad that the words were flowing. "Now … will you show me this room off the schoolroom? Robert will want to unpack and get everything organised."

It was not much of a room, with just space enough for a narrow bed, a wardrobe, a small table and chair, and an armchair beside the fireplace. What a life the governess must have had, her days spent in the schoolroom next door, and her nights alone in her tiny cell. Probably she took her meals there too, neither a servant nor part of the family.

With Robert unpacking, Lily and Poppy making up the bed, and Rose supervising, there was no room for Mel, Margaret and Mr Audley. They retreated therefore to the schoolroom.

"It is late in the day to begin a journey," Mel said to Audley. "Do you still plan to leave today?"

"It will be better for me to extend my stay a little," he said, with a rueful smile. "My purpose in coming was to reassure Lucy — Mrs Price, I mean, that her sister is well. It is difficult to do so when there is a murderer in the house."

"You think there is a risk of further violence?" Mel said. "That had not occurred to me, I confess."

"It depends on why Mrs Herbert was killed," Audley said, grimly. "Until that is known, there can be no safety for anyone at Pendarreth."

Margaret stared at him, wide-eyed. "Oh no!" she whispered. "No, no, no." And she shrank a little closer to Mel, as if his very presence could prevent such horrors. And he could offer her no reassurance on that head.

Rose and the two maids emerged from the bedroom just then to sweep Margaret away to the servants' quarters to be properly congratulated on her marriage. Audley disappeared to send word to Dunton Cross, to make arrangements to stay on for another night or two. Mel was left to consider Audley's grim words. Was there a possibility of another death? And could Margaret be a target? There was no way to be sure, and that meant he could not leave her to sleep alone in her room, without a protector. He had married her to protect her from the unwanted attentions of her avaricious suitors, and how much more strongly would he wish to protect her from physical harm. He recalled his own anger and frustration in finding that she had been kidnapped, and his overwhelming relief at finding her unharmed. He dared not risk leaving her alone and vulnerable to a murderer.

At once, he knew that he must sleep in Margaret's room each night until such time as the murderer were apprehended. Yet not in her bed, not until he was more confident that Lord Delacrost's intentions were settled. If there were a sofa there, or perhaps two chairs, he could make a comfortable enough bed, and his very presence would reassure her. She was not there to ask, so he set off down the corridor to find her room. He knew which one was hers, for it was next door to Mrs Bradwell's room. He pushed open the door and strode inside.

A black-clad figure turned and gazed vaguely at him. "Oh... Mr Haymer."

"Miss Tilford? What are you doing here? This is Mrs Haymer's room."

"Oh, yes, indeed it is. I lent her a book... she has not returned it... so careless."

"Perhaps you should ask her directly," he said shortly. "Margaret knows with precision where everything is. She will be able to return it to you. I shall let her know you were looking for it. What book is it?"

She tittered. "Oh, it is of no consequence, not the least consequence in the world. I had a fancy to read it this afternoon... no matter, I have other books. I would not put her to any inconvenience on my account, you know."

And so saying, she drifted past him into the corridor outside, leaving him bemused.

~~~~~

Dinner was as strange as any that Mel had attended. The early hour meant that many of those who would otherwise have been gone long since were invited to stay and take their pot luck. The viscount and his younger son, Edward, the squire and the doctor all sat down
~~~~~

with the family, and with the addition of Mel and Audley, the absence of Mrs Herbert was less obvious. Fortunately the kitchen servants had anticipated the situation, for there were two substantial courses, with both beef and mutton, and as fine an array of pastries as Mel had seen since the evening party two weeks earlier.

Not much of this fine array was consumed. The Herberts ate little and said less, the young ladies pale and cast down, the young men scowling and whispering together, but still able to drink wine when it was offered. Mrs Fordham kept to her room, too prostrate for company. Margaret was quiet, as always, and the men said little that did not relate to the requirements of the table, in respect for the departed.

Only one person was cheerful. Miss Tilford gleefully placed Margaret at the head of the table, surrendering her own place, and insisted on Mel taking the seat of honour at the foot. "You are the master of Pendarreth now, dear Mel," she said, and when, to avoid discord, he and Margaret did as she bade them, she beamed at them in delight, and chattered away happily throughout the meal.

When the ladies withdrew, the viscount immediately said, "Great heavens, but Pru gets odder by the minute. What do you make of that, Harling?"

The doctor took a long swallow of his port, then said, "It would not be surprising, all things considered, if her mind has become entirely disconnected from the demands of life. She has suffered the death of her sister, and many changes at Pendarreth, changes which, in her fragile state, she is ill-suited to accept with any degree of equanimity. And now a murder in the house. It is astonishing that all the ladies are not overwrought, so delicate as the female constitution is, but in Miss Tilford's case I would venture to suggest that such ill-judged behaviour is exactly as I should expect."

"Truly?" the viscount said. "You expected it? Such levity, when her own niece lies cold and dead, her face mangled beyond all recognition? That is not consistent with sanity."

"I did not say it was," the doctor said complacently, helping himself to some dried apricots. "Her mind is unbalanced, without question. It remains to be seen whether a few weeks or months of tranquillity will restore her to her usual state of mind."

"Well, it is very queer, if you ask me," the viscount said. "Such behaviour is abhorrent to any rational being."

"But harmless," Dr Harling said. "Quite harmless. Have you finished with the port, my lord?"

After dinner, most of the gentlemen departed to their own houses, there to enjoy a second dinner, presumably. The Herberts and Miss Tilford had disappeared, so when Mel and Audley walked into the withdrawing room, only Margaret remained. Her face lit up when she saw them.

"Oh, thank goodness!" She held out her hand to Mel, who took it with a smile, and lifted it to his lips. "Now I feel better! I had begun to wonder where everyone was, and I cannot even while away the time by playing the pianoforte. That makes it feel like a Sunday, so I do not like to read or do any work. I am glad you are still here, Mr Audley."

"My coachman has brought my carriage round from Dunton Cross, so I may stay as long as you wish me to, Mrs Haymer. In fact, he will be enjoying ale and pies and flirting with your maids in the servants' hall, so he will not be at all happy if I leave early."

That brought a smile to her lips. "You are very good, sir."

"May I fetch you a book?" he said. "Shall I read to you? That would distract our minds wonderfully, would it not? Something dramatic, I fancy."

"That reminds me," Mel said. "Dearest, Miss Tilford was in your room this afternoon, trying to find a book she had lent you. She said it did not matter but—"

"A book?" Margaret said. "She has never lent me a book. Indeed, I do not recall that I have ever seen her with a book in her hand. And she was in my room?"

"She was, looking at the books on your shelf."

"And you were in my room too?" she said, but there was no sharpness in her tone. A hint of a smile played about her lips.

Mel tried not to look conscious. "Bearing in mind Audley's thoughts on the possibility of a second murder, I went to see whether there might be a... a chaise longue or sofa that would provide me with a makeshift bed. I am not going to leave you unprotected with a murderer in the house," he added with dignity.

"Thank you, Mel," she said placidly, although her eyes sparkled with mischief. "That was very thoughtful of you. But I have no books in my room apart from a few I borrowed from the library. And the Bible and my psalter, naturally. I cannot imagine what Aunt Pru was looking for."

"It is curious," Audley said. "Mrs Herbert was looking at books when she was killed, and now Miss Tilford is interested in books too."

"There can be no connection, surely?" Mel said, but even as he spoke the words, he was filled with foreboding. There was something not right about this, and Miss Tilford was at the heart of it.

"Aunt Pru *knows*," Margaret said, in a low voice. "Everything that happened twenty nine years ago when you were born, Aunt Pru was here and knows everything. She it was who sent away all the male servants, keeping only the loyal female staff, she it was who took you as a tiny baby over to Norton Forbury, she it was who brought the dead baby back with her and buried him in the woods. She it is who tends the grave, even now. She knows — she has always known — who you are, who your mother was, who your father is. She has always liked you, Mel. She barely tolerates other men, but *you* are always welcome. She is thrilled that you are master of Pendarreth. She once said that Pendarreth should belong to someone who was born here — she meant you! She *wants* you to have Pendarreth."

"But she denied being your mother," Audley said, musingly. Mel held his breath, for Audley was quite sharp enough to work it out. "That seemed truly spoken, to my ears, and—" He stopped, an arrested expression on his face. "Oh, but then... yes, it must have been... her reaction..."

"Audley?" Mel said.

"Mrs Herbert... of course!" Audley said. "Haymer, you perhaps were not observing others in the room yesterday when you made your dramatic announcement, but Mrs Herbert was unduly shocked by it. I did not know her well, having only met her a few days ago, but she did not strike me as a woman of heightened sensibilities, prone to hysteria, yet I would swear she was on the point of collapse when she heard your words. The idea suggests itself, therefore, that *she* was your mother... ah, I see by your faces that I am near the mark. So let me make a further supposition — that the viscount is your father, given the resemblance in your looks. And perhaps neither of them realised it until recently. Mrs Herbert, in fact, knew of it only yesterday. Almost at once, she rushed to the study to find the household record book which would prove... what would it prove?"

"That she was at Pendarreth that fateful year," Margaret said, with a slight smile at this guesswork. "You have missed out a step, Mr Audley. Mrs Herbert went first to the library, to check the date of Mel's birth in Debrett's Peerage, and then to the study to find the proof she sought."

"Where someone hit her over the head with the doorstop," Mel said, "and still we do not know why."

"But I do," Margaret said calmly. "Mrs Herbert had it within her power to prove that you are *not* the legitimate heir to Lord Delacrost. She was killed to prevent that from happening."

"But who cared enough about it to resort to murder?" Mel said.

"Lord Delacrost?" Audley said. "With Mortimer disgraced, he now wants to keep you as his heir. He might have—"

"He was not here," Margaret said. "He was at Norton Forbury all last evening."

"Then who could— oh!" Mel said.

"Exactly," Margaret said. "There is only one person who knew all, and who strongly desired you to be master of Pendarreth *and* to inherit the viscountcy."

A delicate titter caused them to look round. Miss Tilford stood not ten feet away, in her nightgown and robe, her cap slightly askew. "Really, dear, you are becoming so fanciful these days. You should not let your imagination run away with you."

"But it is true," Margaret said, rising to her feet to face her aunt. "You... you..." She reached for Mel's hand, and heaved a deep breath. "*You* killed Mrs Herbert, Aunt Pru."

32: A Celebration Ball (October)

Mel dared not breathe. It was almost impossible to believe, yet it made a dreadful kind of sense. He shifted protectively a little nearer to Margaret, and, on her other side, Audley did the same. Miss Tilford looked harmless enough, just another grey-haired old lady, fragile enough that a puff of wind might blow her over. Yet he remembered all those lengthy walks in the woods, and her maintenance of the grave that still continued, with bracken and brambles and saplings kept away from the precious mound of stones, and the little gap in the surrounding hedge kept open. No, that was not the work of a fragile old lady.

Miss Tilford laughed out loud at Margaret's suggestion. "Killed her? I? What nonsense! It was a burglar, someone who broke into the house."

"It was not a burglar," Margaret said, "and I can prove it. Mrs Herbert was looking for the household record book from twenty nine years ago, to be sure that she was Mel's mother. She did not find it, nor did you, for you were looking for it in my room, were not you? But you did not find it there either."

"Where is it?" she cried. "Where have you hidden it, you wicked girl?"

"It is still in the kitchen. Primrose used it to plan the evening party we held, and she is learning some of the other receipts. Those books are full of wonderful receipts, Aunt Pru."

"The kitchen..."

She turned and would have left the room, but Margaret said quietly, "It will make no difference. I daresay you want to tear out those pages that prove Mrs Herbert was here and burn them, but it does not matter now. No one can prove Mel is not legitimate now, except you. He is quite safe."

"Safe..." she murmured. "That is true. Only me, and I am not telling. No... no one will ever know, not from my lips. And now he is master of Pendarreth, as he should be, and he will be viscount, and I will have my revenge on Matthew." She laughed, a high-pitched giggle that turned Mel cold. She was insane, clearly insane. "He should have married me — he should! He married stupid Eliza instead. Served him right that there was no babe — no heir. But then she had a piece of luck. A babe at last, and it was a boy. I could not allow that, could I?"

"You killed the viscount's real son?" Margaret said, her eyes wide with shock.

"Matthew!" Miss Tilford spat, her face twisting into a horrifying grimace. "She called him Matthew! Matthew was *my* child, mine! But I could never keep him, never watch him grow up, as a mother should. She knew that, she knew that *my* son was Matthew, but she called hers by that name anyway. Melville Matthew. But I had Selina's babe, who had to be got rid of somehow... it was the perfect revenge, was not it? I got my revenge on that *wicked* man. Except that stupid, *stupid* Eliza had to tell him!

Still, he could not set him aside, not legally, so he would still inherit, as was proper. He would be Viscount Delacrost one day. My son... no..." She looked bewildered for a moment. "Not mine... Selina's, but almost mine. It *should* have been my son. And then Letty tricked me and left Pendarreth as she did, and look what happened! Margaret married Mel, who is Letty's grandchild." She laughed hysterically again. "Master of Pendarreth *and* Viscount Delacrost... it is perfect, is it not?"

"But Mrs Herbert would have spoilt it all," Mel said. "So you killed her."

She started, as if she had forgotten he was there. "Spoilt... yes. I could not allow that, could I? *Stupid* Selina, she would have told him, signed things, got my son disinherited—" She broke off, looking round at them in some confusion. Then, perhaps some glimmer of sanity broke through and she realised what she had said. "No, no, I did not mean it. No! You must not look at me that way. No, I am a good girl, truly I am. It was not my fault, *not* my fault. It was *your* fault, you little vixen," she cried, rounding on Margaret. "Coming here with your scheming ways, taking Pendarreth away from me, bringing Selina here and wanting to *change* everything. I hate you!"

Suddenly, terrifyingly, there was the flash of steel in her hand — a dagger! She lunged, but Mel and Audley jumped towards her and she skittered back, leaning against a sideboard, tears in her eyes. "It has all gone *wrong*. If only he had married me, as he should. He ought to have done so, if he had had any honour. Men! None of them are honourable. Not Father. Not Matthew. Not one."

"Miss Tilford, give me the dagger," Mel said firmly, holding out his hand.

She bared her teeth at him like an animal. Then, with devastating speed, she plunged the knife into her own heart.

~~~~~

OCTOBER

Margaret sat at her escritoire, considering. The elegant little writing desk was a wedding present from Mel, who had gone to Ludlow one day with Mrs Simpson and chosen a whole suite of furniture for her boudoir. Mel it was who had sent in painters and carpenters and plasterers and glazers and chimney sweeps, and refurbished the Queen's room for her, and Mel who had discovered the convenient connecting door to the adjoining bedroom, which he had instantly made his own. Her own rooms were finished, but she could hear the men at work next door, hammering and occasionally, when they forgot, whistling. Eventually the whole house would be in full working order, every chimney swept, every wall freshly hung with wallpaper or panelling, every piece of furniture polished and then moved to a different place in the house, so that there would be no reminders of the dreadful events of September. None of them would forget, but they could, as Mr Audley had said, go on with their lives and take pleasure in the good which outweighed the bad.

She had found it easier than expected to go on, but that was Mel's doing, of course. Oh, the comfort of having him right there in the house! And although he was not a man to put himself forward, when a thing needed to be done, he got on and did it, without hesitation or doubt or the shyness that had crippled Margaret for so many years. He had emptied the house of its unwanted guests as soon as it was decent to do so, sent for Mr Williams to repair the coach and barouche in the coach house, bought horses to pull them and engaged grooms. He had taken on two full-time gardeners to
~~~~~

bring order to the grounds, and had a stonemason repairing the walls to the much neglected kitchen garden.

The viscount could not resist interfering, naturally. He had a habit of calling in at unexpected moments, and always brought some little gift — a few pheasant, or some trout from his fish ponds, or a basket of plums, although they had plenty of their own, or a hideous epergne for the dining table, which Margaret promptly hid away in a dark cupboard, never to be used. He sent one of his own coaches for them, and was disgruntled to discover that they were already adequately supplied. He engaged a butler, four footmen and a fearsomely starchy lady's maid. They kept the butler and two footmen, and sent the rest away. He sent barrels of ale and claret, and bottles of brandy, which they accepted gratefully. But they could not be cross at this evidence of good intentions, as if he supposed that trout and brandy could recompense for decades of neglect towards his heir. Nothing now could be done to dislodge Mel from his unwanted rôle as a future viscount, but Mel had accepted it equably, as he accepted everything that happened in the same calm, easy-going manner.

A gentle knock on the door heralded his arrival. "How are you getting on, dearest?"

"Not very well," she said, looking ruefully at the blank sheet of paper before her. "It is so *difficult*. I can never think what to say in a letter, or how to say it. I *feel* so much that I cannot express in words. It would be so much easier to write about the weather. *'We have had much rain lately, but there has been no frost yet.'* "

He laughed. "No, your sisters do not want to hear about the weather. They will want to know all that has happened to you."

"I do not think I have paper enough for that," she said mournfully. "This was supposed to be a quiet, retired life for mousy little Margaret, and we have had murder and kidnapping and a contentious will, and poor, poor Aunt Pru. Whatever can I say about her?"

"The truth," he said softly. "What else?"

She sighed. "It will distress them so. She was so *wicked*, I can scarce believe it myself. I even wonder if she did not kill Aunt Letty, too. It would have been so easy, with her room just across the great hall from Aunt Letty's, and she used to wander about at night, you know. I saw her more than once. So easy..." Another sigh. "So much to tell my sisters and I do not know where to begin. With an apology, I suppose, for not writing to them for all those months. I tried, truly I did, but the words would not obey me. Three letters — no, four, that is all they have had from me, announcing my arrival here, that I had walked to church by myself, Aunt Letty's death and then Aunt Pru's. Four letters in almost a year."

"But everything was read by your aunts — that would be enough to inhibit anyone. Your sisters will understand, they know that it was not your fault, and that you are well and safe. Now all you have to do is to explain all the multitude of extraordinary events that have taken place here, which you did not feel that Audley could do justice to."

"Nor I, I am sure," she said, laughing. "You make it sound so simple, but it is not, not to me. I cannot do this!"

"Of course you can," he said, in his calm way. "Look how far you have progressed already. You have learnt to speak, for one thing."

"And to love," she said, gently touching his dear face with one finger, ending on his soft lips. "And to kiss... and other things."

"We have both learnt other things," he said, smiling affectionately, resting his large hand on her smaller one.

She laughed a little, and allowed him to distract her by kissing each finger in turn. After a while, she said, "This will not do, husband. I learnt to speak because you were in the room with me, but that does not seem to work with letters."

"How did you manage to speak when you were shut up in that tower?" he said. "You talked the Herbert boy out of his wicked scheme, and I was not there with you."

"I imagined you in the room, and then I could speak."

"Perhaps you could imagine your sisters here in this room?" he said. "Let us suppose they are... over there, say, on that sofa. Rosamund on the left, then Annabelle, then Lucy and Fanny on the right. Can you see them?"

"Oh yes! I can!"

"Then let them ask you questions," he said. "Is it Lucy who talks all the time? Well, I daresay she has a thousand questions for you, so all you have to do is to answer them."

"Oh... of course. Lucy..." She dipped her pen into the ink, wiped the nib, chewed the end of the quill, staring at the sofa for inspiration, then, with a smile, bent her head to the paper.

'My dear sister, I cannot believe how much has happened to me these last few months. I did not much enjoy Pendarreth when I first arrived, for I was so lonely without all of you, and although my aunts were not unkind, they were not very interested in me either. I grew accustomed to that. I wrote to tell you that Aunt Letty had died, and again that Aunt Pru had died, but so much happened in between those two events that I do not know where to begin. But do not be alarmed, for I am well and very happy. I am married! I will tell you all about him later, but first let me explain about Aunt Letty's will...'

~~~~~

There was a peculiar delight to Margaret in travelling to an engagement in her own carriage, with her husband by her side. They drove first to collect the Simpsons, and after that they went on very merrily, for there was much news to be exchanged, and although letters had passed between Pendarreth and the parsonage, and they had called on each other, and met twice for dinner, there was still a great deal to be said.

"Have you begun your new book yet?" Margaret asked Mrs Simpson.

"No, and it is all your fault," that lady said, although her laughter made of it a joke. "Every little idea I dream up seems far too tame, when I reflect on all the dramatic happenings at Pendarreth. If one were to make a novel of it, no one would believe a word of it, for it is far too fanciful. I shall have to try my hand at some other amusement altogether, I believe. Poetry, perhaps." And she laughed again.

"I shall pray for a return of your inspiration, then," her husband said. "Your poetry is abominable."

"You say that about my novels, too," she said.

"Not when they put good claret in my cellar, my dear, I assure you."

They passed quickly through the tiny hamlet of Norton Forbury and thence through the gates of the Manor House, standing wide open in the late afternoon sun, still with some warmth, despite the season. Here several of the locals farming families had gathered, the men to bow, the women to curtsy and the children to wave and chase after the carriage.

The viscount himself met them on the steps and showed them to their rooms, for they were to stay the night. Margaret and Mel
~~~~~

were assigned a large room at the front of the house, with windows opening onto a broad balcony lined with pots of roses, and overlooking more rose beds below. Even so late in the year, the air was filled with perfume.

Holly and Robert had arrived that morning with their boxes, so everything was prepared for them to dress for dinner. Margaret was still officially in mourning for Aunt Pru, but under the circumstances she felt that black ribbons were sufficient. Aunt Pru's will had left everything to Mel, including the jewellery she had inherited from Aunt Letty, so Margaret wore the Tilford diamonds, and felt herself to be very grand. But that was appropriate, especially as she was still a bride and was the guest of honour. The evening was an official celebration of the marriage of Lord Delacrost's eldest son and heir.

They emerged just as a lady appeared from a door opposite. Margaret took one look, and then shrieked with glee.

"*Lucy! Lucy!* Oh, Lucy!"

Lucy squealed too, and the two sisters fell on each other with happy cries and copious tears and many, many hugs.

"Oh, Margaret, you look so well!" Lucy cried, as soon as she had caught her breath sufficiently. "Look at you, so grand. And married! Is this the man? Goodness, he is so tall! Leo told me he was, but — goodness! How do you do, Mr Haymer. Oh, Margaret, is this not wonderful? Lord Delacrost invited Leo — he is about somewhere, you will see him shortly — because he was here before, and Leo wrote at once to ask if he might bring me, because he was so sure that you would be glad to see me, and you are, are you not, Margaret? And he said yes, and so here I am! Oh, Margaret!" And here the tears overcame her again.

Between sobs, Margaret said, "Oh, Lucy, I am so happy to see you, I cannot tell you! You must thank Mr Audley for me — oh, here he is now. Mr Audley, I cannot thank you enough for bringing Lucy to see me. May I take it that you are indeed Lucy's Mr Audley now?"

He nodded, with an affectionate glance at Lucy. She, however, was staring at Margaret open-mouthed.

"Margaret!" she said in hushed tones. "Oh, Margaret, you are *talking!"*

"I am," Margaret said, smiling through her tears. "Love is strange, is it not? It mends even a broken creature like me."

"Oh, Margaret!" Lucy wailed, falling on her again with tears of joy. "Dear, dear Margaret."

It was not to be expected that Margaret's new-found powers of speech would enable her to converse easily with anyone within her orbit, and the gathering in the drawing room before dinner and the dinner itself were much the same as always. Even with Mel nearby, she could not muster more than a few words to Lord Delacrost and one of his brothers-in-law, a baron, who sat beside her at table.

But after dinner, they went through to the ballroom, and that was her moment to shine. When the baron led her to the head of the first set, all her shyness and nerves fell away, and there was just the pleasure of the dance. Even the sight of Mel, fumbling his way through the steps with a patient sister of the viscount, could not dent her enjoyment of the evening. She did not intend to sit down all night.

Mel retired with relief after doing his duty with the baron's wife, but Margaret had called upon him to fulfil one more obligation on the dance floor.

"I have never danced the waltz in public," she had said to him when the viscount's invitation had first arrived. "It does not appear to me to be quite seemly, but with my husband it would be perfectly unexceptionable, and I should *so* like to, dear, dear Mel."

"You do know I have two left feet, dearest? I do not even know the steps to the waltz."

"Then let me teach you. *Please.*"

And, as she had known, he had not been able to refuse her. So she had taught him the movements, and they had practised, watched Dr and Mrs Simpson demonstrate, and practised again. And now Mel's feet were to be put to the test.

It would be too much to say that he was graceful, but he executed the proper steps and made the turns in the proper order and only went wrong once or twice. His apologies, at least, were elegant, and Margaret was well satisfied with her big, gentle husband. And having the company of Lucy and Mr Audley at supper, hearing all their news and knowing that they could stay for a whole week made the evening entirely perfect.

~~~~~

Mel woke to darkness, and knew instantly that Margaret was not in bed. As his eyes adjusted to the gloom, he saw that it was not quite dark, for there was light outside the window, and a movement on the balcony.

He slipped out of bed and pulled on his nightshirt against the chill, then padded silently to the open window. She was on the balcony, eyes closed, swaying in the moonlight to some music running through her head. She wore only her nightgown, with her hair loose down her back and reaching almost to her waist. Every little wisp of breeze plucked at stray strands of hair so that they
~~~~~

seemed to float as she moved. The moon lit her with an ethereal glow, like an angel.

Mesmerised, he watched as she spun and arched and straightened, now as upright as a tree, now curled up like a flower, now gliding like a fish. Once she hopped like a little bird. His heart overflowed with love for his dainty wife, this girl-woman who was only just unfurling her petals to the world. She was so fragile on the outside, but inside she had the strength of a well-tempered sword.

She saw him.

"Did I wake you?" she said, running straight to him. "I tried not to, but I was too full of happiness to be still."

"Have you not danced enough tonight?" he said teasingly. "You did not sit down once."

"No, and it was wonderful," she sighed. "I thought my very first ball was impossible to match, but this was so, so much better."

"Because Lucy was there?"

"Partly, but mostly because you were there. Every time I looked, you were watching me, and smiling, and that made me feel as if I could do anything. When I came to Pendarreth, I was terrified, Mel. I had no idea how I would cope, not even able to talk to anyone. But you never made me feel peculiar or of less worth than anyone else. I love you so much."

"And I love you too, dearest. But I shall be very cross if you catch a chill and leave me a widower when we have not been married a month, so will you not come inside out of this cold air? Shall I build up the fire to warm you?"

"I expect the bed is still warm," she said innocently.

He chuckled. "I expect it is, Mrs Haymer. Shall we find out?"

THE END

Thanks for reading!

If you have enjoyed reading this book, please consider writing a short review on Amazon. You can find out the latest news and sign up for the mailing list at the Mary Kingswood website http://marykingswood.co.uk/

Book 4 of the series is *The Seamstress*, featuring romantic Fanny, and you can read a sneak preview of Chapter 1 after the acknowledgements.

Family trees: Hi-res version available at the Mary Kingswood website http://marykingswood.co.uk/

A note on historical accuracy: I have endeavoured to stay true to the spirit of Regency times, and have avoided taking too many liberties or imposing modern sensibilities on my characters. The book is not one of historical record, but I've tried to make it reasonably accurate. However, I'm not perfect! If you spot a historical error, I'd very much appreciate knowing about it so that I can correct it and learn from it. Thank you!

About the series*: When Mr Edmund Winterton of Woodside dies, his daughters find themselves penniless and homeless. What can they do? Unless they wish to live on charity, they will have to find* *genteel employment for themselves. This book is set in England during the Regency period of the early nineteenth century. Book 0 takes place 5 years before books 1-4, and book 5 ten years later.*

Book 0: The Betrothed (Rosamund) (a short novel, free to mailing list subscribers)

Book 1: The Governess (Annabelle)

Book 2: The Chaperon (Lucy)

Book 3: The Companion (Margaret)

Book 4: The Seamstress (Fanny)

Book 5: Woodside

Any questions about the series? Email me - I'd love to hear from you!

About the author

I write traditional Regency romances under the pen name Mary Kingswood, and epic fantasy as Pauline M Ross. I live in the beautiful Highlands of Scotland with my husband. I like chocolate, whisky, my Kindle, massed pipe bands, long leisurely lunches, chocolate, going places in my campervan, eating pizza in Italy, summer nights that never get dark, wood fires in winter, chocolate, the view from the study window looking out over the Moray Firth and the Black Isle to the mountains beyond. And chocolate. I dislike driving on motorways, cooking, shopping, hospitals.

Acknowledgements

Jane Austen and Georgette Heyer, who jointly inspired me to try my hand at writing a Regency romance.

Shayne Rutherford of Darkmoon Graphics for the cover design.

My beta readers: Mary Burnett, Barbara Daniels Dena, Amy DeWitt, Megan Jacobson, Melanie Savage

Last, but definitely not least, my first reader: Amy Ross.

Sneak preview of Book 4: The Seamstress: Chapter 1: A New Home (January)

The Honourable Ferdinand Alphonse Makenham, son of Viscount Craston and grandson of the Earl of Belwarren, was embarrassed. This was not a situation which occurred with frequency, for Ferdy was as socially adept as he was well brought up. He could move with ease in every setting where a gentleman might find himself, and acquit himself well in every one. There was no circumstance which discomfited him, no place where he might not happily pass, no crisis which he could not address with aplomb and grace.

Except for one, and that was his grandfather's house on Christmas Day.

It was the tradition within the family that everyone who was capable of travel converged on Abbeymount at the tail end of the year, there to celebrate every birth and betrothal and marriage in the last twelvemonth, and mourn every death. The house was vast, with entire wings which stood empty for eleven months of the year, but in December every bed was filled and the house was stuffed to the rafters with Makenhams and their cousins the Brants and Marfords and Deans and Carmichaels and Missenthorpes. And Christmas Day brought the dark moment of Ferdy's year, the great feast of Christmas and the reason for his discomfort.

For Ferdy had had the misfortune to be born on Christmas Day twenty five years ago, and that was excuse enough for his every childhood foible, his most unfortunate mishaps and his most excruciating failures to be brought out for inspection, and laughed over, and passed on to the next generation. One day, far in the future, when he was grey and stooped and had finally stepped into his grandfather's shoes as the Earl of Belwarren, his relations would still be chortling over the occasion at the age of two years when he had been violently sick over the Dowager Duchess of Camberley, or when, on his first attempt to mount his pony unassisted, he had contrived to seat himself facing the tail. Would he ever be allowed to forget the time he had teased the peacocks on the south lawn, and one of them had chased him all the way down to the ice house, where he had hidden, terrified, for three hours? And then there was the incident with the Bishop, which even now made Ferdy hot with embarrassment to recall. How he wished that his relations would quietly forget his childhood misdemeanours and treat him as the responsible adult he now was. Or, failing that, that he had been born on any other day of the year.

But there was no escaping it. The aunts sighed over him every year on this day, remembering his auspicious arrival, his father's first child, for coming so soon on the heels of his Uncle Walter's untimely demise it had seemed like the hand of Providence. As one heir departed, another had arrived, and with the whole family gathered to celebrate it. And celebrate it they had, every year thereafter, and if Ferdy had grown somewhat reconciled to the attention, the mortification never diminished.

After the feast was the especial humiliation of his grandfather's speech, which always involved some kind of present. It was never a horse or a curricle or something of the like kind that Ferdy might actually use, or at least exchange for a better version, more to his taste. No, it was always some outlandish piece of jewellery, such as no man had worn anytime these last fifty years, or a book, perhaps, and what need had Ferdy for a book? He already had a Bible, a psalter and a copy of Debrett's Peerage, and he could not see what purpose any additional book might serve. He had left all that nonsense behind when he had waved farewell to his last tutor.

But this time his grandfather surprised him.

"My good people," he bellowed, the better to be heard by the one hundred and twenty persons gathered at his exceedingly large dining table, "we are here today to celebrate two births — that of our Lord Jesus, and that of my grandson and heir, Ferdinand. The former took place this morning in church, and the latter here and now. Let us all drink to Ferdinand's health and wish him a joyous and pleasurable year to come."

That much was entirely as usual. Everyone raised their glasses, and drank, and settled down to hear what present Ferdy was to have this year. But then the earl veered away from the usual speech.

"This year is a very special one for Ferdinand, as it was for Craston and as it was also for me. For today Ferdinand reaches the age of five and twenty, and this is the year he will marry, just as his father did at that age, and just as I did also at the same age. It is the way of the Makenhams, to marry at twenty five, and I have no doubt that Ferdinand will do what is expected of him. To this end, therefore, the present I bestow on him is a very particular one.

Today I present my grandson with the key to his house, number Twenty Five Harlington Terrace, Sagborough, the place where he will bring his bride. Congratulations, Ferdinand."

And so saying, he placed an ornate key, decorated for the occasion with ribbons, on Ferdy's plate. There was a murmuring of approval, and some applause, and someone slapped Ferdy painfully on the back. Ferdy stared at the key before him as if it might jump up and bite him on the nose. To the world it might appear to be only a key, but to him it represented the bars of a cage.

When the ladies had withdrawn, with many a knowing glance at Ferdy, the gentlemen moved around the table and clustered in groupings of their choosing, the grandfathers at one end around the earl, the fathers in the middle and at the further end, the young men gathered around Ferdy in varying degrees of sympathy.

"Lord, Ferdy, you must have guessed how it would be," his cousin Ralph said, reaching a well-manicured hand for the port decanter. "Five and twenty is when the heir marries, and five and twenty you are."

"Oh yes, but... the house!" Ferdy said. "Never expected the house. Bride first, *then* the house, that is the proper way of things."

"Not for the Makenhams," said Edgar, another cousin. Ferdy had a great many cousins, but these two were his particular friends. "Have their own proper way of doing things, the Makenhams."

"Confound it, though," Ferdy said gloomily. "Married! Me! It hardly bears thinking about. I mean, a woman about the place, always."

The others murmured in sympathy.

"Pretty bad," Edgar said. "Horrifying."

"Oh, not *that* bad," Ralph said, with a wink and a grin. "A house of your own, Ferdy, and no need to leave it for a man's pleasures. It could be worse."

"Still horrifying," Edgar said firmly, and Ferdy could not but agree with him.

When the men started to drift away, the earl came and slapped Ferdy on the back. "Come into the book room with me, m'boy, and have a brandy, eh? You too, Craston."

Making a face of mock alarm to his friends, Ferdy followed his father and grandfather out of the Long Gallery, where they dined when the house was full, and then along twisting corridors to the book room. Despite the face-pulling, he was not afraid of his progenitors. His school friends had told dire tales of beatings and worse, of parents who constantly berated them for the smallest misdemeanour, or forced them to follow a particular career against their inclinations. Ferdy had never encountered such difficulties. His parents and grandparents had uniformly applauded his successes, and treated his mishaps lightly, as humorous escapades that might befall anyone. They had never quibbled at his expenditure, or denied him horses or clothes, or looked sternly at him and told him how disappointed they were in him. He got along with them remarkably well, in fact.

But now they wanted him to marry, and Ferdy was not sure he could oblige them.

The earl's book room was tucked away in a secluded part of the house. Unlike the rest of Abbeymount, this part was not built on a grandiose scale, and the book room would not have looked out of place as the housekeeper's room. The furnishings were elderly and worn, the carpet threadbare and the curtains moth-eaten. The shelves held a mismatched assortment of ornaments, including a wooden horse Ferdy had laboriously carved at the age of ten as a present for his grandfather.

The earl turned genially to Ferdy as they entered the room. "There now, we rubbed through that tolerably well, eh, m'boy? Only one mention of the Bishop, eh? 'Pon my soul, you colour up as easy as a girl, sometimes. Craston, do the honours, will you, while Ferdinand and I get comfortable."

Ferdy's father poured the brandy while the earl took the wing chair on one side of the fire, and gestured Ferdy to its partner on the other side, for Ferdy was the guest of honour today. Viscount Craston, having handed round glasses, brought forward a smaller chair.

"Well now, you look as nervous as a kitten, boy," the earl said. "It is not so bad being married, y'know. Not so bad at all, eh, Craston?"

The viscount shook his head. "No, indeed. Best thing I ever did, getting married. You will love it, Ferdy. So comfortable, having a lady to arrange all those delicate little touches that make the place a proper home. Meals always on time, the house run just as it should be, and a nursery filling up, you see. What could be pleasanter?"

Almost anything, in Ferdy's opinion. Instead, he said plaintively, "But who am I to marry?"

"Why, whomsoever you please," the earl said in surprise. "What, did you think we were about to foist some fubsy spinster on you in an arranged marriage? You must think us positively medieval, m'boy." The two men chuckled.

"No one is going to force you into anything you dislike," the viscount said, smiling. "Once you turn your mind to it, however, you will start to view every eligible female in a new light."

"Turn my mind to it?" Ferdy said, dazed. "How do I do that?"

"That part is already accomplished," the earl said smugly. "We have sown the seeds of the idea in your brain, y'know, and you have your house now, all ready and waiting. You will see the ladies differently now."

"You can look around you when you go up to London in April," the viscount said. "You will soon find someone you like, and with your address you will have no trouble fixing your interest."

"Aye, he is very personable, I grant you," the earl said. "He dresses too plain, though. A man needs a bit of colour about him, and a decent quantity of lace. I say nothing about powder and wigs, for good riddance to all that, but I do like to see a bit of lace about the cuffs, if a gentleman is to distinguish himself from his land agent or banker."

Ferdy smiled, and said nothing, perfectly assured that his attire was both fashionable and elegant, in the restrained manner of the London saloons. Here in Yorkshire, the more flamboyant styles could often still be seen, although his grandfather, for all his yearning for lace, restricted his desire for colour to a brocade waistcoat.

"Ah, that is the fashion, these days," the viscount said. "Dark colours everywhere, and only the neckcloth showing any liveliness at all. It is all that fellow Brummell's fault. But Ferdy's style is much admired, and is quite copied by the young bloods, so I am told. And nobody would ever take him for a banker."

Ferdy bowed modestly at this compliment.

The earl grunted. "Well, I have no doubt he can take his pick of the ladies. Once they understand him to be looking to be riveted, they will be all about in a trice, and he may look as high as he pleases. A title in the future, and an excellent fortune — I shall increase your allowance immediately, m'boy. How does fifteen hundred a year suit you? You will need a good income to maintain that house in the proper manner, and do some entertaining, you know. Get Agatha to help you with that. She knows how best to do these things, but do not worry if it gets expensive. If you find you need more, just say so. And when you marry, you will need a great deal more and you will not find me ungenerous, not at all."

"You are too kind, Grandfather," Ferdy murmured. "But how will I choose a wife? What must I look for? What sort of dowry?"

"Ha!" His grandfather took a long swallow of brandy. "That would be very tawdry, to choose a wife for the purse she brings with her. No, m'boy, you may have a free hand to find a woman who pleases you, but you must be very sure that she is the right one for you. It is a lonely business being an earl, and you must have a woman by your side who makes you happy, above all else."

"Happy. I see," Ferdy murmured, wondering how an earl who had just left a dinner for one hundred and twenty relations could describe himself as lonely.

"You must be in love with your wife, of course," his father said.

"In love... But... but how will I know? How can I tell when I am in love?"

His father and grandfather both chuckled. "You will know," his grandfather said. "Twenty four hours after I took possession of the house at Twenty Five Harlington Terrace, I was just emerging from the snuff shop in Sagborough, and almost bumped slap into my Alicia, and I knew at once."

"It was the same with me," the viscount said. "I had barely been in the house a week when I went out, only to the post office, as it happened, and a lady's carriage had become entangled with a pig wagon, and I stopped to render assistance, and there was my dear Louisa."

Ferdy smiled and nodded, having heard the tales before, usually with more embellishments.

"So I will just know..."

His father and grandfather smiled benevolently at him, nodding, but Ferdy was no nearer understanding just how he was to find a wife, or even whether he wanted one.

~~~~~

Fanny was sure she must be the most fortunate creature alive. When poor Papa had died leaving his four unmarried daughters penniless, it had seemed like the end of the world, yet now they were all safely employed in pleasant occupations. Annabelle was to be a governess, and no one could deny her aptitude for books and learning. Lucy, the most sociable of them, was to act as chaperon to two young ladies making their come-out and what could be more romantic? And shy Margaret was to live secluded with two elderly aunts, which would suit her retiring nature admirably.

As for Fanny herself, she was to be of service to Lady Harriet Hay's project helping women who had fallen into difficulties to return to respectability. She was not entirely sure what those difficulties might be or why it rendered them less than respectable, but she was sure that any assistance was to be commended. Lady Harriet once called them *'my fallen women'*, but when Fanny had asked what they had fallen from, Lady Harriet had looked at her thoughtfully for a moment, and then said, "Let us call them *unfortunate*, Fanny. They are unfortunate women, and it is best not to enquire into their histories."

So it was that Fanny found herself travelling north with Lady Harriet in the greatest imaginable comfort, the carriage as snug as
~~~~~

snug could be, every inn perfectly accommodating and every attention paid to them. They travelled with Miss Hay, Lady Harriet's sister-in-law, and Miss Marianne Trivers, whose journey would reunite her with her uncle and aunt, whose heiress she was now become. A second coach conveyed the bulk of the luggage, as well as the lady's maids of Lady Harriet and Miss Trivers.

Fanny had no lady's maid. At home at Woodside, she had shared Janet with her three sisters, but mostly they had laced each other's stays and tended each other's hair. Now there was no one to help her with her curling papers, or advise on which gown to wear. Her sisters were scattered about the country, and Janet was gone with Lucy, and Fanny must learn to do her own hair. It was fortunate, then, that she had nimble fingers and a way with a ribbon or a few beads or a strip of lace, to make something out of nothing. It was, after all, why she had been engaged by Lady Harriet, for her skills with a needle.

"Are you not terrified, Miss Winterton?" Miss Trivers said one evening, as they waited in the private parlour for Lady Harriet and Miss Hay to join them. "Leaving everything you know behind you, and journeying all alone to foreign parts — I should be terrified. Indeed, I *am* terrified, even though I already know my uncle and aunt."

"Oh, I am a little *nervous*, naturally," Fanny said. "Lady Harriet has been so kind to me and I should not like to disappoint her. But there is nothing to terrify one. I am not alone, after all, and Yorkshire is not exactly foreign parts."

"But very wild," Miss Trivers said. "Still, we are both of us alone, in a way, for we have both of us left sisters behind us, and neither of us has any friends in Yorkshire. Not of our own age, I mean. Even Miss Hay is quite old."

"She is eight and twenty," Fanny said, trying not to laugh.

"Exactly! Quite old. Will *you* be my friend, Miss Winterton?"

"Of course I will!" Fanny said at once. "As far as my duties permit, of course. I should be very honoured, Miss Trivers."

"Oh, but you must call me Marianne."

"And you must call me Fanny."

And so it was that Fanny arrived in the small town of Sagborough in the northern county of Yorkshire already in possession of a friend. She thought herself very blessed.

~~~~~

For one reason or another, it was near the end of January before Ferdy took possession of his house. After the celebrations of Christmas at Abbeymount, he spent a week with his parents at Lennister Hall, and then there was an old school friend to be cheered up, recovering from an unfortunate bout of measles, and so the month drifted away. But eventually, he made his way to the unprepossessing market town of Sagborough. It was already showing signs of advancement, in the numerous mills and manufactories lining the canal at the eastern end of town, and the road from York was edged with many new buildings to house the mill workers and managers and engineers such industries required. Further on, the brand new hospital was still being built, and not far away was a new school.

But the centre of the town boasted a number of fine edifices from the medieval period onwards, and on a quiet side street lay the splendid frontage of Harlington Terrace. Ferdy had never seen the house before, for it had been rented out for years, but as his carriage drew up outside number Twenty Five, he had to confess himself rather impressed. The house, like all those in the street, was double-fronted with a porticoed entrance and at least five stories,
~~~~~

not counting the basement and attics. And all of this was his! Naturally, it was not comparable to the vast splendour of Abbeymount, or even the more modest scale of Lennister Hall, but still, it far outclassed his modest rooms in the town house in London.

As his travelling carriage drew up outside, the front door opened and out streamed a line of servants. His grandfather had said airily that the servants were in place, but Ferdy had hardly expected a butler and no fewer than three footmen for a bachelor household. His carriage door was opened by one footman, another let down the steps, and a third offered his arm, a service which Ferdy declined. He descended to the street, gazing up in some awe at the property which was now his.

Voices nearby caused him to turn his head. At the house next door, another carriage was drawn up, and three ladies were alighting, amidst the usual bustle of such occasions. His new neighbours, he supposed. His practised eye weighed them up instantly. One older woman, married, he thought, with clear London style about her. A spinster, with practical garb, who might be a companion, perhaps. And a third, younger than the others, in mourning, her clothes cleverly created but rather plain. The two older women ascended the steps to the front door without looking his way. The younger one hesitated, looking up at the house before her much as Ferdy had looked at his own, with surprise and perhaps a little awe.

And then she turned her head and looked at him, with a delicate little smile playing about her lips.

That smile! Ferdy stood stock still on the pavement, mesmerised by her smile. He had never in his life seen a lady, old or young, married or spinster, rich or poor, with a smile of such enchantment. Her whole expression was filled with sweetness.

She turned and followed her companions up the steps and into the house. The door closed behind her, the carriage rolled away and the street was empty of all but Ferdy's own carriage and servants.

But Ferdy knew. Confound it, his father and grandfather had been absolutely right after all. He had no idea of her name or connections or situation, but he knew. He had met the lady who would be his wife.

END OF SAMPLE CHAPTER of *The Seamstress*

Printed in Great Britain
by Amazon

38842064R00236